S.J.

Nora Roberts is the *New York Times* bestselling author of more than one hundred and ninety novels. A born storyteller, she creates a blend of warmth, humour and poignancy that speaks directly to her readers and has earned her almost every award for excellence in her field. The youngest of five children, Nora Roberts lives in western Maryland. She has two sons.

Visit her website at www.noraroberts.com.

Nora Roberts

The Calhouns:
SUZANNA AND MEGAN

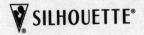

SILHOUETTE®

Silhouette and Colophon are registered trademarks of
Harlequin Books S.A., used under licence.
Silhouette Books, Eton House, 18-24 Paradise Road,
Richmond, Surrey TW9 1SR

THE CALHOUNS: SUZANNA AND MEGAN
© Harlequin Books S.A. 2005

The publisher acknowledges the copyright holder of the
individual works as follows:

Suzanna's Surrender © Nora Roberts 1991
Megan's Mate © Nora Roberts 1996

ISBN: 978 0 263 86741 1

078-0708

Printed and bound in Spain
by Litografía Rosés S.A., Barcelona

CONTENTS

The Calhouns:
Suzanna and Megan

Suzanna's Surrender

For my mother, with love

Prologue

The moment I saw her, my life was changed. More than fifty years have passed since that moment, and I'm an old man whose hair has turned white, whose body has grown frail. Yet my memories are full of color and strength.

Since my heart attack, I am to rest every day. So I have come back here to the island—her island—where it all began for me. It has changed, as I have. The great fire in '47 destroyed much. New buildings, new people have come. Cars crowd the streets without the charm of the jingling carriages. But I am lucky to be able to see it as it was, and as it is.

My son is a man now, a good one who chose to make his living from the sea. We have never understood each other, but have dealt together well enough. He has a quiet, lovely wife and a son of his own. The boy, young Holt, brings me a special kind of joy. Perhaps it is because I can see myself in him so clearly. The impatience, the fire, the passions that were once mine. Perhaps he, too, will feel too much, want too much. Yet I can't be sorry for it. If I could tell him one thing, it would be to grab hold of life and take.

My life has been full, and I'm grateful for the years I had with Margaret. I was no longer young when she became my wife. What we shared was not a blaze, but the quiet warmth of a banked fire. She brought me comfort, and I hope I gave her happiness. She's been gone for nearly ten years, and my memories of her are sweet.

Yet it is the memory of another woman that haunts me. This memory is so painfully clear, so complete. No amount of time could dull it. The years have not faded my image of her, nor have they altered by a single degree the desperate love I felt. Yes, feel still—will always feel though she is lost to me.

Perhaps now that I have brushed so close to death, I can open myself to it again, let myself remember what I have never been able to forget. Once it was too painful, and I lost the pain in a bottle. Finding no comfort there, I at last buried my misery in my work. Painting again, I traveled. But always, always, was pulled back here where I had once begun to live. Where I know I will one day die.

A man loves that way only once, and only if he is fortunate. For me, it was Bianca. It has always been Bianca.

It was June, the summer of 1912, before the Great War ripped the world apart. The summer of peace and beauty, of art and poetry, when the village of Bar Harbor opened itself to the wealthy and gave refuge to artists.

She came to the cliffs where I worked, her hand holding that of a child. I turned from my canvas, the brush still in my hand, the mood of the sea and the painting still on me. There she was, slender and lovely, the sunset hair swept up off her neck. The wind tugged at it, and at the skirts of the pale blue frock she wore. Her eyes were the color of the sea I was so frantically trying to recreate on canvas. They watched me, curious, wary. She had the pale and luminous skin of the Irish.

The moment I saw her, I knew I had to paint her. And I think I knew, as we stood in the wind, that I would have to love her.

She apologized for interrupting my work. The faint and musical lilt of Ireland was in the soft, polite voice. The child now in her arms was her son. She was Bianca Calhoun, another man's wife. Her summer home was on the ridge above. The Towers, the elaborate castle Fergus Calhoun had built. Even though I had only been on Mount Desert Island a short time, I had heard of Calhoun, and his home. Indeed I had admired the arrogant and fanciful lines of it, the turrets and peaks, the towers and parapets.

Such a place suited the woman who stood before me. She had a timeless beauty, a quiet steadiness, a graciousness that could never be taught, and banked passions simmering in her large green eyes. Yes, I was already in love, but then it was only with her beauty. As an artist, I wanted to interpret that beauty in my own way, with paint or pencils. Perhaps I frightened her by staring so intently. But the child, his name was Ethan, was fearless and friendly. She looked so young, so untouched, that it was difficult to believe the child was hers, and that she had two more besides.

She didn't stay long that day, but took her son and

*went home to her husband. I watched her walk through
the wild roses, the sun in her hair.*

*I couldn't paint the sea anymore that day. Her face
had already begun to haunt me.*

Chapter 1

She wasn't looking forward to this. It had to be done, of course. Suzanna dragged a fifty-pound bag of mulch over to her pickup, then muscled it into the bed. That small physical task wasn't the problem. In fact, she was pleased to be able to make the delivery her second stop on her way home.

It was the first stop she wished she could avoid. But for Suzanna Calhoun Dumont, duty could never be avoided.

She'd promised her family that she would speak to Holt Bradford, and Suzanna kept her promises. Or tried to, she thought, and wiped a forearm over her sweaty brow.

But damn it, she was tired. She'd put in a full day in Southwest Harbor, landscaping a new house, and she had a full schedule the next day. That wasn't taking into account that her sister Amanda was getting married in little more than a week, or that The Towers was mass confusion in preparation for the wedding and with the remodeling of the west wing. It didn't even begin to deal with the fact that she had two energetic children at home who would want, and deserved, their mother's time and attention that evening. Or the paperwork that was piling up on her desk—or the fact that one of her part-time employees had quit just that morning.

Well, she'd wanted to start a business, Suzanna reminded herself. And she'd done it. She glanced back at her shop, locked for the night with the display of summer blooms in the window, at the greenhouse just behind the main building. It belonged to her—and the bank, she thought with a little smile—every pansy, petunia and peony. She'd proven she wasn't the incompetent failure her ex-husband had told her she was. Over and over again.

She had two beautiful children, a family who loved her and a landscaping-and-gardening business that was holding its own. She didn't even suppose Bax's claim that she was dull could apply now. Not when she was in the middle of an adventure that had started eighty years before.

There certainly wasn't anything mundane about searching for a priceless emerald necklace, or being dogged by international jewel thieves who would stop at nothing to get their hands on her great-grandmother Bianca's legacy.

Not that she'd been much more than a supporting player so far, Suzanna mused as she climbed into the truck. It had been her sister C.C. who had started it by falling in love with Trenton St. James III, of the St. James Hotels. It had been his idea to turn part of the financially plagued family home into a luxury retreat. In doing so, the old legend of the Calhoun emeralds had leaked to the ever-eager press and had set off a chain reaction that had run a course from the absurd to the dangerous.

It had been Amanda who had nearly been killed when the desperate and obsessed thief going by the name of William Livingston had stolen family papers he'd hoped would lead him to the lost emeralds. And it had been her sister Lilah who had had her life threatened during the latest attempt.

In the week that had passed since that night, the police hadn't turned up a trace of Livingston, or his latest known alias, Ellis Caufield.

It was odd, she thought as she joined the stream of traffic, how The Towers and the lost emeralds had affected the entire family. The Towers had brought C.C. and Trent together. Then Sloan O'Riley had come to design the retreat and had fallen in love with Amanda. The shy history professor, Max Quartermain, had lost his heart to Suzanna's free-spirited sister, Lilah, and both of them had nearly been killed. Again, because of the emeralds.

There were times Suzanna wished they could forget about the necklace that had belonged to her great-grandmother. But she knew, as they all knew, that the necklace Bianca had hidden away before her death was meant to be found.

So they continued, following up every lead, exploring every dusty path. Now it was her turn. During his research, Max had uncovered the name of the artist Bianca had loved.

It was a story that never failed to make Suzanna wistful, but it was just her bad luck that the connection with the artist led to his grandson.

Holt Bradford. She sighed a little as she drove through the traffic-jammed streets of the village. She couldn't claim to know him well—wasn't sure anyone could. But she remembered him as a teenager. Surly, bad tempered and aloof. Of course, girls had been attracted by his go-to-hell attitude. The attraction helped along, no doubt, by the dark, brooding looks and angry gray eyes.

Odd she should remember the color of his eyes, she mused. But then again, the one time she had seen them up close and personal he'd all but burned her alive with them.

He'd probably forgotten the altercation, she assured herself. She hoped so. Altercations made her shaky and sweaty, and she'd had enough of them in her marriage to last a lifetime. Certainly Holt wouldn't still hold a grudge—it had been more than ten years. After all, he hadn't been hurt very much when he'd taken a header off his motorcycle. And it had been his fault, she thought, setting her chin. She'd had the right of way.

In any case, she had promised Lilah she would talk to him. Any connection with Bianca's lost emeralds had to be followed up. As Christian Bradford's grandson, Holt might have heard stories.

Since he'd come back to Bar Harbor a few months before, he had taken up residence in the same cottage his grandfather had lived in during his romance with Bianca. Suzanna was Irish enough to believe in fate. There was a Bradford in the cottage and Calhouns in The Towers. Surely between them, they could find the answers to the mystery that had haunted both families for generations.

The cottage was on the water, sheltered by two lovely old willows. The simple wooden structure made her think of a doll's house, and she thought it a shame that no one had cared enough to plant flowers. The grass was freshly mowed, but her professional eye noted that there were patches that needed reseeding, and the whole business could use a good dose of fertilizer.

She started toward the door when the barking of a dog and the rumble of a man's voice had her skirting around to the side.

There was a rickety pier jutting out above the calm, dark water. Tied to it was a neat little cabin cruiser in gleaming white. He sat in the stern, patiently polishing the brass. He was shirtless, his tanned skin taut over bone and muscle, and gleaming with sweat. His black hair was curled past where his collar would be if he'd worn one. Apparently he didn't find it necessary to cover himself with anything more than a pair of ripped and faded cut-offs. She noticed his hands, limber, long fingered, and wondered if he had inherited them from his artist grandfather.

Water lapped quietly at the boat. Behind it, she saw a fish hawk soar then plummet. It gave a cry of triumph as it rose up again, a silver fish caught wriggling in its claws. The man in the boat continued to work, untouched by or oblivious to the drama of life and death around him.

Suzanna fixed what she hoped was a polite smile on her face and walked toward the pier. "Excuse me."

When his head shot up, she stopped dead. She had the quick but vivid impression that if he'd had a weapon, it would have been aimed at her. In an instant, he had gone from relaxed to full alert, with an edgy kind of violence in the set of his body that had her mouth going dry.

As she struggled to steady her heartbeat, she noted that he had changed. The surly boy was now a dangerous man. There was no other word that came to mind. His face had matured so that it was all planes and angles, sharply defined. The stubble of a two-day beard added to the rough-and-ready look.

But it was his eyes once again, that dried up her throat. A man with eyes that sharp, that potent, needed no weapon.

He squinted at her but didn't rise or speak. He had to give himself a moment to level. If he'd been wearing his weapon, it would have been out and in his hand. That was one of the reasons he was here, and a civilian again.

He might have forced himself to relax—he knew how—but he remembered her face. A man didn't forget that face. God knows, he hadn't. Timeless. In one of his youthful fantasies, he'd imagined her as a princess, lost and lovely in flowing silks. And himself as the knight who would have slain a hundred dragons to have her.

The memory made him scowl.

She'd hardly changed, he thought. Her skin was still pale Irish roses and cream, the shape of her face still classically oval. Her mouth had remained full and romantically soft, her eyes that deep, deep, dreamy blue, luxuriously lashed. They were watching him now with a kind of baffled alarm as he took his time looking her over.

She'd pulled her hair back in a smooth ponytail, but he remembered how it had flowed, long and loose and gleaming blond over her shoulders.

She was tall—all the Calhoun women were—but she was too thin. His scowl deepened at that. He'd heard she'd been married and divorced, and that both had been difficult experiences. She had two children, a boy and girl. It was difficult to believe that the slender wand of a woman in grubby jeans and a sweaty T-shirt had ever given birth.

It was harder to believe, harder to accept, that she could jangle his nerves just by standing ten feet away.

With his eyes still on hers, he went back to his polishing. "Do you want something?"

She let out the breath she hadn't been aware she was holding. "I'm sorry to just drop in this way. I'm Suzanna Dumont. Suzanna Calhoun."

"I know who you are."

"Oh, well…" She cleared her throat. "I realize you're busy, but I'd like to talk with you for a few minutes. If this isn't a good time—"

"What about?"

Since he was being so gracious, she thought, annoyed, she'd get right to the point. "About your grandfather. He was Christian Bradford, wasn't he? The artist?"

"That's right. So?"

"It's kind of a long story. Can I sit down?"

When he only shrugged, she walked to the pier. It groaned and swayed under her feet, and she lowered herself carefully.

"Actually, it started back in 1912 or '13, with my great-grandmother, Bianca."

"I've heard the fairy tale." He could smell her now, flowers and sweat, and it made his stomach tighten. "She was an unhappy wife with a rich and difficult husband. She compensated by taking a lover. Somewhere along the line, she supposedly hid her emerald necklace. Insurance if she got up the guts to leave. Instead of taking off into the sunset with her lover, she jumped out of the tower window, and the emeralds were never found."

"It wasn't precisely—"

"Now your family's decided to start a treasure hunt," he went on as if she hadn't spoken. "Got a lot of press out of it, and more trouble than I imagine you bargained for. I heard you had some excitement a couple of weeks ago.''

"If you can call my sister being held at knifepoint excitement, yes.'' The fire had come into her eyes. She wasn't always good at defending herself, but when it came to her family, she was a scrapper. "The man who was working with Livingston, or whatever the bastard's calling himself now, nearly killed Lilah and her fiancé.''

"When you've got priceless emeralds with a legend attached, the rats gnaw through the woodwork.'' He knew about Livingston. Holt had been a cop for ten years, and though he'd spent most of that time in Vice, he'd read reports on the slick and often violent jewel thief.

"The legend and the emeralds are my family's business.''

"So why come to me? I turned in my shield. I'm retired.''

"I didn't come to you for professional help. It's personal.'' She took another breath, wanting to be clear and concise. "Lilah's fiancé used to be a history professor at Cornell. A couple of months ago, Livingston, going under the name of Ellis Caufield, hired him to go through the family's papers he'd stolen from us.''

Holt continued to polish the brightwork. "Doesn't sound like Lilah developed any taste.''

"Max didn't know the papers were stolen,'' Suzanna said between her teeth. "When he found out, Caufield nearly killed him. In any case, Max came to The Towers and continued his research for us. We've documented the emeralds' existence, and we've even interviewed a servant who worked at The Towers the year Bianca died.''

Holt shifted and continued to work. "You've been busy.''

"Yes. She corroborates the story that the necklace was

hidden, and that Bianca was in love, and planning to leave her husband. The man she was in love with was an artist.'' She waited a beat. ''His name was Christian Bradford.''

Something flickered in his eyes then was gone. Very deliberately he set down his rag. He pulled a cigarette from a pack, flicked on a lighter then slowly blew out a haze of smoke.

''Do you really expect me to believe that little fantasy?''

She'd hoped for surprise, even amazement. She'd gotten boredom. ''It's true. She used to meet him on the cliffs near The Towers.''

He gave her a thin smile that was very close to a sneer. ''Saw them, did you? Oh, I've heard about the ghost, too.'' He drew in more smoke, lazily released it. ''The melancholy spirit of Bianca Calhoun, drifting through her summer home. You Calhouns are just full of—stories.''

Her eyes darkened, but her voice remained very controlled. ''Bianca Calhoun and Christian Bradford were in love. The summer she died, they met often on the cliffs just below The Towers.''

That touched a chord, but he only shrugged. ''So what?''

''So there's a connection. My family can't afford to overlook any connection, particularly one so vital as this one. It's very possible she told him where she put the emeralds.''

''I don't see what a flirtation—an unsubstantiated flirtation—between two people some eighty years ago has to do with emeralds.''

''If you could get past this prejudice you seem to have toward my family, we might be able to figure it out.''

"Not interested in either part." He flipped open the top of a small cooler. "Want a beer?"

"No."

"Well, I'm fresh out of champagne." Watching her, he twisted off the top, tossed it toward a plastic bucket, then drank deeply. "You know, if you think about it, you'd see it's a little tough to swallow. The lady of the manor, well-bred, well-off, and the struggling artist. Doesn't play, babe. You'd be better off dropping the whole thing and concentrating on planting your flowers. Isn't that what you're doing these days?"

He could make her angry, she thought, but he wasn't going to shake her from her purpose. "My sisters' lives were threatened, my home has been broken into. Idiots are sneaking around in my garden and digging up my rosebushes." She stood, tall and slim and furious. "I have no intention of dropping the whole thing."

"Your business." He flicked the cigarette away before jumping effortlessly onto the pier. It shook and swayed beneath them. He was taller than she remembered, and she had to angle her chin to keep her eyes level. "Just don't expect to suck me into it."

"All right then. I'll just stop wasting my time and yours."

He waited until she'd stepped off the pier. "Suzanna." He liked the way it sounded when he said it. Soft and feminine and old-fashioned. "You ever learn to drive?"

Eyes stormy, she took a step back toward him. "Is that what this is all about?" she demanded. "You're still steaming because you fell off that stupid motorcycle and bruised your inflated male ego?"

"That wasn't the only thing that got bruised—or scraped, or lacerated." He remembered the way she'd looked. God, she couldn't have been more than sixteen.

Rushing out of her car, her hair windblown, her face pale, her eyes dark and drenched with concern and fear.

And he'd been sprawled on the side of the road, his twenty-year-old pride as raw as the skin the asphalt had abraded.

"I don't believe it," she was saying. "You're still mad, after what, twelve years, for something that was clearly your own fault."

"My fault?" He tipped the bottle toward her. "You're the one who ran into me."

"I never ran into you or anyone. You fell."

"If I hadn't ditched the bike, you would have run into me. You weren't looking where you were going."

"I had the right of way. And you were going entirely too fast."

"Bull." He was starting to enjoy himself. "You were checking that pretty face of yours in the rearview mirror."

"I certainly was not. I never took my eyes off the road."

"If you'd had your eyes on the road, you wouldn't have run into me."

"I didn't—" She broke off, swore under her breath. "I'm not going to stand here and argue with you about something that happened twelve years ago."

"You came here to try to drag me into something that happened eighty years ago."

"That was an obvious mistake." She would have left it at that, but a very big, very wet dog came bounding across the lawn. With two happy barks, the animal leaped, planting both muddy feet on Suzanna's shirt and sending her staggering back.

"Sadie, down!" As Holt issued the terse command, he

caught Suzanna before she hit the ground. "Stupid bitch."

"I beg your pardon?"

"Not you, the dog." Sadie was already sitting, thumping her dripping tail. "Are you all right?" He still had his arms around her, bracing her against his chest.

"Yes, fine." He had muscles like rock. It was impossible not to notice. Just as it was impossible not to notice that his breath fluttered along her temple, that he smelled very male. It had been a very long time since she had been held by a man.

Slowly he turned her around. For a moment, a moment too long, she was face-to-face with him, caught in the circle of his arms. His gaze flicked down to her mouth, lingered. A gull wheeled overhead, banked, then soared out over the water. He felt her heart thud against his. Once, twice, three times.

"Sorry," he said as he released her. "Sadie still sees herself as a cute little puppy. She got your shirt dirty."

"Dirt's my business." Needing time to recover, she crouched down to rub the dog's head. "Hi, there, Sadie."

Holt pushed his hands into his pockets as Suzanna acquainted herself with his dog. The bottle lay where he'd tossed it, spilling its contents onto the lawn. He wished to God she didn't look so beautiful, that her laugh as the dog lapped at her face didn't play so perfectly on his nerves.

In that one moment he'd held her, she'd fit into his arms as he'd once imagined she would. His hands fisted inside his pockets because he wanted to touch her. No, that wasn't even close. He wanted to pull her inside the cottage, toss her onto the bed and do incredible things to her.

"Maybe a man who owns such a nice dog isn't all

bad.'' She tossed a glance over her shoulder and the cautious smile died on her lips. The way he was looking at her, his eyes so dark and fierce, his bony face so set had the breath backing up in her lungs. There was violence trembling around him. She'd had a taste of violence from a man, and the memory of it made her limbs weak.

Slowly he relaxed his shoulders, his arms, his hands. ''Maybe he isn't,'' he said easily. ''But it's more a matter of her owning me at this point.''

Suzanna found it more comfortable to look at the dog than the master. ''We have a puppy. Well, he's growing by leaps and bounds so he'll be as big as Sadie soon. In fact, he looks a great deal like her. Did she have a litter a few months ago?''

''No.''

''Hmm. He's got the same coloring, the same shaped face. My brother-in-law found him half-starved. Someone had dumped him, I suppose, and he'd managed to get up to the cliffs.''

''Even I draw the line at abandoning helpless puppies.''

''I didn't mean to imply—'' She broke off because a new thought had jumped into her mind. It was no crazier than looking for missing emeralds. ''Did your grandfather have a dog?''

''He always had a dog, used to take it with him wherever he went. Sadie's one of the descendants.''

Carefully she got to her feet again. ''Did he have a dog named Fred?''

Holt's brows drew together. ''Why?''

''Did he?''

Holt was already sure he didn't like where this was leading. ''The first dog he had was called Fred. That was before the First World War. He did a painting of him.

And when Fred exercised the right *de seigneur* around the neighborhood, my grandfather took a couple of the puppies.''

Suzanne rubbed suddenly damp hands on her jeans. It took all of her control to keep her voice low and steady. ''The day before Bianca died, she brought a puppy home to her children. A little black puppy she called Fred.'' She saw his eyes change and knew she had his attention, and his interest. ''She'd found him out on the cliffs—the cliffs where she went to meet Christian.'' She moistened her lips as Holt continued to stare at her and say nothing. ''My great-grandfather wouldn't allow the dog to stay. They argued about it, quite seriously. We were able to locate a maid who'd worked there, and she'd heard the whole thing. No one was sure what happened to that dog. Until now.''

''Even if that's true,'' Holt said slowly, ''it doesn't change the bottom line. There's nothing I can do for you.''

''You can think about it, you can try to remember if he ever said anything, if he left anything behind that could help.''

''I've got enough to think about.'' He paced a few feet away. He didn't want to be involved with anything that would bring him into contact with her again and again.

Suzanna didn't argue. She could only stare at the long, jagged scar that ran from his shoulder to nearly his waist. He turned, met her horrified eyes and stiffened.

''Sorry, if I'd known you were coming to call, I'd have put on a shirt.''

''What—'' She had to swallow the block of emotion in her throat. ''What happened to you?''

''I was a cop one night too long.'' His eyes stayed steady on hers. ''I can't help you, Suzanna.''

She shook away the pity he obviously would detest. "You won't."

"Whatever. If I'd wanted to dig around in other people's problems, I'd still be on the force."

"I'm only asking you to do a little thinking, to let us know if you remember anything that might help."

He was running out of patience. Holt figured he'd already given her more than her share for one day. "I was a kid when he died. Do you really think he'd have told me if he'd had an affair with a married woman?"

"You make it sound sordid."

"Some people don't figure adultery's romantic." Then he shrugged. It was nothing to him either way. "Then again, if one of the partners turns out to be a washout, I guess it's tough to come down on the other for looking someplace else."

She looked away at that, closing in on a private pain. "I'm not interested in your views on morality, Holt. Just your memory. And I've taken up enough of your time."

He didn't know what he'd said to put that sad, injured look in her eyes. But he couldn't let her leave with that haunting him. "Look, I think you're reaching at straws here, but if anything comes to mind, I'll let you know. For Sadie's ancestor's sake."

"I'd appreciate it."

"But don't expect anything."

With a half laugh she turned to walk to her truck. "Believe me, I won't." It surprised her when he crossed the lawn with her.

"I heard you started a business."

"That's right." She glanced around the yard. "You could use me."

The faint sneer came again. "I ain't the rosebush type."

"The cottage is." Unoffended, she fished her keys out of her pocket. "It wouldn't take much to make it charming."

"I'm not in the market for posies, babe. I'll leave the puttering around the rose garden to you."

She thought of the aching muscles she took home with her every night and climbed into the truck to slam the door. "Yes, puttering around the garden is something we women do best. By the way, Holt, your grass needs fertilizer. I'm sure you have plenty to spread around."

She gunned the engine, set the shift in reverse and pulled out.

Chapter 2

The children came rushing out of the house, followed by a big-footed black dog. The boy and the girl skimmed down the worn stone steps with the easy balance and grace of youth. The dog tripped over his own feet and somersaulted. Poor Fred, Suzanna thought as she climbed out of the truck. It didn't look as though he would ever outgrow his puppy clumsiness.

"Mom!" Each child attached to one of Suzanna's jean-clad legs. At six, Alex was already tall for his age and dark as a gypsy. His sturdy tanned legs were scabbed at the knees and his bony elbows were scraped. Not from clumsiness, Suzanna thought, but from derring-do. Jenny, a year younger and blond as a fairy princess, carried the same badges of honor. Suzanna forgot her irritation and fatigue the moment she bent to kiss them.

"What have you two been up to?"

"We're building a fort," Alex told her. "It's going to be impregnant."

"Impregnable," Suzanna corrected, tweaking his nose.

"Yeah, and Sloan said he could help us with it on Saturday."

"Can you?" Jenny asked.

"After work." She bent to pet Fred, who was trying to push his way through the children for his rightful share of affection. "Hello, boy. I think I met one of your relatives today."

"Does Fred have relatives?" Jenny wanted to know.

"It certainly looked that way." She walked over to sit with the children on the steps. It was a luxury to sit, to smell the sea and flowers, to have a child under each arm. "I think I met his cousin Sadie."

"Where? Can she come to visit? Is she nice?"

"In the village," Suzanna said, answering Alex's rapid-fire questions in turn. "I don't know, and yes, she's very nice. Big, like Fred's going to be when he grows into his feet. What else did you do today?"

"Loren and Lisa came over," Jenny told her. "We killed hundreds of marauders."

"Well, we can all sleep easy tonight."

"And Max told us a story about storming the beach at Normally."

Chuckling, Suzanna kissed the top of Jenny's head. "I think that was Normandy."

"Lisa and Jenny played dolls, too." Alex gave his sister a brotherly smirk.

"She wanted to. She got the brand-new Barbie and her car for her birthday."

"It was a Ferrari," Alex said importantly, but didn't want to admit that he and Loren had played with it when the girls were out of the room. He inched closer to toy with his mother's ponytail. "Loren and Lisa are going to Disney World next week."

Suzanna bit back a sigh. She knew her children dreamed of going to that enchanted kingdom in central Florida. "We'll go someday."

"Soon?" Alex prompted.

She wanted to promise, but couldn't. "Someday," she repeated. The weariness was back when she rose to take each child by the hand. "You guys run and tell Aunt Coco I'm home. I need to shower and change. Okay?"

"Can we go to work with you tomorrow?"

She gave Jenny's hand a quick squeeze. "Carolanne's watching the shop tomorrow. I have site work." She felt their disappointment as keenly as her own. "Next week. Go ahead now," she said as she opened the massive front door. "And I'll look at your fort after dinner."

Satisfied with that, they barreled down the hall with the dog at their heels.

They didn't ask for much, Suzanna thought as she climbed the curving stairs to the second floor. And there was so much more she wanted to give them. She knew they were happy and safe and secure. They had a huge family who loved them. With one of her sisters married, and two others engaged, her children had men in their lives. Maybe uncles didn't replace a father, but it was the best she could do.

They hadn't heard from Baxter Dumont for months. Alex hadn't even rated a card on his birthday. The child support check was late again—as it was every month. Bax was too sharp a lawyer to neglect the payment completely, but he made certain it arrived weeks after its due date. To test her, she knew. To see if she would beg for it. Thank God she hadn't needed to yet.

The divorce had been final for a year and a half, but he continued to take out his feelings for her on the chil-

dren—the only truly worthwhile thing they had made together.

Perhaps that was why she had yet to get over the nagging disillusionment, the sense of betrayal and loss and
inadequacy. She no longer loved him. That love had died
before Jenny had been born. But the hurt…Suzanna
shook her head. She was working on it.

She stepped into her room. Like most of the rooms in
The Towers, Suzanne's bedroom was huge. The house
had been built in the early 1900s by her great-grandfather. It had been a showpiece, a testament to his vanity,
his taste for the opulent and his need for status. It was
five stories of somber granite with fanciful peaks and
parapets, two spiraling towers and layering terraces. The
interior was lofty ceilings, fancy woodwork, mazelike
hallways. Part castle, part manor house, it had served first
as summer home, then as permanent residence.

Through the years and financial reversals, the house
had fallen on hard times. Suzanna's room, like the others,
showed cracks in the plaster. The floor was scarred, the
roof leaked and the plumbing had a mind of its own. As
one, the Calhouns loved their family home. Now that the
west wing was under renovation, they hoped it would be
able to pay its own way.

She went to the closet for a robe, thinking that she'd
been one of the lucky ones. She'd been able to bring her
children here, into a real home, when their own had
crumbled. She hadn't had to interview strangers to care
for them while she made a living. Her father's sister, who
had raised Suzanna and her sisters after their parents had
died, was now caring for Suzanna's children. Though
Suzanna was aware that Alex and Jenny were a handful,
she knew there was no one better suited for the task than
Aunt Coco.

And one day soon they would find Bianca's emeralds, and everything would settle back to what passed for normal in the Calhoun household.

"Suze." Lilah gave the door a quick knock then poked her head in. "Did you see him?"

"Yes, I saw him."

"Terrific." Lilah, her red hair curling to her waist, strolled in. She stretched out diagonally on the bed, plumping a pillow against the tiered headboard. Easily she settled into her favorite position. Horizontal. "So tell me."

"He hasn't changed much."

"Oh-oh."

"He was abrupt and rude." Suzanna pulled the T-shirt over her head. "I think he considered shooting me for trespassing. When I tried to explain what was going on, he sneered." Remembering that look, she tugged down the zipper of her jeans. "Basically, he was obnoxious, arrogant and insulting."

"Mmm. Sounds like a prince."

"He thinks we made the whole thing up to get publicity for The Towers when we open the retreat next year."

"What a crock." That stirred Lilah enough to have her sitting up. "Max was nearly killed. Does he think we're crazy?"

"Exactly." With a nod, Suzanna dragged on her robe. "I couldn't begin to guess why, but he seems to have a grudge against the Calhouns in general."

Lilah gave a sleepy smile. "Still stewing because you knocked him off his motorcycle."

"I did not—" On an oath, Suzanna gave up. "Never mind, the point is I don't think we're going to get any help from him." After pulling the band out of her hair, she ran her hands through it. "Though after the business with the dog, he did say he'd think about it."

"What dog?"

"Fred's cousin," she said over her shoulder as she walked into the bath to turn on the shower.

Lilah came to the doorway just as Suzanna was pulling the curtain closed. "Fred has a cousin?"

Over the drum of the water, Suzanna told her about Sadie, and her ancestors.

"But that's fabulous. It's just one more link in the chain. I'll have to tell Max."

With her eyes closed, Suzanna stuck her head under the shower. "Tell him he's on his own. Christian's grandson isn't interested."

He didn't want to be. Holt sat on the back porch, the dog at his feet, and watched the water turn to indigo in twilight.

There was music here, the symphony of insects in the grass, the rustle of wind, the countermelody of water against wood. Across the bay, Bar Island began to fade and merge into dusk. Nearby someone was playing a radio, a lonely alto sax solo that suited Holt's mood.

This was what he wanted. Quiet, solitude, no responsibilities. He'd earned it, hadn't he? he thought as he tipped the beer to his lips. He'd given ten years of his life to other people's problems, their tragedies, their miseries.

He was burned out, bone-dry and tired as hell.

He wasn't even sure he'd been a good cop. Oh, he had citations and medals that claimed he had been. But he also had a twelve-inch scar on his back that reminded him he'd nearly been a dead one.

Now he just wanted to enjoy his retirement, repair a

few motors, scrape some barnacles, maybe do a little boating. He'd always been good with his hands and knew he could make a decent living repairing boats. Running his own business, at his own pace, in his own way. No reports to type, no leads to follow up, no dark alleys to search.

No knife-wielding junkies springing out of the shadows to rip you open and leave you bleeding on the littered concrete.

Holt closed his eyes and took another pull of beer. He'd made up his mind during the long, painful hospital stay. There would be no more commitment in his life, no more trying to save the world from itself. From that point on, he would start looking out for himself. Just himself.

He'd taken the money he'd inherited and had come home, to do as little as possible with the rest of his life. Sun and sea in the summer, roaring fires and howling winds in the winter. It wasn't so damn much to ask.

He'd been settling in, feeling pretty good about himself. Then she'd come along.

Hadn't it been bad enough that he'd looked at her and felt—Lord, the way he'd felt when he'd been twenty years old. Churned up and hungry. He was still hung up on her.

The lovely, and unattainable, Suzanna Calhoun of the Bar Harbor Calhouns. The princess in the tower. She'd lived high up in her castle on the cliffs. And he had lived in a cottage on the edge of the village. His father had been a lobsterman, and Holt had often delivered a catch to the Calhouns' back door—never going beyond the kitchen. But he'd sometimes heard voices or laughter or music. And he had wondered and wanted.

Now she had come to him. But he wasn't a love-struck boy any longer. He was a realist. Suzanna was out of his

league, just as she had always been. Even if it had been
different, he wasn't interested in a woman who had home
and hearth written all over her.

As far as the emeralds went, there was nothing he
could do to help her. Nothing he wanted to do.

He'd known about the emeralds, of course. That particular story had made national press. But the idea that
his grandfather had been involved, had loved and been
loved by a Calhoun woman. That was fascinating.

Even with the coincidence about the dogs, he wasn't
sure he believed it. Holt hadn't known his grandmother,
but his grandfather had been the hero of his childhood.
He'd been the dashing and mysterious figure who had
gone off to foreign places, come back with fabulous
stories. He'd been the man who had been able to perform
magic with a canvas and brush.

He could remember climbing up the stairs to the studio
as a child to watch the tall man with the snow-white hair
at work. Yet it had seemed more like combat than work.
An elegant and passionate duel between his grandfather
and the canvas.

They would take long walks, the young boy and the
old man, along the shore, across the rocks. Up on the
cliffs. With a sigh, Holt sat back. Very often they had
walked to the cliffs just below The Towers. Even as a
child he'd understood that as his grandfather had looked
out to sea, he had gone someplace else.

Once, they had sat on the rocks there and his grandfather had told him a story about the castle on the cliffs,
and the princess who'd lived there.

Had he been talking about The Towers, and Bianca?

Restless, Holt rose to go inside. Sadie glanced up, then
settled her head on her front paws again as the screen
door slammed.

The cottage suited him more than the home he'd grown up in. That had been a neat and soulless place with worn linoleum and dark paneled walls. Holt had sold it after his mother's death three years before. Recently he'd used the profits for some repairs and modernization of the cottage, but preferred keeping the old place much as it had been in his grandfather's day.

It was a boxy house, with plaster walls and wood floors. The original stone fireplace had been pointed up, and Holt looked forward to the first cool night when he could try it out.

The bedroom was tiny, almost an afterthought that jutted out from the main structure. He liked lying in bed at night and listening to rain drumming on the tin roof. The stairs to his grandfather's studio had been reinforced, as well as the railing that skirted along the open balcony. He climbed up now, to look at the wide, airy space, dim with twilight.

Now and then he thought about putting skylights in the angled roof, but he never considered refinishing the floor. The dark old wood was splattered with paint that had dripped from brush or palette. There were streaks of carmine and turquoise, drops of emerald green and canary yellow. His grandfather had preferred the vivid, the passionate, even the violent in his work.

Against one wall, canvases were stacked, Holt's legacy from a man who had only begun to find critical and financial success in his last years. They would, he knew, be worth a hefty sum. Yet as he never considered sanding the paint from the floors, he had never considered selling this part of his inheritance.

Crouching down, he began to look through the paintings. He knew them all, had studied them countless times, wondering how he could have come from a man with such vision and talent. Holt turned over the portrait, knowing that was why he had come up here.

The woman was as beautiful as a dream—the fine-featured oval face, the alabaster skin. Rich red-gold hair was swept up off a graceful neck. Full, soft lips were curved, just a little. But it was the eyes that drew Holt, as they always had. They were green, like a misty sea. It wasn't their color that pulled at him, but the expression in them, the look, the emotion that had been captured by his grandfather's brush and skill.

Such quiet sadness. Such inner grief. It was almost too painful to look at, because to look too long was to feel. He had seen that expression today, in Suzanna's eyes.

Could this be Bianca? he wondered. The resemblance was there, in the shape of the face, the curve of the mouth. The coloring was certainly wrong and the similarities slight. Except the eyes, he thought. When he looked at them, he thought of Suzanna.

Because he was thinking of her too much, he told himself. He rose, but he didn't turn the portrait back to the wall. He stood staring at it for a long time, wondering if his grandfather had loved the woman he'd painted.

It was going to be another hot one, Suzanna thought. Though it was barely seven, the air was already sticky. They needed rain, but the moisture hung in the air and stubbornly refused to fall.

Inside her shop, she checked on the refrigerated blooms and left a note for Carolanne to push the carnations by selling them at half price. She checked the soil in the hanging pots of impatiens and geraniums, then moved on to the display of gloxinia and begonias.

Satisfied, she took her sprayer out to drench the flats of annuals and perennials. The rosebushes and peonies were moving well, she noted. As were the yews and junipers.

By seven-thirty, she was checking on the greenhouse plants, grateful that her inventory was dwindling. What didn't sell, she would winter over. She would also take cuttings for next year's plants. But winter, and that quiet work, was months away.

By eight her pickup was loaded, and she was on her way to Seal Harbor. She would put in a full day's work there on the grounds of a newly constructed home. The buyers were from Boston, and wanted their summer home to have an established yard, complete with shrubs, trees and flower beds.

It would be hot, sweaty work, Suzanne mused. But it would also be quiet. The Andersons were in Boston this week, so she would have the yard to herself. She liked nothing better than working with the soil and living things, tending something she had planted and watching it grow and thrive.

Like her children, she thought with a smile. Her babies. Every time she put them to bed at night or watched them run in the sunlight, she knew that nothing that had happened to her before, nothing that would happen to her in the future would dim that glow of knowing they were hers.

The failed marriage had left her shaken and uncertain, and there were times she still had terrible doubts about herself as a woman. But not as a mother. Her children had the very best she could give them. The bond nourished her, as well as them.

Over the past two years, she'd begun to believe that she could be a success in business. Her flair for gardening had been her only useful skill and had been a kind of salvation during the last months of her dying marriage.

In desperation she had sold her jewelry, taken out a loan and had plunged into Island Gardens.

It had made her feel good to use her maiden name. She hadn't wanted any frivolous or clever name for the business, but something straightforward. The first year had been rough—particularly when she'd been pouring every cent she could spare into legal fees to fight a custody suit.

The thought of that, the memory of it, still made her blood run cold. She couldn't have lost them.

Bax hadn't wanted the children, but he'd wanted to make things difficult for her. When it had been over, she'd lost fifteen pounds, countless hours of sleep and had been up to her neck in debt. But she had her children. The ugly battle had been won, and the price meant nothing.

Gradually she was pulling out. She'd gained back a few of the pounds, had caught up a bit on her sleep and was slowly, meticulously hacking away at the debt. In the two years since she'd opened the business, she'd earned a reputation as dependable, reasonable and imaginative. Two of the resorts had tried her out, and it looked as though they'd be negotiating long-term contracts.

That would mean buying another truck, hiring on full-time labor. And maybe, just maybe, that trip to Disney World.

She pulled up in the driveway of the pretty Cape Cod house. Now, she reminded herself, it meant getting to work.

The grounds took up about a half acre and were gently sloped. She had had three in-depth meetings with the owners to determine the plan. Mrs. Anderson wanted plenty of spring flowering trees and shrubs, and the long-term privacy factor of evergreens. She wanted to enjoy a perennial bed that was carefree and full of summer color. Mr. Anderson didn't want to spend his summers maintaining the yard, particularly the side portion, which fell in a more dramatic grade. There, Suzanna would use ground covers and rockeries to prevent erosion.

By noon, she had measured off each area with stakes and strings. The hardy azaleas were planted. Two long-blooming fairy roses flanked the flagstone walk and were already sweetening the air. Because Mrs. Anderson had expressed a fondness for lilacs, Suzanna placed a trio of compact shrubs near the master bedroom window, where the next spring's breezes would carry the scent indoors.

The yard was coming alive for her. It helped her ignore the aching muscles in her arms as she drenched the new plants with water. Birds were chirping, and somewhere in the near distance, a lawn mower was putting away.

One day, she would drive by and see that the fast-growing hedge roses she had planted along the fence had spread and bloomed until they covered the chain link. She would see the azaleas bloom in the spring and the maple leaves go red in the fall, and know that she'd been part of that.

It was important, more important than she could admit to anyone, that she leave a mark. She needed that to remind herself that she wasn't the weak and useless woman who had been so callously tossed aside.

Dripping with sweat, she picked up her water bottle and shovel and headed around to the front of the house again. She'd put in the first of the flowering almonds and was digging the hole for the second when a car pulled into the driveway behind her truck. Resting on her shovel, Suzanna watched Holt climb out.

She let out a little huff of breath, annoyed that her solitude had been invaded, and went back to digging.

"Out for a drive?" she asked when his shadow fell over her.

"No, the girl at the shop told me where to find you. What the hell are you doing?"

"Playing canasta." She shoveled some more dirt. "What do you want?"

"Put that shovel down before you hurt yourself. You've got no business digging ditches."

"Digging ditches is my business—more or less. Now, what do you want?"

He watched her dig for another ten seconds before he snatched the shovel away from her. "Give me that damn thing and sit down."

Patience had always been her strong point, but she was hard-pressed to find it now. Working at it, she adjusted the brim of the fielder's cap she wore. "I'm on a schedule, and I have six more trees, two rosebushes and twenty square feet of ground cover to plant. If you've got something to say, fine. Talk while I work."

He jerked the shovel out of her reach. "How deep do you want it?" She only lifted a brow. "How deep do you want the hole?"

She skimmed her gaze down, then up again. "I'd say a little more than six feet would be enough to bury you in."

He grinned, surprising her. "And you used to be so sweet." Plunging the shovel in, he began to dig. "Just tell me when to stop."

Normally she repaid kindness with kindness. But she was going to make an exception. "You can stop right now; I don't need any help. And I don't want the company."

"I didn't know you had a stubborn streak." He glanced up as he tossed dirt aside. "I guess I had a hard time getting past that pretty face." That pretty face, he noted, was flushed and damp and had shadows of fatigue under the eyes. It annoyed the hell out of him. "I thought you sold flowers."

"I do. I also plant them."

"Even I know that thing there is a tree."

"I plant those, too." Giving up, she took out a bandanna and wiped at her neck. "The hole needs to be wider, not deeper."

He shifted to accommodate her. Maybe he needed to do a little reevaluating. "How come you don't have anybody doing the heavy work for you?"

"Because I can do it myself."

Yes, there was stubbornness in the tone, and just a touch of nastiness. He liked her better for it. "Looks like a two-man job to me."

"It is a two-man job—the other man quit yesterday to be a rock star. His band got a gig down in Brighton Beach."

"Big time."

"Hmm. That's fine," she said, and turned to heft the three-foot tree by its balled roots. As Holt frowned at her, she lifted it, then set it carefully in the hole.

"Now I guess I fill it back in."

"You've got the shovel," she pointed out. As he worked, she dragged a bag of peat moss closer and began to mix it with the soil.

Her nails were short and rounded, he noted as she dug her already grimed fingers into the soil. There was no wedding ring on her finger. In fact, she wore no jewelry at all, though she had hands that were meant to wear beautiful things.

She worked patiently, her head down, her cap shielding her eyes. He could see the nape of her neck and wondered what it would be like to press his lips there. Her skin would be hot now, and damp. Then she rose, switching on the garden hose to drench the dirt.

"You do this every day?"

"I try to take a day or two in the shop. I can bring the kids in with me." With her feet, she tamped down the damp earth. When the tree was secure, she spread a thick lawyer of mulch, her moves competent and practiced. "Next spring, this will be covered with blooms." She wiped the back of her wrist over her brow. The little tank top she wore had a line of sweat down the front and back that only emphasized her fragile build. "I really am on a schedule, Holt. I've got some aspens and white pine to plant out in back, so if you need to talk to me, you're going to have to come along."

He glanced around the yard. "Did you do all this today?"

"Yes. What do you think?"

"I think you're courting sunstroke."

A compliment, she supposed, would have been too much to ask. "I appreciate the medical evaluation." She put a hand on the shovel, but he held on. "I need this."

"I'll carry it."

"Fine." She loaded the bags of peat and mulch into a wheelbarrow. He swore at her, tossed the shovel on top then nudged her away to push the wheelbarrow himself.

"Where out back?"

"By the stakes near the rear fence."

She frowned after him when he started off, then followed him. He began digging without consulting her so she emptied the wheelbarrow and headed back to her truck. When he glanced up, she was pushing out two more trees. They planted the first one together, in silence.

He hadn't realized that putting a tree in the ground

could be soothing, even rewarding work. But when it stood, young and straight in the dazzling sunlight, he felt soothed. And rewarded.

"I was thinking about what you said yesterday," he began when they set the second tree in its new home.

"And?"

He wanted to swear. There was such patience in the single word, as if she'd known all along he would bring it up. "And I still don't think there's anything I can do, or want to do, but you may be right about the connection."

"I know I'm right about the connection." She brushed mulch from her hands to her jeans. "If you came out here just to tell me that, you've wasted a trip."

She rolled the empty wheelbarrow to the truck. She was about to muscle the next two trees out of the bed when he jumped up beside her.

"I'll get the damn things out." Muttering, he filled the wheelbarrow and rolled it back to the rear of the yard. "He never mentioned her to me. Maybe he knew her, maybe they had an affair, but I don't see how that helps you."

"He loved her," Suzanna said quietly as she picked up the shovel to dig. "That means he knew how she felt, how she thought. He might have had an idea where she would have hidden the emeralds."

"He's dead."

"I know." She was silent a moment as she worked. "Bianca kept a journal—at least we're nearly certain she did, and that she hid it away with the necklace. Christian might have kept one, too."

Annoyed, he grabbed the shovel again. "I never saw it."

She suppressed the urge to snap at him. However much

it might grate, he could be a link. "I suppose most people keep a private journal in a private place. Or he might have kept some letters from her. We found one Bianca wrote him and was never able to send."

"You're chasing windmills, Suzanna."

"This is important to my family." She set the white pine carefully in the hole. "It's not the monetary value of the emeralds. It's what they meant to her."

He watched her work, the competent and gentle hands, the surprisingly strong shoulders. The delicate curve of her neck. "How could you know what they meant to her?"

She kept her eyes down. "I can't explain that to you in any way you'd understand or accept."

"Try me."

"We all seem to have some kind of bond with her— especially Lilah." She didn't look up when she heard him digging the next hole. "We'd never seen the emeralds, not even a photograph. After Bianca died, Fergus, my great-grandfather, destroyed all pictures of her. But Lilah...she drew a sketch of them one night. It was after we'd had a séance."

She did look up then and caught his look of amused disbelief. "I know how it sounds," she said, her voice stiff and defensive. "But my aunt believes in that sort of thing. And after that night, I think she may be right to. My youngest sister, C.C. had an...experience during the séance. She saw them—the emeralds. That's when Lilah drew the sketch. Weeks later, Lilah's fiancé found a picture of the emeralds in a library book. They were exactly as Lilah had drawn them, exactly as C.C. had seen them."

He said nothing for a moment as he set the next tree in place. "I'm not much on mysticism. Maybe one of your sisters saw the picture before, and had forgotten about it."

"If any of us had seen a picture, we wouldn't have forgotten. Still, the point is that all of us feel that finding the emeralds is important."

"They might have been sold eighty years ago."

"No. There was no record. Fergus was a maniac about keeping his finances." Unconsciously she arched her back, rolled her shoulders to relieve the ache. "Believe me, we've been through every scrap of paper we could find."

He let it drop, mulling it over as they planted the last of the trees.

"You know the bit about the needle in the haystack?" he asked as he helped her spread mulch. "People don't really find it."

"They would if they kept looking." Curious, she sat back on her heels to study him. "Don't you believe in hope?"

He was close enough to touch her, to rub the smudge of dirt from her cheek or run a hand down the ponytail. He did neither. "No, only in what is."

"Then I'm sorry for you." They rose together, their bodies nearly brushing. She felt something rush along her skin, something race through her blood, and automatically stepped back. "If you don't believe in what could be, there isn't any use in planting trees, or having children or even watching the sun set."

He'd felt it, too. And resented and feared it every bit as much as she. "If you don't keep your eye on what's real, right now, you end up dreaming your life away. I don't believe in the necklace, Suzanna, or in ghosts, or in eternal love. But if and when I'm certain that my

grandfather was involved with Bianca Calhoun, I'll do
what I can to help you.''

She gave a half laugh. ''You don't believe in hope or
love, or anything else apparently. Why would you agree
to help us?''

''Because if he did love her, he would have wanted
me to.'' Bending, he picked up the shovel and handed it
back to her. ''I've got things to do.''

Chapter 3

Suzanna pulled up to the shop, pleased that she had to squeeze between a station wagon and a hatchback in the graveled parking area. There were a few people wandering around the flats of annuals, and a young couple deliberating over the climbing roses. A woman, hugely pregnant, strolled about, carrying a tray of mixed pots. The toddler by her side held a single geranium like a flag.

Inside, Carolanne was ringing up a sale and flirting with the young man who held a ceramic urn of pink double begonias. ''Your mother will love them,'' she said, and swept her long lashes over doe-colored eyes. ''There's nothing like flowers for a birthday. Or anytime. We're having a special on carnations.'' She smiled and tossed her long, curling brown hair. ''If you have a girl-friend.''

''Well, no...'' He cleared his throat. ''Not really. Right now.''

"Oh." Her smile warmed several degrees. "That's too bad." She gave him his change and a long look. "Come back anytime. I'm usually here."

"Sure. Thanks." He shot a glance over his shoulder, trying to keep her in sight, and nearly ran over Suzanna. "Oh. Sorry."

"That's all right. I hope your mother enjoys them." Chuckling, she joined the pert brunette at the cash register. "You're amazing."

"Wasn't he cute? I love it when they blush. Well." She turned her smile on Suzanna. "You're back early."

"It didn't take as long as I thought." She didn't feel it was necessary to add she'd had unexpected and unwanted help. Carolanne was a hard worker, a skilled salesperson, and an inveterate gossip. "How are things here?"

"Moving along. All this sunshine must be inspiring people to beef up their gardens. Oh, Mrs. Russ was back. She liked the primroses so much, she made her husband build her another window box so she could buy more. Since she was in the mood, I sold her two hibiscus—and two of those terra-cotta pots to put them in."

"I love you. Mrs. Russ loves you, and Mr. Russ is going to learn to hate you." At Carolanne's laugh, Suzanna looked out through the glass. "I'll go and see if I can help those people decide which roses they want."

"The new Mr. and Mrs. Halley. They both wait tables over at Captain Jack's, and just bought a cottage. He's studying to be an engineer, and she's going to start teaching at the elementary school in September."

Shaking her head, Suzanna laughed. "Like I said, you're amazing."

"No, just nosy." Carolanne grinned. "Besides, people buy more if you talk to them. And boy, do I love to talk."

"If you didn't, I'd have to close up shop."

"You'd just work twice as hard, if that's possible." She waved a hand before Suzanna could protest. "Before you go, I asked around to see if anyone needed any part-time work." Carolanne lifted her hands. "No luck yet."

It wasn't any use moaning, Suzanna thought. "This late in the season, everyone's already working."

"If Tommy the creep Parotti hadn't jumped ship—"

"Honey, he had a chance to make a break and do something he's always wanted to do. We can't blame him for that."

"You can't," Carolanne muttered. "Suzanna, you can't keep doing all the site work yourself. It's too hard."

"We're getting by," she said absently, thinking of the help she'd had that day. "Listen, Carolanne, after we deal with these customers, I have another delivery to make. Can you handle things until closing?"

"Sure." Carolanne let out a sigh. "I'm the one with a stool and a fan, you're the one with the pick and the shovel."

"Just keep pushing the carnations."

An hour later, Suzanna pulled up at Holt's cottage. It wasn't just impulse, she told herself. And it wasn't because she wanted to pressure him. Lecturing herself, she climbed out of the truck. It certainly wasn't because she wanted his company. But she was a Calhoun, and Calhouns always paid their debts.

She walked up the steps to the porch, again thinking it was a charming place. A few touches—morning glories climbing up the railing, a bed of columbine and larkspur, with some snapdragons and lavender.

Day lilies along that slope, she thought as she knocked. A border of impatiens. Miniature roses under the win-

dows. And there, where the ground was rocky and uneven, a little herb bed, set off with spring bulbs.

It could be a fairy-tale place—but the man who lived
there didn't believe in fairy tales.

She knocked again, noting that his car was there. As
she had before, she walked around the side, but he wasn't
in the boat this time. With a shrug, she decided she would
do what she'd come to do.

She'd already picked the spot, between the water and
the house, where the shrub could be seen and enjoyed
through what she'd determined was the kitchen window.
It wasn't much, but it would add some color to the empty
backyard. She wheeled around what she needed, then began to dig.

Inside his work shed, Holt had the boat engine broken
down. Rebuilding it would require concentration and
time. Which was just what he needed. He didn't want to
think about the Calhouns, or tragic love affairs, or responsibilities.

He didn't even glance up when Sadie rose from her
nap on the cool cement and trotted outside. He and the
dog had an understanding. She did as she chose, and he
fed her.

When she barked, he kept on working. As a watchdog,
Sadie was a bust. She barked at squirrels, at the wind in
the grass, and in her sleep. A year before there'd been
an attempted burglary in his house in Portland. Holt had
relieved the would-be thief of his stereo equipment while
Sadie had napped peacefully on the living room rug.

But he did look up, he did stop working when he heard
the low, feminine laughter. It skimmed along his skin,
light and warm. When he pushed away from the work-

bench, his stomach was already in knots. When he stood in the doorway and looked at her, the knots yanked tight.

Why wouldn't she leave him alone? he wondered, and shoved his hands into his pockets. He'd told her he'd think about it, hadn't he? She had no business coming here again.

They didn't even like each other. Whatever she did to him physically was his problem, and so far he'd managed quite nicely to keep his hands off her.

Now here she was, standing in his yard, talking to his dog. And digging a hole.

His brows drew together as he stepped out of the shed. "What the hell are you doing?"

Her head shot up. He saw her eyes, big and blue and alarmed. Her face, flushed from the heat and her work, went very pale. He'd seen that kind of look before—the quick, instinctive fear of a cornered victim. Then it was gone, fading so swiftly he nearly convinced himself he'd imagined it. Color seeped slowly into her cheeks again as she managed to smile.

"I didn't think you were here."

He stayed where he was and continued to scowl. "So, you decided to dig a hole in my yard."

"I guess you could say that." Steady now, annoyed with herself for the instinctive jolt, she plunged the shovel in again, braced her foot on it and deepened the hole. "I brought you a bush."

Damned if he was going to take the shovel from her this time and dig the hole himself. But he did cross to her. "Why?"

"To thank you for helping me out today. You saved me a good hour."

"So you use it to dig another hole."

"Uh-huh. There's a breeze off the water today." She lifted her face to it for a moment. "It's nice."

Because looking at her made his palms sweat, he scowled down at the tidy shrub pregnant with sassy yellow blooms. "I don't know how to take care of a bush. You put it there, you're condemning it to death row."

With a laugh, she scooped out the last of the dirt. "You don't have to do much. This one's very hardy, even when it's dry, and it'll bloom for you into the fall. Can I use your hose?"

"What?"

"Your hose?"

"Yeah." He raked a hand through his hair. He hadn't a clue how he was supposed to react. It was certainly the first time anyone had given him flowers—unless you counted the batch the guys at the precinct had brought in when he'd been in the hospital. "Sure."

At ease with her task, she continued to talk as she went to the outside wall to turn on the water. "It'll stay neat. It's a very well behaved little bush and won't get over three feet." She petted Sadie, who was circling the bush and sniffing. "If you'd like something else instead…"

He wasn't going to let himself be touched by some idiotic plant or her misplaced gratitude. "It doesn't matter to me. I don't know one from the other."

"Well, this is a *hypericum kalmianum*."

His lips quirked into what might have been a smile. "That tells me a lot."

Chuckling, she set it in place. "A sunshine shrub in layman's terms." Still smiling, she tilted her head back to look at him. If she didn't know better, she'd have thought he was embarrassed. Fat chance. "I thought you could use some sunshine. Why don't you help me plant it? It'll mean more to you then."

He'd said he wasn't going to get sucked in, and damn it, he'd meant it. "Are you sure this isn't your idea of a bribe? To get me to help you out?"

Sighing a little, she sat back on her heels. "I wonder what makes someone so cynical and unfriendly. I'm sure you have your reasons, but they don't apply here. You did me a favor today, and I'm paying you back. Very simple. Now if you don't want the bush, just say so. I'll give it to someone else."

He lifted a brow at the tone. "Is that how you keep your kids in line?"

"When necessary. Well, what's it to be?"

Maybe he was being too hard on her. She'd made a gesture and he was slapping it back in her face. If she could be casually friendly, so could he. "I've already got a hole in my yard," he pointed out then knelt beside her. The dog lay down in the sunlight to watch. "We might as well put something in it."

And that, she supposed, was his idea of a thank-you. "Fine."

"So how old are your kids?" Not that he cared, he told himself. He was just making conversation.

"Five and six. Alex is the oldest, then Jenny." Her eyes softened as they always did when she thought of them. "They're growing up so fast, I can hardly keep up."

"What made you come back here after the divorce?"

Her hands tensed in the soil, then began to work again. It was a small and quickly concealed gesture, but he had very sharp eyes. "Because it's home."

There was a tender spot, he thought and eased around it. "I heard you're going to turn The Towers into a hotel."

"Just the west wing. That's C.C.'s husband's business."

"It's hard to picture C.C. married. The last time I saw her she was about twelve."

"She's grown up now, and beautiful."

"Looks run in the family."

She glanced up, surprised, then back down again. "I think you've just said something nice."

"Just stating a fact. The Calhoun sisters were always worth a second look." To please himself, he reached out to toy with the tip of her ponytail. "Whenever guys got together, the four of you were definitely topics of conversation."

She laughed a little, thinking how easy life had been back then. "I'm sure we'd have been flattered."

"I used to look at you," Holt said slowly. "A lot."

Wary, she lifted her head. "Really? I never noticed."

"You wouldn't have." His hand dropped away again. "Princesses don't notice peasants."

Now she frowned, not only at the words but at the clipped tone. "What a ridiculous thing to say."

"It was easy to think of you that way, the princess in the castle."

"A castle that's been crumbling for years," she said dryly. "And as I recall, you were too busy swaggering around and juggling girls to notice me."

He had to grin. "Oh, between the swaggering and juggling, I noticed you all right."

Something in his eyes set off a little warning bell. It might have been some time since she'd heard that particular sound, but she recognized it and heeded it. She looked down again to firm the dirt around the bush.

"That was a long time ago. I imagine we've both changed quite a bit."

"Can't argue with that." He pushed at the dirt.

"No, don't shove at it, press it down—firm, but gentle." Scooting closer, she put her hands over his to show him. "All it needs is a good start, and then—"

She broke off when he turned his hands over to grip hers.

They were close, knees brushing, bodies bent toward each other. He noted that her hands were hard, callused, a direct and fascinating contrast to the soft eyes and tea rose complexion. There was a strength in her fingers that would have surprised him if he hadn't seen for himself how hard she worked. For reasons he couldn't fathom, he found it incredibly erotic.

"You've got strong hands, Suzanna."

"A gardener's hands," she said, trying to keep her voice light. "And I need them to finish planting this bush."

He only tightened his grip when she tried to draw away. "We'll get to it. You know, I've thought about kissing you for fifteen years." He watched the faint smile fade away from her face and the alarm shoot into her eyes. He didn't mind it. It might be best for both of them if she was afraid of him. "That's a long time to think about anything."

He released one hand, but before she could let out a sigh of relief, he had cupped the back of her neck. His fingers were firm, his grip determined. "I'm just going to get it out of my system."

She didn't have time to refuse. He was quick. Before she could deny or protest, his mouth was on hers, covering and conquering. There was nothing soft about him. His mouth, his hands, his body when he pulled her against him, were hard and demanding. The swift frisson of fear had her lifting a hand to push against his shoulder. She might as well have tried to move a boulder.

Then the fear turned to an ache. She fisted her hand against him, forced to fight herself now rather than him.

She was taut as a wire. He could feel her nerves sizzle and snap as he clamped her against him. He knew it was wrong, unfair, even despicable, but damn it, he needed to wipe out this fever that continued to burn in him. He needed to convince himself that she was just another woman, that his fantasies of her were only remnants of a boy's foolish dreams.

Then she shuddered. A soft, yielding sound followed. And her lips parted beneath his in irresistible and avid invitation. Swearing, he plunged, dragging her head back by the hair so that he could take more of what she so mindlessly offered.

Her mouth was a banquet, and he too racked with hunger to stem the greed. He could smell her hair, fresh as rainwater, her skin, seductively musky with heat and labor, and the rich and primitive fragrance of earth newly turned. Each separate scent slammed into his system, pumping through his blood, roaring through his head to churn a need he'd hoped to dispel.

She couldn't breathe, or think. All of the weighty and worrisome cares she carried in her vanished. In their place, rioting sensations sprinted. The tensed ripple of muscle under her fingers, the hot and desperate taste of his mouth, the thunder of her heartbeat that raced with dizzying speed. She was wrapped around him now, her fingers digging in, her body straining, her mouth as urgent and impatient as his.

It had been so long since she had been touched. So long since she had tasted a man's desire on her lips. So long since she had wanted any man. But she wanted now—to feel his hands on her, rough and demanding, to have his body cover hers on the soft, sunny grass. To be wild and willful and wanton until this clawing ache was soothed.

The sheer power of that want ripped through her, tearing through her lips in a sobbing moan.

His fingers were curled into her shirt, had nearly ripped it aside before he caught himself, cursed himself. And released her. Her shallow ragged breaths were both condemnation and seduction as he forced himself to pull away. Her eyes had gone to cobalt and were wide with shock.

Small wonder, he thought in livid self-disgust. The woman had nearly been shoved to the ground and ravished in broad daylight.

Her lashes lowered before he could see the shame.

"I hope you feel better now."

"No." His hands were far from steady, so he curled them into fists. "I don't."

She didn't look at him, couldn't. Nor could she afford to think, just at this moment, of what she had done. To comfort herself she began to spread mulch around the newly planted bush. "If it stays dry, you'll have to water this regularly until it's established."

For a second time, he gripped her hands. This time she jolted. "Aren't you going to belt me?"

Using well-honed control, she relaxed and looked up. There was something in her eyes, something dark and passionate, but her voice was very calm. "There doesn't seem to be much point in that. I'm sure you're of the opinion that a woman like me would be...needy."

"I wasn't thinking about your needs when I kissed you. It was a purely selfish act, Suzanna. I'm good at being selfish."

Because his grip was light, she slipped her hands from under his. "I'm sure you are." She brushed her palms on her thighs before she rose. The only thought in her head was of getting away, but she made herself load the wheelbarrow calmly. Until he gripped her arm and whirled her around.

"What the hell is this?" His eyes were stormy, his voice as rough as his hands. He wanted her to rage at him—needed it to soothe his conscience. "I all but took you on the ground, without giving a hell of a lot of consideration to whether you'd have liked it or not, and now you're going to load up your cart and go away?"

She was very much afraid she would have liked it. That was why it was imperative that she stay very calm and very controlled. "If you want to pick a fight or a casual lover, Holt, you've come to the wrong person. My children are expecting me home, and I'm very tired of being grabbed."

Yes, her voice was calm, he thought, even firm, but her arm was trembling lightly under his hold. There was something here, he realized, some secrets she held behind those sad and beautiful eyes. The same stubbornness that had had him pursuing his gold shield made it essential that he discover them.

"Grabbed in general, or just by me?"

"You're the one doing the grabbing." Her patience was wearing thin. The Calhoun temper was always difficult to control. "I don't like it."

"That's too bad, because I have a feeling I'm going to be doing a lot more of it before we're through."

"Maybe I haven't made myself clear. We are through." She shook loose and grabbed the handles of the wheelbarrow.

He simply put his weight on it to stop her. He wasn't

sure if she realized she'd just issued an irresistible challenge. His grin came slowly. "Now you're getting mad."

"Yes. Does that make you feel better?"

"Quite a bit. I'd rather have you claw at me than crawl off like a wounded bird."

"I'm not crawling anywhere," she said between her teeth. "I'm going home."

"You forgot your shovel," he told her, still grinning.

She snatched it up and tossed it into the wheelbarrow with a clatter. "Thanks."

"You're welcome."

He waited until she'd gone about ten feet. "Suzanna."

She slowed but didn't stop, and tossed a look over her shoulder. "What?"

"I'm sorry."

Her temper eased a bit as she shrugged. "Forget it."

"No." He dipped his hands into his pockets and rocked back on his heels. "I'm sorry I didn't kiss you like that fifteen years ago."

Swearing under her breath, she quickened her pace. When she was out of sight, he glanced back at the bush. Yeah, he thought, he was sorry as hell, but planned to make up for lost time.

She needed some time to herself. That wasn't a commodity Suzanna found very often in a house as filled with people as The Towers. But just now, with the moon on the rise and the children in bed, she took a few precious moments alone.

It was a clear night, and the heat of the day had been replaced by a soft breeze that was scented with the sea and roses. From her terrace she could see the dark shadow of the cliffs that always drew her. The distant

murmur of water was a lullaby, as sweet as the call of a
night bird from the garden.

Tonight it wouldn't ease her into sleep. No matter how
tired her body was, her mind was too restless. It didn't
seem to matter how often she told herself she had nothing
to worry about. Her children were safely tucked into bed,
dreaming about the day's adventures. Her sisters were
happy. Each one of them had found her place in the
world, just as each one of them had found a mate who
loved her for who and what she was. Aunt Coco was
happy and healthy and looking forward to the day when
she would become head chef of The Towers Retreat.

Her family, always Suzanna's chief concern, was content and settled. The Towers, the only real home she'd
ever known, was no longer in danger of being sold, but
would remain the Calhoun home. It was pointless to
worry about the emeralds. The family was doing all that
could be done to find the necklace.

If they hadn't been exploring every avenue, she would
never have gone to Holt Bradford. Her fingers curled on
the stone wall. That, she thought, had been a useless ex-
ercise. He was Christian Bradford's grandson, but he
didn't feel the connection. It was obvious that the past
held no interest for him. He thought only about the moment, about himself, about his own comfort and pleasures.

Catching herself, Suzanna sighed and forced herself to
relax her hands. If only he hadn't made her so angry. She
despised losing her temper, and it had come dangerously
close to breaking loose that day. It was her own fault,
and her own problem that something else had broken
loose.

Needs. She didn't want to need anyone but her family—the family she could love and depend on and worry

about. She'd already learned a painful lesson about needing a man, one man. She didn't intend to repeat it.

He'd kissed her on impulse, she reminded herself. It had been a kind of dare to himself. There had certainly been no affection in it, no softness, no romance. The fact that it had stirred her was strictly chemical. She'd cut herself off from men for more than two years. And the last year or so of her marriage—well, there had been no affection, softness or romance there, either. She'd learned to do without those things when it came to men. She could continue to do without them.

If only she hadn't responded to him so…blatantly. He might as well have knocked her over the head with a club and dragged her into a cave by the hair for all the finesse he'd shown. Yet she had thrown herself into the moment, clinging to him, answering those hard and demanding lips with a fervor she'd never been able to show her own husband.

By doing so, she'd humiliated herself and amused Holt. Oh, the way he had grinned at her at the end had had her steaming for hours afterward. That was her problem, too, she thought now. Just as it was her problem that she could still taste him.

Perhaps she shouldn't be so hard on herself. As embarrassing as the moment had been, it had proved something. She was still alive. She wasn't the cold shell of a woman that Bax had tossed so carelessly aside. She could feel, and want.

Closing her eyes, she pressed a hand to her stomach. Want too much, it seemed. It was like a hunger, and the kiss, like a crust of bread after a long fast, had stirred the juices. She could be glad of that—to feel something again besides remorse and disillusionment. And feeling it, she could control it. Pride would prevent her from avoiding

Holt. Just as pride would save her from any new humiliation.

She was a Calhoun, she reminded herself. Calhoun
women went down fighting. If she had to deal with Holt
again in order to widen the trail to the emeralds, then she
would deal with him. She would never, never let herself
be dismissed and destroyed by a man again. He hadn't
seen the last of her.

"Suzanna, there you are."

Her thoughts scattered as she turned to see her aunt
striding through the terrace doors. "Aunt Coco."

"I'm sorry, dear, but I knocked and knocked. Your
light was on so I just peeked in."

"That's all right." Suzanna slipped an arm around
Coco's sturdy waist. This was a woman she'd loved for
most of her life. A woman who had been mother and
father to her for more than fifteen years. "I was lost in
the night, I guess. It's so beautiful."

Coco murmured an agreement and said nothing for a
moment. Of all of her girls, she worried most about Suzanna. She had watched her ride away, a young bride
radiant with hope. She had been there when Suzanna had
come back, barely four years later, a pale, devastated
woman with two small children. In the years since, she'd
been proud to see Suzanna gain her feet, devoting herself
to the difficult task of single parenthood, working hard,
much too hard, to establish her own business.

And she had waited, painfully, for the sad and haunted
look that clouded her niece's eyes, to finally fade forever.

"Couldn't you sleep?" Suzanna asked her.

"I haven't even thought about sleep yet." Coco let out
a huff of breath. "That woman is driving me out of my
mind."

Suzanna managed not to smile. She knew *that woman*

was her great-aunt Colleen, the eldest of Bianca's children, and the sister of Coco's father. The rude, demanding and perpetually cranky woman had descended on them a week before. Coco was certain the move had been made with the sole purpose of making her life a misery.

"Did you hear her at dinner?" Tall and stately in her draping caftan, Coco began to pace. Her complaints were issued in an indignant whisper. Colleen might have been well past eighty, her bedroom may have been two dozen feet away, but she had ears like a cat. "The sauce was too rich, the asparagus too soft. The idea of her telling *me* how to prepare coq au vin. I wanted to take that cane and wrap it around her—"

"Dinner was superb, as always," Suzanna soothed. "She has to complain about something, Aunt Coco, otherwise her day wouldn't be complete. And as I recall, there wasn't a crumb left on her plate."

"Quite right." Coco drew in a deep breath, releasing it slowly. "I know I shouldn't let the woman get on my nerves. The fact is, she's always frightened me half to death. And she knows it. If it wasn't for yoga and meditation, I'm sure I'd have already lost my sanity. As long as she was living on one of those cruise ships, all I had to do was send her an occasional duty letter. But actually living under the same roof." Coco couldn't help it—she shuddered.

"She'll get tired of us soon, and sail off down the Nile or the Amazon or whatever."

"It can't be too soon for me. I'm afraid she's made up her mind to stay until we find the emeralds. Which is what this is all about anyway." Coco calmed herself enough to stand at the wall again. "I was using my crystal to meditate. So soothing, and after an evening with Aunt Colleen—" She broke off because she was clenching her teeth. "In any case, I was just drifting along, when thoughts and images of Bianca filled my head."

"That's not surprising," Suzanne put in. "She's on all of our minds."

"But this was very strong, dear. Very clear. There was such melancholy. I tell you, it brought tears to my eyes." Coco pulled a handkerchief out of her caftan. "Then suddenly, I was thinking of you, and that was just as strong and clear. The connection between you and Bianca was unmistakable. I realized there had to be a reason, and thinking it through, I believe it's because of Holt Bradford." Coco's eyes were shining now with discovery and enthusiasm. "You see, you've spoken to him, you've bridged the gap between Christian and Bianca."

"I don't think you can call my conversations with Holt a bridge to anything."

"No, he's the key, Suzanna. I doubt he understands what information he might have, but without him, we can't take the next step. I'm sure of it."

With a restless move of her shoulders, Suzanna leaned against the wall. "Whatever he understands, he isn't interested."

"Then you have to convince him otherwise." She put a hand on Suzanna's and squeezed. "We need him. Until we find the emeralds, none of us will feel completely safe. The police haven't been able to find that miserable thief, and we don't know what he may try next time. Holt is our only link with the man Bianca loved."

"I know."

"Then you'll see him again. You'll talk to him."

Suzanna looked toward the cliffs, toward the shadows. "Yes, I'll see him again."

I knew she would come back. However unwise, however wrong it might have been, I looked for her every after-

noon. On the days she did not come to the cliffs, I would find myself staring up at the peaks of The Towers, aching for her in a way I had no right to ache for another man's wife. On the days she walked toward me, her hair like melted flame, that small, shy smile on her lips, I knew a joy like no other.

In the beginning, our conversations were polite and distant. The weather, unimportant village gossip, art and literature. As time passed, she became more at ease with me. She would speak of her children, and I came to know them through her. The little girl, Colleen, who liked pretty dresses and yearned for a pony. Young Ethan who only wanted to run and find adventure. And little Sean, who was just learning to crawl.

It took no special insight to see that her children were her life. Rarely did she speak of the parties, the musicals, the social gatherings I knew she attended almost nightly. Not at all did she speak of the man she had married.

I admit I wondered about him. Of course, it was common knowledge that Fergus Calhoun was an ambitious and wealthy man, one who had turned a few dollars into an empire during the course of his life. He commanded both respect and fear in the business world. For that I cared nothing.

It was the private man who obsessed me. The man who had the right to call her wife. The man who lay beside her at night, who touched her. The man who knew the texture of her skin, the taste of her mouth. The man who knew how it felt to have her move beneath him in the dark.

I was already in love with her. Perhaps I had been from the moment I had seen her walking with the child through the wild roses.

It would have been best for my sanity if I had chosen another place to paint. I could not. Already knowing I would have no more of her, could have no more than a few hours of conversation, I went back. Again and again.

She agreed to let me paint her. I began to see, as an artist must see, the inner woman. Beyond her beauty, beyond her composure and breeding was a desperately unhappy woman. I wanted to take her in my arms, to demand that she tell me what had put that sad and haunted look in her eyes. But I only painted her. I had no right to do more.

I have never been a patient or a noble man. Yet with her, I found I could be both. Without ever touching me, she changed me. Nothing would be the same for me after that summer—that all too brief summer when she would come, to sit on the rocks and look out to sea.

Even now, a lifetime later, I can walk to those cliffs and see her. I can smell the sea that never changes, and catch the drift of her perfume. I have only to pick a wild rose to remember the fiery lights of her hair. Closing my eyes, I hear the murmur of the water on the rocks below and her voice comes back as clear and as sweet as yesterday.

I am reminded of the last afternoon that first summer, when she stood beside me, close enough to touch, as distant as the moon.

"We leave in the morning," she said, but didn't look at me. "The children are sorry to go."

"And you?"

A faint smile touched her lips but not her eyes. "Sometimes I wonder if I've lived before. If my home was an island like this. The first time I came here, it was as if I had been waiting to see it again. I'll miss the sea."

Perhaps it was only my own needs that made me think,

when she glanced at me, that she would miss me, as well. Then she looked away again and sighed.

"New York is so different, so full of noise and urgency. It's hard to believe such a place exists when I stand here. Will you stay on the island through the winter?"

I thought of the cold and desolate months ahead and cursed fate for taunting me with what I could never have. "My plans change with my mood." I said it lightly, fighting to keep the bitterness out of my voice.

"I envy you your freedom." She turned away then to walk back to where her nearly completed portrait rested on my easel. "And your talent. You've made me more than what I am."

"Less." I had to curl my hands into fists to keep from touching her. "Some things can never be captured with paint and canvas."

"What will you call it?"

"Bianca. Your name is enough."

She must have sensed my feelings, though I tried desperately to hold them in myself. Something came into her eyes as she looked at me, and the look held longer than it should. Then she stepped back, cautiously, like a woman who had wandered too close to the edge of a cliff.

"One day you'll be famous, and people will beg for your work."

I couldn't take my eyes off her, knowing I might never see her again. "I don't paint for fame."

"No, and that's why you'll have it. When you do, I'll remember this summer. Goodbye, Christian."

She walked away from me—for what I thought was the last time—away from the rocks, through the wild grass and the flowers that fight through both for the sun.

Chapter 4

Coco Calhoun McPike didn't believe in leaving things up to chance—particularly when her horoscope that day had advised her to take a more active part in a family matter and to visit an old acquaintance. She felt she could do both by paying an informal call on Holt Bradford.

She remembered him as a dark, hot-eyed boy who had delivered lobster and loitered around the village, waiting for trouble to happen. She also remembered that he had once stopped to change a flat for her while she'd been struggling on the side of the road trying to figure out which end of the jack to put under the bumper. He'd refused—stiffly, she recalled—her offer of payment and had hopped back on his motorcycle and ridden off before she'd properly thanked him.

Proud, defiant, rebellious, she mused as she maneuvered her car into his driveway. Yet, in a grudging sort of way, chivalrous. Perhaps if she was clever—and Coco thought that she was—she could play on all of those traits to get what she wanted.

So this had been Christian Bradford's cottage, she mused. She'd seen it before, of course, but not since she'd known of the connection between the families. She paused for a moment. With her eyes closed she tried to *feel* something. Surely there was some remnant of energy here, something that time and wind hadn't washed away.

Coco liked to consider herself a mystic. Whether it was a true evaluation, or her imagination was ripe, she was certain she did feel some snap of passion in the air. Pleased with it, and herself, she trooped to the house.

She'd dressed very carefully. She wanted to look attractive, of course. Her vanity wouldn't permit otherwise. But she'd also wanted to look distinguished and just the tiniest bit matronly. She felt the old and classic Chanel suit in powder blue worked very well.

She knocked, putting what she hoped was a wise and comforting smile on her face. The wild barking and the steady stream of curses from within had her placing a hand on her breast.

Five minutes out of the shower, his hair dripping and his temper curdled, Holt yanked open the door. Sadie bounded out. Coco squeaked. Good reflexes had Holt snatching the amorous dog by the collar before she could send Coco over the porch railing.

"Oh my." Coco looked from dog to man, juggling the plate of double-fudge brownies. "Oh, goodness. What a very *large* dog. She certainly does look like our Fred, and I'd so hoped he'd stop growing soon. Why you could practically *ride* her if you liked, couldn't you?" She beamed a smile at Holt. "I'm so sorry, have I interrupted you?"

He continued to struggle with the dog, who'd gotten a

good whiff of the brownies and wanted her share. Now.
"Excuse me?"

"I've interrupted," Coco repeated. "I know it's early,
but on days like this I just can't stay in bed. All this sun
and twittering birds. Not to mention the sawing and hammering. Do you suppose she'd like one of these?" Without waiting for an answer, Coco took one of the brownies
off the plate. "Now you sit and behave."

With what was certainly a grin, Sadie stopped straining, sat and eyed Coco adoringly.

"Good dog." Sadie took the treat politely then padded
back into the house to enjoy it. "Well, now." Pleased
with the situation, Coco smiled at Holt. "You probably
don't remember me. Goodness, it's been years."

"Mrs. McPike." He remembered her, all right, though
the last time he'd seen her, her hair had been a dusky
blond. It had been ten years, he thought, but she looked
younger. She'd either had a first-class face-lift or had
discovered the fountain of youth.

"Why, yes. It's so flattering to be remembered by an
attractive man. But you were hardly more than a boy the
last time. Welcome home." She offered the plate of
brownies.

And left him no choice but to accept it and ask her in.

"Thanks." He studied the plate as she breezed inside.
Between plants and brownies, the Calhouns were making
a habit of bearing gifts. "Is there something I can do for
you?"

"To tell you the truth, I've just been dying to see the
place. To think this is where Christian Bradford lived and
worked." She sighed. "And dreamed of Bianca."

"Well, he lived and worked here anyway."

"Suzanna tells me you're not quite convinced they
loved each other. I can appreciate your reluctance to fall

right in with the story, but you see, it's a part of my family history. And yours. Oh, what a glorious painting!''

She crossed the room to a misty seascape hung above the stone fireplace. Even through the haze of fog, the colors were ripe and vivid, as though the vitality and passion were fighting to free themselves from the thin graying curtain. Turbulent whitecaps, the black and toothy edge of rock, the gloom-crowned shadows of islands marooned in a cold, dark sea.

''It's powerful,'' she murmured. ''And, oh, lonely. It's his, isn't it?''

''Yes.''

She let out a shaky sigh. ''If you'd like to see that view, you've only to walk on the cliffs beneath The Towers. Suzanna walks there, sometimes with the children, sometimes alone. Too often alone.'' Shaking off the mood, Coco turned back. ''My niece seems to feel that you're not particularly interested in confirming Christian and Bianca's relationship, and helping to find the emeralds. I find that difficult to believe.''

Holt set the plate aside. ''It shouldn't be, Mrs. McPike. But what I told your niece was that if and when I was convinced there had been a connection of any importance, I'd do what I could to help. Which, as I see it, is next to nothing.''

''You were a police officer, weren't you?''

Holt hooked his thumbs in his pockets, not trusting the change of subject. ''Yeah.''

''I have to admit I was surprised when I heard you'd chosen that profession, but I'm sure you were well suited to the job.''

The scar on his back seemed to twinge. ''I used to be.''

"And you'd have solved cases, I suppose."

His lips curved a little. "A few."

"So you'd have looked for clues and followed them up until you found the right answer." She smiled at him. "I always admire the police on television who solve the mystery and tidy everything up before the end of the show."

"Life's not tidy."

On certain men, she thought, a sneer was not at all unattractive. "No, indeed not, but we could certainly use someone on our side who has your experience." She walked back toward him, and she was no longer smiling. "I'll be frank. If I had known what trouble it would cause my family, I might have let the legend of the emeralds die with me. When my brother and his wife were killed, and left their girls in my care, I was also left the responsibility of passing along the story of the Calhoun emeralds—when the time was right. By doing what I consider my duty, I've put my family in danger. I'll do anything in my power, and use anyone I can, to keep them from being hurt. Until those emeralds are found, I can't be sure my family is safe."

"You need the police," he began.

"They're doing what they can. It isn't enough." Reaching out, she put a hand on his. "They aren't personally involved, and can't possibly understand. You can."

Her faith and her obstinate logic made him uneasy. "You're overestimating me."

"I don't think so." Coco held his hand another moment, then gave it a brief squeeze before releasing it. "But I don't mean to nag. I only came so I could add my input to Suzanna's. She has such a difficult time pushing for what she wants."

"She does well enough."

"Well, I'm glad to hear it. But with her work and Mandy's wedding, and everything else that's been going on, I know she hasn't had time to speak with you again for the last couple of days. I tell you, our lives have been turned upside down for the last few months. First C.C.'s wedding, and the renovations, now Amanda and Sloan— and Lilah already setting a date to marry Max." She paused and hoped to look wistful. "If I could only find some nice man for Suzanna, I'd have all my girls settled."

Holt didn't miss the speculative look. "I'm sure she'll take care of that herself when she's ready."

"Not when she doesn't give herself a moment to look. And after what that excuse for a man did to her." She cut herself off there. If she started on Baxter Dumont, it would be difficult to stop. And it would hardly be proper conversation. "Well, in any case, she keeps herself too busy with her business and her children, so I like to keep my eye out for her. You're not married, are you?"

At least no one could accuse her of being subtle, Holt thought, amused. "Yeah. I've got a wife and six kids in Portland."

Coco blinked, then laughed. "It was a rude question," she admitted. "And before I ask another, I'll leave you alone." She started for the door, pleased that he had enough manners to accompany her and open it for her. "Oh, by the way, Amanda's wedding is Saturday, at six. We're holding the reception at the ballroom in The Towers. I'd like for you to come."

The unexpected curve had him hesitating. "I really don't think it's appropriate."

"It's more than appropriate," she corrected. "Our families go back quite a long way, Holt. We'd very much

like to have you there.'' She started toward her car then
turned, smiling again. ''And Suzanna doesn't have an
escort. It seems a pity.''

The thief called himself by many names. When he had
first come to Bar Harbor in search of the emeralds, he
had used the name Livingston and had posed as a successful British businessman. He had only been partially
successful and had returned under the guise of Ellis Caufield, a wealthy eccentric. Due to bad luck and his partner's fumbling, he'd had to abandon that particular cover.

His partner was dead, which was only a small incon-
venience. The thief now went under the name of Robert
Marshall and was developing a certain fondness for this
alter ego.

Marshall was lean and tanned and had a hint of a Boston accent. He wore his dark hair nearly shoulder length
and sported a drooping mustache. His eyes were brown,
thanks to contact lenses. His teeth were slightly bucked.
The oral device had cost him a pretty penny, but it had
also changed the shape of his jaw.

He was very comfortable with Marshall, and delighted
to have signed on as a laborer on The Towers renovation.
His references had been forged and had added to his
overhead. But the emeralds would be worth it. He intended to have them, whatever the price.

Over the past months they had gone from being a job
to an obsession. He didn't just want them. He needed
them. He found the risk of working so close to the Calhouns only added spice to the game. He had, in fact,
passed within three feet of Amanda when she had come
into the west wing to talk to Sloan O'Riley. Neither of
them, who had known him only as Livingston, had given
him a second glance.

He did his job well, hauling equipment, cleaning up debris. And he worked without complaint. He was friendly with his co-workers, even joining them occasionally for a beer after work.

Then he would go back to his rented house across the bay and plan.

The security at The Towers posed no problem—not when it would be so easy for him to disengage it from the inside. By working for the Calhouns, he could stay close, he could be certain he would hear about any new developments in their search for the necklace. And with care and skill, he could do some searching on his own.

The papers he had stolen from them had offered no real clue as yet. Unless it came from the letter he'd discovered. One that had been written to Bianca and signed only "Christian." A love letter, Marshall mused as he stacked lumber. It was something he had to look into.

"Hey, Bob. Got a minute?"

Marshall looked up and gave his foreman an affable smile. "Sure, nothing but minutes."

"Well, they need some tables moved into the ballroom for that wedding tomorrow. You and Rick give the ladies a hand."

"Right."

Marshall strolled along, fighting back a trembling excitement at being free to walk through the house. He took his instructions from a flustered Coco, then hefted his end of the heavy hunt table to move it up to the next floor.

"Do you think he'll come?" C.C. asked Suzanna as they finished washing down the glass on the mirrored walls.

"I doubt it."

C.C. brushed back her short cap of black hair as she stood aside to search for streaks. "I don't see why he wouldn't. And maybe if we all gang up on him, he'll break down and join ranks.''

''I don't think he's a joiner.'' Suzanna glanced around and saw the two men struggling in with the table. ''Oh, it goes against that wall. Thanks.''

''No problem,'' Rick managed through gritted teeth. Marshall merely smiled and said nothing.

''Maybe if he sees the picture of Bianca and hears the tape from the interview Max and Lilah had with the maid who used to work here back then, he'll pitch in. He's Christian's only surviving family.''

''Hey!'' Rick muffled a curse when Marshall bobbled the table.

''I don't think he's big on family feeling,'' Suzanna put in. ''One thing that hasn't changed about Holt Bradford is that he's still a loner.''

Holt Bradford. Marshall committed the name to memory before he called across the room. ''Is there anything else we can do for you ladies?''

Suzanna glanced over her shoulder with an absent smile. ''No, not right now. Thanks a lot.''

Marshall grinned. ''Don't mention it.''

''Some lookers, huh?'' Rick muttered as they walked back out.

''Oh, yeah.'' But Marshall was thinking of the emeralds.

''I tell you, bud, I'd like to—'' Rick broke off when two other women and a young boy came to the top of the stairs. He gave them both a big, toothy smile. Lilah gave him a lazy one in return and kept walking.

''Man, oh, man,'' Rick said with a hand to his heart. ''This place is just full of babes.''

''Pardon the leers,'' Lilah said mildly. ''Most of them don't bite.''

The slim strawberry blonde gave a weak smile. At the moment a couple of leering carpenters were the least of her worries. "I really don't want to get in the way," she began in a soft Southwestern drawl. "I know what Sloan said, but I really think it would be best if Kevin and I checked into a hotel for the night."

"This late in the season, you couldn't check into a tent. And we want you here. All of us. Sloan's family is our family now." Lilah smiled down at the dark-haired boy who was gawking at everything in sight. "It's a wild place, isn't it? Your uncle's making sure it doesn't come crashing down on our heads." She walked into the ballroom.

Suzanna was standing on a ladder, polishing glass, while C.C. sat on the floor, hitting the low spots. Lilah bent to the boy. "I was supposed to be in on this," she whispered. "But I played hooky."

The idea made him laugh, and the laughter, so much like Alex's, had Suzanna glancing over.

She was expecting them. Their arrival had been anticipated for weeks. But seeing them here, knowing who they were, had her nerves jolting.

The woman wasn't just Sloan's sister, nor was the boy just his nephew. A short time before, Suzanna had learned that Megan O'Riley had been her husband's lover, and the boy his child. The woman who was staring at her now, the boy's hand gripped in hers, had been only seventeen when Baxter had charmed her into bed and seduced her with vows of love and promises of marriage. And all the while, he had been planning to marry Suzanna.

Which one of us, Suzanna wondered, had been the other woman?

It didn't matter now, she thought, and she climbed

down. Not when she could see the nerves so clearly in
Megan O'Riley's eyes, the tension in the set of her body,
and the courage in the angle of her chin.

Lilah made introductions so smoothly that an outsider
might have thought there was nothing but pleasantries in
the ballroom. As Suzanna offered a hand, all Megan
could think was that she had overdressed. She felt stiff
and foolish in the trim bronze-colored suit, while Suzanna seemed so relaxed and lovely in faded jeans.

This was the woman she had hated for years, for taking
away the man she'd loved and stealing the father of her
child. Even after Sloan had explained Suzanna's innocence, even knowing the hate had been wasted, Megan
couldn't relax.

"I'm so glad to meet you." Suzanna put both hands
over Megan's stiff one.

"Thank you." Feeling awkward, Megan drew her
hand away. "We're looking forward to the wedding."

"So are we all." After a bracing breath, Suzanna let
herself look down at Kevin, the half brother to her children. Her heart melted a little. He was taller than her son,
and a full year older. But they had both inherited their
father's dark good looks. Unconsciously Suzanna reached
out to brush back the lock of hair that fell, the twin of
Alex's, over Kevin's brow.

Megan's arm came around his shoulders in an instinctive move of defense. Suzanna let her hand drop to her
side.

"It's nice to meet you, Kevin. Alex and Jenny could
hardly sleep last night knowing you'd be here today."

Kevin gave her a fleeting smile, then glanced up at his
mother. She'd told him he was going to meet his half
brother and sister, and he wasn't too sure he was happy
about it. He didn't think his mother was, either.

"Why don't we go down and find them?" C.C. put a hand on Suzanna's shoulder, gently rubbing. Megan noted that Lilah had already flanked her sister's other side. She didn't blame them for sticking together against an outsider, and her chin came up to prove it.

"It might be best if we—"

She never got to finish. Alex and Jenny came clattering down the hall to burst into the room, breathless and flushed. "Is he here?" Alex demanded. "Aunt Coco said he was, and we want to see—" He cut himself off, skidding to a halt on the freshly polished floor.

The two boys eyed each other, interested and cautious, like two terriers. Alex wasn't sure he was pleased that his new brother was bigger than he was, but he'd already decided it would be neat to have something besides a sister.

"I'm Alex and this is Jenny," Alex said, taking over introductions. "She's only five."

"Five and a half," Jenny put in, and marched up to Kevin. "And I can beat you up if I have to."

"Jenny, I don't think that'll be necessary." Suzanna spoke mildly, but the lifted brows said it all.

"Well, I could," Jenny muttered, still sizing him up. "But Mom says we have to be nice 'cause we're family."

"Do you know any Indians?" Alex demanded.

"Yeah." Kevin was no longer gripping his mother's hand for dear life. "Lots of them."

"Want to see our fort?" Alex asked.

"Yeah." He sent a pleading glance at his mother. "Can I?"

"Well, I—"

"Lilah and I'll take them out." C.C. gave Suzanna's shoulder a final squeeze.

"They'll be fine," Suzanna assured Megan as her sisters hustled the children along. "Sloan designed the fort, so it's sturdy." She picked up her rag again to run it through her hands. "Does Kevin know?"

"Yes." Megan turned her purse over and over in restless hands. "I didn't want him to meet your children without understanding." She took a deep breath and prepared to launch into the speech she'd prepared. "Mrs. Dumont—"

"Suzanna. This is hard for you."

"I don't imagine it's easy, or comfortable for either of us. I wouldn't have come," she continued, "if it hadn't been so important to Sloan. I love my brother, and I won't do anything to spoil his wedding, but you must see that this is an impossible situation."

"I can see it's a painful one for you. I'm sorry." Her hands lifted then fell. "I wish I had known sooner, about you, about Kevin. It's unlikely that I could have made any difference as far as Bax is concerned, but I wish I had known." She glanced down at the rag she was gripping too tightly, then put it aside. "Megan, I realize that while you were giving birth to Kevin, alone, I was in Europe, honeymooning with Kevin's father. You're entitled to hate me for that."

Megan could only stare and shake her head. "You're nothing like I expected. You were supposed to be cool and remote and resentful."

"It would be hard to resent a seventeen-year-old girl who was betrayed and left alone to raise a child. I wasn't much older than that when I married Bax. I understand how charming he could be, how persuasive. And how cruel."

"I thought we'd live happily ever after," Megan said with a sigh. "Well, I grew up quickly, and I learned fast.'' She let out another long breath as she studied Suzanna. ''I hated you, for having everything I thought I wanted. Even when I'd stopped loving him, it helped get me through to hate you. And I was terrified of meeting you.''

''That's something else we have in common.''

''I can't believe I'm here, talking to you like this.'' To relieve her nerves she wandered around the ballroom. ''I imagined it so many times all those years ago. I'd face you down, demand my rights.'' She gave a soft laugh. ''Even today, I had a whole speech planned out. It was very sophisticated, very mature—maybe just a little vicious. I didn't want to believe that you hadn't known about Kevin, that you'd been a victim, too. Because it was so much easier to think of myself as the only one who'd been betrayed. Then your children came in.'' She closed her eyes. ''How do you deal with the hurt, Suzanna?''

''I'll let you know when I figure it out.''

Smiling a little, Megan glanced out of the window. ''It hasn't affected them. Look.''

Suzanna walked over. Down in the yard she could see her children, and Megan's son, climbing into the plywood fort.

Holt gave it a lot of thought. Up until the moment when he dragged the suit out of his closet, he'd been certain he wasn't going. What the devil was he supposed to do at a society wedding? He didn't like socializing or making small talk or picking at those tiny little canapés. You never knew what the hell was in them anyway.

He didn't like strangling himself with a tie or having to iron a shirt.

So why was he doing it?

He loosened the hated knot of the tie and frowned at himself in the dusty mirror over the bureau. Because he was an idiot and couldn't resist an invitation to the castle on the cliffs. Because he was twice an idiot and wanted to see Suzanna again.

It had been over a week since they had planted the yellow bush. A week since he'd kissed her. And a week since he'd admitted that one kiss, however turbulent, wasn't going to be enough.

He wanted to get a handle on her and thought the best way was to observe her in the midst of the family she seemed to love so much. He wasn't quite sure if she was the cool and remote princess of his youth, the hot-blooded woman he'd held in his arms or the vulnerable one whose eyes were haunting his dreams.

Holt was a man who liked to know exactly what he was up against, whether it was a suspect, a dinky motor or a woman. Once he had Suzanna pegged, he'd move at his own pace.

He didn't want to admit that she'd gotten to him with her fervent belief in the connection between his grandfather and her ancestor. More, he hated to admit that the visit by Coco McPike had made him feel guilty and responsible.

He wasn't going to the wedding to help anyone, he reminded himself. He wasn't making any commitments. He was going to please himself. This time he didn't have to stop at the kitchen door.

It wasn't a long drive, but he took his time, drawing it out. His first glimpse of The Towers bounced him back a dozen years. It was, as it had always been, a fanciful place, a maze of contrasts. It was built of somber stone, yet it was flanked with romantic towers. From one angle, it seemed formidable, from another graceful. At the moment, there was scaffolding on the west side, but instead of looking unsightly, it simply looked productive.

The sloped lawn was emerald green and guarded by gnarled and dignified trees, dashed with fragile and fragrant flowers. There was already a crowd of cars, and Holt felt foolish handing over the keys to his rusted Chevy to the uniformed valet.

The wedding was to take place on the terrace. Since it was about to begin, Holt kept well to the back of the crowd of people. There was organ music, very stately. He had to force himself not to drag at his tie and light a cigarette. There were a few murmured comments and sighs as the bridesmaids started down a long white runner spread over the lawn.

He barely recognized C.C. as the stunning goddess in the long rose-colored dress. Yeah, the Calhoun girls had always been lookers, he thought, and skimmed his gaze over the woman who walked behind her. Her dress was the color of sea foam, but he hardly noticed. It was the face—the face in the portrait in his grandfather's loft. Holt let out the breath between his teeth. Lilah Calhoun was a dead ringer for her great-grandmother. And Holt wasn't going to be able to deny the connection any longer.

He stuffed his hands into his pockets, wishing he hadn't come after all.

Then he saw Suzanna.

This was the princess of his youthful imagination. Her pale gold hair fell in soft curls to her shoulders under a fingertip veil of misty blue. The dress of the same color flowed around her, skirts billowing in the breeze as she walked. She carried flowers in her hands; more were scattered in her hair. When she passed him, her eyes as soft

and dreamy as the dress, he felt a longing so deep, so
intense, he could barely keep from speaking her name.

He remembered nothing about the brief and lovely cer-
emony except how her face had looked when the first
tear slipped down her cheek.

As it had been so many years ago, the ballroom was
filled with light and music and flowers. As for the food,
Coco had outdone herself. The guests were treated to
lobster croquettes, steamship round, salmon mousse and
champagne by the bucket. Dozens of chairs had been set
up in corners and along the mirrored walls, and the terrace doors had been thrown open to allow the guests to
spill outside.

Holt held himself apart, sipping the cold, frothy wine
and using the time to observe. As his first visit to The
Towers, it was quite a show, he decided. Mirrors tossed
back the reflection of women in pastel dresses as they
stood or sat or were lured out to dance. Music and the
scent of gardenias filled the air.

The bride was stunning, tall and regal in white lace,
her face luminous as she danced with the big, bronzed
man who was now her husband. They looked good together, Holt thought idly. The way people were meant
to, he supposed, when they were in love. He saw Coco
dancing with a tall, fair man who looked as if he'd been
born in a tuxedo.

Then he looked back, as he already had several times,
at Suzanna. She was leaning over now, saying something
to a dark-haired little boy. Her son? Holt wondered. It
was obvious the kid was on the verge of some kind of
rebellion. He was shuffling his feet and tugging at the
bow tie. He had Holt's sympathy. There couldn't be anything much worse for a kid on a summer evening then

being stuck in a mini tuxedo and having to hang around with adults. Suzanna whispered something in his ear, then tugged on it. The boy's mutinous expression turned into a grin.

"Still brooding in corners, I see."

Holt turned and was once again struck by Lilah Calhoun's resemblance to the woman his grandfather had painted. "Just watching the show."

"It is worth the price of a ticket. Max." Lilah laid a hand on the arm of the tall, lanky man at her side. "This is Holt Bradford, whom I was madly in love with for about twenty-four hours some fifteen years ago."

Holt's brow lifted. "You never told me."

"Of course not. At the end of the day I decided I didn't want to be in love with the surly, dangerous sort after all. This is Max Quartermain, the man I'm going to love for the rest of my life."

"Congratulations." Holt took Max's offered hand. Firm grip, Holt mused, steady eyes and a slightly embarrassed smile. "You're the teacher, right?"

"I was. And you're Christian Bradford's grandson."

"That's right," Holt agreed, and his voice had cooled.

"Don't worry, we're not going to hound you as long as you're a guest." Studying him, Lilah ran a fingertip around the rim of her glass. "We'll do that later. I'll have Max show you the scar he got while we were having our little publicity stunt."

"Lilah." Max's voice was soft with an underlying command.

Lilah merely shrugged and sipped champagne. "You remember C.C." She gestured as her sister joined them.

"I remember a gangly kid with engine grease on her face." He relaxed enough to smile. "You look good."

"Thanks. My husband, Trent. Holt Bradford."

It was Coco's dance partner, Holt noted as the two men summed each other up during the polite introductions.

"And the bride and groom," Lilah announced, toasting the couple before she drank again.

"Hello, Holt." Though she was still glowing, Amanda's eyes were steady and watchful. "I'm glad you could come." As she introduced Sloan, Holt realized he'd been surrounded quite neatly. They didn't press. No, the emeralds were never mentioned. But they'd joined ranks, he thought, in a solid wall of determination he had to admire, even as he resented it.

"What is this, a family meeting?" Suzanna hurried up. "You're supposed to be mingling, not huddling in a corner. Oh. Holt." Her smile wavered a bit. "I didn't know you were here."

"Your aunt invited me."

"Yes, I know, but—" She broke off and put her hostess's smile back in place. "I'm glad you could make it."

Like hell, he thought and lifted his glass. "It's been...interesting so far."

At some unspoken signal, her family drifted away, leaving them alone in the corner beside a tub of gardenias. "I hope they didn't make you uncomfortable."

"I can handle it."

"That may be, but I wouldn't want you badgered at my sister's wedding."

"But it doesn't bother you if it's someplace else."

Before she could retort, small impatient hands were tugging at her skirt. "Mom, when can we have the cake?"

"When Amanda and Sloan are ready to cut it." She skimmed a finger down Alex's nose.

"But we're hungry."

"Then go over to the buffet table and stuff your little face."

He giggled at that but didn't relent. "The cake—"

"Is for later. Alex, this is Mr. Bradford."

Not particularly interested in meeting another adult who would pat his head and tell him what a big boy he was, Alex pouted up at Holt. When he was offered a very manly handshake, he perked up a bit.

"Are you the policeman?"

"I used to be."

"Did you ever get shot in the head?"

Holt muffled a chuckle. "No, sorry." For some reason he felt as though he'd lost face. "I did catch one in the leg once."

"Yeah?" Alex brightened. "Did it bleed and bleed?"

He had to grin. "Buckets."

"Wow. Did you shoot lots of bad guys?"

"Dozens of them."

"Okay! Wait a minute." He raced off.

"I'm sorry," Suzanna began. "He's going through a murder-and-mayhem stage."

"I'm sorry I didn't get shot in the head."

She laughed. "Oh, that's all right, you made up for it by telling him you shot lots of bad guys." She wondered, but didn't ask, if he'd been telling the truth.

"Suzanna, would—"

"Hey." Alex skidded to a halt, with two other children in tow. "I told them how you got shot in the leg."

"Did it hurt?" Jenny wanted to know.

"Some."

"It bled and bled," Alex said with relish. "This is Jenny, she's my sister. And this is my brother, Kevin."

Suzanna wanted to kiss him. She wanted to pull Alex up in her arms and smother him with kisses for accepting so easily what adults had made so complicated. Instead, she brushed a hand over his hair.

The three of them bombarded Holt with questions until Suzanna called a halt. "I think that's enough gore for now."

"But, Mom—"

"But, Alex," she mimicked. "Why don't you go get some punch?"

Since it seemed like a pretty good idea, they trooped off.

"Quite a brood," Holt murmured, then looked back at Suzanna. "I thought you had two kids."

"I do."

"Seems to me I just saw three."

"Kevin is my ex-husband's son," she said coolly. "Now, if you'll excuse me."

He put a hand on her arm. Another secret, he thought, and decided he would dig up that answer, as well. Not now. Now he was going to do something he'd thought about doing since he'd seen her walk down the white satin runner in the floaty blue dress.

"Would you like to dance?"

Chapter 5

She couldn't quite relax in his arms. She told herself it was foolish, that the dance was just a casual social gesture. But his body was so close, so firm, the hand at her back so possessive. It reminded her too clearly of the moment he had pulled her against him to send her soaring into a kiss.

"It's quite a house," he said, and gave himself the pleasure of feeling her hair against his cheek. "I always wondered what it was like inside."

"I'll have to give you a tour sometime."

He could feel her heart thud against his. Experimenting, he skimmed his hand up her spine. The rhythm quickened. "I'm surprised you haven't been back to nag me."

There was annoyance in her eyes as she drew her head back. "I have no intention of nagging you."

"Good." He brushed his thumb over her knuckles and felt her tremble. "But you will come back."

"Only because I promised Aunt Coco."

"No." He increased the pressure on her spine and brought her an inch closer. "Not only because of that. You wonder what it would be like, the same way I've wondered half my life."

A little line of panic followed his fingers up her spine. "This isn't the place."

"I choose my own ground." His lips hovered bare inches from hers. He watched her eyes darken and cloud. "I want you, Suzanna."

Her heart had leaped up to throb in her throat so that her voice was husky and uneven. "Am I supposed to be flattered?"

"No. You'd be smart to be scared. I won't make things easy on you."

"What I am," she said with more control, "is uninterested."

His lips curved. "I could kiss you now and prove you wrong."

"I won't have a scene at my sister's wedding."

"Fine, then come to my place tomorrow morning."

"No."

"All right then." He lowered his head. She turned hers away so that his lips brushed her temple, then nibbled on her ear.

"Stop it. My children—"

"Should hardly be shocked to see a man kiss their mother." But he did stop, because his knees were going weak. "Tomorrow morning, Suzanna. There's something I need to show you. Something of my grandfather's."

She looked up again, struggling to steady her pulse. "If this is some sort of game, I don't want to play."

"No game. I want you, and this time I'll have you.

But there is something of my grandfather's you have the right to see. Unless you're afraid to be alone with me."

Her spine stiffened. "I'll be there."

The next morning, Suzanna stood on the terrace with Megan. They watched their children race across the lawn with Fred.

"I wish you could stay longer."

With a half laugh, Megan shook her head. "I'm surprised to say I wish I could, too. I have to be back at work tomorrow."

"You and Kevin are welcome here anytime. I want you to know that."

"I do." Megan shifted her gaze to meet Suzanna's. There was a sadness there she understood, though she rarely allowed herself to feel it. "If you and the kids decide to visit Oklahoma, you've got a home with us. I don't want to lose touch. Kevin needs to know this part of his family."

"Then we won't." She stooped to pick up a rose petal that had drifted from a bouquet to float to the terrace. "It was a beautiful wedding. Sloan and Mandy are going to be happy—and we'll have nieces and nephews in common."

"God, the world's a strange place." Megan took Suzanna's hand. "I'd like to think we can be friends, not only for our children's sakes or for Sloan and Amanda."

Suzanna smiled. "I think we already are."

"Suzanna!" Coco signaled from the kitchen door. "A phone call for you." She was chewing her lip when Suzanna reached her. "It's Baxter."

"Oh." Suzanna felt the simple pleasure of the morning drain. "I'll take it in the other room."

She braced herself as she walked down the hallway.

He couldn't hurt her any longer, she reminded herself. Not physically, not emotionally. She slipped into the library, took a long, steadying breath, then picked up the phone.

"Hello, Bax."

"I suppose you considered it sly to keep me waiting on the phone."

And there it was again, she thought, that clipped, critical tone that had once made her shiver. Now she only sighed. "I'm sorry. I was outside."

"Digging in the garden, I suppose. Are you still pretending to make a living pruning rosebushes?"

"I'm sure you didn't call to see how my business is going."

"Your business, as you call it, is nothing to me but a slight embarrassment. Having my ex-wife selling flowers on the street corner—"

"Clouds your image, I know." She passed a hand over her hair. "We're not going to go through that again, are we?"

"Quite the little shrew these days." She heard him murmur something to someone else, then laugh. "No, I didn't call to remind you you're making a fool of yourself. I want the children."

Her blood turned to ice. "What?"

The shaky whisper pleased him enormously. "I believe it states quite clearly in the custody agreement that I'm entitled to two weeks during the summer. I'll pick them up on Friday."

"You...but you haven't—"

"Don't stammer, Suzanna. It's one of your more annoying traits. If you didn't comprehend, I'll repeat. I'm exercising my parental rights. I'll pick the children up on Friday, at noon."

"You haven't seen them in nearly a year. You can't just pick them up and—"

"I most certainly can. If you don't choose to honor the agreement, I'll simply take you back to court. It isn't legal or wise for you to try to keep the children from me."

"I've never tried to keep them from you. You haven't bothered with them."

"I have no intention of rearranging my schedule to suit you. Yvette and I are going to Martha's Vineyard for two weeks, and have decided to take the children. It's time they saw something of the world besides the little corner you hide in."

Her hands were shaking. She gripped the receiver more tightly. "You didn't even send Alex a card on his birthday."

"I don't believe there's anything in the agreement about birthday cards," he said shortly. "But it is very specific on visitation rights. Feel free to check with your lawyer, Suzanna."

"And if they don't want to go?"

"The choice isn't theirs—or yours." But his, he thought, which was exactly as he preferred it. "I wouldn't try to poison them against me."

"I don't have to," she murmured.

"See that they're packed and ready. Oh, and Suzanna, I've been reading quite a bit about your family lately. Isn't it odd that there wasn't any mention of an emerald necklace in our settlement agreement?"

"I didn't know it existed."

"I wonder if the courts would believe that."

She felt tears of frustration and rage fill her eyes. "For God's sake, didn't you take enough?"

"It's never enough, Suzanna, when you consider how

very much you disappointed me. Friday,'' he said.
"Noon." And hung up.

She was trembling. Even when she lowered carefully
into a chair, she couldn't stop. She felt as though she'd
been jerked back five years, into that terrible helplessness. She couldn't stop him. She'd read the custody
agreement word for word before signing it, and he was
within his rights. Oh, technically she could have demanded more notice, but that would only postpone the
inevitable. If Bax had made up his mind, she couldn't
change it. The more she fought, the more she argued, the
harder he would twist the knife.

And the more difficult he would make it on the children.

Her babies. Rocking, she covered her face with her
hands. It was only for a short time—she could survive it.
But how would they feel when she shipped them off,
giving them no choice?

She would have to make it sound like an adventure.
With the right tone, the right words, she could convince
them this was something they wanted to do. Pressing her
lips together, she rose. But not now. She would never be
able to convince them of anything but her own turmoil
if she spoke with them now.

"Damn place is like Grand Central Station." The familiar thump of a cane nearly had Suzanna sinking back
into the chair again. "People coming and going, phone
ringing. You'd think nobody ever got married before."
Suzanna's great-aunt Colleen, her magnificent white hair
swept back and diamonds glittering at her ears, stopped
in the doorway. "I'll have you know those little monsters
of yours tracked dirt up the stairs."

"I'm sorry."

Colleen only huffed. She enjoyed complaining about

the children, because she had grown so fond of them. "Hooligans. The one blessed day of the week there's not hammering and sawing every minute, and there's packs of children shrieking through the house. Why the hell aren't they in school?"

"Because it's July, Aunt Colleen."

"Don't see what difference that makes." Her frown deepened as she studied Suzanna. "What's the matter with you, girl?"

"Nothing. I'm just a little tired."

"Tired my foot." She recognized the look. She'd seen it before—the weary desperation and helplessness—in her own mother's eyes. "Who was that on the phone?"

Suzanna's chin came up. "That, Aunt Colleen, is none of your business."

"Well, you've climbed on your high horse." And it pleased her. She preferred that her grandniece bite back rather than take a slap. Besides, she'd just badger Coco until she learned what was going on.

"I have an appointment," Suzanna said as steadily as possible. "Would you mind telling Aunt Coco that I've gone out?"

"So now I'm a messenger boy. I'll tell her, I'll tell her," Colleen muttered, waving her cane. "It's high time she fixed me some tea."

"Thank you. I won't be long."

"Go out and clear your head," Colleen said as Suzanna started by. "There's nothing a Calhoun can't handle."

Suzanna sighed and kissed Colleen's thin cheek. "I hope you're right."

She didn't allow herself to think. She left the house and climbed into her pickup, telling herself she would handle whatever needed to be handled—but she would calm herself first.

She had become very skilled at pulling in her emotions. A woman couldn't sit in a courtroom with her children's futures hanging in the balance and not learn control.

It was possible to feel panic or rage or misery and function normally. When she was certain she could, she would speak with the children.

There was an appointment to be kept. Whatever Holt had to show her might distract her enough to help her keep control of her emotions until they leveled.

She thought she was calm when she pulled up at his house. As she got out of the truck, she combed a hand through her windblown hair. When she realized she was gripping her keys too hard she deliberately relaxed her fingers. She slid the keys into her pocket and knocked.

The dog sent up a din. Holt had one hand on Sadie's collar as he opened the door. "You made it. I thought I might have to come after you."

"I told you I'd be here." She stepped inside. "What do you have to show me?"

When he was sure Sadie would do no more than sniff and whine for attention, he released her. "Your aunt showed a lot more interest in the cottage."

"I'm a little pressed for time." After giving the dog an absent pat, she stuck her hands into the pockets of her baggy cotton slacks. "It's very nice." She glanced around, took in nothing. "You must be comfortable here."

"I get by," he said slowly, his eyes keen on her face. There wasn't a trace of color in her cheeks. Her eyes were too dark. He'd wanted to make her aware of him, maybe uncomfortably aware, but he hadn't wanted to make her sick with fear at the thought of seeing him again.

"You can relax, Suzanna." His voice was curt and dismissive. "I'm not going to jump you."

Her nerves stretched taut on the thin wire of control. "Can we just get on with this?"

"Yeah, we can get on with it, as soon as you stop standing there as if you're about to be chained and beaten. I haven't done anything—yet—to make you look at me that way."

"I'm not looking at you in any way."

"The hell you're not. Damn it, your hands are shaking." Furious, he grabbed them. "Stop it," he demanded. "I'm not going to hurt you."

"It has nothing to do with you." She yanked her hands away, hating the fact that she couldn't stop them from trembling. "Why should you think that anything I feel, any way I look depends on you? I have my own life, my own feelings. I'm not some weak, terrified woman who falls apart because a man raises his voice. Do you really think I'm afraid of you? Do you really think you could hurt me after—"

She broke off, appalled. She'd been shouting, and the furious tears were still burning her eyes. Her stomach was clenched so tight she could hardly breathe. Sadie had retreated to a corner and sat quivering. Holt stood a foot away, staring at her, eyes narrowed in speculation.

"I have to go," she managed, and bolted for the door. His hand slapped the wood and held it shut. "Let me go." When her voice broke, she bit down on her lip. She struggled with the door then whirled on him, eyes blazing. "I said let me go."

"Go ahead," he said with surprising calm, "take a

punch at me. But you're not going anywhere while you're churned up like this.''

"If I'm churned up, it's my own business. I told you, this has nothing to do with you.''

"Okay, so you're not going to hit me. Let's try another release valve.'' He put his hands firmly on either side of her face and covered her mouth with his.

It wasn't a kiss meant to soothe or comfort. It did neither. This was raw and turbulent emotion and matched her own feelings completely.

Her arms were caught between them, her hands still fisted. Her body trembled; her skin heated. At the first flicker of response, he dived into the rough, desperate kiss until he was certain the only thing she was thinking about was him.

Then he took a moment longer, to please himself. She was a volcano waiting to erupt, a storm ready to blow. Her pent-up passion packed a punch more stunning than her fist could have. He intended to be around for the explosion, but he could wait.

When he released her, she leaned back against the door, her eyes closed, breath hitching. Watching her, he realized he'd never seen anyone fight so hard for control.

"Sit down.'' She shook her head. "All right, stand.'' With a dismissive shrug, he moved away to light a cigarette. "Either way you're going to tell me what set you off.''

"I don't want to talk to you.''

He sat on the arm of a chair and blew out a stream of smoke. "Lots of people haven't wanted to talk to me. But I usually find out what I want to know.''

She opened her eyes. They were dry now, which relieved him considerably. "Is this an interrogation?''

With another shrug, he brought the cigarette to his lips

again. It wouldn't do her any good if he caved in and offered soft words. He wasn't even sure he had them. "It can be."

She thought about pulling the door open and leaving. But he would only stop her. She'd learned the hard way that there were some battles a woman couldn't win.

"It isn't worth it," she said wearily. "I shouldn't have come while I was upset, but I thought I had gotten myself under control."

"Upset about what?"

"It isn't important."

"Then it shouldn't be a problem to tell me."

"Bax called. My ex-husband." To comfort herself she began to roam the room.

Holt studied the tip of his cigarette, reminding himself that jealousy was out of place. "Looks like he can still stir you up."

"One phone call. One, and I'm back under his thumb." There was a bitterness in her voice he hadn't expected from her. He said nothing. "There's nothing I can do. Nothing. He's going to take the children for two weeks. I can't stop him."

Holt let out an impatient breath. "For God's sake, is that what all this hysteria's about? So the kids go off with Daddy for a couple of weeks." Disgusted, he crushed out his cigarette. And to think he'd been worried about her. "Save the vindictive-wife routine, babe. He's got a right."

"Oh yes, he's got the right." Her voice shook with an emotion so deep that Holt's head snapped up again. "Because it says so on a piece of paper. And he was there when they were conceived, so that makes him their father. Of course, that doesn't mean he has to love them, or worry about them or struggle to raise them without malice. It doesn't mean he has to remember Christmas or birthdays. It's just as Bax told me on the phone. There's nothing in the custody agreement that obligates him to send birthday cards. But it does obligate me to turn the children over to him when he has the whim.''

There were tears threatening again, but she refused them. Tears in front of a man never brought anything but humiliation. ''Do you think this is about me? He can't hurt me anymore. But my children don't deserve to be used so that he can try to pay me back for being so much less than he wanted.''

Holt felt something hot and lethal spread in his gut. ''He did a good job on you, didn't he?''

''That isn't the point. Alex and Jenny are the point. Somehow I have to convince them that the father who hasn't bothered to contact them in months, who could barely tolerate them when they lived under the same roof, is going to take them on a wonderful two-week vacation.'' Suddenly tired, she pushed her hands through her hair. ''I didn't come here to talk about this.''

''Yes, you did.'' Calmer, Holt lit another cigarette. If he didn't do something with his hands, he was going to touch her again, and he wasn't sure either of them could handle it. ''I'm not family, so I'm safe. You can dump on me and figure I won't lose any sleep over it.''

She smiled a little. ''Maybe you're right. Sorry.''

''I didn't ask for an apology. How do the kids feel about him?''

''He's a stranger.''

''Then they probably don't have any preset expectations. Seems to me they might think of the whole thing as an adventure—and that you're letting him push your buttons. If he is using them to get to you, he hit a bull's-eye.''

"I'd already come to those same conclusions myself. I needed to vent some excess frustration." She tried a smile again. "Usually I just pull some weeds."

"I think kissing me worked better."

"It was different anyway."

He tapped out his cigarette and rose. The hell with what they could handle. "Is that the best description you can come up with?"

"Off the top of my head. Holt," she began when he slid his arms around her.

"Yeah?" He nipped at her chin, then her mouth.

"I don't want to be held." But she did, too much.

"That's too bad." His arms tightened, bringing her closer.

"You asked me to come here so you could…" She made a little sound of distress when he closed his teeth over her earlobe. "You could show me something of your grandfather's."

"That's right." Her skin smelled like the air high on the cliffs—laced with the sea and wildflowers and hot summer sunlight. "I also asked you here so I could get my hands on you again. We'll just take one thing at a time."

"I don't want to get involved." But even as she said it, her mouth was moving to meet his.

"Me, either." He changed the angle and sucked on her bottom lip.

"This is just—oh—chemistry." Her fingers tangled in his hair.

"You bet." His rough-palmed hands slipped under her shirt to explore.

"It can't go anywhere."

"It already has."

He was right about that, as well. For one brief moment

she let herself fall into the kiss, into the heat. She needed something, someone. If she couldn't have comfort or compassion, she would take desire. But the more she took, the more her body strained for something just out of reach. Something she couldn't afford to want or need again.

"This is too fast," she said breathlessly, and struggled away. "I'm sorry, I realize it must seem as though I'm sending you mixed signals."

He was watching her eyes, just her eyes, as his body pulsed. "I think I can sort them out."

"I don't want to start something I won't be able to finish." She moistened her lips still warm from his. "And I have too many responsibilities, too much to worry about right now to even think about having…"

"An affair?" he finished. "You're going to have to think about it." With his eyes still on hers, he gathered her hair in his hand. "Go ahead, take a few days. I can afford to be patient as long as I get what I want. And I want you."

Nerves skittered along her spine. "Just because I find you attractive, physically, doesn't mean I'm going to jump into bed with you."

"I don't much care whether you jump, crawl or have to be dragged. We can decide on the method later." Before she could think of a name to call him, he grinned, kissed her then stepped back. "Now that that's settled, I'll take you up and show you the portrait."

"If you think it's settled because you—what portrait?"

"You take a look, then tell me."

He led the way up into the loft. Torn between curiosity and fury, Suzanna followed him. The only thing she was certain of at the moment was that since she'd met Holt Bradford again, her emotions had been on a roller coaster. All she wanted out of life was a nice smooth, uneventful ride.

"He worked up here."

The simple statement captured her attention and her interest. "Did you know him well?"

"I don't think anyone did." Holt moved over to open a tilt-out window. "He came and went pretty much as he pleased. He'd come back here for a few days, or a few months. I'd sit up here sometimes and watch him work. If he got tired of me hanging around, he'd send me out with the dog, or into the village for ice cream."

"There's still paint on the floor." Unable to resist, Suzanna bent down to touch. She glanced up, met Holt's eyes and understood.

He'd loved his grandfather. These splotches of paint, more than the cabin itself, were memories. She reached a hand out for his, rising when their fingers linked. Then she saw the portrait.

The canvas was tilted against the wall, its frame old and ornate. The woman looked back at her, with eyes full of secrets and sadness and love.

"Bianca," Suzanna said, and let her own tears come. "I knew he must have painted her. He'd have had to."

"I wasn't certain until I saw Lilah yesterday."

"He never sold it," Suzanna murmured. "He kept it, because it was all he had left of her."

"Maybe." He wasn't entirely comfortable that the exact thought had occurred to him. "I've got to figure there was something between them. I don't see how that helps you get any closer to the emeralds."

"But you'll help."

"I said I would."

"Thank you." She turned to face him. Yes, he would

help, she thought. He wouldn't break his word no matter how much it annoyed him to keep it.

"The first thing I have to ask you, is if you'll bring the portrait to The Towers so my family can see it. It would mean a great deal to them."

At Suzanna's insistence, they took Sadie as well. She rode in the back of the pickup, grinning into the wind. When they arrived at The Towers, they saw Lilah and Max sitting out on the lawn. Fred, spotting the truck, tore across the yard, then came to a stumbling halt when Sadie leaped nimbly out of the back.

Body aquiver, he approached her. The dogs gave each other a thorough sniffing over. With a flick of her tail, Sadie pranced across the yard. She sent Fred one come-hither look over her shoulder that had him scrambling after her.

"Looks like love at first sight for old Fred," Lilah commented as she walked with Max to the truck. "We wondered where you'd gone." She ran a hand down Suzanna's arm, letting her know without words that she knew about the call from Bax.

"Are the kids around?"

"No, they went into the village with Megan and her parents to help Kevin pick out some souvenirs before they leave."

With a nod, Suzanna took her hand. "There's something you have to see." Stepping back, she gestured. Through the open door of the truck, Lila saw the painting. Her fingers tightened on her sister's.

"Oh, Suze."

"I know."

"Max, can you see?"

"Yes." Gently he kissed the top of her head and

looked at the portrait of a woman who was the double for the one he loved. "She was beautiful. This is a Bradford." He glanced at Holt with a shrug. "I've been studying your grandfather's work for the past couple of weeks."

"You've had this all along," Lilah began.

Holt let the accusation in the tone roll off him. "I didn't know it was Bianca until I saw you yesterday."

She subsided, studying his face. "You're not as nasty as you'd like people to think. Your aura's much too clear."

"Leave Holt's aura alone, Lilah," Suzanna said with a laugh. "I want Aunt Coco to see this. Oh, I wish Sloan and Mandy hadn't left on their honeymoon."

"They'll only be gone two weeks," Lilah reminded her.

Two weeks. Suzanna struggled to keep the smile in place as Holt carried the portrait inside.

The moment she saw it, Coco wept. But that was only to be expected. Holt had propped the painting on the love seat in the parlor, and Coco sat in the wing chair, drenching her handkerchief.

"After all this time. To have part of her back in this house."

Lilah touched her aunt's shoulder. "Part of her has always been in the house."

"Oh, I know, but to be able to look at her." She sniffled. "And see you."

"He must have loved her so much." Damp eyed, C.C. rested her head on Trent's shoulder. "She looks just as I imagined her, just as I knew she looked that night when I felt her."

Holt kept his hands in his pocket. "Look, sentiment

and séances aside, it's the emeralds you need. If you want my help, then I need to know everything.''

"Séance." Coco dried her eyes. ''We should hold another one. We'll hang the portrait in the dining room. With that to focus on we're bound to be successful. I've got to check the astrological charts.'' She got up and hurried out of the room.

''And she's off and running,'' Suzanna murmured.

Trent nodded. ''Not to discredit Coco, but it might be best if I filled in Holt in a more conventional way.''

''I'll make some coffee.'' Suzanna sent one last glance at the portrait before heading for the kitchen.

There wasn't so very much Trent could tell him, she thought as she ground beans. Holt already knew about the legend, the research they'd done, the danger her sisters had faced. It was possible that he might make more of it, with his training, than they had. But would he care, even a fraction of the amount her family did?

She understood that emotional motivation could change lives. And that without it, nothing worthwhile could be accomplished.

He had passion. But could his passions run deeper than a physical need? Not for her, she assured herself, measuring the coffee carefully. She'd meant what she'd said about not wanting to become involved. She couldn't afford to love again.

She was afraid he was right about an affair. If she couldn't be strong enough to resist him, she hoped she could be strong enough to hold her heart and her body separate. It couldn't be wrong to need to be touched and wanted. Perhaps by giving herself to him, in a physical way, she could prove to herself that she wasn't a failure as a woman.

God, she wanted to feel like a woman again, to experience that rush of pleasure and release. She was nearly thirty, she thought, and the only man with whom she'd been intimate had found her wanting. How much longer could she go on wondering if he was right?

She jolted when hands came down on her shoulders.

Slowly, aware of how easily she paled, Holt turned her to face him. "Where were you?"

"Oh. Up to my ears weeding pachysandra."

"That's a pretty good lie if you'd put more flare into it." But he let it go. "I'm going to run down and talk with Lieutenant Koogar. Rain check the coffee."

"All right, I'll drive you down."

"I'm hitching a ride with Max and Trent."

Her brow lifted. "Men only, I take it."

"Sometimes it works better that way." He rubbed a thumb over the line between her brows in a gentle gesture that surprised them both. Catching himself, he dropped his hand again. "You worry too much. I'll be in touch."

"Thank you. I won't forget what you're doing for us."

"Forget it." He hauled her against him and kissed her until she went limp. "I'd rather you remember that."

He strode out, and she sank weakly into a chair. She wouldn't have any choice but to remember it.

Chapter 6

He wasn't playing Good Samaritan, Holt assured himself. After getting a clearer handle on the situation, he was doing what he felt was best. Somebody had to keep an eye on her until Livingston was under wraps. The best way to keep an eye on her was to stick close.

Swinging into the graveled lot, he pulled up next to her pickup. He saw that she was outside the shop with customers, so amused himself by roaming around.

He'd driven by Island Gardens before but had never stopped in. There hadn't been any reason to. There were a lot of thriving blossoms crowded on wooden tables or sitting in ornamental pots. Though he couldn't tell one from the other, he could appreciate their appeal. Or maybe it was the fact that the air smelled like Suzanna.

It was obvious she knew what she was doing here, he reflected. There was a tidiness to the place, enhanced by a breezy informality that invited browsers to browse even as it tempted them to buy.

Colorful pictures were set up here and there, describing certain flowers, their planting instructions and maintenance. Along the side of the main building were stacks of fifty- and hundred-pound bags of planting medium and mulch.

He was looking over a tray of snapdragons when he heard a rustle in the bush behind him. He tensed automatically, and his fingers jerked once toward the weapon he no longer wore. Letting out a quiet breath, he cursed himself. He had to get over this reaction. He wasn't a cop anymore, and no one was likely to spring at his back with an eight-inch buck knife.

He turned his head slightly and spotted the young boy crouched behind a display of peonies. Alex grinned and popped up. "I got you!" He danced gleefully around the peonies. "I was a pygmy and I zapped you with my poison blow dart."

"Lucky for me I'm immune to pygmy poison. If it'd been Ubangi poison, I would've been a goner. Where's your sister?"

"In the greenhouse. Mom gave us seeds and stuff, but I got bored. It's okay for me to come out here," he said quickly, knowing how fast adults could make things tough for you. "As long as I don't go near the street or knock over anything."

He wasn't about to give the kid a hard time. "Have you killed many customers today?"

"It's pretty slow. 'Cause it's Monday, Mom says. That's why we can come to work with her and Carolanne can have the day off."

"You like coming here?"

Holt wasn't sure how it had happened, but he and the boy were walking among the flats of flowers, and Alex's hand was in his.

"Sure, it's neat. We get to plant things. Like, see those?" He pointed at an edging of multicolored flowers that sprang up beside the gravel. "Those are zinnias, and I planted them myself, so I get to water them and stuff. Sometimes we get to carry things to the car for people, and they give you quarters."

"Sounds like a good deal."

"And Mom closes up at lunchtime and we walk down the street and get pizza and play the video games. We get to come almost every Monday. Except—" He broke off and kicked at the gravel.

"Except what?"

"Next week we'll have to be on vacation, and Mom won't come."

Holt looked down at the boy's bent head and wondered what the hell to do. "I, ah, guess she's pretty busy here."

"Carolanne or somebody could work, and she could come. But she won't."

"Don't you figure she'd go with you if she could?"

"I guess." Alex kicked at the gravel again and, when Holt didn't scold, kicked a third time. "We have to go to somebody named Martha's yard, with my father and his new wife. Mom says it'll be fun, and we'll go to the beach and have ice cream."

"Sounds pretty good."

"I don't want to go. I don't see how come I have to. I want to go to Disney World with Mom."

When the little voice broke, Holt let out a deep breath and crouched down. "It's tough having to do things you don't want to. I guess you'll have to look after Jenny while you're gone."

Alex shrugged and sniffled. "I guess. She's scared to go. But she's only five."

"She'll be okay with you. Tell you what, I'll look after your mom while you're gone."

"Okay." Feeling better, Alex wiped his nose with the back of his hand. "Can I see on your leg where they shot you?"

"Sure." Holt pointed to a scar about six inches above his kneecap on his left leg.

"Wow." Since Holt didn't seem to mind, Alex ran a fingertip over it. "I guess since you were a policeman and all, you'll take good care of Mom."

"Sure I will."

Suzanna wasn't sure what she felt when she saw Holt and her son, dark heads bent close. But she knew something warm stirred when Holt lifted a hand and brushed it through Alex's hair.

"Well, what's all this?"

Both males looked over then back at each other to exchange a quick and private look before Holt rose. "Man talk," he said, and gave Alex's hand a squeeze.

"Yeah." Alex pushed out his chest. "Man talk."

"I see. Well, I hate to interrupt, but if you want pizza, you'd better go wash your hands."

"Can he come?" Alex asked.

"His name," Suzanna said, "is Mr. Bradford."

"His name is Holt." Holt sent Alex a wink and got a grin in return.

"Can he?"

"We'll see."

"She says that a lot," Alex confided, then raced off to find his sister.

"I suppose I do." Suzanna sighed then turned back to Holt. "What can I do for you?"

She was wearing her hair loose, with a little blue cap over it that made her look about sixteen. Holt suddenly felt as foolish and awkward as a boy asking for his first date.

"Do you still need part-time help?"

"Yes, without any luck." She began to pinch off begonias. "All the high school and college kids are set for the summer."

"I can give you about four hours a day."

"What?"

"Maybe five," he continued as she stared at him. "I've got a couple of repair jobs, but I call my own hours."

"You want to work for me?"

"As long as I only have to haul and plant the things. I ain't selling flowers."

"You can't be serious."

"I mean it. I won't sell them."

"No, I mean about working for me at all. You've already started up your own business, and I can't afford to pay more than minimum wage."

His eyes went very dark, very fast. "I don't want your money."

Suzanna blew the hair out of her eyes. "Now, I am confused."

"Look, I figured we could trade off. I'll do some of the heavy work for you, and you can fix up my yard some."

Her smile bloomed slowly. "You'd like me to fix up your yard?"

Women always made things complicated, he thought and stuffed his hands into his pockets. "I don't want you to go crazy or anything. A couple more bushes maybe. Now do you want to make a deal or don't you?"

Her smile turned to a laugh. "One of the Andersons'

neighbors admired our team effort. I'm scheduled to start tomorrow." She held out a hand. "Be here at six."

He winced. "A.M.?"

"Exactly. Now, how about lunch?"

He put his hand in hers. "Fine. You're buying."

Good God, the woman worked like an elephant. She worked like two elephants, Holt corrected as the sweat poured down his back. He had a pick or shovel in his hand so often, he might as well be on a chain gang.

It should've been cooler up here on the cliffs. But the lawn they were landscaping—attacking, he thought as he brought the pick down again—was nothing but rock.

In the three days he'd worked with her, he'd given up trying to stop her from doing any of the heavy work. She only ignored him and did as she pleased. When he went home in the midafternoon, every muscle twinging, he wondered how in holy hell she kept it up.

He couldn't put in more than four or five hours and juggle his own jobs. But he knew she worked eight to ten every day. It wasn't difficult to see that she was throwing herself into her work to keep from thinking about the fact that the kids were leaving the next day.

He brought the pick down again, hit rock. The shock sang up his arms. At the low, steady swearing, Suzanna glanced up from her own work. "Why don't you take a break. I can finish that."

"Did you bring the dynamite?"

The smile touched her lips for only a moment. "No, really. Go get a drink out of the cooler. We're nearly ready to plant."

"Fine." He hated to admit that the whole business was wearing him out. There were blisters on top of his blisters, his muscles felt as though he'd gone ten rounds with the champ—and lost. Wiping his face and neck dry, he walked over to the cooler they'd set in the shade of a beech tree. As he pulled out a ginger ale, he heard the pick ring against the rocky soil. It was no use telling her she was crazy, he thought as he guzzled down the cold liquid. But he couldn't help it.

"You're a lunatic, Suzanna. This is the kind of work they give to people with numbers across their chest."

"What we have here," she said in a thick Southern drawl, "is a failure to communicate."

Her quote of the line from *Cool Hand Luke* made him grin, but only for an instant. "Stark, raving mad," he continued, watching her swing the pick. "What the hell do you think's going to grow in that rock?"

"You'd be surprised." She took a moment to wipe at the sweat that was dripping in her eyes. "See those lilies on the bank there?" She gave a little grunt as she dislodged a rock. "I planted them two years ago in September."

He glanced at the profusion of tall, colorful flowers with grudging admiration. He had to admit that they were an improvement over the rough, rocky soil, but was it worth it?

"The Snyders gave me my first real job." She hefted a rock and tossed it into the wheelbarrow. Stretching her back, she listened to the fat bees buzzing in the gaillardia. "A sympathy job, seeing as they were friends of the family and poor Suzanna needed a break." Her breath whooshed out as she struck soil, and she blinked away the little red dots in front of her eyes. "Surprised them that I knew what I was doing, and I've been working here on and off ever since."

"Great. Would you put that damn thing down a minute?"

"Almost done."

"You won't be done until you keel over. Who's going to see a few posies wilting all the way up here?"

"The Snyders will see them, their guests will see them." She shook her head to clear a haze brought on by the heat. "The photographer from *New England Gardens* will see them." Lord, the bees were loud, she thought as the buzzing filled her head. "And nothing's going to wilt. I'm putting in pinks and campanula and some coreopsis, some lavender for scent and monarda for the hummingbirds." She pressed a hand to her head, ran it over her eyes. "In September we'll plant some bulbs. Dwarf irises and windflowers. Some tuberoses and…" She staggered under a hot wave of dizziness. Holt made the dash from shade to sun as the pick slid out of her hands. When he grabbed her she seemed to melt into his arms.

Cursing her helped relieve the fright as he carried her over and laid her down under the tree. Her body was like hot wax he could all but pour onto the cool grass. "That's it." He plunged his hand into the cooler then rubbed icy water over her face. "You're finished, do you understand? If I see a pick in your hands again, I'll murder you."

"I'm all right." Her voice was weak, but the irritation was clear enough. "Just a little too much sun." The water on her face felt heavenly, even if his hands were a bit rough. She took the ginger ale from him and drank carefully.

"Too much sun," he was ranting, "too much work. And not enough food or sleep from the look of you. You're a mess, Suzanna, and I'm tired of it."

"Thank you very much." She pushed his hands away and leaned back against the tree. She needed a minute, she'd admit. But she didn't need a lecture. "I should have taken a break," she said in disgust. "I know better, but I've got things on my mind."

"I don't care what you've got on your mind." God, she was white as a sheet. He wanted to hold her until the color came back into her cheeks, to stroke her hair until she was strong and rested again. But the concern came out in fury. "I'm taking you home and you're going to bed."

Steadier, she set the bottle aside. "I think you're forgetting who works for whom."

"When you pass out on me, I take over."

"I didn't pass out," she said irritably. "I got dizzy. And nobody takes over for me, not now, not ever again. Stop splashing water in my face, you're going to drown me."

She was recovering fast enough, he thought, but it didn't cool his temper. "You're stubborn, hardheaded and just plain stupid."

"Fine. If you've finished yelling at me, I'm going to take my lunch break." She knew she had to eat. She didn't mind being stubborn or hardheaded, but she did mind being stupid. Which, she thought as she snatched a sandwich out of the cooler, was exactly what she had been to skip breakfast.

"Maybe I haven't finished yelling."

She shrugged as she unwrapped the sandwich. "Then you can yell while I eat. Or you can stop wasting time and have some lunch."

He considered dragging her to the truck. He liked the idea, but the benefits would only be short-term. Short of tying her up and locking her in a room, he couldn't stop her from working herself into the ground.

At least she was eating, he reflected. And the color had

seeped back into her cheeks. Maybe there was another tack to getting his way. Casually he took out a sandwich.

"I've been thinking about the emeralds."

The change in topic and attitude surprised her. "Oh?"

"I read the transcript Max put together from the interview with Mrs. Tobias, the maid. And I listened to the tape."

"What do you think?"

"I think she's got a good memory, and that she was impressed by Bianca. From her viewpoint, the setup was that Bianca was unhappy in her marriage, devoted to her children and in love with my grandfather. She and Fergus were already on shaky ground when they had the blowout over the dog. We'll figure that was the straw that broke it. She decided to leave him, but she didn't go that night. Why?"

"Even if she'd finally made the decision," Suzanna said slowly, "there would have been arrangements to make. She'd have had to consider the children." This she understood all too well. "Where could she take them? How could she be certain she could provide for them? Even if the marriage was a disaster, she would have to plan carefully how to tell them she was taking them away from their father."

"So when Fergus left for Boston after they fought, she started to work it out. We have to figure she went to my grandfather, because he ended up with the dog."

"She loved him," Suzanna murmured. "She would have gone to him first. And he loved her, so he would have wanted to go away with her and the children."

"If we go with that, we take it to the next step. She went back to The Towers to pack, to get the kids together. But instead of meeting my grandfather and riding off into the sunset, she takes a jump out of the tower window. Why?''

''She was in turmoil.'' With her eyes half-closed, Suzanna stared into the sunlight. ''She was about to take a step that would end her marriage, separate her children from their father. Break her vows. It's so difficult, so frightening. Like dying. Maybe she thought she was a failure, and when her husband came home, and she had to face him and herself, she couldn't.''

Holt ran a hand over her hair. ''Is that what it was like for you?''

Her shoulders stiffened. ''We're talking about Bianca. And I don't see what her reasons for killing herself have to do with the emeralds.''

Holt took his hand away. ''First we decide why she hid them, then we go for where.''

Slowly she relaxed again. ''Fergus gave them to her when their first son was born. Not their first child. A girl didn't rate.'' She took another sip of her ginger ale and washed away some of her own bitterness. ''She would have resented that, I think. To be rewarded—like a prize mare—for producing an heir. But, they were hers because the child was hers.''

Because her eyes were heavy, she let them drift closed. ''Bax gave me diamonds when Alex was born. I didn't feel guilty about selling them to start the business. Because they were mine. She might have felt the same way. The emeralds would have bought a new life for her, for the children.''

''Why did she hide them?''

''To make certain he didn't find them if he stopped her from leaving. So that she knew she'd have something of her own.''

"Did you hide your diamonds, Suzanna?"

"I put them in Jenny's diaper bag. The last place Baxter would look." With a half laugh, she plucked at the grass. "That sounds so melodramatic."

But he wasn't smiling or sneering, she noted. He was frowning out at the dianthiums where the bees hovered and hummed. "It sounds damn smart to me. She spent a lot of time in the tower, right?"

"We've looked there."

"We'll look again, and take her bedroom apart."

"Lilah will love that." Suzanna closed her eyes again. The food and the shade were making her sleepy. "It's her bedroom now. And we've looked there, too."

"I haven't."

"No." She decided it wouldn't hurt to stretch out while they finished talking it through. The grass was blissfully cool and soft. "If we found her journal, we'd know the answers. Mandy went through every book in the library, just in case it got mixed in like the purloined letter."

He began to stroke her hair again. "We'll take another look."

"Mandy wouldn't have missed anything. She's too organized."

"I'd rather check over old ground than depend on a séance."

She made a sound that was half laugh and half sigh. "Aunt Coco'll talk you into it." Her voice grew heavy with fatigue. "We need to plant the pinks first."

"Okay." He'd moved his hands down and was gently massaging her shoulders.

"It'll trail right over the rocks and down the bank. It doesn't give up," she murmured, and was asleep.

"You're telling me."

He left her there in the shade and walked back into the sunlight.

The grass was tickling her cheek when she woke. She'd rolled over onto her stomach and had slept like a stone. Groggy, she opened her eyes. She saw Holt sitting back against the tree, his legs crossed at the ankles. He was watching her as he brought a cigarette to his lips.

"I must have dozed off."

"You could say that."

"Sorry." She pushed herself up on her elbow. "We were talking about the emeralds."

He flicked the cigarette away. "We've talked enough for now." In one swift move, he hooked his hands under her arms and pulled her against him. Before she was fully awake, she was in his lap and his mouth was on hers.

He'd watched her sleep. And as he had watched her sleep, the need to touch her had boiled inside him until his blood was like lava. She'd looked so perfect, the sleeping princess, creamy skin dappled by hazy shade, her cheek resting on her hand, her hand on the grass.

He'd wanted those soft, warm lips under his, to feel that long, fragile body molded to him, to hear that quick little catch in her breathing. So he took, feverishly.

Disarmed, disoriented, she struggled back. Her blood had gone from slow and cool to rapid and hot. Her body, relaxed by sleep, was now taut as a bow. She dragged in a single ragged breath. All she could see was his face, his eyes dark and dangerous, his mouth hard and hungry. Then all was a blur as his lips brushed down on hers again.

She let him take what he seemed to need to take so desperately. Under the shade of the beech she pressed against him, answering each demand. When the dizziness came again, she reveled in it. This was not a weakness she had to fight. It was one she had wanted to feel as long as she could remember.

On an oath, he buried his face at her throat where her pulse jackhammered. Nothing and no one had ever made him feel like this. Frantic and shaky. Each time his mouth came back to hers it was with a new edge of desperation, each keener than the last. Dozens of sensations knifed into him, all sharp and deadly. He wanted to shove her aside, walk away before they cut him to ribbons. He wanted to roll with her on the cool, soft grass and drive out all the aches and jagged needs.

But her arms were around him, her hands moving restlessly through his hair while her body trembled. Then her cheek was against his, nuzzling there in a gesture that was almost unbearably sweet.

"What are we going to do?" she murmured. Wanting comfort, she turned her lips to his skin and sighed.

"I think we both know the answer to that."

Suzanna closed her eyes. It was so simple for him. She rested against him a moment, listening to the bees buzz in the flowers. "I need time."

He put his hands on her shoulders, pushing her back until they were face-to-face. "I may not be able to give it to you. We're not children anymore, and I'm tired of wondering what it would be like."

She let out a shaky breath. The turmoil wasn't only hers, she realized. She could feel it, shimmering out of him. "If you ask for more than I can give, we'll both be disappointed. I want you." She bit back a gasp when his fingers tightened. "But I can't make another mistake."

His eyes darkened and narrowed. "Do you want promises?"

"No," she said quickly. "No, I don't. But I have to

keep the ones I made to myself. If I come to you, I have to be sure it's not just something I want, but something I can live with.'' Reaching out, she laid a hand on his cheek. ''The one thing I can promise you is that if we're lovers, I won't regret it.''

He couldn't argue, not when she looked at him that way. ''When,'' he corrected.

''When,'' she said with a nod, then rose. Her legs weren't as shaky as she'd thought they would be. She felt stronger. *When,* she thought again. Yes, she'd already accepted that it was only a matter of time. ''But for now, we'll have to take things as they come. We've got a job to finish.''

''It's finished.'' He pulled himself to his feet as she turned.

The plants were in place, the ground smoothed and mulched. Where there had only been rocks and thin, thirsty soil were bright hopeful young flowers and tender green leaves.

''How?'' she began, already hurrying over to study his work.

''You slept three hours.''

''Three—'' Appalled, she looked back at him. ''You should have woken me up.''

''I didn't,'' he said simply. ''Now I've got to get back, I'm running late.''

''But you shouldn't have—''

''It's done.'' Impatience shimmered around him. ''Do you want to rip the damn things out and do it yourself?''

''No.'' As she studied him she realized he wasn't just angry, he was embarrassed. Not only had he done something sweet and considerate, but he'd spent three hours planting what he still sneeringly called posies.

So he stood there, she thought, looking very male and

ruffled in the streaming sun, the charming rockery at his feet and his rough, clever hands stuffed in his pockets. Thank me and I'll snarl, he seemed to say.

It was then, facing him on the rocky slope, that she realized what she had refused to admit in his arms. What she had insisted was only passion and need. She loved him. Not just for the hot-blooded kisses or the demanding hands. But for the man beneath. The man who would run a careless hand over her son's hair or answer her little girl's incessant questions. The man who would leave paint splattered on the floor in memory of his grandfather.

The one who would plant flowers for her while she slept.

As she continued to stare, Holt shifted uncomfortably. "Look, if you're going to faint again, I'm going to leave you where you fall. I haven't got time to play nursemaid."

A smile moved slowly, beautifully over her face, confusing him. She loved him for that, too—that snapping impatience that covered the compassion. She would need time to think, of course. Time to adjust. But for now, for this moment, she could simply hold tight to this rush of feeling and be content.

"You did a good job."

He glanced back at the flowers, certain he'd rather cut out his tongue than admit how much he'd enjoyed the work. "You stick them in and cover them up." He moved his shoulders in dismissal. "I put the tools and stuff in the truck. I've got to go."

"I put the Bryce job off until Monday. Tomorrow—I have to be home tomorrow."

"All right. See you later."

As he walked off to his car, Suzanna knelt down to touch the fragile new blooms.

* * *

In the cottage near the water, the man who called himself Marshall completed a thorough search. He found a few things of minor interest. The ex-cop liked to read and didn't cook. There were shelves of well-worn books in the bedroom, and only a few scattered supplies in the kitchen. He kept his medals in a box tossed in the bottom of a drawer, and a loaded .32 at the ready in the nightstand.

After rifling through a desk, Marshall discovered that Christian's grandson had made a few shrewd investments. He found it amusing that a former Vice cop had had the sense to create a tidy nest egg. He also found it interesting that training had caused Holt to write up a detailed report on everything he knew about the Calhoun emeralds.

His temper threatened as he read of the interview with the former servant—the servant that Maxwell Quartermain had located. That grated. Quartermain should have been working for him. Or he should have been dead. Marshall was tempted to wreck the place, to toss furniture, break lamps. To give in to an orgy of destruction.

But he forced himself to stay calm. He didn't want to tip his hand. Not yet. Perhaps he hadn't found anything particularly enlightening, but he knew as much as the Calhouns did.

Very carefully, he put the papers back in place, shut the drawers. The dog was beginning to bark out in the yard. He detested dogs. Sneering at the sound, he rubbed at the scar on his leg where the little Calhoun mutt had bitten him. They would have to pay for that. They would all have to pay.

And so they would, he thought. When he had the emeralds.

He left the cottage precisely as he had found it.

* * *

I will not write of the winter. That is not a memory I wish to relive. But I did not leave the island. Could not leave it. She was never out of my mind in those months. In the spring, she remained with me. In my dreams.

And then, it was summer.

It isn't possible for me to write how I felt when I saw her running to me. I could paint it, but I could never find the words. I haunted those cliffs, waiting for her, hoping for her. It had become easy to convince myself that it would be enough just to see her, just to speak with her again. If she would only walk down the slope, through the wildflowers and sit on the rocks with me.

Then all at once, she was calling my name, running, her eyes so filled with joy. She was in my arms, her mouth on mine. And I knew she had suffered as I had suffered. She loved as I loved.

We both knew it was madness. Perhaps I could have been stronger, could have convinced her to go and leave me. But something had changed in her over the winter. No longer would she be content with only emptiness, as I learned her marriage was for her. Her children, so dear to her, could not forge a bond between her and the husband who wanted only obedience and duty. Yet I could not allow her to give herself to me, to take the step that could cause her guilt or shame or regret.

So we met, day after day on the cliffs, in all innocence. To talk and laugh, to pretend the summer was endless. Sometimes she brought the children, and it was almost as if we were a family. It was reckless, but somehow we didn't believe anything could touch us while we stood, cupped between sky and sea, with the peaks of the house far up at our backs.

We were happy with what we had. There have been no happier days in my life before or since. Love like that has no beginning or end. It has no right or wrong. In those bright summer days, she was not another man's wife. She was mine.

A lifetime later, I sit here in this aging body and look out at the water. Her face, her voice, come so clearly to me.

She smiled. "I used to dream of being in love."

I had taken the pins from her hair so that my hands could lose themselves in it. A small, precious pleasure. "Do you still?"

"Now I don't have to." She bent toward me, to touch her lips to mine. "I'll never have to dream again. Only wish."

I took her hand to kiss it, and we watched an eagle soar. "There's a ball tonight. I'll wish you were there, to waltz with me."

I got to my feet, drew her to hers and began to dance with her through the wild roses. "Tell me what you'll wear, so I can see you."

Laughing, she lifted her face to mine. "I shall wear ivory silk with a low bodice that bares my shoulders and a draped beaded skirt that catches the light. And my emeralds."

"A woman shouldn't look sad when she speaks of emeralds."

"No." She smiled again. "These are very special. I've had them since Ethan was born, and I wear them to remind me."

"Of what?"

"That no matter what happens, I've left something behind. The children are my real jewels." As a cloud came over the sun she pressed her head to my shoulder. "Hold me closer, Christian."

Neither of us spoke of the summer that was so quickly

coming to an end, but I know we both thought of it at that moment when my arms held her tight and our hearts beat together in the dance. The fury of what I was soon to lose again rushed through me.

"I would give you emeralds, and diamonds, sapphires." I crushed my mouth to hers. "All that and more, Bianca, if I could."

"No." She brought her hands to my face, and I saw the tears sparkling in her eyes. "Only love me," she said.

Only love me.

Chapter 7

Holt was home for less than three minutes when he knew someone had broken in. He might have turned in his shield, but he still had cop's eyes. There was nothing obviously out of place—but an ashtray was closer to the edge of the table, a chair was pulled at a slightly different angle to the fireplace, a corner of the rug was turned up.

Braced and at alert, he moved from the living room into the bedroom. There were signs here, as well. He noted them—the fractional rearrangement of the pillows, the different alignment of the books on the shelves—as he crossed to get his gun from the drawer. After checking the clip, he took his weapon with him as he searched the house.

Thirty minutes later, he replaced the gun. His face was set, his eyes flat and hard. His grandfather's canvases had been moved, not much, but enough to tell Holt that someone had touched them, studied them. And that was a violation he couldn't tolerate.

Whoever had tossed the place had been a pro. Nothing had been taken, little had been disturbed, but Holt was certain every inch of the cottage had been combed.

He was also certain who had done the combing. That meant that Livingston, by whatever guise he was using, was still close. Close enough, Holt thought, that he had discovered the Bradford connection to the Calhouns. And the emeralds.

Now, he decided as he dropped a hand on the head of the dog who whined at his feet, it was personal.

He went through the kitchen door to sit on the porch with his dog and a beer and watch the water. He would let his temper cool and his mind drift, sorting through all the pieces of the puzzle, arranging and rearranging until a picture began to form.

Bianca was the key. It was her mind, her emotions, her motivations he had to tap into. He lit a cigarette, resting his crossed ankles on the porch rail as the light began to soften and pearl toward twilight.

A beautiful woman, unhappily married. If the current crop of Calhoun women were anything to go by, Bianca would also have been strong willed, passionate and loyal. And vulnerable, he added. That came through strongly in the eyes of the portrait, just as it came through strongly in Suzanna's eyes.

She'd also been on the upper rungs of society's ladder, one of the privileged. A young Irishwoman of good family who had married extremely well.

Again, like Suzanna.

He drew on the cigarette, absently stroking Sadie's ears when she nuzzled her head into his lap. His gaze was drawn toward the little yellow bush, the slice of sunshine Suzanna had given him. According to the interview with the former maid, Bianca had also had a fondness for flowers.

She had had children, and by all accounts had been a good and devoted mother, while Fergus had been a strict and disinterested father. Then Christian Bradford had come into the picture.

If Bianca had indeed taken him as a lover, she had also taken an enormous social risk. Like Caesar's wife, a woman in her position was expected to be unblemished. Even a hint of an affair—particularly with a man beneath her station—and her reputation would have been in tatters.

Yet she had become involved.

Had it all grown to be too much for her? Holt wondered. Had she been eaten up by guilt and panic, hidden the emeralds away as some kind of last-ditch show of defiance, only to despair at the thought of the disgrace and scandal of divorce. Unable to face her life, she had chosen death.

He didn't like it. Shaking his head, Holt blew out a slow stream of smoke. He just didn't like the rhythm of it. Maybe he was losing his objectivity, but he couldn't see Suzanna giving up and hurling herself onto the cliffs. And there were too many similarities between Bianca and her great-granddaughter.

Maybe he should try to get inside Suzanna's head. If he understood her, maybe he could understand her star-crossed ancestor. Maybe, he admitted with a pull on the beer, he could understand himself. His feelings for her seemed to undergo radical changes every day, until he no longer knew exactly what he felt.

Oh, there was desire, that was clear enough. But it wasn't simple. He'd always counted on it being simple.

What made Suzanna Calhoun Dumont tick? Her kids,

Holt thought immediately. No contest there, though the rest of her family ran a dead heat. Her business. She would work herself ragged making it run. But Holt suspected that her thirst to succeed in business doubled right back around to her children and family.

Restless, he rose to pace the length of the porch. A whippoorwill came to roost in the old wind-bent maple and lifted its voice in its three-note call. Roused, the insects began to whisper in the grass. The first firefly, a lone sentinel, flickered near the water that lapped the bank.

This, too, was something he wanted. The simple quiet of solitude. But as he stood, looking out into the night, he thought of Suzanna. Not just the way she had felt in his arms, the way she made his blood swim. But what it would be like to have her beside him now, waiting for moonrise.

He needed to get inside her head, to make her trust him enough to tell him what she felt, how she thought. If he could make the link with her, he would be one step closer to making it with Bianca.

But he was afraid he was already in too deep. His own thoughts and feelings were clouding his judgment. He wanted to be her lover more than he had ever wanted anything. To sink into her, to watch her eyes darken with passion until that sad, injured look was completely banished. To have her give herself to him the way she had never given herself to anyone—not even the man she had married.

Holt pressed his hands to the rail, leaned out into the growing dark. Alone, with night to cloak him, he admitted that he was following the same pattern as his grandfather.

He was falling in love with a Calhoun woman.

It was late before he went back inside. Later still before he slept.

Suzanna hadn't slept at all. She had lain awake all night trying not to think about the two small suitcases she had packed. When she managed to get her mind off that, it had veered toward Holt. Thoughts of him only made her more restless.

She'd been up at dawn, rearranging the clothes she'd already packed, adding a few more things, checking yet again to be sure she had included a few of their favorite toys so that they wouldn't feel homesick.

She'd been cheerful at breakfast, grateful that her family had been there to add support and encouragement. Both children had been whiny, but she'd nearly joked them out of it by noon.

By one, her nerves had been frayed and the children were cranky again. By two she was afraid Bax had forgotten the entire thing, then was torn between fury and hope.

At three the car had come, a shiny black Lincoln. Fifteen horrible minutes later, her children were gone.

She couldn't stay home. Coco had been so kind, so understanding, and Suzanna had been afraid they would both dissolve into puddles of tears. For her aunt's sake as much as her own, she decided to go to work.

She would keep herself busy, Suzanna vowed. So busy that when the children got back, she hardly would have noticed they'd been gone.

She stopped by the shop, but Carolanne's sympathy and curiosity nearly drove her over the edge.

"I don't mean to badger you," Carolanne apologized when Suzanna's responses became clipped. "I'm just worried about you."

"I'm fine." Suzanna was selecting plants with almost obsessive care. "And I'm sorry for being short with you. I'm feeling a little rough today."

"And I'm being too nosy." Always good-natured, Carolanne shrugged. "I like the salmon-colored ones," she said as Suzanna debated over the group of New Guinea impatiens. "Listen, if you want to blow off some steam, just call me. We can have a girls' night out."

"I appreciate that."

"Anytime," Carolanne insisted. "It'll be fine. That's a really nice grouping," she added as Suzanna began to load her choices into the truck. "Are you putting in another bed?"

"Paying off a debt." Suzanna climbed into the truck, gave a wave then drove off. On the way to Holt's, she busied her mind by designing and redesigning the arrangement for the flower bed. She'd already scouted out the spot, bordering the front porch so he could enjoy it whenever he came or went from the cottage. Whether he wanted to or not.

The job would take her the rest of the day, then she would unwind by walking along the cliffs. Tomorrow she would put in a full day at the shop, then spend the cool of the evening working the gardens at The Towers.

One by one, the days would pass.

She didn't bother to announce herself after she'd parked the truck, but set right to work staking out the bed. The result was not what she'd hoped for. As she dug and hoed and worked the soil there was no soothing response. Her mind didn't empty of worries and fill with the pleasure of planting. Instead a headache began to work nastily behind her eyes. Ignoring it, she wheeled over a load of planting medium and dumped it. She was raking it smooth when Holt stepped out.

He'd watched her from the window for nearly ten minutes, hating the fact that the strong shoulders were slumped and her eyes dull with sadness.

"I thought you were taking the day off."

"I changed my mind." Without glancing up, she rolled the wheelbarrow back to the truck and loaded it with flats of plants.

"What the hell are all of those?"

"Your paycheck." She started with snapdragons, delphiniums and bright shasta daisies. "This was the deal."

Frowning, he came down a couple of steps. "I said maybe you could put in a couple of bushes."

"I'm putting in flowers." She packed down the soil. "Anyone with an ounce of imagination can see that this place is crying for flowers."

So she wanted to fight, he noted, rocking back on his heels. Well, he could oblige her. "You could have asked before you dug up the yard."

"Why? You'd just sneer and make some nasty macho remark."

He came down another step. "It's my yard, babe."

"And I'm planting flowers in it. *Babe*." She tossed her head up. Yeah, she was mad enough to spit nails, he noted. And she was also miserable. "If you don't want to bother to give them any water or care, then I will. Why don't you go back inside and leave me to it?"

Without waiting for a response, she went back to work. Holt took a seat while she added lavender and larkspur, dahlias and violas. He smoked lazily, noting that her hands were as sure and graceful as usual.

"Planting posies doesn't seem to be improving your mood today."

"My mood is just fine. In fact, it's dandy." She snapped a sprig off some freesia and swore. "Why shouldn't it be, just because I had to watch Jenny get in that damn car with tears running down her cheeks? Just because I had to stand there and smile when Alex looked back at me, his little mouth quivering and his eyes begging me not to make him go.''

When her eyes filled, she shook the tears away. ''And I had to stand there and take it when Bax accused me of being an overprotective, smothering mother who was turning his children, *his* children into timid weaklings.''

She hacked her spade into the dirt. ''They're not timid or weak,'' she said viciously. ''They're just children. Why shouldn't they be afraid to go with him, when they hardly know him? And with his wife who stood there in her silk suit and Italian heels looking distressed and helpless. She won't have a clue what to do if Jenny has a bad dream or Alex gets a stomachache. And I just let them go. I just stood there and let them get in that awful car with two strangers. So I'm feeling just fine. I'm feeling terrific.''

She sprang up to shove the wheelbarrow back to the truck. When she came back to do the mulching, he was gone. She forced herself to do the work carefully, reminding herself that at least here, over this one thing, she had control.

Holt came back, dragging the hose from around the other side of the house and holding two beers. ''I'll water them. Have a beer.''

Swiping a hand over her brow, she frowned at the bottles. ''I don't drink beer.''

''That's all I've got.'' He shoved one into her hand, then pushed the lever for the sprayer. ''I think I can handle this part by now,'' he said dryly. ''Why don't you have a seat?''

Suzanna walked to the steps and sat. Because she was

thirsty she took one long sip, then rested her chin on her hand and watched him. He'd learned not to drown the plants, or pound them with a heavy spray. She let out a little sigh, then sipped again.

No words of sympathy, she thought. No comforting pats or claims to understand just how she felt. Instead, he'd given her exactly what she'd needed, a silent wall to hurl her misery and anger against. Did he know he'd helped her? She couldn't be sure. But she knew she had come here, to him, not only to plant flowers, not only to get out of the house, but because she loved him.

She hadn't given herself time to think about that, not since the feeling had opened and bloomed inside of her. Nor had she given herself a chance to wonder what it would mean to either of them.

It wasn't something she wanted. She wanted never to love again, never to risk hurt and humiliation at a man's hands again. But it had happened.

She hadn't looked for it. She had looked only for peace of mind, for security for her children, for simple contentment for herself. Yet she had found it.

And what would his reaction be if she told him. Would it please his ego? Would it shock or appall or amuse? It didn't matter, Suzanna told herself as she slipped an arm around the dog who had come to join her. For now, perhaps for always, the love was hers. She no longer expected emotions to be shared.

Holt shut off the spray. The colorful bed added charm to the simple wooden cottage. It even pleased him that he recognized some of the blooms by name. He wasn't going to ask her about the ones that were unfamiliar. But he'd look them up.

"It looks pretty good."

"They're mostly perennials," she said in the same casual tone. ''I thought you might find it rewarding to see them come back year after year.''

He might, but he also thought he would remember, much too vividly, how hurt and unhappy she'd looked when she'd planted them. He didn't dare dwell on how much it upset him to picture Alex and Jenny climbing tearfully into a car and driving away.

''They smell okay.''

''That's the lavender.'' She took a deep breath of it herself before rising. ''I'll go around and turn off the hose.'' She'd nearly turned the corner when he called her name.

''Suzanna. They'll be all right.''

Not trusting her voice, she nodded and continued around back. She was crouched down, the dog's face in hers when he joined her.

''You know, if you put some day lilies and some sedum on that bank, you'd solve most of the erosion problem.''

He cupped a hand under her elbow to pull her to her feet. ''Is working the only thing you use to take your mind off things?''

''It does the job.''

''I've got a better idea.''

Her heart gave a quick jolt. ''I really don't—''

''Let's go for a ride.''

She blinked. ''A ride?''

''In the boat. We've got a couple of hours before dark.''

''A ride in the boat,'' she said, unaware that she amused him with her long, relieved sigh. ''I'd like that.''

''Good.'' He took her hand and pulled her to the pier. ''You cast off.'' When the dog jumped in beside him, Suzanna realized this was an old routine. For a man who didn't want to appear to have any sentiment, it was a telling thing that he took a dog along for company when he set out to sea.

The engine roared to life. Holt waited only until Suzanna had climbed on board before he headed into the bay.

The wind slapped against her face. Laughing, she clapped a hand to her cap to keep it from flying off. After she'd pulled it on more securely, she joined him at the wheel.

"I haven't been out on the water in months," she shouted over the engine.

"What's the use of living on an island if you never go out on the water?"

"I like to watch it."

She turned her head and caught the bright glint of window glass from the secluded houses on Bar Island. Overhead gulls wheeled and screamed. Sadie barked at them, then settled on the boat cushions with her head on the side so that the wind could send her ears flying.

"Has she ever jumped out?" Suzanna asked him.

He glanced back at the dog. "No. She just looks stupid."

"You'll have to bring her by the house again. Fred hasn't been the same since he met her."

"Some women do that to a man." The salt breeze was carrying her scent to him, wrapping it around his senses so that he drew her in with every breath. She was standing close, braced against the boat's motion. The expression in her eyes was still far off and troubled, and he knew she wasn't thinking of him. But he thought of her.

He moved expertly through the bay traffic, keeping the speed slow and steady as he maneuvered around other boats, passed a hotel terrace where guests sat under striped umbrellas drinking cocktails or eating an early dinner. Far to starboard, the island's three-masted schooner streamed into port with its crowd of waving tourists.

Then the bay gave way to the sea and the water became less serene. The cliffs roared up into the sky. Arrogantly, defiantly, The Towers sat on its ridge overlooking village and bay and sea. Its somber gray stone mirrored the tone of the rain clouds out to the west. Its old, wavy glass glinted with fanciful rainbows. Like a mirage, there were streaks and blurs of color that were Suzanna's garden.

"Sometimes when I went lobstering with my father, I'd look up at it." And think of you. "Castle Calhoun," Holt murmured. "That's what he called it."

Suzanna smiled, shading her eyes with the flat of her hand as she studied the imposing house on the cliffs. "It's just home. It's always been home. When I look up at it I think of Aunt Coco trying out some new recipe in the kitchen and Lilah napping in the parlor. The children playing in the yard or racing down the stairs. Amanda sitting at her desk and working her meticulous way through the mounds of bills it takes to hold a home together. C.C. diving under the hood of the old station wagon to see if she could make a miracle happen and get one more year out of the engine. Sometimes I see my parents laughing at the kitchen table, so young, so alive, so full of plans." She turned around to keep the house in sight. "So many things have changed, and will change. But the house is still there. It's comforting. You understand that or you wouldn't have chosen to live in Christian's cottage, with all his memories."

He understood exactly, and it made him uneasy. "Maybe I just like having a place on the water."

Suzanna watched Bianca's tower disappear before she

shifted to face him. "Sentiment doesn't make you weak, Holt."

He frowned out over the water. "I could never get close to my father. We came at everything from different directions. I never had to explain or justify anything I felt or wanted to my grandfather. He just accepted. I guess I figured there was a reason he left me the place when he died, even though I was only a kid."

It moved her in a very soft, very lovely way that he had shared even that much with her. "So you came back to it. We always come back to what we love." She wanted to ask him more, what his life had been like during the span of years he'd been away. Why he had turned his back on police work to repair boat motors and props. Had he been in love, or had his heart broken? But he hit the throttle and sent the boat streaking out over the wide expanse of water.

He hadn't come out to think deep thoughts, to worry or to wonder. He had come to give her, and himself, an hour of relaxation, a respite from reality. Wind and speed worked that particular miracle for him. It always had. When he heard her laugh, when she tossed her face up into the sun, he knew he'd chosen well.

"Here, take the wheel."

It was a challenge. She could hear the dare in his voice, see it in his eyes when he grinned at her. Suzanna didn't hesitate, but took his place at the helm.

She gloried in the control, in the power vibrating under her fingertips. The boat sliced through the water like a blade, racing to nowhere. There was only sea and sky and unlimited freedom. The Atlantic roughened, adding a dash of danger. The air took on a bite that shivered along the skin and made each breath a drink of icy wine.

Her hands were firm and competent on the wheel, her

body braced and ready. The wistful look in her eyes had been replaced by a bright fearlessness that quickened his blood. Her face was flushed with excitement, dampened by the spray. She didn't look like a princess now, but like a queen who knew her own power and was ready to wield it.

He let her race where she chose, knowing that she would end where he had wanted her for most of his life. He wouldn't wait another day. Not even another hour.

She was breathless and laughing when she gave him the wheel again. "I'd forgotten what it was like. I haven't handled a boat in five years."

"You did all right." He kept the speed high as he turned the boat in a wide half circle.

Still laughing, she rubbed her hands over her arms. "Lord, it's freezing."

He glanced toward her and felt the punch low in his gut. She was glowing—her eyes as blue as the sky and only more vital, the thin cotton pants and blouse plastered against her slender body, her hair streaming out from under the cap.

When his palms grew damp and unsteady on the wheel, he looked away. Not falling in love, he realized. He'd stopped falling and had hit the ground with a fatal smack. "There's a jacket in the cabin."

"No, it feels wonderful." She closed her eyes and let the sensations hammer her. The wild wind, the golden evening sun, the smell of salt and sea and the man beside her, the roar of the motor and the churning wake. They might have been alone, completely, with nothing but excitement and speed, with either of them free to take the wheel and spear off into that fabulous aloneness.

She didn't want to go back. Suzanna drank deeply of the tangy air and thought how liberating it would be to race and race in no direction at all, then to drift wherever the current took her.

But the air was already warming. They were no longer alone. She heard the long, droning horn of a tourist boat as Holt cut the speed and glided toward the harbor.

This too was lovely, she thought. Coming home. Knowing your place, certain of your welcome. She let out a little sigh at the simple familiarity. The blue water of Frenchman Bay deepening now with evening, the buildings crowded with people, the clang of buoys. It was all the more comforting after the frantic race to nowhere.

They said nothing as he navigated across the bay and circled around to drift to his pier. But she was relaxed when she jumped out to secure the lines, when she ran her hands over the dog who leaned against her legs, begging for attention.

"You're quite the sailor, aren't you, girl?" She crouched down to give the dog a good rub. "I think she wants to go again."

Holt stepped nimbly to the dock and stood a foot apart. "There's a storm coming in."

Suzanna glanced up and saw that the clouds were blowing slowly but determinedly inland. "You're right. We can certainly use the rain." Foolish, she thought, to feel awkward now and start talking of the weather. She rose, uncertain of her moves now that he was standing here, tension in every line of his body, his eyes dark and intent on hers. "Thanks for the ride. I really enjoyed it."

"Good." The pier swayed when he started forward. Suzanna took two steps back and felt better when her feet hit solid ground.

"If you get a chance, maybe you can bring Sadie to visit Fred this weekend. He'll be lonely without the kids around."

"All right."

She was halfway across the yard, and he was still a foot away. If it hadn't seemed so paranoid, she would have said he was stalking her. "The bush is doing well." She ran her fingers over it as she passed. "But you really need to feed this lawn. I could recommend a simple and inexpensive program."

His lips curved slightly, but his eyes stayed on hers. "You do that."

"Well, I…it's getting late. Aunt Coco—"

"Knows you're a big girl." He took her arm to hold her still. "You're not going anywhere tonight, Suzanna."

Perhaps if she'd been wiser or more experienced, she would have gauged his mood before he touched her. There was no mistaking it now, not when his fingers had closed over her with taut possession, not when his needs, and his intention of satisfying them, were so clear in those deep gray eyes.

She wished she could have been so certain of her own mood and her own needs.

"Holt, I told you I needed time."

"Time's up," he said simply, with an underlying edge that had her pulse jerking.

"This isn't something I intend to take casually."

Heat flashed into his eyes. From miles away came the violent rumble of thunder. "There's nothing casual about it. We both know that."

She did know it, and the knowledge was terrifying. "I think—"

He swore and swept her into his arms. "You think too much."

The moment the shock wore off she began to struggle. By then he had already carried her onto the back porch. "Holt. I won't be pressured." The screen door slammed behind them. Didn't he know she was afraid? That she was so afraid if she took this step he would find her dull, shrug her off and leave her shattered? "I'm not going to be rushed into this."

"If you had your way, it would take another fifteen years." He kicked open the door to the bedroom then dropped her onto the bed. It wasn't what he had planned, but he was too knotted up with terror and longings to struggle with soft words.

She was off the bed in a shot to stand beside it, slim and straight as an arrow. The lowering light, already gathering gloom, crept through the window at her back. "If you think you can cart me in here and throw me on the bed—"

"That's exactly what I've done." His eyes stayed hard on hers as he pulled his shirt over his head. "I'm tired of waiting, Suzanna, and I'm damn tired of wanting you. We're going to do this my way."

It had been like this for her before, she thought as her heart sank to her stomach like a stone. Only then it had been Bax, ordering her into bed, peeling off his clothes before he climbed on top of her to take his marital rights, quick and hard and without affection. And after, there would come his derision and disgust for her.

"Your way's hardly new," she said tightly. "And it doesn't interest me. I'm not obligated to go to bed with you, Holt. To let you demand and take and tell me I'm not good enough to satisfy. I'm not going to be used again, by anyone."

He caught her arms before she could storm from the room, dragged her struggling and swearing against him to crush his heated mouth to hers. The force of it sent her reeling. She would have stumbled away if his arms hadn't banded her so tightly.

Over the fear and the anger her own needs swelled. She wanted to scream at him for pulling them from her, for leaving her raw and naked and defenseless. But she could only hold on.

He yanked her away, arm's length, his breath already ragged and shallow. Her eyes were dark as midnight and held as many secrets. He would uncover them, that he promised himself. One by one he would learn them all. And tonight, he would begin.

"No one is going to be used here, and I'm only going to take what you give." His tensed fingers flexed on her arms. "Look at me, Suzanna. Look at me and tell me you don't want me, and I'll let you go."

Her lips parted on a shaky breath. She loved him, and she was no longer a girl who could hold love to herself like a comforting pillow in the night. If she was not as strong as she hoped and able to hold her heart and body separate, then she had no choice but to unite them. If that heart was broken, she would survive.

Hadn't she promised them both there would be no regrets?

She lifted a hand to his gently though she expected no gentleness in return. The choice was one she made freely.

"I can't tell you I don't want you. There's no need to wait any longer."

Chapter 8

If his nerves hadn't been so tangled, if the need hadn't been so acute, he might have been able to show her tenderness. If his blood hadn't been so hot, desire so greedy, he would have tried to give her some romance. But he was certain if he didn't possess now, possess quickly, he would shatter into hundreds of jagged shards of desperation.

So his mouth was fevered with impatience, his hands rough with urgency. At the first potent taste he understood she was already his. But it wasn't enough. Maybe it could never be enough.

She didn't tremble or hesitate. The vulnerability was cloaked inside a generosity that urged him to take his fill. As her hands roamed restlessly over his back he felt only her hunger, and none of her doubt.

He pushed the cap from her hair, then yanked the band from it so that his hands could take fistfuls of honey-colored silk. And the hands that gripped were unsteady, even as his mouth ruthlessly devoured hers.

She opened for him, releasing a soft and sultry moan of pleasure as his tongue plunged to duel with hers. He wanted so badly, and that want vibrating from him aroused her own. She had risen on her toes, unaware that she was fighting to meet him flare for flare. Her body was quaking with passions long suppressed.

And there was fear in that, fear in not knowing what would become of her if she lost that last toehold on control. She had to show him that she could give pleasure, make him enjoy and continue to want. If she fumbled now, lessened her grip on proving herself a woman, might he not find her less than his fantasy?

Yet she had never been wanted like this. Not like this with the violence of desire pulsing in the air so that every breath was like breathing temptation. She strained against him, hoping what she had to give would be enough while her system jolted along the battering tide of sensations.

His mouth raced over her face, down her throat where his teeth and the rough stubble of beard scraped. And his hands—Lord, his hands were fast and lethal.

She had to keep her head, but her knees were watery and her mind was spinning from the onslaught. Desperately she dug her nails into his back as she struggled away from the edge and tried to remember what a man would like.

She was quivering like a plucked bow, so tensed and wired he thought she might snap in two in his hands. She was holding back. The knowledge that she could do so when he was half-crazed brought on a kind of virulent fury. He tore the blouse aside as he pushed her onto the bed.

"Damn you, I want it all." Breath heaving, he encircled her wrists and dragged her arms over her head. "I'll have it all." When his mouth swooped down to capture hers, her hands strained under his grip, her pulse jittering in quick, rabbit jumps under his fingers.

His body was like a furnace, hot damp flesh fusing with hers in a way that made her shudder from the sheer wonder of it. Like iron, his fingers clamped hers still while his free hand raked over her in a merciless assault. She could feel the anger, taste the frustrated and furious desire. Desperate, she tried to pull in a breath to beg him to wait, to give her a moment, but all she could manage were jagged moans.

The wind kicked the curtains aside, letting dusk pour through. The first drops of rain hit the roof, sounding to her sensitized ears like gunshots that echoed the war he was waging on her. Again thunder rumbled, closer now, warning of a reckless power.

When his mouth found her breast, he let out a hot groan of pleasure. Here she was as soft as a summer breeze and as potent as whiskey. As she writhed beneath him, he dampened and tugged on the taut nipple, losing himself in the taste and texture while her heartbeat hammered against his mouth.

And she wanted as he wanted. He could feel the urgent excitement raging through her, hear it in her quick, sobbing breaths. Her hips arched and plunged against his until he was senseless. He ranged lower, his teeth nipping at her rib cage, his tongue laying a line of wet heat over her belly.

Her hands were free now and her fingers gripped his hair, then tore at the bedspread. She couldn't breathe. She needed to tell him. Her body was too full of aches and heat. She needed...

She needed.

Someone cried out. Suzanna heard the quick desperate sound, felt it tear from her own throat as her body arched up. Whole worlds exploded inside of her with a roar more huge than the thunder that stalked just overhead. Stunned, she lay shuddering under him as he lifted his head to stare at her.

Her eyes were dark, her face flushed with fresh fever. Beneath his, her body shook with aftershocks even as her hands slipped limply from his back to the ravaged bed. He hadn't guessed what it would do to him to see that kind of dazed pleasure on her face.

But he knew he wanted more.

He was driving her up again before she could recover. Now she could only embrace the speed and the thrill of danger. As the rain began to pound, she rolled with him, too giddy to be shocked by her own greed. Her hands were as rough and ready as his now, her mouth as merciless. When he dragged the slacks down her legs, her quick gasp was one of triumph. Her fingers were equally impatient as they yanked the denim over his hips, as they streaked and pressed over slick, heated flesh.

She wanted to touch as urgently as she needed to be touched. To possess even as she was possessed. She craved the madness, the turbulent hunger she hadn't known she could feel, and this tempestuous desire that reared up like a wild wolf to consume.

There was no thought of control now, not from either of them. When he sent her racing up again, then again, she rode each slashing crest only frantic for more. More was what he wanted to give her, and what he wanted to take. As the blood fired through his veins he drove himself into her, claiming possession in a frenzy of speed and heat. She matched him, beat for wild beat, the long, nurturing fingers digging into his hips.

They were alone again, but this time the sea was violently churning and the air was flaming hot. Here, at last was the power and the freedom. The speed was reckless, the journey a glorious risk. She felt him shudder, bury his face in her hair as he reached the end. Suzanna locked tight around him, and followed.

He'd wondered what it would be like for fifteen years. From boy to man he had dreamed about her, imagined her, wanted her. None of his fantasies had come close. She had been like a volcano, smoldering and shuddering, then erupting hot. Now she lay like warm wax beneath him, her body meltingly soft with passions spent. Her hair smelled of sun and sea. He thought he could stay just so for eternity, molded against her with the rain drumming on the roof and the wind blowing the curtains.

But he wanted to see her.

When he shifted, she made a small sound of protest and reached out. He said nothing, only kissed her until she relaxed again. Her eyes were drifting shut when he turned the lamp beside the bed on low.

Lord, she was beautiful, with her hair fanned out on the pillows, her skin glowing, her mouth soft and full. She tensed, but he ignored her discomfort as he took a long, silent study of the rest of her.

"Like I said," he murmured when his eyes came back to hers. "The Calhoun women are all lookers."

She didn't know what she was supposed to say or how she was expected to act. She knew that he had taken her to a new place, an extraordinary place, but she had no idea if he had experienced the same mind-spinning ride. Then he frowned and her stomach twisted. With his eyes narrowed, he traced a finger down her throat, over the swell of her breasts.

"I should have shaved," he said abruptly, hating the fact that he'd scraped and reddened her skin. "You could have told me I was hurting you."

"I guess I didn't notice."

"Sorry." He touched his lips gently to her throat. Her look of dazed surprise made him feel like an idiot. When he rolled away, she reached out tentatively for his hand.

"You didn't hurt me," she said softly. "It was wonderful." And she waited, hopeful that he would tell her the same.

"I've got to let the dog in." His voice was rough, but he gave her fingers a quick squeeze before he left the room.

Suzanna heard it now, the whining howls, the scratching at the screen. She told herself it wasn't a rejection. It only meant that he could go from passion to practicality more quickly than she. They had shared something, something vital. She could cling to that. She sat up, more than a little amazed to see the state of the bed. The spread was a heap on the floor, the sheets a tangled knot at the foot. Her clothes—what was left of them—were scattered with his.

She rose and, uncomfortable naked, tugged on his shirt before she lifted her own. One button out of five remained, hanging by a thread. Laughing, she hugged it to herself. To have been wanted like that. With a little sigh, she bent down to search for her buttons. Maybe now he could be cool and collected, maybe his life hadn't been changed as hers had, but she had been wanted, desperately. She would never forget it.

"What are you doing?"

She looked up to see him standing in the doorway. Obviously walking around buck naked didn't concern him in the least, she thought and felt her steady pulse jerk and dance again. He looked angry. She wished she understood what she had done, or hadn't done, to put that scowl on his face.

"My blouse," she said. "I found the buttons." She gripped them in one hand, the thin cotton in the other. "Do you have a needle and thread?"

"No." Didn't she know what she did to him, standing there in nothing but his shirt, her hair tousled, her eyes heavy? Did she want him to get down on his knees and beg?

"Oh." She swallowed and tried to smile. "Well, I can fix it at home. If I could just borrow your shirt. I'd better get back."

He closed the door behind him. "No," he said again, and crossed the room to take her.

The rain stopped at dawn, leaving the air washed clean. Suzanna awoke to the lazy music of water dripping from the gutters. Before her mind had adjusted to where she was, her mouth was captured in a hot, hungry kiss. Her body catapulted from sleep to desire in one breathless leap.

He'd awakened wanting her. That burning need wouldn't ease no matter how much he took, how willingly she gave. There were no words, none he knew, that could express what she had come to mean to him. From a boy's fantasy to a man's salvation.

He could only show her.

He covered her. He filled her. Watching her face in the watery morning sunlight, he knew he would never be content unless she was with him.

"You're mine." He threw the words out like a curse as her body shuddered beneath his. "Say it." His hands fisted on the sheets and he buried his face against her throat. "Damn it, Suzanna, say it."

She could say nothing but his name as he dragged her over the edge.

When her hands slid limply from his back, he rolled over, locking her close so that she lay over him. He could be content with her head resting on his heart. He told himself that he'd already pushed her hard and fast enough. But he'd wanted badly to hear the words.

His hands were fisted in her hair. As if, she thought dizzily, he would yank her back if she tried to move. Her body felt achy and bruised and glorious. She smiled, listening to the rapid thud of his heart and the liquid beauty of morning birdsong.

Her eyes flew open, her head up. He did pull her hair, but more from reflex than intent. "It's morning," Suzanna said.

"That usually happens when the sun comes up."

"No, I—ouch."

"Sorry," he muttered, and reluctantly released her hair.

"I must have fallen asleep."

"Yeah." He ran his hands up and down her back. He liked the long, smooth feel of it. "You dozed off before I could interest you in another round."

Her color fluctuated, but when she tried to scramble up, he held her firmly in place.

"Going somewhere?"

"I have to get home. Aunt Coco must be frantic."

"She knows where you are." Because it was easier to keep her in place, he reversed positions again and began to nibble at her throat. Nothing could have pleased him more than feeling the instant quickening of her pulse under his lips. "And in all likelihood, she's got a pretty good idea what you've been up to."

Without much hope of dislodging him, she pushed at his shoulder. "I didn't tell her where I was going."

"I called her last night when I let Sadie in. Scratch my back, will you? Base of the spine."

She obliged automatically, even while her thoughts spun. "You—you told my aunt that I…"

"I told her you were with me. I figure she could put the rest together. That's good. Thanks."

Suzanna let out a long breath. Oh yes, Aunt Coco wouldn't have any trouble adding two and two. And there was absolutely no reason to feel uncomfortable or embarrassed. But she was both. Not only relating to her aunt but to the man whose naked body was spread over hers.

It had been one thing to face him at night. But the morning…

He lifted his head to study her. "What's the problem?"

"Nothing." When he lifted a brow she shifted in what passed for a shrug. "It's just that I'm not sure what to do now. I've never done this before."

He grinned at her. "How'd you get two kids?"

"I don't mean that I've never…I mean I've never…"

His grin only widened. "Well, get used to it, babe." Considering, he trailed a finger over her jawline. "Want me to help you out with morning-after etiquette?"

"I want you to stop leering at me."

"No, you see that's part of the form." He replaced his trailing finger with a light nip of his teeth. "I'm supposed to leer at you in the morning so you don't start feeling that you look like a hag."

"A—" The word caught in her throat. "A hag?"

"And you're supposed to tell me I was incredible."

Her brow lifted. "I am?"

"That, and any other superlatives you can come up with. Then—" he rolled her over again "—you're supposed to go fix me breakfast, to show me your talents are versatile."

"I can't tell you how grateful I am that you're filling me in on the procedure."

"No problem. And after you fix me breakfast, you should seduce me back into bed."

She laughed and pressed her cheek to his in a move that disarmed and delighted him. "I'll have to practice up on that, but I could probably handle a couple of scrambled eggs."

"Let me know if you find any."

"Have you got a robe?"

"What for?"

She looked up again. He was still leering. "Never mind." Sliding away, she instinctively turned her back as she groped on the floor for his shirt. "And what do you do while I'm fixing breakfast?"

He caught the ends of her hair, let them shift through his fingers. "I watch you."

And he enjoyed it, seeing her move around his kitchen, his shirt skimming her thighs with the scent of coffee ripening the air and her voice low and amused as she spoke to the dog.

She felt more at ease here, with familiar chores. The bush they had planted was a cloud of sunlight outside the window, and the breeze still smelled of rain.

"You know," she said as she grated cheese into the eggs, "you could use more than a toaster, one pot and a skillet."

"Why?" He kicked back in the chair and took a comfortable drag on his cigarette.

"Well, some people actually use this room to prepare entire meals."

"Only if they haven't heard of take-out." He saw that the coffee had dripped through and rose to pour them both a cup. "What do you take in this?"

"Just black. I need the kick."

"If you ask me, what you need is more sleep."

"I have to be at work in an hour or so." With the bowl of eggs in her hands, she stopped to stare out of the window. He recognized the look in her eyes and rubbed a hand over her shoulder.

"Don't."

"I'm sorry." She turned to the stove to pour the beaten eggs into the skillet. "I can't help but wonder what they're doing, if they're having a good time. They've never been away before."

"Hasn't he taken them for a weekend?"

"No, just a couple of afternoons that weren't terribly successful." She made an effort to shake the mood as she stirred the eggs. "Well, there's only thirteen days left to go."

"You're not helping them or yourself by getting worked up." His impotence grated as he fought to massage the tension from her shoulders.

"I'm fine. I will be fine," she corrected. "I've got more than enough to keep me busy for the next couple of weeks. And with the kids gone, I can put in more time trying to find the emeralds."

"You leave that to me."

She glanced over her shoulder. "This is a team effort, Holt. It always has been."

"I'm involved now, and I'll handle it."

She dished the eggs up as carefully as she chose her words. "I appreciate your help. All of us do. But they're called the Calhoun emeralds for a reason. Two of my sisters have been threatened because of them.''

"Exactly my point. You're out of your league with Livingston, Suzanna. He's smart and he's brutal. He won't ask you nicely to get out of his way.''

Turning, she handed him his plate. ''I'm accustomed to smart, brutal men, and I've already spent enough of my life being afraid.''

"What's that supposed to mean?''

"Just what I said.'' She lifted her plate, and the mug of coffee. ''I won't let some thief intimidate me or make me afraid to do what's best for myself and my family.''

But Holt was shaking his head. That wasn't the answer he'd wanted. ''Are you afraid of Dumont? Physically?''

Her gaze wavered then leveled. ''We're talking about the emeralds.'' She tried to move by him, but Holt blocked her path. His eyes had gone dark, but when he spoke his voice was softer, more controlled than she had ever heard it.

"Did he hit you?''

Her color deepened, then raced away from her cheeks. ''What?''

"I want to know if Dumont ever hit you.''

Nerves were tightening her throat. No matter how quiet his voice, there was a terrible gleam of violence in his eyes. ''The eggs are getting cold, Holt, and I'm hungry.''

He fought back the urge to hurl the plate against the wall. He sat, waited for her to take the seat across from him. She looked very frail and very composed in the stream of sunlight. ''I want an answer, Suzanna.'' He picked up his coffee and sipped as she toyed with her food. He knew how to wait and how to push.

"No.'' Her voice was flat as she took the first bite. ''He never hit me.''

"Just knocked you around?" He kept his voice casual and ate without tasting. Her gaze flicked up to his, then away.

"There are a lot of ways to intimidate and demoralize, Holt. After that, humiliation is a snap." Picking up a slice of toast, she buttered it carefully. "You're nearly out of bread."

"What did he do to you?"

"Let it go."

"What," he repeated slowly, "did he do to you?"

"He made me face facts."

"Such as?"

"That I was pitifully inadequate as a wife of a corporate lawyer with social and political ambitions."

"Why?"

She slammed down the knife. "Is this how you interrogate suspects?"

Anger, he thought. That was better. "It's a simple question."

"And you want a simple answer? Fine. He married me because of my name. He thought there was a bit more money as well as prestige attached to it, but the Calhoun name was more than adequate. Unfortunately it became quickly apparent that I wasn't the social boon he'd imagined. My dinner party conversation was pedestrian at best. I could be dressed up to look the part of the prominent wife of a politically ambitious attorney, but I could never quite pull it off. It was, as he told me often, a huge disappointment that I couldn't get it through my head what was expected of me. That I was boring, in the drawing room, the dining room and the bedroom."

She sprang up to scrape the rest of her meal into Sadie's bowl. "Does that answer your question?"

"No." Holt pushed his plate away and pulled out a

cigarette. "I'd like to know how he convinced you that you were at fault."

Keeping her back to him, she straightened. "Because I loved him. Or I loved the man I thought I'd married, and I wanted, very badly, to be the woman he'd be proud of. But the harder I tried, the more I failed. Then I had Alex, and it seemed…I had done something so incredible. I'd brought that beautiful baby into the world. And it was so easy, so natural for me to be a mother. I never had any doubts, any missteps. I was so happy, so focused on the child and the family we'd begun, that I didn't realize that Bax was discreetly finding more exciting companionship. Not until I found out I was going to have Jenny."

"So he cheated on you." His voice was deceptively mild. "What did you do about it?"

She didn't turn around, but began to run water in the sink to wash the dishes. "You can't understand what it's like to be betrayed that way. To already feel as though you're inadequate. To be carrying a man's child and find out that you've already been replaced."

"No, I can't. But it seems to me I'd be ticked off."

"Was I angry?" She nearly laughed. "Yes, I was angry, but I was also…wounded. I don't like to remember how easy it was for him to shatter me. Alex was only a few months old, and Jenny hadn't been planned. But I was so happy to be pregnant. He didn't want her. Nothing he'd done to me before had hurt or shocked me the way his reaction did when I told him I was pregnant again. He wasn't angry so much as…irked." She decided on a half laugh and plunged her hands into the soapy water.

"He had a son," she continued, "so the Dumont name would continue. He didn't intend to clutter up his life with children, and he certainly didn't want to have to drag me around the social wheel a second time while I was fat and tired and unattractive. The most practical solution was to terminate the pregnancy. We fought horribly about that. It was the first time I'd had the nerve to stand up to him—which only made it worse. Bax was used to getting his own way, he always had. Since he couldn't force me to do what he wanted, he paid me back, expertly.''

Calmer now, she set the dish aside to drain and began to wash out the skillet. ''He was still discreet publicly with his affairs, but he made sure I knew about them, and how sadly I compared to the women he slept with. He took my name off the checking and charge accounts so that I had to ask him whenever I needed money. That was one of his more subtle humiliations. The night Jenny was born, he was with another woman. He made certain I knew about that when he came to the hospital so the press could snap his picture while he played the proud father.''

Holt hadn't moved. He didn't trust himself to move. ''Why did you stay with him?''

''At first, because I kept hoping I would wake up beside the man I'd fallen in love with. Then, when I started to consider that my marriage was a failure, I had one child and was pregnant with another.'' She picked up a cloth and began to dry the dishes. ''And I stayed because for a long time, a very long time I was convinced he was right about me. I wasn't clever and witty and sharp. I wasn't sexy or seductive. So the least I could be was loyal. When I realized I couldn't even be that, I had to consider the effect on the children. They weren't to be hurt. I couldn't have stood it if dissolving my marriage to Bax had hurt them. One day, I suddenly understood that it was all for nothing, that I was not only wasting my life but probably doing more harm to Alex and Jenny by pretending there was a marriage. Bax paid little attention to his son, and none at all to his daughter. He spent a great deal more time with his lover than he did with his family.''

She sighed, set the dishes down. ''So I hid my diamonds in Jenny's diaper bag and asked for a divorce.'' When she turned, the weariness was back on her face. ''Does that answer your question?''

Very slowly, his eyes on hers, he rose. ''Did it ever occur to you, did it ever once cross your mind that he was inadequate, that he was a failure? That he was a spoiled, selfish bastard?''

Her lips curved a little. ''Well, the last part certainly occurred to me. It also occurs to me that my little story is one-sided. I imagine Bax's view of our relationship would differ from mine, and not without some merit.''

''He's still pushing your buttons,'' Holt said with barely suppressed fury. ''So you're not clever? I guess anyone could manage to raise two kids and run a business. Dull, too?'' He took a step toward her, only more furious when he saw her instinctive move to brace. ''Yeah, I don't know when I've been so bored by anyone, but then most men are bored with women with brains and guts, especially when they're softhearted and hardheaded. Nothing puts me to sleep faster than a woman who'll sweat all day to make sure her kids are provided for. God knows you're not sexy. I just didn't have anything better to do last night than to spend it going crazy over you.''

He'd trapped her against the sink with his body and with an anger so ripe she could almost taste it. ''You asked and I answered. I don't know what you want me to say now.''

"I want you to say you don't give a damn about him."
He grabbed her by the shoulders, his face close to hers.
"I want you to tell me what I told you to tell me when
I was inside you, when I was so full of you I couldn't
breathe. You're mine, Suzanna. Nothing that happened
before counts because you're mine now. That's what I
want to hear."

His hands slipped down to clamp over her wrists. Even
as she opened her mouth to speak he saw the quick wince
of pain. Swearing, he looked down and saw the bruises
he'd already put on her. He jerked back as if she'd
slapped him.

"Holt—"

He raised a hand to silence her, turning away until he
could clear the red haze of fury from his mind. He'd put
marks on her skin. It had been done in passion and without intention, but that didn't erase them. By putting them
there, he was no better than the man who had bruised her
soul.

He jammed his hands into his pockets before he turned.
"I've got things to do."

"But—"

"We got off the track, Suzanna. My fault. I know you
have to get to work, and so do I."

So that was that, she thought. She'd bared her soul,
now he would walk away. "All right. I'll see you on
Monday."

With a nod, he headed for the back door, then swore,
stopping with his hand on the screen. "Last night meant
something to me. Do you understand that?"

She let out a quiet breath. "No."

His hand curled into a fist on the screen. "You're important to me. I care about you, and having you here, this
way, is…I need you. Is that clear enough?"

She studied him—a fist on the door, impatience in his eyes, his body rigid with passions she couldn't quite understand. It was enough, she realized. For now it was more than enough.

"Yes, I think it's clear."

"I don't want it to end there." He turned his head, and his eyes were dark and fierce again. "It's not going to end there."

She continued to study his face, keeping her voice calm. "Are you asking me to come back?"

"You know damn well—" He cut himself off and closed his eyes. "Yes, I'm asking you to come back. And I'm asking you to think about spending time with me that isn't at work or in bed. If that doesn't spell it out for you, then—"

"Would you like to come to dinner?"

He gave her a blank stare. "What?"

"Would you like to come to dinner, tonight? Maybe we could take a drive after."

"Yeah." He dragged a hand through his hair, not sure if he was relieved or uneasy that it had been so simple. "That would be good."

Yes, it would be good, she thought and smiled. "I'll see you about seven then. Bring Sadie if you like."

Chapter 9

It wasn't candlelight and moonbeams, Suzanna thought, but it was a romance. She hadn't believed she would find it again, or want it. Flexing her back as she drove up the curving road to The Towers, she smiled.

Of course, a relationship with Holt Bradford was lined with rough edges, but it had its softer moments. She'd had a lovely time discovering them over the past few days. And nights.

There was the way he'd shown up at the shop once or twice, just before lunchtime. He hadn't said anything about the children, or her missing the routine—just that he'd come into the village for some parts and felt like eating.

Or how he'd come up behind her at odd moments to rub the tension out of her shoulders. The evening he'd surprised her after a particularly grueling day by dragging her and a wicker basket filled with cold chicken into the boat.

He was still demanding, often abrupt, but he never made her feel less than what she wanted to be. When he loved her, he loved her with an urgency and ferocity that left no doubt as to his desire.

No, she hadn't been looking for romance, she thought as she parked the truck behind Holt's car. But she was terribly glad she'd found it.

The moment she opened the door, Lilah pounced. ''I've been waiting for you.''

''So I see.'' Suzanna lifted a brow. Lilah was still in her park service uniform. Knowing her schedule, Suzanna was sure her sister had been home nearly an hour. As a matter of routine, Lilah should have been in her most comfortable clothes and spread out dozing on the handiest flat surface. ''What's up?''

''Can you do anything with that surly hulk you've gotten tangled up with?''

''If you mean Holt, not a great deal.'' Suzanna pulled off her cap to run her hands through her hair. ''Why?''

''Right now, he's upstairs, taking my room apart inch by inch. I couldn't even change my clothes.'' She aimed a narrowed glance up the steps. ''I told him we'd already looked there, and that if I'd been sleeping in the same room as the emeralds all these years, I'd know it.''

''And he ignored you.''

''He not only ignored me, he kicked me out of my own bedroom. And Max.'' She let out a hiss of breath and sat on the stairs. ''Max grinned and said it was a damn good idea.''

''Want to gang up on them?''

A wicked gleam came into Lilah's eyes. ''Yeah.'' She rose then swung an arm over Suzanna's shoulders as they started up. ''You're really serious about him, aren't you?''

"I'm taking it one step at a time."

"Sometimes when you love someone it's better to take it by leaps and bounds." Then she yawned and swore. "I missed my nap. It'd be satisfying if I could say I disliked that pushy jerk, but I can't. There's something too solid and steady under the bad manners."

"You've been looking at his aura again."

Lilah laughed and stopped at the top of the stairs. "He's a good guy, as much as I'd like to belt him right now. It's good to see you happy again, Suze."

"I haven't been unhappy."

"No, just not happy. There's a difference."

"I suppose there is. Speaking of happy, how are the wedding plans coming?"

"Actually, Aunt Coco and the relative from hell are in the kitchen arguing over them right now." She turned laughing eyes to her sister. "And having a delightful time. Our great-aunt Colleen is pretending she simply wants to make certain the event will live up to the Calhoun reputation, but the fact is, she's getting a big kick out of making guest lists and shooting down Aunt Coco's menus."

"As long as she's entertained."

"Wait until she gets hold of you," Lilah warned. "She has some very creative ideas for floral arrangements."

"Terrific." Suzanna stopped in Lilah's doorway. Holt was definitely hard at work. Never particularly ordered, Lilah's room looked as though someone had scooped up every piece of furniture and dropped it down again like pick-up sticks. At the moment, he had his head in the fireplace, and Max was crawling on the floor.

"Having fun, boys?" Lilah said lazily.

Max looked up and grinned. She was mad, all right, he thought. He'd learned to handle and enjoy her temper.

"I found that other sandal you've been looking for. It was under the cushion of the chair."

"There's good news." She lifted a brow, noting that Holt was now sitting on Lilah's hearth, looking at Suzanna. And Suzanna was looking at him. "You need a break, Max."

"No, I'm fine."

"You definitely need a break." She walked in to take his hand and pull him to his feet. "You can come back and help Holt invade my privacy later."

"I told you she wouldn't like it," Suzanna said when Lilah dragged Max from the room.

"That's too bad."

With her hands on her hips she surveyed the damage. "Did you find anything?"

"Not unless you count the two odd earrings and one of those lacy things we found behind the dresser." He tilted his head. "You got any of those lacy things?"

"Not really." She looked down at her sweaty T-shirt. "Up until a few days ago, I didn't think I'd need any."

"You've got a real nice way of wearing denim, babe." He rose, and since she wasn't coming any closer, moved to her. "And..." He ran his hands over her shoulders, down her back to her hips. "I get a real charge out of taking it off you." He kissed her hard, in the deep and urgent way she'd come to expect. Then he nipped her bottom lip and grinned. "But anytime you want to borrow one of those lacy things from Lilah..."

She laughed and gave him a quick, affectionate hug, the kind she gave so freely that never failed to warm him from the inside out. "Maybe I'll surprise you. How long have you been here?"

"I came straight from the site. Did you get the rest of those whatdoyoucallits in?"

"Russian olives, yes." And her back was still aching. "You were a lot of help on the retaining wall."

"You were out of your mind to think you could build that thing on your own."

"I had a part-time laborer when I contracted."

He shook his head and went back to searching the fireplace. "You may be tough, Suzanna, but you're not equipped to haul around lumber and swing a sledgehammer."

"I'd have done it—"

"Yeah." He glanced around. "I know." He tested another brick. "It did look pretty good."

"It looked terrific. And since you didn't swear at me more than half a dozen times when you were hefting landscape timbers, why don't I reward you?"

"Oh, yeah?" He lost his interest in the bricks.

"I'll go get you a beer."

"I'd rather have—"

"I know." She laughed as she walked out. "But you'll have to settle for a beer. For now."

It felt good, she thought, to be able to joke like that. Not to be embarrassed or edgy. There was no need to feel anything but content, knowing he cared for her. In time, they might have something deeper.

Full of energy and hope, she rounded the last step and turned into the hall. All at once, there was chaos. She heard the dogs first, Fred and Sadie, barking fiendishly, then the clatter of feet on the porch and two high bellowing shouts.

"Mom!" Both Jenny and Alex yelled the single syllable as they burst into the house.

The rich and fast joy came first as she bent to scoop them up in her arms. Laughing, she smothered them both with kisses as the dogs dashed in mad circles.

"Oh, I missed you. I missed you both so much. Let me look at you." When she drew them back arm's length, her smile faltered. They were both on the edge of tears. "Baby?"

"We wanted to come home." Jenny's voice trembled as she buried her face against her mother's shoulder. "We hate vacation."

"Shh." She stroked Jenny's hair as Alex rubbed a fist under his eyes.

"We were unmanageable and bad," he said in a trembly voice. "And we don't care, either."

"Just the attitude I've come to expect," Bax said as he walked through the open front door. Jenny's arms tightened around Suzanna's neck, but Alex turned and threw out his Calhoun chin.

"We didn't like the dumb party, and we don't like you, either."

"Alex!" Her tone sharp, she dropped a hand on his shoulder. "That's enough. Apologize."

His lips quivered, but the stubborn gleam remained in his eyes. "We're sorry we don't like you."

"Take your sister upstairs," Bax said tightly. "I want to speak with your mother in private."

"You and Jenny go in the kitchen." Suzanna brushed a hand over Alex's cheek. "Aunt Coco's there."

Bax took a careless swipe at Fred with his foot. "And take these damn mutts with you."

"Chéri?" This from the svelte brunette who continued to hover in the doorway.

"Yvette." Keeping her arms around the children, Suzanna rose. "I'm sorry, I didn't see you."

The Frenchwoman waved distracted hands. "I beg your pardon, it's so confusing, I see. I just wondered— Bax, the children's bags?"

"Have the driver bring them in," he snapped. "Can't you see I'm busy?"

Suzanna sent the frazzled woman a look of sympathy. "He can just leave them here in the hall. If you'd like to come into the parlor…go see Aunt Coco," she told the children. "She'll be so happy you're back."

They went, holding each other's hand, with the dogs prancing at their heels.

"If you could spare a moment of your time," Bax said, then cast a glance up and down her work clothes, "out of your obviously fascinating day."

"The parlor," she repeated and turned. She struggled for calm, knowing it was essential. Whatever had caused him to change his plans and bring the children home a full week early was undoubtedly going to fall on her head. That she could handle. But the fact that the children had been upset was a different matter.

"Yvette—" Suzanna gestured to a chair "—can I get you something?"

"Oh, if you would be so kind. A brandy?"

"Of course. Bax?"

"Whiskey, a double."

She went to the liquor cabinet and poured, grateful her hands were steady. As she served Yvette, she thought she caught a glance of apology and embarrassment.

"Well, Bax, would you like to tell me what happened?"

"What happened began years ago when you had the mistaken idea you could be a mother."

"Bax," Yvette began, and was rounded on.

"Get out on the terrace. I prefer to do this privately."

So that hadn't changed, Suzanna thought. She gripped her hands together as Yvette crossed the room and exited through the glass doors.

"At least this little experiment should have rid her of the notion of having a child."

"Experiment?" Suzanna repeated. "Your visit with the children was an experiment?"

He sipped at the whiskey and watched her. He was still a striking man with a charmingly boyish face and fair hair. But temper, as it always had, added an edge to his looks that was anything but appealing.

"My reasons for taking the children are my concern. Their unforgivable behavior is yours. They haven't any conception of how to act in public and in private. They have the manners and dispositions of heathens and as little control. You've done a poor job, Suzanna, unless it was your intention to raise two miserable brats."

"Don't think you can stand here and speak about them that way in my house." Eyes dangerously bright, she walked toward him. "I don't give a damn if they fit your standards or not. I want to know why you've brought them back this way."

"Then listen," he suggested, and shoved her into a chair. "Your precious children don't have a clue what's expected of a Dumont. They were loud and unmanageable in restaurants, whiny and fidgety on the drive. When corrected they became defiant or sulky. At the resort, among several of my acquaintances, their behaviour was an embarrassment."

Too incensed for fear, Suzanna pulled herself out of the chair. "In other words, they were children. I'm sorry your plans were upset, Baxter, but it's difficult to expect a five- and six-year-old to present themselves as socially correct on all occasions. Even more difficult when they're thrust into a situation that wasn't any of their doing. They don't know you."

He swirled whiskey, swallowed. "They're perfectly

aware that I'm their father, but you've seen to it that they have no respect for that relationship."

"No, you've seen to it."

Deliberately he set the whiskey aside. "Do you think I don't know what you tell them? Sweet, harmless little Suzanna." She stepped back automatically, pleasing him.

"I don't tell them anything about you," she said, furious with herself for retreating.

"Oh, no? Then you didn't mention the fact that they had a bastard brother out in Oklahoma?"

So that was it, she realized, struggling to settle. "Megan O'Riley's brother married my sister. There was no way to keep the situation a secret, even if I had wanted to."

"And you just couldn't wait to sling my name around." He gave her another shove that sent her stumbling back.

"The boy's their half brother. They accept that, and they're too young to understand what a despicable thing you did."

"My affairs are mine. Don't you forget it." Gripping her shoulders, he pushed her up against the wall. "I have no intention of letting you get away with your pitiful plots for revenge."

"Take your hands off me." She twisted, but he forced her back again.

"When I'm damn good and ready. Let me warn you, Suzanna. I won't have you spreading my private business around. If even a hint of this gets out, I'll know where it started, and you know who'll pay for it."

She kept herself rigid, kept her eyes steady. "You can't hurt me anymore."

"Don't count on it. You make sure your children keep this business of half brothers to themselves. If it's mentioned again—'' he tightened his grip and jerked her up on her toes ''—ever, you'll be very sorry.''

''Take your threats and get out of my house.''

''Yours?'' He closed a hand around her throat. ''Remember, it's only yours because I didn't want this crumbling anachronism. Push me, and I'll have you back in court in a heartbeat. And I'll have it all this time. Those children might benefit from a nice, Swiss boarding school, which is exactly where they'll be if you don't watch your step.''

He saw her eyes change, but it wasn't the fear he'd expected. It was fury. She lifted a hand, but before she could strike out, he was jerked away and tumbling to the floor. She watched Holt drag him up again by the collar, then send him crashing into a Louis Quinze table.

She'd never seen murder in a man's eyes before, but she recognized it in Holt's as he pounded a fist into Baxter's face.

''Holt, don't—''

She started forward only to have her arm gripped with surprising strength. ''Let him alone,'' Colleen said, her mouth grim, her eyes bright.

He wanted to kill him, and might have, if the man had fought back. But Bax slumped in his hold, nose and mouth seeping blood. ''You listen to me, you bastard.'' Holt slammed him against the wall. ''Put your hands on her again, and you're dead.''

Shaken, hurting, Bax fumbled for a handkerchief. ''I can have you arrested for assault.'' Holding the cloth to his nose, he looked around and saw his wife standing inside the terrace doors. ''I have a witness. You assaulted me and threatened my life.'' It was his first taste of humiliation, and he detested it. His glance veered toward Suzanna. ''You'll regret this.''

"No, she won't," Colleen put in before Holt could give in to the satisfaction of smashing his fist into the sneering mouth. "But you will, you miserable, quivering, spineless swine." She leaned heavily on her cane as she walked toward him. "You'll regret it for what's left of your worthless life if you ever lay hands on any member of my family again. Whatever you think you can do to us, I can do only more viciously to you. If you're unclear about my abilities, my name is Colleen Theresa Calhoun, and I can buy and sell you twice over."

She studied him, a pitiful man in a rumpled suit, bleeding into a silk handkerchief. "I wonder what the governor of your state—who happens to be my godchild—will have to say if I mention this scene to him." She gave a slow, satisfied nod when she saw she was understood. "Now get your miserable hide out of my house. Young man—" she inclined her head to Holt "—you'll be so kind as to show our guest to the door."

"My pleasure." Holt dragged him into the hall. The last thing Suzanna saw when she ran from the house was Yvette's fluttering hands.

"Where did she go?" Holt demanded when he found Colleen alone in the parlor.

"To lick her wounds, I suppose. Get me a brandy. Damn it, she'll keep a minute," she muttered when he hesitated. Colleen eased herself into a chair and waited for her heart rate to settle. "I knew she'd had a difficult time, but I wasn't fully aware of the extent of it. I've had this Dumont looked into since the divorce." She took the brandy and drank deeply. "Pitiful excuse for a man. I still wasn't aware he had abused her. I should have been, the first time I saw that look in her eyes. My mother had the same look." She closed her own and leaned back. "Well, if he doesn't want to see his political ambitions go up in smoke, he'll leave her be.'' Slowly she opened her eyes and gave Holt a steely look. ''You did well for yourself—I admire a man who uses his fists. I only regret I didn't use my cane on him.''

''I think you did better. I just broke his nose, you scared the—''

''I certainly did.'' She smiled and drank again. ''Damn good feeling, too.'' She noted that Holt was staring at the open terrace doors, his hands still fisted. Suzanna could do worse, she thought and swirled the remaining brandy. ''My mother used to go to the cliffs. You might find Suzanna there. Tell her the children are having cookies and spoiling their dinner.''

She had gone to the cliffs. She didn't know why when she'd needed to run, that she had run there. Only for a moment, she promised herself. She would only need a moment alone.

She sat on a rock, covered her face and wept out the bitterness and shame.

He found her like that, alone and sobbing, the wind carrying off the sounds of her grief, the sea pounding restlessly below. He didn't know where to begin. His mother had always been a sturdy woman, and whatever tears she had shed, had been shed in private.

Worse, he could still see Suzanna pushed against the wall, Dumont's hand on her throat. She'd looked so fragile, and so brave.

He stepped closer, laid a hesitant hand on her hair. ''Suzanna.''

She was up like a shot, choking back tears, wiping them from her damp face. ''I have to get back in. The children—''

"Are in the kitchen stuffing themselves with cookies. Sit down."

"No, I—"

"Please." He sat, easing her down beside him. "I haven't been here in a long time. My grandfather used to bring me. He used to sit right here and look out to sea. Once he told me a story about a princess in the castle up on the ridge. He must have been talking about Bianca, but later, when I remembered it, I always thought of you."

"Holt, I'm so sorry."

"If you apologize, you're only going to make me mad."

She swallowed another hot ball of tears. "I can't stand that you saw, that anyone saw."

"What I saw was you standing up to a bully." He turned her face to his. When he saw the fading red marks on her throat, he had to force back an oath. "He's never going to hurt you again."

"It was his reputation. The children must have talked about Kevin."

"Are you going to tell me?"

She did, as clearly as she was able. "When Sloan told me," she finished, "I knew it was important that the children understand they had a brother. What Bax doesn't realize is that I never thought about him, never cared. It was the children who mattered, all of them. The family."

"No, he wouldn't understand that. Or you." He brought her hand to his lips to kiss it gently. The stunned look on her face had him scowling out to sea. "I haven't been Mr. Sensitivity myself."

"You've been wonderful."

"If I had you wouldn't look like I hit you with a rock when I kiss your hand."

"It just isn't your style."

"No." He shrugged and dug out a cigarette. "I guess it's not." Then he changed his mind and slipped an arm around her shoulders instead. "Nice view."

"It's wonderful. I've always come here, to this spot. Sometimes…"

"Go ahead."

"You'll just laugh at me, but sometimes it's as if I can almost see her. Bianca. I can feel her, and I know she's here, waiting." She rested her head on his shoulder and shut her eyes. "Like right now. It's so warm and real. Up in the tower, her tower, it's bittersweet, more of a longing. But here, it's anticipation. Hope. I know you think I'm crazy."

"No." When she started to shift, he pulled her closer so that her head nestled back on his shoulder. "No, I can't. Not when I feel it, too."

From the west tower, the man who called himself Marshall watched them through field glasses. He didn't worry about being disturbed. The family no longer came above the second floor in the west wing, and the crew had knocked off thirty minutes before. He'd hoped to take advantage of the time that Sloan O'Riley was away with his new bride on his honeymoon to move more freely around the house. The Calhouns were so accustomed to seeing men in tool belts that they rarely gave him a second glance.

And he was interested, very interested in Holt Bradford, finding it fascinating that he was being drawn into this generation of Calhouns. It pleased him that he could continue his work right under the nose of an ex-cop. Such irony added to his vanity.

He would continue to keep tabs, he thought, while the

cop completed his search. And he would be there to take
what was his the moment the treasure was found. Whoever was in the way would simply be eliminated.

Suzanna spent all evening with her children, soothing
ruffled feathers and trying to turn their unhappy experience into a silly misadventure. By the time she got them
tucked into bed, Jenny was no longer clinging and Alex
had rebounded like a rubber ball.

"We had to ride in the car for hours and hours." He
bounced on his sister's bed while Suzanna smoothed
Jenny's sheets. "And they had dumb music on the radio
the *whole* time. People were singing like this." He
opened his mouth wide and let out what he thought
passed for an operatic aria. "And you couldn't understand a word."

"Not like that, like this." Jenny let out a screech that
could have shattered crystal. "And we had to be quiet
and appreciate."

Suzanna held her temper and tweaked her daughter's
nose. "Well, you appreciated that it was awful, didn't
you?"

That made Jenny giggle and reach up for another kiss.
"Yvette said we could play a word game, but he said it
gave him a headache, so she went to sleep."

"And that's what you should do, right now."

"I liked the hotel," Alex continued, hoping to postpone the inevitable. "We got to jump on the beds when
nobody was looking."

"You mean like you do in your room?"

He grinned. "They had little bars of soap in the bath-
room, and they put candy on your pillow at night."

Suzanna cocked her head. "You can forget that idea,
toadface."

After Jenny was settled with her night-light and army of stuffed animals, Suzanna carried Alex to his room. He didn't let her pick him up and cuddle often anymore, but tonight, he seemed to need it as much as she did.

"You've been eating bricks again," she murmured, and nuzzled his neck.

"I had five bricks for lunch." He flew out of her arms and onto the bed. She wrestled with him until he was breathless. He flopped back, laughing, then leaped out of bed again.

"Alex—"

"I forgot."

"You've already stretched it tonight, kid. In the bed or I'll have you cooked over a slow fire."

He pulled something out of the jeans he'd been wearing when he'd come home. "I saved it for you."

Suzanna took the flattened, broken chocolate wrapped in gold paper. It was more than a little melted, certainly inedible and more precious than diamonds.

"Oh, Alex."

"Jenny had one, too, but she lost it."

"That's all right." She brought him close for a fierce hug. "Thanks. I love you, you little worm."

"I love you, too." It didn't embarrass him to say it as it sometimes did, and he cuddled against her a moment longer. When his mother tucked him into bed, he didn't complain when she stroked his hair. "Night," he said, ready to sleep.

"Good night." She left him alone, weeping a little over the smashed mint. In her room, she opened the little case that had once held her diamonds, and tucked her son's gift inside.

She undressed then slipped into a thin white nightgown. There was paperwork waiting on her desk in the

corner, but she knew her mind and nerves were still too
rattled. To soothe herself, she opened the terrace doors
and, taking her brush, walked outside to feel the night.

There was an owl hooting, crickets singing, the quiet
whoosh of the sea. Tonight the moon was gilded and its
light clear as glass. Smiling to herself, she lifted her face
to it and skimmed the brush lazily through her hair.

Holt had never seen anything more beautiful than Suzanna brushing her hair in the moonlight. He knew he
made a poor Romeo and was deathly afraid he'd make a
fool of himself trying, but he had to give her something,
to somehow show her what it meant to have her in his
life.

He came out of the garden and started up the stone
steps. He moved quietly, and she was dreaming. She
didn't know he was there until he said her name.

"Suzanna."

She opened her eyes and saw him standing only a foot
away, his hair ruffled by the breeze, his eyes dark in the
shimmering light. "I was thinking about you. What are
you doing here?"

"I went home, but...I came back." He wanted her to
go on brushing her hair, but was certain the request
would sound ridiculous. "Are you all right?"

"I'm fine, really."

"The kids?"

"They're fine, too. Sleeping. I didn't even thank you
before. Maybe it's petty, but now that I've had a chance
to settle, I can admit I really enjoyed seeing Bax's nose
bleed."

"Anytime," Holt said, and meant it.

"I don't think it'll be necessary again, but I appreciate
it." She reached out to touch his hand, and pricked her
finger on a thorn. "Ow."

"That's a hell of a start," he mumbled, and thrust the rose at her. "I brought you this."

"You did?" Absurdly touched, she brushed the petals to her cheek.

"I stole it out of your garden." He stuck his hands into his pockets and wished for a cigarette. "I don't guess it counts."

"It certainly does." She had had two gifts that night, she thought, from the two men she loved. "Thank you."

He shrugged and wondered what to do next. "You look nice."

She smiled and glanced down at the simple white gown. "Well, it's not lacy."

"I watched you brushing your hair." His hand came out of his pocket of its own volition to touch. "I just stood there, down at the edge of the garden and watched you. I could hardly breathe. You're so beautiful, Suzanna."

Now it was she who couldn't breathe. He'd never looked at her just this way. His voice had never sounded so quiet. There was a reverence in it, as in the hand that stroked over her hair.

"Don't look at me like that." His fingers tightened in her hair and he had to force them to relax again. "I know I've been rough with you."

"No, you haven't."

"Damn it, I have." He fought against a welling impatience as she only stared at him. "I've pushed you around and grabbed on. I ripped your blouse."

A smile touched her lips. "When I sewed the buttons back on I remembered that night, and what it felt like to be needed that way." More than a little baffled, she shook her head. "I'm not fragile, Holt."

Couldn't she see how wrong she was? Didn't she know

how she looked right now, her hair smooth and shining in the moonlight, the thin white gown flowing down?

"I want to be with you tonight." He slid his hand down to touch her cheek. "Let me love you tonight."

She couldn't have denied him anything. When he lifted her to carry her in, she pressed her lips to his throat. But his mouth didn't turn hot and ready to hers. He laid her down carefully, took the brush and rose from her to set it on the nightstand. Then he turned the lights low.

When his mouth came to hers at last, it was soft as a whisper. His hands didn't race to excite, but moved with exquisite patience to seduce.

He felt her confusion, heard it in the unsteady murmur of his name, but he only rubbed his lips over hers, tracing the shape with his tongue. His strong hands moved with an artist's grace over the tensed slope of her shoulders.

"Trust me." He took his mouth on a slow, quiet journey over her face. "Let go and trust me, Suzanna. There's more than one way." Over her jaw, down the line of her throat, back to her trembling lips his mouth whispered. "I should have showed you before."

"I can't..." Then his kiss had her sinking, deep, deeper still into some thick velvet haze. She couldn't right herself. Didn't want to. Surely this endless, echoing tunnel was paradise.

He touched, hardly touching at all, and left her weak. His mouth, gliding like a cool breeze over her flesh, was rapture. She could hear him murmur to her, incredible promises, soft, lovely words. There was passion in them, in the fingertips that seemed designed only to bring her pleasure, yet this was a passion to give she had never expected.

He stroked her through the thin cotton, delighting in the liquid movements of her body beneath his hands. He could watch her face in the lamplight, feed on that alone, knowing she was steeped in him, in what he offered her. There was no need to strap down greed, desire was no less, but it had taken a different hue.

When she sighed, he brought his lips back to hers to swallow the flavor of his name.

He undressed her slowly, bringing the gown down inch by inch, wallowing in the delight of warming newly bared skin. Fascinated with each tremor he brought her, he lingered. Then took her gently over the first crest.

Unbearably sweet. Each movement, each sigh. Exquisitely tender. Every touch, every murmur. He had imprisoned her in a world of silk, gently bringing dozens of pulses to a throbbing ache that was like music. Never had she been more aware of her body than now as he explored it so thoroughly, so patiently.

At last she felt his flesh against hers, the warm, hard body she had come to crave. Opening heavy eyes, she looked. Lifting weighted limbs, she touched.

He hadn't known a need could be so strong yet so quiet. She enfolded him. He slipped into her. For both, it was like coming home.

I could not have foreseen that the day would be my last with her. Would I have looked more closely, held more tightly? The love could have been no greater, but could it have been treasured more completely?

There is no answer.

We found the little dog, cowering and half-starved in the rocks by our cliffs. Bianca found such pleasure in him. It was foolish, I suppose, but I think we both felt this was something we could share, since we had found him together.

We called him Fred, and I must admit I was sad to see

*him go when it was time for her to return to The Towers.
Of course it was right that she take the orphaned pup to
her children so that they could make him a family. I went
home alone, to think of her, to try to work.*

*When she came to me, I was stunned that she should
have taken such a risk. Only once before had she been
to the cottage, and we had not dared chance that again.
She was frantic and overwrought. Under her cloak, she
carried the puppy. Because she was pale as a ghost, I
made her sit and poured her brandy.*

*She told me, as I sat, hardly daring to speak, of the
events that had taken place since we'd parted.*

*The children had fallen in love with the dog. There had
been laughter and light hearts until Fergus had returned.
He refused to have the dog, a stray mutt, in his home.
Perhaps I could have forgiven him for that, thought of
him only as a rigid fool. Bianca told me that he had
ordered the dog destroyed, holding firm even on the tears
and pleas of his children.*

*On the girl, young Colleen, he had been the hardest.
Fearing a harsher, perhaps a physical reprisal, Bianca
had sent the children and the dog up to their nanny.*

*The argument that had followed was bitter. She did not
tell me all, but her tremors and the flash of fear in her
eyes said enough. In his fury, he had threatened and
abused her. It was then I saw in the light of my lamp,
the marks on her throat where his hands had squeezed.*

*I would have gone then. I would have killed him. But
her terror stopped me. Never before and never again in
my life have I felt a rage such as that. To love as I loved,
to know that she had been hurt and frightened. There are
times I wish to God I had gone, and had killed. Perhaps
things would have been different. But I'll never be sure.*

I didn't leave her, but stayed while she wept and told

*me that he had gone to Boston, and that when he re-
turned he intended to bring a new governess of his choos-
ing. He had accused her of being a poor mother, and
would take the care and control of the children from her.*

*If he had threatened to cut out her heart, he could not
have done more damage. She would not see her children
raised by a paid servant, overseen by a cold, ambitious
father. She feared most for her daughter, knowing if nothing was done, Colleen would one day be bartered off into
marriage—even as her mother had been.*

*It was this great fear that forced her decision to leave
him.*

*She knew the risks, the scandal, the position she would
be giving up. Nothing could sway her. She would take
her children away where she knew they would be safe.
Her wish was for me to go with them, but she did not
beg or call upon my love.*

She did not need to.

*I would make the arrangements the next day, and she
would prepare the children. Then she asked me to make
her mine.*

*For so long I had wanted her. Yet I had promised my-
self I would not take her. That night I broke one promise,
and I made another. I would love her eternally.*

*I still remember how she looked, her hair unbound, her
eyes so dark. Before I touched her I knew how she would
feel. Before I laid her in my bed, I knew how she would
look there. Now it is only a dream, the sweetest memory
of my life. The sound of the water and the crickets, the
smell of wildflowers.*

*In that timeless hour, I had everything a man could
want. She was beauty and love and promise. Seductive
and innocent, shy and wanton. Even now, I can taste her
mouth, smell her skin. And ache for her.*

Then she was gone. What I had thought was a beginning was an end.

I took what money I had, sold paints and canvases for more and bought four tickets on the evening train. She did not come. There was a storm brewing. Hot lightning, vicious thunder, heavy wind. I told myself it was the weather that turned my blood so cold. But God help me, I think I knew. There was such a sharp, terrifying pain, such unreasonable fear. It consumed me.

For the first time, and the last, I went to The Towers. The rain began to slash as I beat on the door. The woman who answered was hysterical. I would have pushed past her, run through the house calling for Bianca, but at that moment, the police arrived.

She had jumped from the tower, thrown herself through the window onto the rocks. This is unclear now, as it was even then. I remember running, shouting for her over the howling wind. The lights of the house were blinding, slashing through the gloom. Men were already scrambling on the ridge and below with lanterns. I stood, looking down at her. My love. Taken from me. Not by her own hand. I could never accept that. But gone. Lost.

I would have leaped off that ridge myself. But she stopped me. I will swear it was her voice that stopped me. Instead, I sat on the ground, the rain pouring over me.

I could not join her then. Somehow I would have to live out my life without her. I have done so, and perhaps some good has come from the time I have spent here. The boy, my grandson. How Bianca would have loved him. There are times I take him to our cliffs and I'm sure she's there with us.

There are still Calhouns in The Towers. Bianca would have wanted that. Her children's children, and theirs.

Perhaps one day another lonely young woman will walk those cliffs. I hope her fate is a kinder one.

I know, in my heart, that it is not ended yet. She waits for me. When my time comes at last, I will talk with Bianca again. I will love her as I once promised. Eternally.

Chapter 10

Holt waited for Trent in the pergola along the seawall. Lighting a cigarette, he looked over the wide lawn to The Towers. One of the gargoyles along the center peak had lost its head while the other sat grinning down, more charming than ferocious. There were clematis—he recognized it now—and roses climbing up to the first terrace. The old stone glowered in the hazy sunlight. There was really no other word for it, but the flowers gave it a kind of magical, Sleeping Beauty aura. Towers and turrets speared up, arrogant of form, dignified with age.

Scaffolding bracketed the west end, and the high whine of a power saw cut the air. A lift truck was parked under the balcony, its mechanism groaning as it hefted its load of equipment to a trio of bare-backed men. A radio jolted out hard rock.

Maybe it was right and just that the house held so tenaciously to the past even while it accepted the present, Holt mused. If it was possible for stone and mortar to absorb emotion and memory, The Towers had done so. Already he felt as though it harbored some of his.

The windows of the room where he had spent most of the night with Suzanna winked back at him. He remembered every second of those hours, every sigh, every movement. He also remembered that he had confused her. No, tenderness wasn't his style, he thought, but it had been easy with her.

She hadn't asked him for softness. She hadn't asked him for anything. Was that why he felt compelled to give? Without trying, she had tapped into something inside him he hadn't known was there—and was still more than a little uncomfortable with. Finding it, feeling it left him as vulnerable as she. He'd yet to work out the right way to tell her.

She deserved the music, the candlelight, the flowers. She deserved the soft poetic words. He was going to try to give them to her, no matter how big a fool it made him feel.

In the meantime, he had a job to do. He was going to find those damn emeralds for her. And he was going to put Livingston behind bars.

Holt tossed the cigarette away as he saw Trent come out of the house. In the pergola, they would have relative privacy. The clatter of construction echoed in countertime to the beat and drum of waves. Whatever they said wouldn't carry above ten feet. Anyone looking out of the house would see two men sharing a late-afternoon beer, away from the women.

Trent stepped inside and offered a bottle.

"Thanks." Holt leaned negligently against a post and lifted the beer. "Did you get the list?"

"Yeah." Trent took a seat on one of the stone benches

so that he could watch the house as he drank. "We've only signed on four new men in the last month."

"References?"

"Of course." The faint annoyance in his tone was instinctive. "Sloan and I are well aware of security."

Holt merely shrugged. "A man like Livingston wouldn't have any problem getting references. They'd cost him." Holt drank deeply. "But he'd get them."

"You'd know more about that sort of thing than I." Trent's eyes narrowed as he watched two of the men replacing shingles on the roof of the west wing. "But I have a hard time buying that he could be here, working right under our noses."

"Oh, he's here." Holt took out another cigarette, lighted it, then took a thoughtful drag. "Whoever tossed my place knew about the connection almost as soon as you did. Since none of you go around talking about the situation at cocktail parties, he'd have heard something here, in the house. He didn't sign on at the start of the job, because he was busy elsewhere. But the last few weeks…" He paused as the children ran out, dogs in tow, to race to their fort. "He wouldn't just sit and wait, not as long as there's a possibility you could knock out a wall and have the emeralds fall into your hand. And where better to keep an eye on things than inside?"

"It fits," Trent admitted. "But I don't like the idea of my wife, or any of the others, being that close." He thought of C.C., the baby she carried, and his eyes darkened. "If there's a chance you're right, I want to move on it."

"Give me the list, and I'll check it out. I've still got connections." Holt's gaze remained on the children. "He's not going to hurt any of them. That's a fact."

Trent nodded. He was a businessman and had never

done anything more violent than a little boxing in college. But he would do whatever it took to protect his wife and unborn child. "I filled Max in, and Sloan and Amanda decided to break off their honeymoon. They should be here in a couple of hours."

That was good, Holt thought. It was best having the family all in one place. "What did Sloan tell her?"

"That there was some problem with the job." More comfortable now that wheels were in motion, Trent grinned a little. "If she finds out he's stringing her along, there'll be hell to pay."

"The less the women know, the better."

This time Trent laughed. "If any of them heard you say that, you'd lose three layers of skin. They're a tough bunch."

Holt thought of Suzanna. "They think they are."

"No, they are. It took me quite a while to accept it. Individually they're strong—velvet-coated steel. Not to mention stubborn, impulsive and feverishly loyal. Together…" Trent smiled again. "Well, I'll admit I'd rather face a pair of sumo wrestlers than the Calhoun women on a roll."

"When it's over, they can be as mad as they want."

"As long as they're safe," Trent finished, and noted that Holt was watching the children. "Great kids," he commented.

"Yeah. They're okay."

"They've got a hell of a mother." Trent drank contemplatively. "Too bad they don't have a real father."

Even the thought of Baxter Dumont made Holt's blood boil. "How much do you know about him?"

"More than I like. I know he put Suzanna through hell. He nearly broke her with the custody suit."

"Custody suit?" Stunned, Holt looked back. "He went after the kids?"

"He went after her," Trent corrected. "What better way? She doesn't talk about it. I got the story from C.C. Apparently he was annoyed that she filed for the divorce. Not good for his image, particularly since he's got his eye on a senate seat. He dragged her through a long, ugly court battle, trying to prove she was unstable and unfit."

"Bastard." Choking on rage, Holt turned away to flick the cigarette onto the rocks.

"He didn't want them. The idea was to ship them off to a boarding school. Or that was the threat. He backed off when Suzanna made the settlement."

His hands were on the stone rail now, fingers digging in. "What settlement?"

"She gave him damn near everything. He dropped the case so the arrangements could be made privately. He got the house, all the property, along with a chunk of her inheritance. She could have fought it, but she and the kids were already an emotional mess. She didn't want to take any chances with them, or put them through any more stress."

"No, she wouldn't." Holt drank in a futile attempt to wash the bitterness from his throat. "He's not going to hurt her or the kids anymore. I'll see to it."

"I thought you would." Trent rose, satisfied. He pulled a list out of his pocket and exchanged it for Holt's empty bottle. "Let me know what you find out."

"Yeah."

"The séance tonight." Trent saw Holt grimace and laughed again. "It may surprise you."

"The only thing that surprises me is that Coco talked me into it."

"If you plan on sticking around, you'll have to get used to being talked into all manner of things."

He was going to stick around, all right, Holt thought as Trent walked away. He just needed to find the right way to tell Suzanna. After glancing at the names on the list, Holt tucked it away. He'd make a couple of calls and see what he could dig up.

As he started across the lawn, the dogs galloped up to him, Fred devotedly pressing to Sadie's side. When they stopped jumping long enough to be petted, Fred lapped frantically at her face. Sadie tolerated it, then turned away and ignored him.

"They've got a name for women like you," Holt told her.

"Remember the Alamo!" Alex shouted. He stood spread legged on the roof of his fort, a plastic sword in his hand. Because he counted on his challenge being answered, his eyes gleamed as they met Holt's. "You'll never take us alive."

"Oh yeah?" Unable to resist, Holt moved closer. "What makes you think I want you, monkey brain?"

"'Cause we're the patriots and you're the evil invaders."

Jenny popped her head through an opening that served as a window. Before Holt could evade it, he was hit dead center of the chest with a splat of water from her pistol. Alex let out a triumphant hoot as Holt scowled down at his shirt.

"I suppose you know," Holt said slowly, "this means war."

As Jenny shrieked, he grabbed her and pulled her through the window. To her delight, he held her upside down so that her two blond ponytails brushed the grass.

"He's taken a hostage!" Alex bellowed. "Death to the

last man.'' He scrambled inside then burst out of the doorway, brandishing his sword. Holt barely had time to right Jenny before the little missile plowed into him. ''Off with his head,'' Alex chanted, echoed by his sister. Holt let his body go lax and took them both to the ground with him.

There were screams and giggles as he wrestled with them. It wasn't as easy as he'd supposed. They were both agile and slick, wriggling out of his hold to attack. He found himself at a disadvantage as Alex sat on his chest and Jenny found a spot on his ribs to tickle.

''I'm going to have to get rough,'' he warned them. When he took a spray of water in the face, he swore, making them both howl with laughter. A quick roll and he dislodged the pistol, then snatched it up to drench them both. With shrieks and giggles, they fell on him.

It was a wet and messy battle, and when he finally managed to pin them, they were all out of breath.

''I massacred you both,'' Holt managed. ''Say uncle.'' Jenny poked a finger in his ribs, making him twitch. In defense he lowered his cheek to her neck and rubbed a day's worth of stubble over her skin.

''Uncle, uncle, uncle!'' She screamed, gurgling with laughter. Satisfied, he used the same weapon on Alex until victorious, he rolled over and lay stomach down on the grass.

''You killed us,'' Alex admitted, not displeased. ''But you're morally wounded.''

''Yeah, but I think you mean mortally.''

''Are you going to take a nap?'' Jenny climbed onto his back to bounce. ''Lilah sleeps in the grass sometimes.''

''Lilah sleeps anywhere,'' Holt muttered.

''You can take a nap in my bed if you want,'' she

invited, then pressed a curious finger on the edge of the scar she saw beneath his hitched-up T-shirt. "You have a hurt on your back."

"Uh-huh."

Alex was already scrambling to look. "Can I see?"

Holt tensed automatically, then forced himself to relax. "Sure."

As Alex pushed up the shirt, both children's eyes widened. It wasn't like the neat little scar they had both admired on his leg. This was long and jagged and mean, slashing from the waist so high up on his back they couldn't push the shirt up enough to see the end of it.

"Gee," was all Alex could think to say. He swallowed, then gamely touched a finger to the scar. "Did you get in a big fight?"

"Not exactly." He remembered the pain, the incredible flash of white heat. "One of the bad guys got me," he said, and hoped it would satisfy. When he felt Jenny's little mouth lower to his back, he went very still.

"Does it feel better now?" she asked.

"Yeah." He had to let out a long breath to steady his voice. "Thanks." Turning over, he sat up to brush a hand through her hair.

Suzanna stood a few feet away, watching them with her heart in her throat. She'd seen the battle from the kitchen doorway. It had touched her to see how easily Holt had joined in the game with her children. She'd been smiling when she'd started out to join them—then she had watched Jenny and Alex examining the scar on Holt's back, and Jenny's kiss to make it better. She had seen the look of ragged emotion on Holt's face when he'd turned to sweep his hand over her little girl's hair.

Now the three of them were on the grass, Jenny cuddled on his lap, Alex's arm slung affectionately around his shoulder. She took a moment to make certain her eyes were dry before she continued toward them.

"Is the war over?" she asked, and three pair of eyes lifted.

"He won," Alex told her.

"It doesn't look as though it was an easy victory." She scooped Jenny up when the girl lifted her arms. "You're all wet."

"He blasted us—but I got him first."

"That's my girl."

"And he's ticklish," Jenny confided. "*Real* ticklish."

"Is that so?" Suzanna sent Holt a slow smile. "I'll keep that in mind. Now you two scat. I noticed nobody put away the game you were playing."

"But, Mom—" Alex had his excuses ready, but she stopped them with a look.

"If you don't clean it up, I will," she said mildly. "But then I'll have your share of strawberry shortcake tonight."

That was a tough one. Alex agonized over it for a minute, then caved in. "I'll do it. Then I get Jenny's share."

"Do not." Jenny sprinted toward the house with her brother giving chase.

"Very smooth, Mom," Holt commented as he rose.

"I know their weaknesses." She put her arms around him, surprising and pleasing him. It was very rare for her to make the first move. "You're all wet, too."

"Sniper fire, but I picked them off like flies." Bringing her closer, he rested his cheek on her hair. "They're terrific kids, Suzanna. I'm, ah…" He didn't know how to tell her he'd fallen in love with them, any more than he knew how to tell her he'd fallen in love with their mother. "I'm getting you wet." Feeling awkward, he drew away.

Smiling, she touched a hand to his cheek. "Want to take a walk?"

He thought of the list in his pocket. It could wait an hour, he decided, and took her hand.

He'd known she would head to the cliffs. It seemed right that they would walk there as the shadows lengthened and the air cooled toward evening. She talked a little of the job she'd finished that day, he of the hull he'd repaired. But their minds weren't on work.

"Holt." She looked out to sea, her hand in his. "Will you tell me why you resigned from the force?" She felt his fingers stiffen, but didn't turn.

"It's done," he said flatly. "There's nothing to tell."

"The scar on your back—"

"I said it's done." He withdrew and pulled out a cigarette.

"I see." She absorbed the rejection. "Your past and your personal feelings about it are none of my business."

He took an impatient drag. "I didn't say that."

"You certainly did. You have the right to know all there is to know about me. I'm supposed to trust you with everything, unquestioningly. But I'm not to pry into what's yours."

He turned angry eyes on her. "What is this, some kind of test?"

"Call it what you like," she tossed back. "I'd hoped you trusted me by now, that you cared enough to let me in."

"I do care, damn it. Don't you know it still rips me up to remember it? Ten years of my life, Suzanna. Ten years." He whirled away to flick the cigarette over the edge.

"I'm sorry." Instinctively she put her hands on his shoulders to soothe. "If anyone knows how painful it is to dredge up old wounds, it's me. Why don't we go back? I'll see if I can find you a clean shirt.''

''No.'' His jaw was clenched, his body tight as a spring. ''You want to know, you've got a right. I tossed it in because I couldn't handle it. I spent ten years telling myself I could make a difference, that none of the crap I had to wade through would affect me. I could rub shoulders with dealers and pimps and victims all day and not lose any sleep at night. If I had to kill somebody, it was line of duty. Not something you want to think about too much, but something you live with. I saw a few cops burn out along the way, but it wasn't going to happen to me.''

She said nothing, just continued to rub at the knotted muscles of his shoulders while she waited for him to go on. He kept looking out to sea, smelling her, and the dusky scent of the wild roses that were at peak.

''Vice takes you into the pits, Suzanna. You get so you understand the people you're trying to wipe out. You think like them. You have to when you go under, or you don't come out again. There are things I'm never going to tell you, because I do care. Ugly things, and I just...'' He closed his eyes, and jammed his hands into his pockets. ''I just didn't want to see it anymore. I was already thinking about coming back here—just sort of kicking it around.''

Suddenly weary, he lifted his hands to rub the heels over his eyes. ''I was tired, Suzanna, and I wanted to live like a normal person again. The kind who doesn't strap on a gun every day or make deals with slime in back rooms. We were on a routine investigation, looking for a small-time dealer who we thought we could pressure information out of. Doesn't matter why,'' he said impatiently. ''Anyway, we got a tip where to find him, and when we cornered him in this little dive, he snapped. Turned out the jerk had about twenty thousand in coke strapped under his clothes, and more than a couple lines in his system. He panicked. He dragged some half-stoned woman with him and bolted.''

His palms were beginning to sweat, so he wiped them against his jeans. ''My partner and I separated to cut him off. He pulled the woman out in the alley. With us on either end, he didn't have any hope of getting away. I had my weapon out. It was dark. The garbage had turned.''

He could still smell it, rank and fetid, as the sweat began to run down his back. ''I could hear my partner coming up the other side, and hear the woman crying. He'd sliced her up a little and she was balled up on the concrete. I couldn't be sure how bad she was hurt. I remember thinking the creep was going to be up for more than distribution. Then he jumped me. He had the knife in before I could get off a shot.''

He could still feel it ripping through his flesh, still smell his own blood. ''I knew I was dead, and I kept thinking that I wouldn't be able to come home. That I was going to die in that damn alley with the stink of that garbage. I killed him as I went down. That's what they told me. I don't remember. The thing I remember next was waking up in the hospital feeling like I'd been sliced in half and sewn back together. I told myself that if I made it, I was coming back here. Because I knew if I had to walk down another alley, I wouldn't come back out.''

Suzanna had her arms tight around him now, her cheek pressed against his back. ''Do you think because you came home instead of facing another alley, you failed?''

''I don't know.''

"I did, for a long time. No one had put a knife in my back, but I came to understand that if I stayed with Bax, if I'd kept that promise, part of me would die. I chose survival, do you think I should be ashamed of that?"

"No." He turned, taking her shoulder. "No."

She lifted her hands to cup his face. In her eyes was understanding, and the sympathy he couldn't have accepted even a week before. "Neither do I. I hate what happened to you, but I'm glad it brought you here." Offering comfort, she touched her lips to his. Slowly, with a sweetness that was unbearably moving, she felt him let go.

His body relaxed against hers even as he pulled her closer. His mouth softened even as it heated. Here, at last, was the next level. There was not only passion, not only tenderness, but trust. As the wind whispered through the wild grass and the bright, brave flowers, she thought she heard something else, something so quiet and lovely that it brought tears to her eyes. When he lifted his head, when she saw his face, she knew he'd heard it, too. She smiled.

"We're not alone here," she murmured. "They must have stood in this same spot, holding each other like this. Wanting each other like this." Filled with the moment, she pressed his hand to her lips. "Holt, do you believe that fate and time can run in a circle?"

"I'm beginning to."

"They still come here, to wait. I wonder if they ever find each other. I think they will, if we can make things right." She kissed him again, then slipped an arm around his waist. "Let's go home. I have a feeling it's going to be an interesting evening."

"Suzanna," he began as they started back. "After the

séance…'' He trailed off, looking pained, and made her laugh.

"Don't worry, at The Towers we only have friendly ghosts."

"Right. Just don't expect me to put much stock in chanting and trances, but anyway, I was wondering if after—look, I know you don't like to leave the kids, but I thought you could come back to my place for a little while. There's some stuff I want to talk to you about."

"What stuff?"

"Just—stuff," he said lamely. If he was going to ask her to marry him, he wanted to do it right. "I'd appreciate it if you could get away for an hour or two."

"All right, if it's important. Is it about the emeralds?"

"No. It's…I'd rather wait, okay? Listen, I've got a couple of things to do before we start calling up spirits."

"Aren't you going to stay for dinner?"

"I can't. I'll be back." As they came up the slope and passed the stone wall, he pulled her against him for a brief hard kiss. "See you later."

She frowned after him and might have pursued, but her name was called from the second-level terrace. Shading her eyes, she saw her sister.

"Amanda!" With a laugh, she raced across the lawn and up the stone steps. "What are you doing back?" She gathered the new bride into her arms and squeezed. "You look wonderful—but you were supposed to be gone nearly another week. Is anything wrong?"

"No, nothing." She kissed both of Suzanna's cheeks. "Come on, I'll fill you in."

"Where are we going?"

"Bianca's tower. Family meeting."

They climbed up, then went inside to ascend the narrow circular stairs that led to the tower. C.C. and Lilah were already waiting.

"Aunt Coco?" Suzanna asked.

"We'll let her know what we discuss," Amanda answered. "But it would look too suspicious if we pulled her up here now."

With a nod, Suzanna took a seat on the floor at Lilah's feet. "So I take it this is women only?"

"No more than they deserve," C.C. said, and crossed her arms. "They've been skulking off to have their boy's club meetings for days now. It's time we set things straight."

"Max has definitely got something up his sleeve," Lilah put in. "He's acting much too innocent. And, he's been hanging around the construction crew for the last couple of days."

"I don't suppose he wants to learn how to set tile," Suzanna murmured.

"If he did, he'd have twenty books on it by now." Lilah rolled her shoulders and leaned back. "And this afternoon when I got home from work, I saw Trent and Holt powwowing in the pergola. Somebody who didn't know better might have thought they were just hanging out and having a beer, but something was going on."

"So they know something they're not telling us." Thoughtful, Suzanna drummed her fingers on her knees. She'd had a feeling something was going on, but Holt had done such a good job of distracting her, she hadn't acted on it.

"Sloan had a long, mumbling conversation with Trent on the phone two days ago. He claimed there was some problem with materials that he had to see to personally." Tossing her hair, Amanda gave a sniff. "And he thought I was stupid enough to buy it. He wanted to get back because they're on to something—and they want to keep the little women out of the way.''

''Fat chance,'' C.C. muttered. ''I'm for marching downstairs right now and demanding they tell us whatever they know. If Trent thinks I'm going to sit around twiddling my thumbs while he handles Calhoun business, he's got another think coming.''

''Bamboo shoots and brass knuckles,'' Lilah mused, not terribly displeased with the image. ''That'll just make them more stubborn. Male egos on the line, ladies. Get out your hard hats and flak jackets.''

Suzanna laughed and patted her leg. ''You've got a point. Let's see what we know... Sloan gets called back so they must think they're getting close. I can't see them being secretive if they thought they'd hit on the location of the emeralds.''

''Neither can I.'' Because she thought best on her feet, Amanda paced. ''Remember how stiff-necked they got when we decided to look for the yacht Max had jumped off? Sloan threatened to...what was it? Hog-tie,'' she said viciously. ''Yes, that was it. He threatened to hog-tie me if I so much as thought about trying to find Livingston on my own.''

''Trent won't even discuss Livingston with me,'' C.C. added, then wrinkled her nose. ''It isn't good for me to be upset in my delicate condition.''

From her sprawled perch on the window seat, Lilah gave a hoot. ''I'd like to see any man go through childbirth then have the nerve to call a woman delicate.''

''Holt says that Livingston is out of our league. *Ours*,'' Suzanna explained, making a circular motion with her finger. ''Not his.''

''Jerk.'' C.C. plopped down on the window seat beside

Lilah. "So are we agreed? They've got a line on Livingston and they're keeping it to themselves."

The vote was unanimous.

"Now, we need to find out what they know." Amanda stopped pacing and tapped her foot. "Suggestions?"

"Well…" Suzanna looked down at her nails and smiled. "I say divide and conquer. The four of us should be able to dig information out of them—each in our own way. Then we rendezvous here, tomorrow, same time, and put the pieces together."

"I like it." Lilah sat up to put a hand on Suzanna's shoulder. "The poor guys haven't got a chance."

Suzanna reached up to lay her hand on Lilah's as Amanda and C.C. added theirs. "And when it's over," she said, "maybe they'll realize the Calhoun women take care of their own."

Chapter 11

Holt had never felt more ridiculous in his life. He was about to take part in a séance. If that wasn't bad enough, before the night was over, he was going to ask the woman who was currently laughing at him, to be his wife.

"It isn't a firing squad." Chuckling, Suzanna patted his cheek. "Relax."

"Damn foolishness is what it is." From the foot of the table, Colleen scowled at everyone in general. "The idea of talking to spirits. Hogwash. And you—" She stabbed a finger toward Coco. "Not that you ever kept an ounce of sense in that flighty head of yours, but I'd have thought even you would know better than to raise these girls on such bilge."

"It isn't bilge." As always, the steely gaze made Coco tremble, but she felt fairly safe with the length of the table between them. "You'll see after we begin."

"What I see is a table full of dolts." Though her face

remained in stern lines, Colleen's heart melted as she looked up at the portrait of her mother, which had been hung over the fireplace. "I'll give you ten thousand for it."

Holt shrugged. She'd been dogging him for days about buying the painting. "It isn't for sale."

"If you think you're going to hose me, young man, you're mistaken. I know a hustle."

He grinned at her. He would have bet his last nickel she'd hustled plenty herself. "I'm not selling it."

"It's worth more, anyway," Lilah put in, unable to resist. "Isn't that right, Professor?"

"Well, actually, yes." Max cleared his throat. "Christian Bradford's early work is increasing in value. At Sotheby's two years ago, one of his seascapes went for thirty-five thousand."

"What are you," Colleen snapped, "his agent?"

Max swallowed a grin. "No, ma'am."

"Then hush. Fifteen thousand, and not a penny more."

Holt ran his tongue around his teeth. "Not interested."

"Maybe if we got on with the matter at hand." Coco held her breath, waiting for her aunt's wrath to fall. When Colleen only muttered and scowled, she relaxed. "Amanda, dear, light the candles. Now we must all try to empty our minds of all worries, all doubts. Concentrate on Bianca." When the candles were glowing, and the chandelier extinguished, she gave a last glance around the table. "Join hands."

Holt grumbled under his breath but took Suzanna's hand in his right, Lilah's in his left.

"Focus on the picture," Coco whispered, closing her eyes to bring it into her mind since it was behind her on the wall. Tingles of anticipation raced up and down her spine. "She's close to us, very close to us. She wants to help."

Holt let his mind drift because it helped him forget what he was doing. He tried to imagine what it would be like when he and Suzanna were alone in the cottage. He'd bought candles. Not the sturdy type he kept in the kitchen drawer for power outages, but slender white tapers that smelled of jasmine.

There was champagne chilling beside the six-pack in his refrigerator, and two new clear flutes beside his coffee mugs. Even now the jeweler's box was burning a hole in his hip pocket.

Tonight, he thought, he'd take the step. The words would come exactly as he planned. The music would be playing. She would open the box, look inside….

Her hands were draped with emeralds. He frowned, giving himself a little shake. That wasn't right. He hadn't bought her emeralds. But the image focused so clearly. Suzanna on her knees holding emeralds. Three glittering tiers flanked by icy diamonds and centered by a glowing teardrop stone of dreamy green.

The Calhoun necklace. He felt the chill on his neck and ignored it. He'd seen the picture Max had found in the old library book. He knew what the emeralds looked like. It was the atmosphere, the humming silence and the flickering candles that made him think of them. That made him see them.

He didn't believe in visions. But when he closed his eyes to clear it from his mind, it seemed imprinted there. Suzanna kneeling on the floor with emeralds dripping from her fingers.

He felt a hand on his shoulder and looked around. There was no one there, only shadows and light thrown by the candles. But the feeling remained, with an urgency that had his hackles rising.

It was crazy, he told himself. And it was time to put an end to the whole insane business.

"Listen," he began. And the portrait of Bianca crashed to the floor.

Coco gave a piping squeak and jolted out of the chair. "Oh, my. Oh, my goodness," she murmured, patting her speeding heart.

Amanda was already racing forward. "Oh, I hope it isn't damaged."

"I don't think it will be." Lilah released Holt's hand. "Do you?"

The clear and steady gaze made him uncomfortable. Ignoring her, he turned to Suzanna. Her hand was like ice in his. "What is it? What's wrong?"

"Nothing." But she gave a quick shudder. "I think you'd better check the portrait."

He rose to go over where the others were crouched. As he did, Suzanna looked down the length of the table at her great-aunt. Colleen's white skin had paled like glass. Her eyes were dark and damp. Without a word, Suzanna rose and poured her a brandy. "It's going to be all right," she murmured, laying a hand on the thin shoulder.

"The frame cracked." Sloan ran a finger along it before he rose. "Funny that it would fall that way. Those nails are sturdy."

Holt started to shrug it off, but when he bent closer to where the frame had separated from the backing, he went very still. "There's something between the canvas and the back." Hefting the portrait, he laid it facedown on the table. "I need a knife."

Sloan pulled out his pocketknife and offered it. Holt made a long thin slit just beneath the cracked frame and slid out several sheets of paper.

"What is it?" The question was muffled as Coco had her hands pressed to her mouth.

"It's my grandfather's writing." The emotion sprang up strong and fast. It churned in Holt's eyes as he lifted them to Suzanna's. "It looks like a kind of diary. It's dated 1965."

"Sit down, dear." Coco put a comforting hand on his shoulder. "Trent, would you pour the brandy? I'll brew some tea for C.C."

He did need to sit, and he hoped the drink would steady him. For now, he could only stare at the papers and see his grandfather. Sitting on the back porch of the cottage, watching the water. Standing in his loft, slashing paint on canvas. Walking on the cliffs, telling a young boy stories.

When Suzanna came back to lay a hand on his, he turned his palm up and gripped her fingers. "It's been there all this time, and I didn't know."

"You weren't meant to know," she said quietly. "Until tonight." When he looked at her again, she curled her fingers tight around his. "Some things we just have to take on faith."

"Something happened tonight. Something upset you."

"I'll tell you. Not yet."

Composed, Coco brought in the tea, then took her seat. "Holt, whatever your grandfather wrote belongs to you. No one here will ask you to share it. If after you read it, you feel you prefer to keep it to yourself, we'll understand."

He glanced down at the papers again, then lifted the

first sheet. "We'll read it together." He took a long breath, kept Suzanna's hand tight in his. "'The moment I saw her, my life changed.'"

No one spoke as Holt read through his grandfather's memories. But around the table, hands linked again. There was no sound but his voice and the wind breathing through the trees outside the windows. When he was finished, the room remained silent.

Lilah spoke first, her voice thick with tears while others slid down her cheeks. "He never stopped loving her. Always, even though he made a life for himself, he loved her."

"How he must have felt, to come here that night and find out she was gone." Amanda leaned her head on Sloan's shoulder.

"But he was right." Suzanna watched one of her tears drop on the back of Holt's hand. "She didn't take her own life. She couldn't have. Not only did she love him too much, but she would have tolerated anything to protect her children."

"No, she didn't jump." Colleen whispered the words. She lifted her snifter with a trembling hand, then set it down again. "I've never spoken of that night, not to anyone. Through the years I've sometimes thought what I saw was a dream. A terrible, terrible nightmare."

Determined, she cleared her blurred vision and strengthened her voice. "He understood her, her Christian. He couldn't have written about her that way and not have known her heart. She was beautiful, but she was also kind and generous. I have never been loved as I was loved by my mother. And I have never hated as I hated my father."

She straightened her shoulders. Already the burden had

lessened. "I was too young to understand her unhappiness or her desperation. In those days a man ruled his home, his family, as he chose. No one dared to question my father. But I remember the day she brought the puppy home, the little puppy my father would not have in his home. She did send us upstairs, but I hid at the top and listened. I had never heard her raise her voice to him before. Oh, she was valiant. And he was cruel. I didn't understand the names he called her. Then."

She paused to drink again, for her throat was dry and the memory bitter. "She defended me against him, knowing as even I knew he barely tolerated me, a female. When he left the house after the argument, I was glad. I prayed that night he would never come back. The next day, my mother told me we were going to take a trip. She hadn't told my brothers yet, but I was the eldest. She wanted me to understand that she would take care of us, that nothing bad would happen.

"Then, he came back. I knew she was upset, even frightened. I was to stay in my room until she came for me. But she didn't come. It grew late, and there was a storm. I wanted my mother." Colleen pressed her lips together. "She wasn't in her room, so I went up to the tower where she often spent her time. I heard them as I crept up the stairs. The door was open and I heard them. The terrible argument. He was raging, crazed with fury. She told him that she would no longer live with him, that she wanted nothing from him but her children and her freedom."

Because Colleen was shaking, Coco rose and walked down to take her hand.

"He struck her. I heard the slap and raced to the door. But I was afraid, too afraid to go in. She had a hand to her cheek, and her eyes were blazing. Not with fear, with fury. I will always remember that there was no fear in her at the end. He threatened her with scandal. He screamed at her that if she left his house, she would never lay eyes on any of his children again. She would never ruin his reputation. She would never throw an obstacle in the path of his ambitions.''

Though her lips trembled, Colleen lifted her chin. ''She did not beg. She did not weep. She hurled words back at him like thunderbolts.'' Fisting a hand, she pressed it to her mouth to smother her own tears. ''She was magnificent. Her children would never be taken from her, and scandal be damned. Did he think she cared what people thought of her? Did he think she feared his power to have society shun her? She would take her children and she would make a life where both she and they could be loved. And I think it was that which drove him mad. The idea that she would choose another man over him. Over him. Fergus Calhoun. That she would toss his money and power and position back at him, rather than bow to his wishes. He grabbed her, lifting her from her feet, shaking her, screaming into her face while his own purpled with rage. I think I screamed then, and hearing me, she began to fight. When she struck him, he threw her aside. I heard the crash of the glass. He ran to it, roaring for her, but she was gone. How long he stood there while the wind and rain poured in, I don't know. When he turned his face was white, his eyes glazed. He walked past me without even seeing me. I went inside, over to the broken window and looked down until Nanny came and carried me away.''

Coco pressed a kiss to the white hair, then gently

stroked. "Come with me, dear. I'll take you upstairs. Lilah will bring you a nice cup of tea."

"Yes, I'll be right there." Lilah wiped her cheeks dry. "Max?"

"I'll come with you." He slipped an arm around her waist as Coco led Bianca's daughter from the room.

"Poor little girl," Suzanna murmured, and let her head rest on Holt's shoulder as he drove away from The Towers. "To have seen something so horrible, to have had to live with it all of her life. I think of Jenny—"

"Don't." He put a firm hand over hers. "You got out. Bianca didn't." He waited a moment. "You knew, didn't you? Before Colleen told us the story."

"I knew she hadn't committed suicide. I can't explain how, but tonight, I knew. It was as if she was standing right behind me."

He thought of the sensation of having a hand on his shoulder. "Maybe she was. After a night like this, it's hard for me to convince myself the picture falling off the wall was a coincidence."

Suzanna closed her eyes. "It was beautiful, what your grandfather wrote about her. If we never find the emeralds, we have that—we'll know she had that. To love that way," she said on a sigh. "It hardly seems possible. I don't want to think of the tragedy or sadness, but of the time they had together. Dancing in the wild roses."

He'd never danced with her in the sunlight, Holt thought. Or read her poetry or promised her eternal love.

When they reached the cottage, Sadie leaped out the back window of the car to race around the yard and sniff at the flower bed she'd planted for him. When Holt leaned across her, Suzanna looked down in surprise.

"What are you doing?"

"I'm opening the door for you." He shoved it open. "If I'd gotten out to do it, you wouldn't have waited."

Amused, Suzanna stepped out. "Thank you."

"You're welcome." When he reached the house, he unlocked the front door, then held that open. Keeping her face sober, Suzanna inclined her head as she slipped past him.

"Thank you."

Holt just let the screen slam shut. Brow lifted, Suzanna scanned the room.

"You've done something different."

"I cleaned it up," he muttered.

"Oh. It looks nice. You know, Holt, I've been meaning to ask you if you think Livingston is still on the island."

"Why? Did something happen?"

His response was much too abrupt, Suzanna noted and moved casually around the room. "No, I've just been wondering where he may be staying, what his next move might be." She ran a fingertip down one of the candles he'd bought. "Any ideas?"

"How should I know?"

"You're the expert on crime."

"And I told you to leave Livingston to me."

"And I told you I couldn't do that. Maybe I'll start poking around on my own."

"Try it and I'll handcuff you and lock you in a closet."

"The urban counterpart to hog-tying," she murmured. "I wouldn't have to try it if you'd tell me what you know. Or what you think."

"What brought this up now?"

She moved her shoulder. "Since we have a little time to ourselves, I thought we could talk about it."

"Look, why don't you just sit down?" He pulled out his lighter.

"What are you doing?"

"I'm lighting candles." His nerves were stretching like taffy. "What does it look like I'm doing?"

She did sit, and steepled her hands. "Since you're so cranky, I have to assume that you do know something."

"You don't have to assume anything except that you're ticking me off." He stalked to the stereo.

"How close are you?" she asked as a bluesy sax filled the air.

"I'm nowhere." Since that was a lie, he decided to temper it with part of the truth. "I think he's in the area because he broke in here and took a look around a couple of weeks ago."

"What?" She catapulted out of the chair. "A couple of weeks ago, and you didn't tell me?"

"What were you going to do about it?" he countered. "Pull out a magnifying glass and deer-hunter's hat?"

"I had a right to know."

"Now you know. Just sit down, will you? I'll be back in a minute."

He stalked out and she began to pace. Holt knew more than he was saying, but at least she'd annoyed a piece from him. Livingston was close, close enough that he'd known Holt might have something of interest. The fact that Holt was wound like a top at the moment made her think something more was working on him. It shouldn't be difficult, she thought, now that she already had him irritated, to push a little more out of him.

The candles were scented, she noted, and smiled to

herself. She couldn't imagine that he'd bought jasmine candles on purpose. Especially a half a dozen of them. She traced a finger over the calla lilies he'd stuck—not very artistically—in a vase. Maybe working with flowers was getting to him, she thought. He wasn't pretending so hard not to like them.

When he came back in, she smiled then looked puzzled. "Is that champagne?"

"Yeah." And he was thoroughly disgusted. He'd imagined she'd be charmed. Instead she questioned everything. "Do you want some or not?"

"Sure." The curt invitation was so typical she didn't take offense. After he'd poured, she tapped her glass absently against his. "Now, if you're sure it was Livingston who broke in, I think—"

"One more word," he said with dangerous calm. "One more word about Livingston and I'll pour the rest of the bottle over your hard head."

She sipped, knowing she'd have to be careful if she didn't want to waste a bottle of champagne and end up with sticky hair. "I'm only trying to get a clear picture."

He let out what was close to a roar of frustration and spun away. Champagne sloshed over his glass as he paced. "She wants a clear picture, and she's blind as a bat. I shoveled two months' worth of dust out of this place. I bought candles and flowers. I had to listen to some jerk try to teach me about wine. That's the picture, damn it."

She'd wanted to irritate information from him, not infuriate him. "Holt—"

"Just sit down and shut up. I should have known this would get screwed up. God knows why I tried to do it this way."

A light dawned, and she smiled. He'd set the stage, but she'd been too focused on her own scheme to take note. "Holt, it's very sweet of you to do all of this. I'm sorry if I didn't seem to appreciate it. If you wanted me to come here tonight so we could make love—"

"I don't want to make love with you." He swore, viciously. "Of course I want to make love with you, but that's not it. I'm trying to ask you to marry me, damn it, so will you sit *down!*"

Since her legs had dissolved from knees to toe, she slid into a chair.

"This is perfect." He gulped down champagne and started pacing again. "Just perfect. I'm trying to tell you that I'm crazy about you, that I don't think I can live without you, and all you can do is ask me what I'm doing and nag me about some obsessed jewel thief."

Cautiously she brought the glass to her lips. "Sorry."

"You should be sorry," he said bitterly. "I was ready to make a fool of myself tonight for you, and you won't even let me do that. I've been in love with you nearly half my life. Even when I moved away, I couldn't get you out of my mind. You spoiled every other woman for me. I'd start to get close to someone, and then...they weren't you. They just weren't you, and I'd never even gotten past your back door."

In love. The two words reeled in her head. *In love.* "I thought you didn't even like me."

"I couldn't stand you." He raked his free hand through his hair. "Every time I looked at you I wanted you so much I couldn't breathe. My mouth would go dry and my stomach would knot, and you'd just smile and keep walking." His dark and turbulent eyes locked on hers. "I wanted to strangle you. Then you ran into me and knocked me off my bike and I was lying there bleeding and—and mortified. You were leaning over me, smelling like heaven and running your hands over me to see if anything was broken. One more minute of that and I'd have dragged you onto the asphalt with me." He rubbed his hand over his face. "Lord, you were only sixteen."

"You swore at me."

His face was a picture of anger and disgust. "Damn right, I swore at you. You were better off with that than with what I wanted to do to you." He was calming, little by little. He sipped again but kept pacing. "I talked myself into believing it was just an adolescent fantasy. Even a crush, and that was tough to swallow. Then you came walking across my yard. I looked at you and my throat went dry, my stomach knotted up. We were both past being adolescents."

He set his glass down, noting that she was gripping hers with both hands. Her eyes were huge and fixed on his. Cursing both of them, he fumbled for a cigarette then tossed it aside.

"I'm not good at this, Suzanna. I thought I could pull it off. Set the mood, you know? And after you'd had enough champagne, I'd convince you I could make you happy."

She couldn't relax her grip. She tried but couldn't. "I don't need champagne and candlelight, Holt."

He smiled a little. "Babe, you were born for it. I could lie to you and tell you I'll remember to give it to you every night. But I won't."

She looked down at her glass and wondered if she was ready to take this sort of chance again. Loving him was one thing. Being loved by him was incredible. But marriage… "Why don't you just tell me the truth then?"

He walked over to sit on the arm of the couch and face her. "I love you. I've never felt about anyone the way I feel about you. Whatever happens, I'll never feel like this about anyone else again. There's no taking back what's happened to either of us in the last few years, but maybe we can make things better for both of us. For the kids."

Her eyes changed, darkened. "It may never be easy. Bax would always be their legal father."

"He wouldn't be the one who loved them." When her eyes filled, he shook his head. No, she hadn't needed candlelight and champagne to make her vulnerable and open to his needs. Only a mention of her children. "I won't use them to get to you. I know I could, but first it has to be between you and me. Maybe I'm stuck on them, and I want to—I think I could be pretty good at being their father, but I don't want you to marry me for them."

She took a deep breath. Odd, her fingers had relaxed on the stem of the glass without her being aware. "I never wanted to love anyone again. And I certainly never wanted to get married." Her lips curved. "Until you." Setting the glass aside, she reached for his hand. "I can't claim to have loved you as long, but you couldn't love me more than I love you."

He didn't settle for her hand, but pulled her into his arms. When he at last managed to tear his mouth from hers, he buried his face in her hair. "Don't tell me you need to think about it, Suzanna."

"I don't need to think about it." She couldn't remember the last time her heart and mind had been so at peace. "I'll marry you."

Before the words were out of her mouth, she was tumbling with him onto the couch. She was laughing as they tugged at each other's clothes, laughing still when the frantic movements sent them rolling onto the floor.

"I knew it." She nipped his bare shoulder. "You did bring me here to make love."

"Can I help it if you can't keep your hands off me?" He trailed a necklace of quick kisses around her throat.

She smiled, tilting her head to give him easy access. "Holt, did you really think about pulling me down on the street after you'd fallen off your bike?"

"After you'd run into me," he corrected, nuzzling her ear. "Yeah. Let me show you what I had in mind."

Later they lay like rag dolls on the floor, a tangle of limbs. When she could manage it, she lifted her head from his chest. "It was much better that we didn't try that twelve years ago."

Lazily he opened his eyes. She was smiling down at him, her hair brushing his shoulders, the candlelight glowing in her eyes. "Much better. I wouldn't have had any skin left on my back."

She chuckled then shifted to trace the shape of his face. "You always scared me a little. Looking so dark and dangerous. And, of course, the girls used to talk about you."

"Oh, yeah? What did they say?"

"I'll tell you when you're sixty. You could probably use it then." He pinched her, but she only laughed then rested her cheek on his. "When you're sixty, we'll be an old married couple with grandchildren."

He liked the thought of it. "And you still won't be able to keep your hands off me."

"And I'll remind you of the night you asked me to

marry you, when you gave me flowers and candlelight, then shouted at me and raged up and down the room, making me love you even more.''

''If that's all it takes, you'll be delirious about me by the time I'm sixty.''

''I already am.'' She lowered her mouth to his.

''Suzanna.'' He drew her closer, started to roll her under him, then swore. ''It's your own fault,'' he said as he nudged her aside.

''What?''

''You were supposed to be sitting over there, dazed by my romantic abilities.'' He fought to untangle his jeans and pull the jeweler's box from the pocket. ''Then I was going to get down on one knee.''

Eyes wide, she stared at the box, then at him. ''You were not.''

''Yes, I was. I was going to feel like an idiot, but I was going to do it. You've got no one to blame but yourself that we're lying naked on the floor. Here.''

''You bought me a ring,'' she whispered.

''There could be a frog in there for all you know.'' Impatient with her, he flipped up the top himself. ''I didn't want to give you diamonds.'' He shrugged when she said nothing, only stared into the box. ''I figured you'd already had those. I thought about emeralds, but those are something you will have. And this is more like your eyes.''

When the tears blurred her vision, the light refracted. There were diamonds, tiny, lovely stones in a heart shape about the deep and brilliant sapphire. They weren't cold, as the ones she had sold, but warmed by the rich blue fire they encircled.

Holt watched the first tear fall with a great deal of

Suzanna's Surrender

discomfort. "If you don't like it, we can take it back. You can pick out what you want."

"It's beautiful." She dashed a tear away with the back of her hand. "I'm sorry. I hate to cry. It's just so beautiful, and you bought it for me because you love me. And when I put it on—" she lifted drenched eyes to his "—I'm yours."

He dropped his brow to hers. Those were the words he'd wanted. The ones he'd needed. Taking the ring from the box, he slipped it onto her finger. "You're mine." He kissed her fingers, then her lips. "I'm yours." Bringing her close again, he remembered his grandfather's words. "Eternally."

Chapter 12

Suzanna took the children to the shop with her in the morning. She couldn't tell the rest of her family the news until she'd gauged Alex's and Jenny's feelings. The day was bright and hot. Knowing it would be a busy one, she arrived a full hour before opening. Because they wanted to check the herbs they had planted, she took them into the greenhouse to look at the tender shoots.

She let them argue for a while over whose plants would be the biggest or the best, supervising as they gave the shoots their morning drink.

"Do you guys like Holt?" she asked casually, nerves drumming.

"He's neat." Alex was tempted to turn the sprayer on his sister, but he'd gotten in trouble the last time he'd indulged himself.

"He plays with us sometimes." Jenny danced from foot to foot, waiting her turn. "I like when he throws me up in the air."

"I like him, too." Suzanna relaxed a little.

"Does he throw you up in the air?" Jenny wanted to know.

"No." With a laugh, Suzanna ruffled her hair.

"He could. He's got big muscles." Reluctantly Alex passed the sprayer to his sister. "He let me feel them." Screwing up his face, Alex flexed his own. Obliging, Suzanna pinched the tiny biceps.

"Wow. You're pretty tough."

"That's what he said."

"I was wondering…" Suzanna wiped nervous hands on her jeans. "How would you feel if he lived with us, all the time?"

"That'd be good," Jenny decided. "He plays with us even when we don't ask."

One down, Suzanna thought and turned to her son. "Alex?"

He shuffled his feet, frowning a little. "Are you going to get married like C.C. and Amanda?"

Sharp little devil, she thought, and crouched down. "I was thinking about it. What do you think?"

"Do I have to wear a dumb tuxedo again?"

She smiled and stroked his cheek. "Probably."

"Is he going to be our uncle, like Trent and Sloan and Max?" Jenny asked.

Suzanna got up to turn off the spray before answering her daughter. "No. He'd be your stepfather."

Brother and sister exchanged looks. "Would he still like us?"

"Of course he would, Jenny."

"Would we have to go away and live someplace else?"

She sighed and combed a hand through Alex's hair.

"No. He would come to live with us at The Towers, or maybe we'd go and live with him at his cottage. We'd be a family."

Alex thought it over. "Would he be Kevin's stepfather, too?"

"No." She had to kiss him. "Megan's Kevin's mom, and maybe one day she'll fall in love and get married. Then Kevin will have a father."

"Did you fall in love with Holt?" Jenny asked.

"Yes, I did." She felt Alex shift uncomfortably and smiled. "I'd like to marry him so we could all live together. But Holt and I both wanted to see how you felt about it."

"I like him," Jenny announced. "He lets me ride on his shoulders."

Alex shrugged, a bit more cautious. "Maybe it's okay."

Concerned, Suzanna rose. "We can talk about it some more. Let's go set up."

They stepped out of the greenhouse just as Holt pulled up in the graveled lot. He knew he'd told her he'd wait until lunchtime, but he hadn't been able to. He'd awakened realizing he'd rather face another alley than those two kids who could so easily reject him. He stuffed his hands into his pockets and tried to look casual.

"Hi."

"Hi." Suzanna wanted to reach out to him, but her children held her hands.

"I thought I'd drop by and...how's it going?"

Jenny gave him a shy smile and huddled closer to her mother. "Mom says you're going to get married and be our stepfather and live with us."

Holt had to knock back an urge to shuffle his feet. "That's the plan."

Alex tightened his fingers around Suzanna's as he stared up at Holt. "Are you going to yell at us?"

After a quick glance at Suzanna, Holt stooped down until he was eye to eye with the boy. "Maybe. If you need it."

Alex trusted that answer more than he would have an unqualified no. "Do you hit?" He remembered the swats he'd received during his vacation. They'd insulted more than hurt, but he still resented it.

Holt put a hand under the boy's chin and held it firm. "No," he said, and the look in his eyes made Alex believe. "But I might hang you up by your thumbs, or boil you in oil. If I get really mad, I'll stake you to an anthill."

Alex's lips twitched, but he wasn't finished with the interrogation. "Are you going to make Mom cry like he did?"

"Alex," Suzanna began, but Holt cut her off.

"I might sometimes, if I'm stupid. But not on purpose. I love her a lot, so I want to make her happy. Sometimes I might screw up."

Alex frowned and considered. "Are you going to do all that kissing stuff? Since Trent and Sloan and Max came, there's always kissing."

"Yeah." Holt's face relaxed into a smile. "I'm going to do all that kissing stuff."

"But you won't like it," Alex said, hopeful. "You'll just do it 'cause Mom likes it."

"Sorry, I like it, too."

"Jeez," Alex muttered, deflated.

"Do it now." Jenny danced and giggled. "Do it now so I can see."

Willing to oblige, Holt straightened and pulled Suzanna close. When he took his lips from Suzanna's, Alex was red faced and Jenny was clapping. ''I hate to tell you,'' Holt said soberly. ''but one day you'll like it, too.''

''Uh-uh. I'd rather eat dirt.''

With a laugh, Holt hoisted him up, relieved and delighted when Alex slung a friendly arm around his neck. ''Tell me that in ten years.''

''I like it,'' Jenny insisted, and tugged on his leg. ''I like it now. Kiss me.'' He hauled her in his other arm and kissed her tiny, waiting lips. She smiled, big blue eyes beaming. ''You kissed Mom different.''

''That's 'cause she's the mom and you're the kid.''

She liked the way he smelled, the way his arm supported her. When she rubbed a hand over his cheek, she was a little disappointed that it was smooth today. ''Can I call you Daddy?'' she asked, and Holt felt his heart lurch in his chest.

''I—ah—sure. If you want.''

''Daddy's for babies,'' Alex said in disgust. ''But you can be Dad.''

''Okay.'' He looked over at Suzanna. ''Okay.''

Holt wished he could have spent the day with them, but there were things that had to be done. He had a family now—it still dazed him—and he meant to protect them. He'd already put in calls to his contacts in Portland and was awaiting the rundowns on the four names from Trent's list. While he waited, he put in calls to the Department of Motor Vehicles, the credit bureau and the Internal Revenue, stretching it a bit by giving his old badge number and rank.

Between information and instinct, he whittled the four names down to two. While he waited for another call back, he read over his grandfather's diary.

He understood the feelings beneath the words, the

longing, the devotion. He understood the rage his grandfather had felt when he'd learned the woman he loved
had suffered abuse by the hands of the man she'd married. Was it coincidence or fate that his relationship with
Suzanna had so many similarities to that of their ancestors? At least this time, the tale would have a happy ending.

Suzanna's diamonds, he thought, drumming his fingers
on the pages. Bianca's emeralds. Suzanna had hidden her
jewels, the one material thing she felt belonged to her
from the marriage, as security for her children. He had
to believe Bianca had done the same.

So, where was the equivalent of Jenny's diaper bag?
he wondered.

When the phone rang, he snatched it up on the first
ring. Before he hung up again, Holt had little doubt he
had his man. Going into the bedroom, he checked his
weapon, balancing the familiar weight in his hand. He
strapped it to his calf.

Fifteen minutes later, he was walking through the
chaos of construction in the west wing. He found Sloan
in what was a nearly completed two-level suite. There
was a smell of new lumber and male sweat. Sloan, in a
tool belt and jeans, was supervising the construction of a
new staircase.

"I didn't know architects swung hammers," Holt commented.

Sloan grinned. "I got a personal interest in this job."

Nodding, Holt scanned the crew. "Which one's Marshall?"

Alerted, Sloan unbuckled the tool belt. "He's up on
the next level."

"I'd like to have a little talk with him."

Sloan's eyes flashed, but he merely nodded again. "I'll

go with you.'' He waited until they were out of range of the crew. ''You think he's the one?''

''Robert Marshall didn't apply for a Maine driver's license until six weeks ago. He's never paid taxes under the name and social security number he's using. Employers don't usually check with the DMV or IRS when they hire a laborer.''

Sloan swore and flexed his fingers. He could still see Amanda racing along the terrace pursued by a man holding a gun. ''I get first crack at him.''

''I appreciate the sentiment, but you'll have to strap it in.''

The hell he would, Sloan thought, and signaled the foreman. ''Marshall,'' he said briefly.

''Bob?'' The foreman pulled out a bandanna to wipe his neck. ''You just missed him. I had him drive Rick into Emergency. Rick took a pretty good slice out of his thumb, figured he needed stitches.''

''How long ago?'' Holt demanded.

'''Bout twenty minutes, I guess. Told them to take the rest of the day, since we're knocking off at four.'' He stuffed the bandanna back into his pocket. ''Problem?''

''No.'' Sloan bit down on temper. ''Let me know if Rick's okay.''

''Sure thing.'' He shouted at one of the carpenters, then lumbered off.

''I need an address,'' Holt said.

''Trent's got the paperwork.'' They started out. ''Are you going to turn it over to Lieutenant Koogar?''

''No,'' Holt said simply.

''Good.''

They found Trent in the office he'd thrown together on the first floor, a stack of files at his fingertips, a phone at his ear. He took one look at the two men. ''I'll get back to you,'' he said into the phone and hung up. ''Who is it?''

''He's using the name Robert Marshall.'' Holt pulled out a cigarette. ''Foreman let him go early. I want an address.''

Saying nothing, Trent crossed to a file cabinet to pull out a folder. ''Max is upstairs. He has a stake in this, too.''

Holt skimmed the information in Marshall's file. ''Then get him. We'll do this together.''

The apartment Marshall had listed was on the edge of the village. The woman who opened the door after Holt's third booming knock was bent and withered and out of sorts.

''What? What?'' she demanded. ''I'm not buying any encyclopedias or vacuum cleaners.''

''We're looking for Robert Marshall,'' Holt told her.

''Who? Who?'' She peered through the thick lenses of her glasses.

''Robert Marshall,'' he repeated.

''I don't know any Marshalls,'' she grumbled. ''There's a McNeilly next door and a Mitchell down below, but no Marshalls. I don't want to buy any insurance, either.''

''We're not selling anything,'' Trent said in his most patient voice. ''We're looking for a man named Robert Marshall who lives at this address.''

''I told you there's no Marshalls here. I live here. Lived here for fifteen years, since that worthless clot I married passed on and left me with nothing but bills. I know you,'' she said abruptly, pointing a gnarled finger at Sloan. ''Saw your picture in the paper.'' Reaching to the table beside the door, she hefted an iron bookend. ''You robbed a bank.''

"No, ma'am." Later, Sloan thought, much later, he might find the whole business amusing. "I married Amanda Calhoun."

The woman held on to the bookend while she considered. "One of the Calhoun girls. That's right. The youngest one—no, not the youngest one, the next one." Satisfied, she set the bookend down again. "Well, what do you want?"

"Robert Marshall," Holt said again. "He gave this building and this apartment as his address."

"Then he's a liar or a fool, because I've lived here for fifteen years ever since that no-account husband of mine caught pneumonia and died. Here one day, gone the next." She snapped her bent fingers. "And good riddance."

Thinking it was a dead end, Holt glanced at Sloan. "Give her a description."

"He's about thirty, six feet tall, trim, black hair, shoulder length, big droopy moustache."

"Don't know him. The boy downstairs, the Pierson boy's got hair past his shoulders. A disgrace if you ask me. Bleaches it, too, just like a girl. He's no more'n sixteen. You'd think his mother would make him cut that hair, but no. Plays the music so loud I have to bang on the floor."

"Excuse me," Max put in and described the man he had known as Ellis Caufield.

"Sounds like my nephew. Lives in Rochester with his second wife. Sells used cars."

"Thanks." Holt wasn't surprised the thief had given a phony address, but he was annoyed. As they came out of the building, he dug a quarter from his pocket.

"I guess we wait until morning," Max was saying.

"He doesn't know we're on to him, so he'll show up for work."

"I'm finished waiting." Holt headed for a phone booth. After dropping in the coin, he punched in numbers. "This is Detective Sergeant Bradford, Portland P.D., badge number 7375. I need a cross-check." He reeled off the phone number from Marshall's file. Then he held on with a cop's patience while the operator set her computer to work. "Thanks." He hung up and turned to the three men. "Bar Island," he said. "We'll take my boat."

While their men prepared to sail across the bay, the Calhoun women met in Bianca's tower. "So," Amanda began, pad and pencil at the ready. "What do we know?"

"Trent's been cross-checking the personnel files," C.C. supplied. "He claimed there was some hitch in withholding taxes, but that's bull."

"Interesting," Lilah mused. "Max stopped me from going over to the west wing this morning. I'd wanted to see how things were going, and he made all kinds of lame excuses why I shouldn't distract the men while they were working."

"And Sloan shoved a couple of files into a drawer, and locked it when I came into the room last night." Amanda tapped her pencil on the pad. "Why wouldn't they want us to know if they're checking up on the crews?"

"I think I have an idea," Suzanna said slowly. She'd been chewing it over most of the day. "Last night I found out that Holt's cottage had been broken into and searched."

Her three sisters pounced on that, hammering her with questions.

"Just wait." She lifted a hand. "He was irritated with me, which is why it came out. He was even more irritated that it had. But he did tell me, because he wanted to scare me into backing off, that he was certain it was Livingston."

"Which means," Amanda concluded, "that our old friend knows Holt's connected. Who else knows besides us?" In her organized way, she began to list names.

"Oh, stop fussing," Lilah said with a negligent wave of her hand. "No one knows except the family. None of us have mentioned it outside of this house."

"Maybe he found out the same way Max did," C.C. suggested. "From the library."

"Max checked out the books." Lilah shook her head. "Maybe he found the information in the papers he stole from us."

"It's possible." Amanda noted it down. "But he's had the papers for weeks. When did he break into the cottage?"

"A couple weeks ago, but I don't think he made the connection that way. I think he got it from us."

There was an instant argument. Suzanna stood, throwing up both hands to cut it off. "Listen, we're agreed that none of us have discussed this outside of the house. And we're agreed that the men are trying to keep us from finding out they're checking out the crews. Which means—"

"Which means," Amanda interrupted and shut her eyes. "The bastard's working for us. Like a fly on the wall, so he can pick up little pieces of information, poke around the house. We're so used to seeing guys hauling lumber, we wouldn't give him a second look."

"I think Holt already came to that conclusion." Suzanna lifted her hands again. "The question is, what do we do about it?"

"We give the construction boys a thrill tomorrow, and visit the west wing." Lilah straightened from the window seat. "I don't care what he's made himself look like this time, I'll know him if I get close enough." With that settled, she sat back. "Now, Suzanna, why don't you tell us when bad boy Bradford asked you to marry him?"

Suzanna grinned. "How did you know?"

"For an ex-cop, he's got great taste in jewelry." She took Suzanna's hand to show off the ring to her other sisters.

"Last night," she said as she was hugged and kissed and wept over. "We told the kids this morning."

"Aunt Coco's going to go through the roof." C.C. gave Suzanna another squeeze. "All four of us in a matter of months. She'll be in matchmaker heaven."

"All we need now is to get that creep behind bars and find the emeralds." Amanda dashed a tear away. "Oh, no! Do you realize what this means?"

"It means you have to organize another wedding," Suzanna answered.

"Not just that. It means we're going to be stuck with Aunt Colleen at least until the last handful of rice gets tossed."

Holt returned to The Towers in a foul mood. They'd found the house. Empty. They had no doubt that Livingston was living there. Bending the law more than a little, he had broken in and given the place as meticulous a search as Livingston had given his cottage. They'd found the stolen Calhoun papers, the lists the thief had made and a copy of the original blueprints of The Towers.

They'd also found a typed copy of each woman's

weekly schedule, along with handwritten comments that left no doubt as to the fact that Livingston had followed and observed each one of them. There was a well-ordered inventory of the rooms he had searched and the items he'd felt valuable enough to steal.

They had waited an hour for his return, then uneasy about leaving the women alone, had phoned in the information to Koogar. While the police staked out the rented house on Bar Island, Holt and his companions returned to The Towers.

It was only a matter of waiting now. That was something he had learned to do well in his years on the force. But now it wasn't a job, and every moment grated.

"Oh, my dear, dear boy." Coco flew at him the moment he stepped into the house. He caught her by her sturdy hips as she covered his face with kisses.

"Hey," was all he could manage as she wept against his shoulder. Her hair, he noted, was no longer gleaming black but fire-engine red. "What'd you do to your hair?"

"Oh, it was time for a change." She drew back to blow her nose into her hankie, then fell into his arms again. Helpless, he patted her back and looked at the grinning men around him for assistance.

"It looks okay," he assured her, wondering if that was what she was weeping about. "Really."

"You like it?" She pulled back again, fluffing at it. "I thought I needed a bit of dash, and red's so cheerful." She buried her face in the soggy hankie. "I'm so happy," she sobbed. "So very happy. I had hoped, you see. And the tea leaves indicated that it would all work out, but I couldn't help but worry. She's had such a dreadful time, and her sweet little babies, too. Now everything's going to be all right. I'd thought it might be Trent, but he and C.C. were so perfect. Then Sloan and Amanda. Then almost before I could blink, our dear Max and Lilah. Is it any wonder I'm overwhelmed?''

''I guess not.''

''To think, all those years ago when you'd bring lobsters to the back door. And that time you changed a tire for me and were too proud to even let me thank you. And now, now, you're going to marry my baby.''

''Congratulations.'' Trent grinned and slapped Holt on the back while Max dug out a fresh handkerchief for Coco.

''Welcome to the family.'' Sloan offered a hand. ''I guess you know what you're getting into.''

Holt studied the weeping Coco. ''I'm getting the picture.''

''Stop all that caterwauling.'' Colleen clumped down the stairs. ''I could hear you wailing all the way up in my room. For heaven's sake, take that mess into the kitchen.'' She gestured with her cane. ''Pour some tea into her until she pulls herself together. Out, all of you,'' she added. ''I want to talk to this boy here.''

Like rats deserting a sinking ship, Holt thought as they left him alone. Gesturing for him to follow, Colleen strode into the parlor.

''So, you think you're going to marry my grandniece.''

''No. I am going to marry her.''

She sniffed. Damned if she didn't like the boy. ''I'll tell you this, if you don't do better by her than that scum she had before, you'll answer to me.'' She settled into a chair. ''What are your prospects?''

''My what?''

''Your prospects,'' she said impatiently. ''Don't think you're going to latch on to my money when you latch on to her.''

His eyes narrowed, pleasing her. "You can take your money and—"

"Very good," she said with an approving nod. "How do you intend to keep her?"

"She doesn't need to be kept." He whirled around the room. "And she doesn't need you or anyone else poking into her business. She's managed just fine on her own, better than fine. She came out of hell and managed to put her life together, take care of the kids and start a business. The only thing that's going to change is that she's going to stop working herself into the ground, and the kids'll have someone who wants to be their father. Maybe I won't be able to give her diamonds and take her to fancy dinner parties, but I'll make her happy."

Colleen tapped her fingers on the head of her cane. "You'll do. If your grandfather was anything like you, it's no wonder my mother loved him. So…" She started to rise, then saw the portrait over the mantel. Where her father's stern face had been was her mother's lovely one. "What's that doing there?"

Holt dipped his hands into his pockets. "It seemed to me that was where it belonged. That's where my grandfather would have wanted it."

Colleen eased herself back into the chair. "Thank you." Her voice was strained, but her eyes remained fierce. "Now go away. I want to be alone."

He left her, amazed that he was growing fond of her. Though he didn't look forward to another scene, he started toward the kitchen to ask Coco where he could find Suzanna.

But he found her himself, following the music that drifted down the hall. She was sitting at a piano, playing some rich, haunting melody he didn't recognize. Though the music was sad, there was a smile on her lips and one in her eyes. When she looked up, her fingers stilled, but the smile remained.

"I didn't know you played."

"We all had lessons. I was the only one they stuck with." She reached out a hand for his. "I was hoping we'd have a minute alone, so I could tell you how wonderful you were with the kids this morning."

With his fingers meshed with hers, he studied the ring he'd given her. "I was nervous." He laughed a little. "I didn't know how they'd take it. When Jenny asked if she could call me Daddy...it's funny how fast you can fall in love. Suzanna." He kept toying with her hands, studying the ring. "I think I understand now what a parent would feel, what he'd go through to make sure his kids were safe. I'd like to have more. I know you'd need to think about it, and I don't want you to feel that I would care less about Alex and Jenny."

"I don't have to think about it." She pressed a kiss to his cheek. "I've always wanted a big family."

He drew her close so her head rested on his shoulder. "Suzanna, do you know where the nursery was when Bianca lived here?"

"On the third floor of the east wing. It's been used as a storeroom as long as I can remember." She straightened. "You think she hid the necklace there?"

"I think she hid them somewhere Fergus wouldn't look, and I can't see him spending a lot of time in the nursery."

"No, but you'd think someone would have come across them. I don't know why I say that," she corrected. "The place is filled with boxes and old furniture. The Tower's version of a garage sale."

"Show me."

It was worse than he'd imagined. Even overlooking

the cobwebs and dust, it was a mess. Boxes, crates, rolled-up rugs, broken tables, shadeless lamps stood, sat or reclined over every inch of space. Speechless, he turned to Suzanna who offered a sheepish grin.

"A lot of stuff collects in eighty-odd years," she told him. "Most of what's valuable's been culled out, and a lot of that was sold when we were—well, when things were difficult. This floor's been closed off for a long time, since we couldn't afford to heat it. We had to concentrate on keeping up the living space. Once we got everything under some kind of control, we were going to kind of attack the other sections a room at a time."

"You need a bulldozer."

"No, just time and elbow grease. We had plenty of the latter, but not nearly enough of the former. Over the last couple of months, we've gone through a lot of the old rooms, inch by inch, but it's a slow process."

"Then we might as well get started."

They worked for two grueling and dirty hours. They found a tattered parasol, an amazing collection of nineteenth-century erotica, a trunk full of musty clothes from the twenties and a box of warped phonograph records. There was also a crate filled with toys, a miniature locomotive, a sad, faded rag doll, assorted yo-yos and tops. Among them was a set of lovely old fairy-tale prints that Suzanna set aside.

"For our nursery," she told him. "Look." She held up a yellow christening gown. "It might have been my grandfather's."

"You'd have thought this stuff would have been packed up with more care."

"I don't think Fergus ran a very tidy household after Bianca died. If any of this stuff belonged to his children,

I'd wager the nanny bundled it away. He wouldn't have cared enough.''

"No." He pulled a cobweb out of her hair. "Listen, why don't you take a break?''

"I'm fine."

It was useless to remind her that she'd been working all day, so he used another tactic. "I could use a drink. You think Coco's got anything cold in the refrigerator— maybe a sandwich to go with it?''

"Sure. I'll go check."

He knew that her aunt would insist on putting the quick meal together, and Suzanna would get that much time to sit and do nothing. "Two sandwiches," he added, and kissed her.

"Right." She rose, stretching her back. "It's sad to think about those three children, lying in here at night knowing their mother wasn't going to come and tuck them in again. Speaking of which, I'd better tuck in my own before I come back.''

"Take your time." He was already headfirst in another crate.

She started out, thinking wistfully of Bianca's babies. Little Sean, who'd barely have been toddling, Ethan, who would grow up to father her father, Colleen, who was even now downstairs surely finding fault with something Coco had done. How the woman had ever been a sweet little girl…

A little girl, Suzanna thought, stopping on the second-floor landing. The oldest girl who would have been five or six when her mother died. Suzanna detoured and knocked on her great-aunt's door.

"Come in, damn it. I'm not getting up."

"Aunt Colleen." She stepped, amused to see the old

woman was engrossed in a romance novel. "I'm sorry to disturb you."

"Why? No one else is."

Suzanna bit the tip of her tongue. "I was just wondering, the summer…that last summer, were you still in the nursery with your brothers?"

"I wasn't a baby, no need for a nursery."

"So you had your own room," Suzanna prompted, struggling to contain the excitement. "Near the nursery?"

"At the other end of the east wing. There was the nursery, then Nanny's room, the children's bath, and the three rooms kept for children of guests. I had the corner room at the top of the stairs." She frowned down at her book. "The next summer, I moved into one of the guest rooms. I didn't want to sleep in the room my mother had decorated for me, knowing she wouldn't come back to it."

"I'm sorry. When Bianca told you that you were going away, did she come to your room?"

"Yes. She let me pick out a few of my favorite dresses, then she packed them herself."

"Then after—I suppose they were unpacked again."

"I never wore those dresses again. I never wanted to. Shoved the trunk under my bed."

"I see." So there was hope. "Thank you."

"Moth-eaten by now," Colleen grumbled as Suzanna went out again. She thought of her favorite white muslin with its blue satin sash and with a sigh got up to walk to the terrace.

Dusk was coming early, she thought. Storm brewing. She could smell it in the wind, see it in the bad-tempered clouds already blocking the sun.

Suzanna raced up the stairs again. The sandwiches

would have to wait. She pushed open the door of Colleen's old room. It too had been consigned to storage,
but being smaller than the nursery wasn't as cramped.
The wallpaper, perhaps the same that Bianca had picked
for her daughter, was faded and spotted, but Suzanna
could still see the delicate pattern of rosebuds and violets.

She didn't bother with the cases or boxes, but dragged
or pushed them aside. She was looking for a traveling
trunk, suitable for a young girl. What better place? she
thought as she pushed aside a crate marked Winter Drap-
eries. Fergus hadn't cared for his daughter. He would
hardly have bothered to look through a trunk of dresses,
particularly when that trunk had been shoved out of sight
by a traumatized young girl.

It had no doubt been opened in later years. Perhaps
someone—Suzanna's own mother?—had shaken out a
dress or two, then finding them quaint but useless, had
designated them to storage.

It could be anywhere, of course, she mused. But what
better place to start than the source?

Her heart pounded dully as she stumbled across an old
leather-strapped truck. Pulling it open, she found bolts of
material carefully folded in tissue. But no little girl's
dresses. And no emeralds.

Because the light was growing dim, she rose and
started toward the door. She would get Holt, and a flashlight, before continuing. In the gloom, she rapped her
shin sharply. Swearing, she looked down and saw the
small trunk.

It had once been a glistening white, but now it was
dull with age and dust. It had been shoved to the side,
piled with other boxes and nearly hidden by them and a
faded tapestry. Kneeling in the half-light, Suzanna un-

covered it. She flexed her unsteady fingers then opened the lid.

There was a smell of lavender, sealed inside perhaps for decades. She lifted the first dress, a frilly white muslin, going ivory with time and banded by a faded blue satin sash. Suzanna set it carefully aside and drew out another. There were leggings and ribbons, pretty bows and a lacy nightie. And there, at the bottom, beside a small stuffed bear, a box and a book.

Suzanna put a trembling hand to her lips, then slowly reached down to lift the book.

Her journal, she thought as tears misted her eyes. Bianca's journal. Hardly daring to breathe, she turned the first page.

Bar Harbor, June 12, 1912
I saw him on the cliffs, overlooking Frenchman Bay

Suzanna let out an unsteady breath and laid the book in her lap. This was not for her to read alone. It would wait for her family. Heart pounding, she reached down to take the box from the trunk. She knew before she opened it. She could feel the change in the room, the trembling of the air. As the first tear slid down her cheek, she opened the lid and uncovered Bianca's emeralds.

They pulsed like green suns, throbbing with life and passion. She lifted the necklace, the glorious three tiers, and felt the heat on her hands. Hidden eighty years before, in hope and desperation, they were now free. The gloom that filled the room was no match for them.

As she knelt, the necklace dripping from her fingers, she reached into the box and took out the matching earrings. Strange, she thought. She'd all but forgotten them.

They were lovely, exquisite, but the necklace dominated. It was made to dominate.

Stunned, she stared down at the power in her hands. They weren't just gems, she realized. They were far from being simply beautiful stones. They were Bianca's passions and hopes and dreams. From the time she had placed them in the box until now, when they had been lifted out by her descendant, they had waited to see the light again.

"Oh, Bianca."

"A charming sight."

Her head jerked up at the voice. He stood in the doorway, hardly more than a shadow. When he stepped into the room, she saw the glint of the gun in his hand.

"Patience pays off," Livingston said. "I watched you and the cop go into the room down the hall. I've been losing quite a bit of sleep wandering these rooms at night."

As he came closer, she stared at him. He didn't look like the man she remembered. His coloring was wrong, even the shape of his face. She rose very slowly, clutching the book and earrings in one hand, the necklace in the other.

"You don't recognize me. But I know you. I know all of you. You're Suzanna, just one of the Calhouns who owes me quite a bit."

"I don't know what you're talking about."

"Three months of my time, and not a little trouble. Then there was the loss of Hawkins, of course. He wasn't much of a partner, but he was mine. Just as those are mine." He looked down at the necklace and his mouth watered. They dazzled him. More than he had dreamed, more than he had imagined. Everything he wanted. His fingers trembled lightly on the gun as he reached out.

Suzanna jerked away. He lifted a brow. "Do you really think you can keep them from me? They're meant to be mine. And when they are, everything they are will be mine."

He stepped closer, and as she looked around for the best route of escape, his hand closed over her hair. "Some stones have power," he told her softly. "Tragedy seeps into them, making them stronger. Death and grief. It hones them. Hawkins didn't understand that, but he was a simple man."

And the one she was facing was a mad one. "The necklace belongs to the Calhouns. It always has. It always will."

He jerked her hair hard and fast. She would have yelped, but the gun was now pressed against the racing pulse in her throat. "It belongs to me. Because I've been clever enough, I've been determined enough to wait for it. The moment I read about it, I knew. Now tonight, it's done."

She wasn't certain what she would have done—given it to him, tried to reason. But at the moment, her little girl moved into the doorway. "Mom." Her voice trembled as she rubbed her eyes. "It's thundering. You're supposed to come get me when it thunders."

It happened fast. He turned, swinging the gun. With all her strength, Suzanna hurled herself at him, blocking his aim. "Run!" she screamed to Jenny. "Run down the hall to Holt." She shoved, and raced after her daughter. The decision had to be made the minute she hit the doorway. As she watched Jenny streak toward the right and— she hoped—safety, Suzanna plunged in the opposite direction.

He would follow her, not the child, she told herself. Because she still had the necklace. The next decision had to be made at the steps. To go down to her family and risk them. Or to go up, alone.

She was halfway up the stairs when she heard him pounding behind her. She jerked in shock as a bullet plowed into the plaster an inch from her shoulder.

Breathless, she streaked up, only now hearing the boom of thunder that had frightened Jenny and made her look for her mother. Her single thought was to put as much distance between the madman behind her and her child. Her feet clattered on the winding metal staircase that led to Bianca's tower.

His fingers darted through the open treads and snatched at her ankle. With a sound of terror and fury, she kicked out, dislodging them, then stumbled up the rest of the way. The door was shut. She nearly wept as she threw her weight against the thick wood. It gave, with painful slowness, then allowed her to fall inside. But before she could slam it closed, he was hurtling in.

She braced, certain it would be only seconds before she felt the bullet. He was panting, sweating, his eyes glazed. At the corner of his mouth, a muscle ticked and jerked. "Give it to me." The gun shook as he advanced on her. A flash of lightning had him looking wildly around the shadowy room. "Give it to me now."

He's afraid, she realized. Of this room. "You've been in here before."

He had, only once, and had run out again, terrified. There was something here, something that hated him. It crawled cold as ice along his skin. "Give me the necklace, or I'll just kill you and take it."

"This was her room," Suzanna murmured, keeping her eyes on his. "Bianca's room. She died when her husband threw her from that window."

Unable to resist, he looked at the glass, dark with gloom, then away again.

"She still comes here, to wait, and to watch the cliffs." She heard, as she had known she would, the sound of Holt racing up the steps. "She's here now. Take them." She held the emeralds out. "But she won't let you leave with them."

His face was bone white and sheened with sweat as he reached for the necklace. He gripped it, but rather than the heat Suzanna had felt, he felt only cold. And a terror.

"They're mine now." He shivered and stumbled.

"Suzanna," Holt said quietly from the doorway. "Move away from him." His weapon was drawn, gripped in both hands. "Move away," he repeated. "Slow."

She took one step back, then two, but Livingston paid no attention to her. He was wiping his gun hand over his dry lips.

"It's over," Holt told him. "Drop the gun, kick it aside." But Livingston continued to stare at the necklace, breathing raggedly. "Drop it." Braced, Holt moved closer. "Get out, Suzanna."

"No, I'm not leaving you."

He didn't have time to swear at her. Though he was prepared to kill, he could see that the man was no longer concerned with his weapon, or with escape. Instead, Livingston merely stared down at the emeralds and trembled.

With his eyes trained on Livingston, Holt reached up to grasp the wrist of his gun hand. "It's over," he said again.

"It's mine." Wild with rage and fear, Livingston lunged. He fired once into the ceiling before Holt disarmed him. Even then he struggled, but the struggle was brief. With the next crash of thunder, he howled, striking out wildly even as the others raced into the room. Disoriented or terrified, stunned by Holt's blow to his jaw or no longer sane, he whirled.

There was the crash of breaking glass. Then a sound Suzanna would never forget. A man's horrified scream. Even as Holt leaped forward to try to save him, Livingston pinwheeled through the broken window and tumbled to the rain-swept rock below.

"My God." Suzanna pressed back against the wall, her hands over her mouth to stop her own screams. There were arms around her, a babble of voices.

Her family poured into the tower room. She bent to her children, pressing kisses on their cheeks. "It's all right," she soothed. "It's all right now. There's nothing to be afraid of." She looked up at Holt. He stood facing her, the black space at his back, the glitter of emeralds at his feet. "Everything's all right now. I'm going to take you downstairs."

Holt pushed the gun back in its holster. "We'll take them down."

An hour later, when the children were soothed and sleeping, he took her by the arm and pulled her out on the terrace. All the fear and rage he'd felt since Jenny had run crying down the hallway came pouring out.

"What the hell did you think you were doing?"

"I had to keep him away from Jenny." She thought she was calm, but her hands began to shake. "I suddenly had an idea about the emeralds. It was so simple, really. And I found them. Then he was there—and Jenny. He had a gun, and God, oh God, I thought he would kill her."

"All right, all right," Holt said. Suzanna didn't choke back the tears this time, but clung to him as they shuddered out of her. "The kids are fine, Suzanna. Nobody's going to hurt them. Or you."

"I didn't know what else to do. I wasn't trying to be brave or stupid."

"You were both. I love you." He framed her face in his hands and kissed her. "Did he hurt you?"

"No." She sniffled a little and wiped her eyes. "He chased me up there, and then…he snapped. You saw how he was when you came in."

"Yeah." Two feet away from her, with a gun in his hand. Holt's fingers tightened on her shoulders. "Don't you ever scare me like that again."

"It's a deal." She rubbed her cheek against his, for comfort and for love. "It's really over now, isn't it?"

He kissed the top of her head. "It's just beginning."

Epilogue

It was late when the family gathered together in the parlor. The police had finally finished and left them alone. They were drawn together, a solid, united front beneath the portrait of Bianca.

Colleen sat, a dog at her feet, the emeralds in her lap. She had shed no tears when Suzanna had explained how and where she had found them, but took comfort in having that small, precious memory of her mother.

There was no talk of death.

Holt keep Suzanna close, his arm firm around her. The storm had passed, and the moon had risen. The parlor was washed with light. The only sound was Suzanna's soft, clear voice as she read from Bianca's journal.

She turned the last page and spoke of Bianca's thoughts as she'd prepared to hide the emeralds.

"'I didn't think of their monetary value as I took them out, held them in my hands and watched them gleam in the light of the lamp. They would be a legacy for my children, and their children, a symbol of freedom, and of hope. And with Christian, of love.

"'As dawn broke, I decided to put them, together with this journal, in a safe place until I joined Christian again.'"

Slowly, quietly Suzanna closed the book. "I think she's with him now. That they're with each other."

She smiled when Holt's fingers gripped hers. Looking around the room, she saw her sisters, the men they loved, her aunt smiling through tears, and Bianca's daughter, gazing up at the portrait that had been painted with unconquerable love.

"It was Bianca, more than the emeralds, who brought us all together. I like to think that by finding them, by bringing them back, we've helped them find each other."

Beyond the house, the moon glimmered on the cliffs far above where the sea churned and fought with the rocks. The wind whispered through the wild roses and warmed the lovers who walked there.

Megan's Mate

For Washington Romance Writers
My extended family

Chapter 1

She wasn't a risk-taker. She was always absolutely sure a step was completed before she took the next. It was part of her personality—at least it had been for nearly ten years. She'd trained herself to be practical, to be cautious. Megan O'Riley was a woman who double-checked the locks at night.

To prepare for the flight from Oklahoma to Maine, she had meticulously packed carry-on bags for herself and her son, and had arranged for the rest of their belongings to be shipped. It was foolish, she thought, to waste time at baggage claim.

The move east wasn't an impulse. She had told herself that dozens of times during the past six months. It was both a practical and an advantageous step, not only for herself, but for Kevin, too. The adjustment shouldn't be too difficult, she thought as she glanced over to the window seat where her son was dozing. They had family in Bar Harbor, and Kevin had been beside himself with ex-

citement ever since she'd told him she was considering
moving near his uncle and his half brother and sister. And
cousins, she thought. Four new babies had been born
since she and Kevin had first flown to Maine, to attend
her brother's wedding to Amanda Calhoun.

She watched him sleep, her little boy. Not so little
anymore, she realized. He was nearly nine. It would be
good for him to be a part of a big family. The Calhouns
were generous, God knew, with their affection.

She would never forget how Suzanna Calhoun Dumont, now Bradford, had welcomed her the year before.
Even knowing that Megan had been Suzanna's husband's
lover just prior to Suzanna's marriage, had borne Baxter
Dumont a child, Suzanna had been warm and open.

Of course, Megan was a poor example of the classic
other woman. She hadn't known Suzanna even existed
when she fell for Baxter. She'd been only seventeen, naive, and ready to believe all the promises and the vows
of undying love. No, she hadn't known Bax was engaged
to Suzanna Calhoun.

When she'd given birth to Baxter's child, he'd been
on his honeymoon. He had never seen or acknowledged
the son Megan O'Riley had borne him.

Years later, when fate tossed Megan's brother, Sloan,
and Suzanna's sister Amanda together, the story had
come out.

Now, through the twists and turns of fate, Megan and
her son would live in the house where Suzanna and her
sisters had grown up. Kevin would have family—a half
brother and sister, cousins, and a houseful of aunts and
uncles. And what a house.

The Towers, Megan mused. The glorious old stone
structure Kevin still called a castle. She wondered what
it would be like to live there, to work there. Now that

the renovations on The Towers Retreat were completed, a large portion of the house served as a hotel. A St. James hotel, she added thoughtfully, the brainstorm of Trenton St. James III, who had married the youngest Calhoun, Catherine.

St. James hotels were known worldwide for their quality and class. The offer to join the company as head accountant had, after much weighing and measuring, simply been too good to resist.

And she was dying to see her brother, Sloan, the rest of the family, The Towers itself.

If she was nervous, she told herself it was foolish to be. The move was a very practical, very logical step. Her new title, accounts manager, soothed frustrated ambitions, and though money had never been a problem, her new salary didn't hurt the ego, either.

And most important of all, she would have more time to spend with Kevin.

As the approach for landing was announced, Megan reached over, brushed a hand through Kevin's hair. His eyes, dark and sleepy, blinked open.

"Are we there yet?"

"Just about. Put your seat back up. Look, you can see the bay."

"We're going to go boating, right?" If he'd been fully awake, he might have remembered he was too old to bounce on his seat. But he bounced now, his face pressed to the window in his excitement. "And see whales. We'll go on Alex's new dad's boat."

The idea of boating made her stomach turn, but she smiled gamely. "You bet we will."

"And we're really going to live in that castle?" He turned back to her, her beautiful boy with his golden skin and tousled black hair.

"You'll have Alex's old room."

"And there's ghosts." He grinned, showing gaps where baby teeth had been.

"So they say. Friendly ones."

"Maybe not all of them." At least Kevin hoped not. "Alex says there's lots of them, and sometimes they moan and scream. And last year a man fell right out of the tower window and broke all his bones on the rocks."

She shuddered, knowing that part was sterling truth. The Calhoun emeralds, discovered a year before, had drawn out more than a legend and romance. They'd drawn out a thief and a murderer.

"That's over with now, Kevin. The Towers is safe."

"Yeah." But he was a boy, after all, and hoped for at least a little danger.

There was another boy who was already plotting adventures. It felt as though he'd been waiting forever at the airport gate for his brother to arrive. Alex had one hand in his mother's, the other in Jenny's—because, as his mother had told him, he was the oldest and had to keep his sister close.

His mother was holding the baby, his brand-new brother. Alex could hardly wait to show him off.

"Why aren't they here yet?"

"Because it takes time for people to get off the plane and out the gate."

"How come it's called a gate?" Jenny wanted to know. "It doesn't look like a gate."

"I think they used to have gates, so they still call them that." It was the best Suzanna could come up with after a frazzling half hour at the airport with three children in tow.

Then the baby cooed and made her smile.

"Look, Mom! There they are!"

Before Suzanna could respond, Alex had broken away and made a beeline toward Kevin, Jenny hot on his heels. She winced as they barely missed plowing into other passengers, then raised a resigned hand to wave at Megan.

"Hi!" Alex, having been schooled in airport procedure by his mother, manfully took Kevin's carry-on. "I'm supposed to take this 'cause we're picking you up." It bothered him a little that, even though his mother claimed he was growing like a weed, Kevin was still taller.

"Have you still got the fort?"

"We got the one at the big house," Alex told him. "*And* we got a new one at the cottage. We live at the cottage."

"With our dad," Jenny piped up. "We got new names and everything. He can fix anything, and he built me a new bedroom."

"It has pink curtains," Alex said with a sneer.

Knowing a brawl was dangerously close, Suzanna neatly stepped between her two children. "How was your flight?" She bent down, kissed Kevin, then straightened to kiss Megan.

"It was fine, thanks." Megan still didn't know quite how to respond to Suzanna's easy affection. There were still times she wanted to shout, *I slept with your husband. Don't you understand? Maybe he wasn't your husband yet, and I didn't know he would be, but facts are facts.* "A little delayed," she said instead. "I hope you haven't been waiting long."

"Hours," Alex claimed.

"Thirty minutes," Suzanna corrected with a laugh. "How about the rest of your stuff?"

"I had it shipped. This is it for now." Megan tapped her garment bag. Unable to resist, she peeked down at the bright-eyed baby in Suzanna's arms. He was all pink and smooth, with the dark blue eyes of a newborn and a shock of glossy black hair. She felt the foolish smile that comes over adults around babies spread over her face as he waved an impossibly small fist under her nose.

"Oh, he's beautiful. So tiny."

"He's three weeks old," Alex said importantly. "His name is Christian."

"'Cause that was our great-grandfather's name," Jenny supplied. "We have new cousins, too. Bianca and Cordelia—but we call her Delia—and Ethan."

Alex rolled his eyes. "Everybody had babies."

"He's nice," Kevin decided after a long look. "Is he my brother, too?"

"Absolutely," Suzanna said, before Megan could respond. "I'm afraid you've got an awfully big family now."

Kevin gave her a shy look and touched a testing finger to Christian's waving fist. "I don't mind."

Suzanna smiled over at Megan. "Want to trade?"

Megan hesitated a moment, then gave in. "I'd love to." She cradled the baby while Suzanna took the garment bag. "Oh, Lord." Unable to resist, she nuzzled. "It's easy to forget how tiny they are. How wonderful they smell. And you…" As they walked through the terminal, she took a good look at Suzanna. "How can you look so terrific, when you had a baby only three weeks ago?"

"Oh, bless you. I've been feeling like such a frump. Alex, no running."

"Same goes, Kevin. How's Sloan taking to fatherhood?" Megan wanted to know. "I hated not coming out when Mandy had the baby, but with selling the house and getting things in order to make the move, I just couldn't manage it.''

"Everyone understood. And Sloan's a terrific daddy. He'd have Delia strapped on his back twenty-four hours a day if Amanda let him. He designed this incredible nursery for the babies. Window seats, cubbyholes, wonderful built-in cupboards for toys. Delia and Bianca share it, and when C.C. and Trent are in town—which, since The Retreat opened, is more often than not—Ethan's in there, too.''

"It's wonderful that they'll all grow up together.'' She looked at Kevin, Alex and Jenny, thinking as much about them as about the babies.

Suzanna understood perfectly. "Yes, it is. I'm so glad you're here, Megan. It's like getting another sister.'' She watched Megan's lashes lower. Not quite ready for that, Suzanna surmised, and switched subjects. "And it's going to be a huge relief to hand over the books to you. Not only for The Retreat, but for the boat business, too.''

"I'm looking forward to it.''

Suzanna stopped by a new minivan, unlocked the doors. "Pile in,'' she told the kids, then slipped the baby out of Megan's arms. "I hope you say that after you get a look at the ledgers.'' Competently she strapped the baby into his car seat. "I'm afraid Holt's a pathetic record keeper. And Nathaniel…''

"Oh, that's right. Holt has a partner now. What did Sloan tell me? An old friend?''

"Holt and Nathaniel grew up together on the island. Nathaniel moved back a few months ago. He used to be in the merchant marine. There you go, sweetie.'' She kissed the baby, then shot an eagle eye over the rest of the children to make sure seat belts were securely buckled. She clicked the sliding door into place, then rounded the hood as Megan took the passenger seat. "He's quite a character," Suzanna said mildly. "You'll get a kick out of him."

The character was just finishing up an enormous lunch of fried chicken, potato salad and lemon meringue pie. With a sigh of satisfaction, he pushed back from the table and eyed his hostess lustfully.

"What do I have to do to get you to marry me, darling?"

She giggled, blushed and waved a hand at him. "You're such a tease, Nate."

"Who's teasing?" He rose, grabbed her fluttering hand and kissed it lavishly. She always smelled like a woman—soft, lush, glorious. He winked and skimmed his lips up to nibble on her wrist. "You know I'm crazy about you, Coco."

Cordelia Calhoun McPike gave another delighted giggle, then patted his cheek. "About my cooking."

"That, too." He grinned when she slipped away to pour him coffee. She was a hell of a woman, he thought. Tall, stately, striking. It amazed him that some smart man hadn't scooped up the widow McPike long ago. "Who do I have to fight off this week?"

"Now that The Retreat's open, I don't have time for romance." She might have sighed over it if she wasn't so pleased with her life. All her darling girls were married and happy, with babies of their own. She had grandnieces and grandnephews to spoil, nephews-in-law to coddle, and, most surprising of all, a full-fledged career as head chef for the St. James Towers Retreat. She offered Nathaniel the coffee and, because she caught him eyeing the pie, cut him another slice.

"You read my mind."

Now she did sigh a little. There was nothing quite so comforting to Coco as watching a man enjoy her food. And he was some man. When Nathaniel Fury rolled back into town, people had noticed. Who could overlook tall, dark and handsome? Certainly not Coco McPike. Particularly not when the combination came with smoky gray eyes, a cleft chin and wonderfully golden skin over sharp cheekbones—not to mention considerable charm.

The black T-shirt and jeans he wore accented an athletic, rangy body—broad shoulders, muscular arms, narrow hips.

Then there was that aura of mystery, a touch of the exotic. It went deeper than his looks, though the dark eyes and the waving mane of deep mahogany hair was exotic enough. It was a matter of presence, she supposed, the culmination of what he'd done and what had touched him in all those years he traveled to foreign ports.

If she'd been twenty years younger... Well, she thought, patting her rich chestnut hair, maybe ten.

But she wasn't, so she had given Nathaniel the place in her heart of the son she'd never had. She was determined to find the right woman for him and see him settled happily. Like her beautiful girls.

Since she felt she had personally arranged the romances and resulting unions of all four of her nieces, she was confident she could do the same for Nathaniel.

"I did your chart last night," she said casually, and checked the fish stew she had simmering for tonight's menu.

"Oh, yeah?" He scooped up more pie. God, the woman could cook.

"You're entering a new phase of your life, Nate."

He'd seen too much of the world to totally dismiss astrology—or anything else. So he smiled at her. "I'd

say you're on target there, Coco. Got myself a business,
a house on land, retired my seabag.''

"No, this phase is more personal." She wiggled her
slim brows. "It has to do with Venus."

He grinned at that. "So, are you going to marry me?"

She wagged a finger at him. "You're going to say that
to someone, quite seriously, before the summer's over.
Actually, I saw you falling in love twice. I'm not quite
sure what that means." Her forehead wrinkled as she
considered. "It didn't really seem as if you'd have to
choose, though there was quite a bit of interference. Perhaps even danger."

"If a guy falls for two women, he's asking for trouble." And Nathaniel was content, at least for the moment,
to have no females in his life. Women simply didn't
come without expectations, and he planned to fulfill none
but his own. "And since my heart already belongs to
you…" He got up to go to the stove and kiss her cheek.

The tornado blew in without warning. The kitchen
door slammed open, and three shrieking whirlwinds spun
through.

"Aunt Coco! They're here!"

"Oh, my." Coco pressed a hand to her speeding heart.
"Alex, you took a year off my life." But she smiled,
studying the dark-eyed boy beside him. "Can this be
Kevin? You've grown a foot! Don't you have a kiss for
Aunt Coco?"

"Yes, ma'am." He went forward dutifully, still unsure
of his ground. He was enveloped against soft breasts, in
soft scents. It eased his somewhat nervous stomach.

"We're so glad you're here." Coco's eyes teared up
sentimentally. "Now the whole family's in one place.
Kevin, this is Mr. Fury. Nate, my grandnephew."

Nathaniel knew the story, how the scum Baxter Dumont had managed to get some naive kid pregnant shortly before he married Suzanna. The boy was eyeing him now, nervous but contained. Nathaniel realized Kevin knew the story, as well—or part of it.

"Welcome to Bar Harbor." He offered his hand, which Kevin took politely.

"Nate runs the boat shop and stuff with my dad." The novelty of saying "my dad" had yet to wear thin with Alex. "Kevin wants to see whales," he told Nathaniel. "He comes from Oklahoma, and they don't have any. They hardly have any water at all."

"We've got some." Kevin automatically defended his homeland. "And we've got cowboys," he added, one-upping Alex. "You don't have any of those."

"Uh-huh." This from Jenny. "I got a whole cowboy suit."

"Girl," Alex corrected. "It's a cowgirl, 'cause you're a girl."

"It is not."

"Is too."

Her eyes narrowed dangerously. "Is not."

"Well, I see everything's normal in here." Suzanna entered, aiming a warning look at both of her children. "Hello, Nate. I didn't expect to see you here."

"I got lucky." He slipped an arm around Coco's shoulders. "Spent an hour with my woman."

"Flirting with Aunt Coco again?" But Suzanna noted that his gaze had already shifted. She remembered that look from the first time they'd met. The way the gray eyes measured, assessed. Automatically she put a hand on Megan's arm. "Megan O'Riley, Nathaniel Fury, Holt's partner—and Aunt Coco's latest conquest."

"Nice to meet you." She was tired, Megan realized. Had to be, if that clear, steady gaze put her back up. She dismissed him, a little too abruptly for politeness, and smiled at Coco. "You look wonderful."

"Oh, and here I am in my apron. I didn't even freshen up." Coco gave her a hard, welcoming hug. "Let me fix you something. You must be worn-out after the flight."

"Just a little."

"We took the bags up, and I put Christian in the nursery." While Suzanna herded the children to the table and chatted, Nathaniel took a good long survey of Megan O'Riley.

Cool as an Atlantic breeze, he decided. A little frazzled and unnerved at the moment, he thought, but not willing to show it. The peach-toned skin and long, waving strawberry blond hair made an eye-catching combination.

Nathaniel usually preferred women who were dark and sultry, but there was something to be said for all that rose and gold. She had blue eyes, the color of a calm sea at dawn. Stubborn mouth, he mused, though it softened nicely when she smiled at her son.

A bit on the skinny side, he thought as he finished off his coffee. Needed some of Coco's cooking to help her fill out. Or maybe she just looked skinny—and prim—because she wore such a severely tailored jacket and slacks.

Well aware of his scrutiny, Megan forced herself to keep up her end of the conversation with Coco and the rest. She'd grown used to stares years before, when she was young, unmarried, and pregnant by another woman's husband.

She knew how some men reacted to her status as a single mother, how they assumed she was an easy mark. And she knew how to disabuse them of the notion.

She met Nathaniel's stare levelly, frostily. He didn't

look away, as most would, but continued to watch her, unblinkingly, until her teeth clenched.

Good going, he thought. She might be skinny, but she had grit. He grinned, lifted his coffee mug in a silent toast, then turned to Coco. "I've got to go, got a tour to do. Thanks for lunch, Coco."

"Don't forget dinner. The whole family will be here. Eight o'clock."

He glanced back at Megan. "Wouldn't miss it."

"See that you don't." Coco looked at her watch, closed her eyes. "Where is that man? He's late again."

"The Dutchman?"

"Who else? I sent him to the butcher's two hours ago."

Nathaniel shrugged. His former shipmate, and The Towers' new assistant chef, ran on his own timetable. "If I see him down at the docks, I'll send him along."

"Kiss me goodbye," Jenny demanded, delighted when Nathaniel hauled her up.

"You're the prettiest cowboy on the island," he whispered in her ear. Jenny shot a smug look at her brother when her feet touched the floor again. "You let me know when you're ready for a sail," he said to Kevin. "Nice meeting you, Ms. O'Riley."

"Nate's a sailor," Jenny said importantly when Nathaniel strolled out. "He's been everywhere and done everything."

Megan didn't doubt it for a minute.

So much had changed at The Towers, though the family rooms on the first two floors and the east wing were much the same. Trent St. James, with Megan's brother, Sloan, as architect, had concentrated most of the time and effort on the ten suites in the west wing, the new guest dining area and the west tower. All of that area comprised the hotel.

From the quick tour Megan was given, she could see that none of the time and effort that had gone into the construction and renovations had been wasted.

Sloan had designed with an appreciation for the original fortresslike structure, retaining the high-ceilinged rooms and circular stairs, ensuring that the many fireplaces were working, preserving the mullioned windows and French doors that led out onto terraces, balconies, parapets.

The lobby was sumptuous, filled with antiques and designed with a multitude of cozy corners that invited guests to lounge on a rainy or wintry day. The spectacular views of bay or cliffs or sea or Suzanna's fabulous gardens were there to be enjoyed, or tempted guests to stroll out onto terraces and balconies.

When Amanda, as hotel manager, took over the tour, Megan was told that each suite was unique. The storage rooms of The Towers had been full of old furniture, mementos and art. What hadn't been sold prior to Trent's having invested the St. James money in the transformation now graced the guest rooms.

Some suites were two levels, with an art deco staircase connecting the rooms, some had wainscoting or silk wallpaper. There was an Aubusson rug here, an old tapestry there. And all the rooms were infused with the legend of the Calhoun emeralds and the woman who had owned them.

The emeralds themselves, discovered after a difficult and dangerous search—some said with the help of the spirits of Bianca Calhoun and Christian Bradford, the artist who had loved her—resided now in a glass case in the lobby. Above the case was a portrait of Bianca, painted by Christian more than eighty years before.

"They're gorgeous," Megan whispered. "Stunning." The tiers of grass green emeralds and white diamonds almost pulsed with life.

"Sometimes I'll just stop and look at them," Amanda admitted, "and remember all we went through to find them. How Bianca tried to use them to escape with her children to Christian. It should make me sad, I suppose, but having them here, under her portrait, seems right."

"Yes, it does." Megan could feel the pull of them, even through the glass. "But isn't it risky, having them out here this way?"

"Holt arranged for security. Having an ex-cop in the family means nothing's left to chance. The glass is bulletproof." Amanda tapped her finger against it. "And wired to some high-tech sensor." Amanda checked her watch and judged that she had fifteen minutes before she had to resume her managerial duties. "I hope your rooms are all right. We've barely scratched the surface on the family renovations."

"They're fine." And the truth was, it relaxed Megan a bit to see cracked plaster and gnawed woodwork. It made it all less intimidating. "Kevin's in paradise. He's outside with Alex and Jenny, playing with the new puppy."

"Our Fred and Holt's Sadie are quite the proud parents." With a laugh, Amanda tossed back her swing of sable hair. "Eight pups."

"As Alex said, everyone's having babies. And your Delia is beautiful."

"She is, isn't she?" Maternal pride glowed in Amanda's eyes. "I can't believe how much she's grown already. You should have been around here six months ago. All four of us out to here." She laughed again as she held out her arms. "Waddling everywhere. The men strutting. Do you know they took bets to see if Lilah or I would deliver first? She beat me by two days." And since she'd bet twenty on herself, it still irritated her a little. "It's the first time I've known her to be in a hurry about anything."

"Her Bianca's beautiful, too. She was awake and howling for attention when I was in the nursery. Your nanny has her hands full."

"Mrs. Billows can handle anything."

"Actually, I wasn't thinking about the babies. It was Max." She grinned remembering how Bianca's daddy had come running in, abandoning his new novel on the typewriter to scoop his daughter out of her crib.

"He's such a softie."

"Who's a softie?" Sloan strode into the room to swing his sister off her feet.

"Not you, O'Riley," Amanda murmured, watching the way his face softened like butter as he pressed his cheek to Megan's.

"You're here." He twirled her again. "I'm so glad you're here, Meg."

"Me too." She felt her eyes tear and squeezed him tight. "Daddy."

With a laugh, he set her down, slipped his free arm around his wife. "Did you see her yet?"

Megan feigned ignorance. "Who?"

"My girl. My Delia."

"Oh, her." Megan shrugged, chuckled, then kissed Sloan on his sulking mouth. "Not only did I see her, I held her, I sniffed her, and have already decided to spoil her at every opportunity. She's gorgeous, Sloan. She looks just like Amanda."

"Yeah, she does." He kissed his wife. "Except she's got my chin."

"That's a Calhoun chin," Amanda claimed.

"Nope, it's O'Riley all the way. And speaking of O'Rileys," he continued, before Amanda could argue, "where's Kevin?"

"Outside. I should probably go get him. We haven't even unpacked yet."

"We'll go with you," Sloan said.

"You go. I'm covering." Even as Amanda spoke, the phone on the mahogany front desk rang. "Break's over. See you at dinner, Megan." She leaned up to kiss Sloan again. "See you sooner, O'Riley."

"Mmm…" Sloan gave a satisfied sigh as he watched his wife stride off. "I do love the way that woman eats up the floor."

"You look at her just the way you did a year ago, at your wedding." Megan tucked her hand in his as they walked out of the lobby and onto the stone terrace steps. "It's nice."

"She's…" He searched for a word, then settled on the simplest truth. "Everything. I'd like you to be as happy as I am, Megan."

"I am happy." A breeze flitted through her hair. On it carried the sound of children's laughter. "Hearing that makes me happy. So does being here." They descended another level and turned west. "I have to admit I'm a little nervous. It's such a big step." She saw her son scramble to the top of the fort in the yard below, arms raised high in victory. "This is good for him."

"And you?"

"And me." She leaned against her brother. "I'll miss Mom and Dad, but they've already said that with both of us out here, it gives them twice as much reason to visit twice as often.'' She pushed the blowing hair from her face while Kevin played sniper, fighting off Alex and Jenny's assault on the fort. "He needs to know the rest of his family. And I...needed a change. And as to that—'' she looked back at Sloan ''—I tried to get Amanda to show me the setup.''

"And she told you that you couldn't sharpen your pencils for a week.''

"Something like that.''

"We decided at the last family meeting that you'd have a week to settle in before you started hammering the adding machine.''

"I don't need a week. I only need—''

"I know, I know. You'd give Amanda a run for the efficiency crown. But orders are you take a week off.''

She arched a brow. "And just who gives the orders around here?''

"Everybody.'' Sloan grinned. "That's what makes it interesting.''

Thoughtful, she looked out to sea. The sky was as clear as blown glass, and the breeze warm with early summer. From her perch at the wall, she could see the small clumps of islands far out in the diamond-bright water.

A different world, she thought, from the plains and prairies of home. A different life, perhaps, for her and her son.

A week. To relax, to explore, to take excursions with Kevin. Tempting, yes. But far from responsible. "I want to pull my weight.''

"You will, believe me.'' He glanced out at the clear sound of a boat horn. "That's one of Holt and Nate's,'' Sloan told her, pointing to the long terraced boat that was gliding across the water. "The *Mariner*. Takes tourists out for whale-watching.''

The kids were all atop the fort now, shouting and waving at the boat. When the horn blasted again, they cheered.

"You'll meet Nate at dinner," Sloan began.

"I met him already."

"Flirting a meal out of Coco?"

"It appeared that way."

Sloan shook his head. "That man can eat, let me tell you. What did you think?"

"Not much," she muttered. "He seemed a little rough-edged to me."

"You get used to him. He's one of the family now."

Megan made a noncommittal sound. Maybe he was, but that didn't mean he was part of hers.

Chapter 2

As far as Coco was concerned, Niels Van Horne was a
thoroughly unpleasant man. He did not take constructive
criticism, or the subtlest of suggestions for improvement,
well at all. She tried to be courteous, God knew, as he
was a member of the staff of The Towers and an old,
dear friend of Nathaniel's.

But the man was a thorn in her side, an abrasive grain
of sand in the cozy slipper of her contentment.

In the first place, he was simply too big. The hotel
kitchen was gloriously streamlined and organized. She
and Sloan had worked in tandem on the design, so that
the finished product would suit her specifications and
needs. She adored her huge stove, her convection and
conventional ovens, the glint of polished stainless steel
and glossy white counters, and her whisper-silent dish-
washer. She loved the smells of cooking, the hum of her
exhaust fans, the sparkling cleanliness of her tile floor.

And there was Van Horne—or Dutch, as he was

called—a bull in her china shop, with his redwood-size shoulders and cinder-block arms rippling with tattoos. He refused to wear the neat white bib aprons she'd ordered, with their elegant blue lettering, preferring his rolled-up shirts and tatty jeans held up by a hank of rope.

His salt-and-pepper hair was tied back in a stubby ponytail, and his face, usually scowling, was as big as the rest of him, scored with lines around his light green eyes. His nose, broken several times in the brawls he seemed so proud of, was mashed and crooked. His skin was brown, and leathery as an old saddle.

And his language… Well, Coco didn't consider herself a prude, but she was, after all, a lady.

But the man could cook. It was his only redeeming quality.

As Dutch worked at the stove, she supervised the two line chefs. The specials tonight were her New England fish stew and stuffed trout *à la franqise*. Everything appeared to be in order.

"Mr. Van Horne," she began, in a tone that never failed to put his back up. "You will be in charge while I'm downstairs. I don't foresee any problems, but should any arise, I'll be in the family dining room."

He cast one of his sneering looks over his shoulder. Woman was all slicked up tonight, like she was going to some opera or something, he thought. All red silk and pearls. He wanted to snort, but knew her damned perfume would interfere with the pleasure he gained from the smell of his curried rice.

"I cooked for three hundred men," he said in his raspy, sandpaper-edged voice, "I can deal with a couple dozen pasty-faced tourists."

"Our guests," she said between her teeth, "may be

slightly more discriminating than sailors trapped on some
rusty boat.''

One of the busboys swung through, carrying plates.
Dutch's eyes zeroed in on one that still held half an en-
trée. On *his* ship, men had cleaned their plates. ''Not too
damn hungry, were they?''

''Mr. Van Horne.'' Coco drew air through her nose.
''You will remain in the kitchen at all times. I will not
have you going out into the dining room again and be-
rating our guests over their eating habits. A bit more gar-
nish on that salad, please,'' she said to one of the line
chefs, and glided out the door.

''Can't stand fancy-faced broads,'' Dutch muttered.
And if it wasn't for Nate, he thought sourly, Dutch Van
Horne wouldn't be taking orders from a dame.

Nathaniel didn't share his former shipmate's disdain of
women. He loved them, one and all. He enjoyed their
looks, their smells, their voices, and was more than satisfied to settle in the family parlor with six of the best-
looking women it had been his pleasure to meet.

The Calhoun women were a constant delight to him.
Suzanna, with her soft eyes, Lilah's lazy sexuality,
Amanda's brisk practicality, C.C.'s cocky grin, not to
mention Coco's feminine elegance.

They made The Towers Nathaniel's little slice of
heaven.

And the sixth woman… He sipped his whiskey and
water as he watched Megan O'Riley. Now there was a
package he thought might be full of surprises. In the
looks department, she didn't take second place to the fabulous Calhouns. And her voice, with its slow Oklahoma
drawl, added its own appeal. What she lacked, he mused,
was the easy warmth that flowed from the other women.

He hadn't decided as yet whether it was the result of a cold nature or simple shyness. Whatever it was, it ran deep. It was hard to be cold or shy in a room filled with laughing people, cooing babies and wrestling children.

He was holding one of his favorite females at the moment. Jenny was bouncing on his lap and barraging him with questions.

"Are you going to marry Aunt Coco?"

"She won't have me."

"I will." Jenny beamed up at him, an apprentice heart-breaker with a missing front tooth. "We can get married in the garden, like Mom and Daddy did. Then you can come live with us."

"Now that's the best offer I've had in a long time." He stroked a callused finger down her cheek.

"But you have to wait until I get big."

"It's always wise to make a man wait." This from Lilah, who slouched on a sofa, her head in the crook of her husband's arm, a baby in her own. "Don't let him rush you into anything, Jenny. Slow is always best."

"She'd know," Amanda commented. "Lilah's spent her life studying slow."

"I'm not ready to give up my girl." Holt scooped Jenny up. "Especially to a broken-down sailor."

"I can outpilot you blindfolded, Bradford."

"Nuh-uh." Alex popped up to defend the family honor. "Daddy sails the best. He can sail better than anybody. Even if bad guys were shooting at him." Territorial, Alex wrapped an arm around Holt's leg. "He even got shot. He's got a bullet hole in him."

Holt grinned at his friend. "Get your own cheering gallery, Nate."

"Did you ever get shot?" Alex wanted to know.

"Can't say that I have." Nathaniel swirled his whiskey. "But there was this Greek in Corfu that wanted to slit my throat."

Alex's eyes widened until they were like saucers. From his spot on the rug, Kevin inched closer. "Really?" Alex looked for signs of knife wounds. He knew Nathaniel had a tattoo of a fire-breathing dragon on his shoulder, but this was even better. "Did you stab him back and kill him dead?"

"Nope." Nathaniel caught the look of doubt and disapproval in Megan's eyes. "He missed and caught me in the shoulder, and the Dutchman knocked him cold with a bottle of ouzo."

Desperately impressed, Kevin slid closer. "Have you got a scar?"

"Sure do."

Amanda slapped Nathaniel's hand before he could tug up his shirt. "Cut it out, or every man in the room will be stripping to show off war wounds. Sloan's really proud of the one he got from barbed wire."

"It's a beaut," Sloan agreed. "But Meg's is even better."

"Shut up, Sloan."

"Hey, a man's gotta brag on his only sister." Enjoying himself, Sloan draped an arm around her shoulders. "She was twelve—hardheaded little brat. We had a mustang stallion nearly as bad-tempered as she was. She snuck him out one day, determined that she could break him. Well, she got about a half a mile before he shook her off."

"He did not shake me off," Megan said primly. "The bridle snapped."

"That's her story." Sloan gave her a quick squeeze. "Fact is, that horse tossed her right into a barbed-wire fence. She landed on her rump. I don't believe you sat down for six weeks.''

"It was two," she said, but her lips twitched.

"Got herself a hell of a scar." Sloan gave her butt a brotherly pat.

"Wouldn't mind taking a look at it," Nathaniel said under his breath, and earned an arched-eyebrow look from Suzanna.

"I think I'll put Christian down before dinner."

"Good idea." C.C. took Ethan from Trent just as the baby began to fuss. "Somebody's hungry."

"I know I am." Lilah rose.

Megan watched mothers and babies head upstairs to nurse, and was surprised by a quick tug of envy. Funny, she mused, she hadn't even thought of having more babies until she came here and found herself surrounded by them.

"So sorry I'm late." Coco glided into the room, patting her hair. "We had a few problems in the kitchen."

Nathaniel recognized the look of frustration on her face and fought back a grin. "Dutch giving you trouble, darling?"

"Well…" She didn't like to complain. "We simply have different views on how things should be done. Oh, bless you, Trent," she said when he offered her a glass. "Oh, dear, where is my head? I forgot the canapés."

"I'll get them." Max unfolded himself from the sofa and headed toward the family kitchen.

"Thank you, dear. Now…" She took Megan's hand, squeezed. "We've hardly had a moment to talk. What do you think of The Retreat?"

"It's wonderful, everything Sloan said it would be. Amanda tells me all ten suites are booked."

"It's been a wonderful first season." She beamed at

Trent. "Hardly more than a year ago, I was in despair, so afraid my girls would lose their home. Though the cards told me differently. Did I ever tell you that I foresaw Trent in the tarot? I really must do a spread for you, dear, and see what your future holds."

"Well..."

"Perhaps I can just look at your palm."

Megan let go with a sigh of relief when Max came back with a tray and distracted Coco.

"Not interested in the future?" Nathaniel murmured.

Megan glanced over, surprised that he had moved beside her without her being aware of it. "I'm more interested in the present, one step at a time."

"A cynic." He took her hand and, though it went rigid in his, turned it palm up. "I met an old woman on the west coast of Ireland. Molly Duggin was her name. She said I had the sight." His smoky eyes stayed level with hers for a long moment before they shifted to her open palm. Megan felt something skitter down her spine. "A stubborn hand. Self-sufficient, for all its elegance."

He traced a finger over it. Now there was more than a skitter. There was a jolt.

"I don't believe in palmistry."

"You don't have to. Shy," he said quietly. "I wondered about that. The passions are there, but repressed." His thumb glided gently over her palm's mound of Venus. "Or channeled. You'd prefer to say channeled. Goal-oriented, practical. You'd rather make decisions with your head, no matter what your heart tells you." His eyes lifted to hers again. "How close am I?"

Much too close, she thought, but drew her hand coolly from his. "An interesting parlor game, Mr. Fury."

His eyes laughed at her as he tucked his thumbs in his pockets. "Isn't it?"

* * *

By noon the next day, Megan had run out of busywork. She hadn't the heart to refuse Kevin's plea to be allowed to spend the day with the Bradfords, though his departure had left her very much to her own devices.

She simply wasn't used to free time.

One trip to the hotel lobby had aborted her idea of convincing Amanda to let her study the books and files. Amanda, she was told by a cheerful desk clerk, was in the west tower, handling a small problem.

Coco wasn't an option, either. Megan had halted just outside the door of the kitchen when she heard the crash of pots and raised voices inside.

Since Lilah had gone back to work as a naturalist in the park, and C.C. was at her automotive shop in town, Megan was left on her own.

In a house as enormous as The Towers, she felt like the last living soul on the island.

She could read, she mused, or sit in the sun on one of the terraces and contemplate the view. She could wander down to the first floor of the family area and check out the progress of the renovations. And harass Sloan and Trent, she thought with a sigh, as they tried to get some work done.

She didn't consider disturbing Max in his studio, knowing he was working on his book. As she'd already spent an hour in the nursery playing with the babies, she felt another visit was out.

She wandered her room, smoothed down the already smooth coverlet on the marvelous four-poster. The rest of her things had arrived that morning, and in her perhaps too-efficient way, she'd already unpacked. Her clothes were neatly hung in the rosewood armoire or folded in the Chippendale bureau. Framed photos of her family smiled from the gateleg table under the window.

Her shoes were aligned, her jewelry was tucked away and her books were stored on the shelf.

And if she didn't find something to do, she would go mad.

With this in mind, she picked up her briefcase, checked the contents one last time and headed outside, to the car Sloan had left at her disposal.

The sedan ran like a top, courtesy of C.C.'s mechanical skills. Megan drove down the winding road toward the village.

She enjoyed the bright blue water of the bay, and the colorful throngs of tourists strolling up and down the sloped streets. But the glistening wares in the shop windows didn't tempt her to stop and do any strolling of her own.

Shopping was something she did out of necessity, not for pleasure.

Once, long ago, she'd loved the idle pleasure of window-shopping, the careless satisfaction of buying for fun. She'd enjoyed empty, endless summer days once, with nothing more to do than watch clouds or listen to the wind.

But that was before innocence had been lost, and responsibilities found.

She saw the sign for Shipshape Tours by the docks. There were a couple of small boats in drydock, but the *Mariner* and its sister ship, the *Island Queen,* were nowhere to be seen.

Her brows knit in annoyance. She'd hoped to catch Holt before he took one of the tours out. Still, there was no reason she couldn't poke inside the little tin-roofed building that housed the offices. After all, Shipshape was now one of her clients.

Megan pulled the sedan behind a long, long T-Bird

convertible. She had to admire the lines of the car, and the glossy black paint job that highlighted the white interior.

She paused a moment, shielding her eyes as she watched a two-masted schooner glide over the water, its rust-colored sails full, its decks dotted with people.

There was no denying the beauty of the spot, though the smell and look of the water was so foreign, compared to what she'd known most of her life. The midday breeze was fresh and carried the scent of the sea and the aromas of lunch from the restaurants nearby.

She could be happy here, she told herself. No, she *would* be happy here. Resolutely she turned toward the building and rapped on the door.

"Yeah. It's open."

There was Nathaniel, his feet propped on a messy and ancient metal desk, a phone at his ear. His jeans were torn at the knee and smeared with something like motor oil. His mane of dark mahogany hair was tousled by the wind, or his hands. He crooked his finger in a come-ahead gesture, his eyes measuring her as he spoke on the phone.

"Teak's your best bet. I've got enough in stock, and can have the deck finished in two days. No, the engine just needed an overhaul. It's got a lot of life left in it. No problem." He picked up a smoldering cigar. "I'll give you a call when we're finished."

He hung up the phone, clamped the cigar between his teeth. Funny, he thought, Megan O'Riley had floated into his brain that morning, looking very much as she did at this moment. All spit and polish, that pretty rose-gold hair all tucked up, her face calm and cool.

"Just in the neighborhood?" he asked.

"I was looking for Holt."

"He's out with the *Queen*." Idly Nathaniel checked the diver's watch on his wrist. "Won't be back for about an hour and a half." His cocky mouth quirked up. "Looks like you're stuck with me."

She fought back the urge to shift her briefcase from hand to hand, to back away. "I'd like to see the books."

Nathaniel took a lazy puff on his cigar. "Thought you were on vacation."

She fell back on her best defense. Disdain. "Is there a problem with the books?" she said frostily.

"Couldn't prove it by me." In a fluid move, he reached down and opened a drawer in the desk. He took out a black-bound ledger. "You're the expert." He held it out to her. "Pull up a chair, Meg."

"Thank you." She took a folding chair on the other side of the desk, then slipped dark-framed reading glasses from her briefcase. Once they were on, she opened the ledger. Her accountant's heart contracted in horror at the mess of figures, cramped margin notes and scribbled-on Post-its®. "These are your books?"

"Yeah." She looked prim and efficient in her practical glasses and scooped-up hair. She made his mouth water. "Holt and I sort of take turns with them—that's since Suzanna tossed up her hands and called us idiots." He smiled charmingly. "We figured, you know, with her being pregnant at the time, she didn't need any more stress."

"Hmmm…" Megan was already turning pages. For her, the state of the bookkeeping didn't bring on anxiety so much as a sense of challenge. "Your files?"

"We got 'em." Nathaniel jerked a thumb at the dented metal cabinet shoved in the corner. There was a small, greasy boat motor on top of it.

"Is there anything in them?" she said pleasantly.

"Last I looked there was." He couldn't help it. The more prim and efficient her voice, the more he wanted to razz her.

"Invoices?"

"Sure."

"Expense receipts?"

"Absolutely." He reached in another drawer and took out a large cigar box. "We got plenty of receipts."

She took the box, opened the lid and sighed. "This is how you run your business?"

"No. We run the business by taking people out to sea, or repairing their boats. Even building them." He leaned forward on the desk, mostly so he could catch a better whiff of that soft, elusive scent that clung to her skin. "Me, I've never been much on paperwork, and Holt had his fill of it when he was on the force." His smile spread. He didn't figure she wore prim glasses, pulled-back hair and buttoned-up blouses so that a man would yearn to toss aside, muss up and unbutton. But the result was the same. "Maybe that's why the accountant we hired to do the taxes this year developed this little tic." He tapped a finger beside his left eye. "I heard he moved to Jamaica to sell straw baskets."

She had to laugh. "I'm made of sterner stuff, I promise you."

"Never doubted it." He leaned back again, his swivel chair squeaking. "You've got a nice smile, Megan. When you use it."

She knew that tone, lightly flirtatious, unmistakably male. Her defenses locked down like a vault. "You're not paying me for my smile."

"I'd rather it came free, anyhow. How'd you come to be an accountant?"

"I'm good with numbers." She spread the ledger on

the desk before opening her briefcase and taking out a calculator.

"So's a bookie. I mean, why'd you pick it?"

"Because it's a solid, dependable career." She began to run numbers, hoping to ignore him.

"And because numbers only add up one way?"

She couldn't ignore that—the faint hint of amusement in his voice. She slanted him a look, adjusted her glasses. "Accounting may be logical, Mr. Fury, but logic doesn't eliminate surprises."

"If you say so. Listen, we may have both come through the side door into the Calhouns' extended family, but we're there. Don't you feel stupid calling me Mr. Fury?"

Her smile had all the warmth of an Atlantic gale. "No, I don't."

"Is it me, or all men, you're determined to beat off with icicles?"

Patience, which she'd convinced herself she held in great store, was rapidly being depleted. "I'm here to do the books. That's all I'm here for."

"Never had a client for a friend?" He took a last puff on the cigar and stubbed it out. "You know, there's a funny thing about me."

"I'm sure you're about to tell me what it is."

"Right. I can have a pleasant conversation with a woman without being tempted to toss her on the floor and tear her clothes off. Now, you're a real treat to look at, Meg, but I can control my more primitive urges— especially when all the signals say stop."

Now she felt ridiculous. She'd been rude, or nearly so, since the moment she'd met him. Because, she admitted to herself, her reaction to him made her uncomfortable.

But, damn it, he was the one who kept looking at her as though he'd like to nibble away.

"I'm sorry." The apology was sincere, if a trifle stiff. "I'm making a lot of adjustments right now, so I haven't felt very congenial. And the way you look at me puts me on edge."

"Fair enough. But I have to tell you I figure it's a man's right to look. Anything more takes an invitation—of one kind or the other."

"Then we can clear the air and start over, since I can tell you I won't be putting out the welcome mat. Now, Nathaniel—" it was a concession she made with a smile "—do you suppose you could dig up your tax returns?"

"I can probably put my hands on them." He scooted back his chair. The squeak of the wheels ended on a high-pitched yelp that had Megan jolting and scattering papers. "Damn it—forgot you were back there." He picked up a wriggling, whimpering black puppy. "He sleeps a lot, so I end up stepping on him or running the damn chair over his tail," he said to Megan as the pup licked frantically at his face. "Whenever I try to leave him home, he cries until I give in and bring him with me."

"He's darling." Her fingers were already itching to stroke. "He looks a lot like the one Coco has."

"Same litter." Because he could read the sentiment in Megan's eyes perfectly, Nathaniel handed the pup across the desk.

"Oh, aren't you sweet? Aren't you pretty?"

When she cooed to the dog, all defenses dropped, Nathaniel noted. She forgot to be businesslike and cool, and instead was all feminine warmth—those pretty hands stroking the pup's fur, her smile soft, her eyes alight with pleasure.

He had to remind himself the invitation was for a dog, not for him.

"What's his name?"

"Dog."

She looked up from the puppy's adoring eyes. "Dog? That's it?"

"He likes it. Hey, Dog." At the sound of his master's voice, Dog immediately cocked his head at Nathaniel and barked. "See?"

"Yes." She laughed and nuzzled. "It seems a bit unimaginative."

"On the contrary. How many dogs do you know named Dog?"

"I stand corrected. Down you go, and don't get any ideas about these receipts."

Nathaniel tossed a ball, and Dog gave joyful chase. "That'll keep him busy," he said as he came around the desk to help her gather up the scattered papers.

"You don't seem the puppy type to me."

"Always wanted one." He crouched down beside her and began to toss papers back into the cigar box. "Fact is, I used to play around with one of Dog's ancestors over at the Bradfords', when I was a kid. But it's hard to keep a dog aboard a ship. Got a bird, though."

"A bird?"

"A parrot I picked up in the Caribbean about five years ago. That's another reason I bring Dog along with me. Bird might eat him."

"Bird?" She glanced up, but the laugh froze in her throat. Why was he always closer than she anticipated? And why did those long, searching looks of his slide along her nerve ends like stroking fingers?

His gaze dropped to her mouth. The hesitant smile was still there, he noted. There was something very appealing about that touch of shyness, all wrapped up in stiff-necked confidence. Her eyes weren't cool now, but wary. Not an invitation, he reminded himself, but close. And damn tempting.

Testing his ground, he reached out to tuck a stray curl behind her ear. She was on her feet like a woman shot out of a cannon.

"You sure spook easily, Megan." After closing the lid on the cigar box, he rose. "But I can't say it isn't rewarding to know I make you nervous."

"You don't." But she didn't look at him as she said it. She'd never been a good liar. "I'm going to take all this back with me, if you don't mind. Once I have things organized, I'll be in touch with you, or Holt."

"Fine." The phone rang. He ignored it. "You know where to find us."

"Once I have the books in order, we'll need to set up a proper filing system."

Grinning, he eased a hip onto the corner of the desk. Lord, she was something. "You're the boss, sugar."

She snapped her briefcase closed. "No, you're the boss. And don't call me 'sugar.'" She marched outside, slipped into her car and eased away from the building and back into traffic. Competently she drove through the village, toward The Towers. Once she'd reached the bottom of the long, curving road that led home, she pulled the car over and stopped.

She needed a moment, she thought, before she faced anyone. With her eyes closed, she rested her head against the back of the seat. Her insides were still jittering, dancing with butterflies that willpower alone couldn't seem to swat away.

The weakness infuriated her. Nathaniel Fury infuriated her. After all this time, she mused, all this effort, it had taken no more than a few measuring looks to remind her, all too strongly, that she was still a woman.

Worse, much worse, she was sure he knew exactly what he was doing and how it affected her.

She'd been susceptible to a handsome face and smooth words before. Unlike those who loved her, she refused to blame her youth and inexperience for her reckless actions. Once upon a time, she'd listened to her heart, had believed absolutely in happy-ever-after. But no longer. Now she knew there were no princes, no pumpkins, no castles in the air. There was only reality, one a woman had to make for herself—and sometimes had to make for her child, as well.

She didn't want her pulse to race or her muscles to tense. She didn't want to feel that hot little curl in her stomach that was a yearning hunger crying to be filled. Not now. Not ever again.

All she wanted was to be a good mother to Kevin, to provide him with a happy, loving home. To earn her own way through her own skills. She wanted so badly to be strong and smart and self-sufficient.

Letting out a long sigh, she smiled to herself. And invulnerable.

Well, she might not quite achieve that, but she would be sensible. Never again would she permit a man the power to alter her life—and certainly not because he'd made her glands stand at attention.

Calmer, more confident, she started the car. She had work to do.

Chapter 3

"Have a heart, Mandy." Megan had sought her sister-in-law out the moment she returned to The Towers. "I just want to get a feel for my office and the routine."

Cocking her head, Amanda leaned back from her own pile of paperwork. "Horrible when everyone's busy and you're not, isn't it?"

Megan let out a heartfelt sigh. A kindred spirit. "Awful."

"Sloan wants you to relax," Amanda began, then laughed when Megan rolled her eyes. "But what does he know? Come on." Ready to oblige, she pushed back from the desk, skirted it. "You're practically next door." She led the way down the corridor to another thick, ornately carved door. "I think you've got just about everything you'll need. But if we've missed something, let me know."

Some women felt that frisson of excitement and anticipation on entering a department store. For some, that sensory click might occur at the smell of fresh paint, or the glint of candlelight, or the fizz of champagne just opened.

For Megan, it was the sight of a well-ordered office that caused that quick shiver of pleasure.

And here was everything she could have wanted.

The desk was glorious, gleaming Queen Anne, with a spotless rose-toned blotter and ebony desk set already in place. A multilined phone and a streamlined computer sat waiting.

She nearly purred.

There were wooden filing cabinets still smelling of lemon oil, their brass handles shining in the sunlight that poured through the many-paned windows. The Oriental rug picked up the hues of rose and slate blue in the upholstered chairs and love seat. There were shelves for her accounting books and ledgers, and a hunt table that held a coffeemaker, fax and personal copier.

Old-world charm and modern technology blended into tasteful efficiency.

"Mandy, it's perfect."

"I'd hoped you'd like it." Fussing, Amanda straightened the blotter, shifted the stapler. "I can't say I'm sorry to be handing over the books. It's more than a full-time job. I've filed everything, invoices, expenses, credit-card receipts, accounts payable, et cetera, by department." She opened a file drawer to demonstrate.

Megan's organized heart swelled at the sight of neatly color-coded file folders. Alphabetized, categorized, cross-referenced.

Glorious.

"Wonderful. Not a cigar box in sight."

Amanda hesitated, and then threw back her head and

laughed. "You've seen Holt and Nate's accounting system, I take it."

Amused, and comfortable with Amanda, Megan patted her briefcase. "I *have* their accounting system." Unable to resist, she sat in the high-backed swivel chair. "Now this is more like it." She took up a sharpened pencil, set it down again. "I don't know how to thank you for letting me join the team."

"Don't be silly. You're family. Besides, you may not be so grateful after a couple of weeks in chaos. I can't tell you how many interruptions—" Amanda broke off when she heard her name bellowed. Her brow lifted. "See what I mean?" She swung to the door to answer her husband's shout. "In here, O'Riley." She shook her head as Sloan and Trent trooped up to the door. Both of them were covered with dust. "I thought you were breaking down a wall or something."

"We were. Had some more old furniture to haul out of the way. And look what we found."

She examined what he held in his hands. "A moldy old book. That's wonderful, honey. Now why don't you and Trent go play construction?"

"Not just a book," Trent announced. "Fergus's account book. For the year of 1913."

"Oh." Amanda's heart gave one hard thud as she grabbed for the book.

Curiosity piqued, Megan rose to join them in the doorway. "Is it important?"

"It's the year Bianca died." Sloan laid a comforting hand on Amanda's shoulder. "You know the story, Meg. How Bianca was trapped in a loveless, abusive marriage. She met Christian Bradford, fell in love. She decided to take the children and leave Fergus, but he found out.

They argued up in the tower. She fell through the window."

"And he destroyed everything that belonged to her." Amanda's voice tightened, shook. "Everything—her clothes, her small treasures, her pictures. Everything but the emeralds. Because she'd hidden those. Now we have them, and the portrait Christian had painted. That's all we have of her." She let out a long breath. "I suppose it's fitting that we should have this of his. A ledger of profit and loss."

"Looks like he wrote in the margins here and there." Trent reached over to flip a page open. "Sort of an abbreviated journal."

Amanda frowned and read a portion of the cramped handwriting aloud.

"Too much waste in kitchen. Fired cook. B. too soft on staff. Purchased new cuff links. Diamond. Good choice for opera tonight. Showier than J. P. Getty's."

She let out a huff of breath. "It shows just what kind of man he was, doesn't it?"

"Darling, I wouldn't have brought it out if I'd known it would bother you."

Amanda shook her head. "No, the family will want it." But she set it down, because her fingers felt coated with more than dust and mold. "I was just showing Megan her new domain."

"So I see." Sloan's eyes narrowed. "What happened to relaxing?"

"This is how I relax," Megan responded. "Now why don't you go away and let me enjoy myself?"

"An excellent idea." Amanda gave her husband a kiss

and a shove. "Scram." Even as she was hurrying the men along, Amanda's phone rang. "Give me a call if you need anything," she told Megan, and rushed to answer.

Feeling smug, Megan shut the door of her office. She was rubbing her hands together in anticipation as she crossed to her briefcase. She'd show Nathaniel Fury the true meaning of the word *shipshape*.

Three hours later, she was interrupted by the thunder of little feet. Obviously, she thought even before her door crashed open, someone had given Kevin the directions to her office.

"Hi, Mom!" He rushed into her arms for a kiss, and all thoughts of balancing accounts vanished from her mind. "We had the best time. We played with Sadie and Fred and had a war in the new fort. We got to go to Suzanna's flower place and water millions of plants."

Megan glanced down at Kevin's soggy sneakers. "And yourselves, I see."

He grinned. "We had a water battle, and I won."

"My hero."

"We had pizza for lunch, and Carolanne—she works for Suzanna—said I was a bottomless pit. And tomorrow Suzanna has to landscape, so we can't go with her, but we can go out on the whale boat if you want. You want to, don't you? I told Alex and Jenny you would."

She looked down at his dark, excited eyes. He was as happy as she'd ever seen him. At that moment, if he'd asked if she wanted to take a quick trip to Nairobi and hunt lions, she'd have been tempted to agree.

"You bet I do." She laughed when his arms flew around her and squeezed. "What time do we sail?"

* * *

At ten o'clock sharp the next morning, Megan had her three charges on the docks. Though the day was warm and balmy for June, she'd taken Suzanna's advice and brought along warm jackets and caps for the trip out into the Atlantic. She had binoculars, a camera, extra film.

Though she'd already downed a dose of motion-sickness pills, her landlubber's stomach tilted queasily as she studied the boat.

It looked sturdy. She could comfort herself with that. The white paint gleamed in the sun, the rails shone. When they stepped on board, she saw that there was a large interior cabin ringed with windows on the first deck. For the less hearty, she assumed. It boasted a concession stand, soft-drink machines and plenty of chairs and benches.

She gave it a last longing look as the children pulled her along. They wouldn't settle for a nice cozy cabin.

"We get to go to the bridge." Alex strutted along importantly, waving to one of the mates. "We own the *Mariner.* Us and Nate."

"Daddy says the bank owns it." Jenny scrambled up the iron steps, a red ribbon trailing from her hair. "But that's a joke. Dutch says it's a crying shame for a real sailor to haul around weak-bellied tourists. But Nate just laughs at him."

Megan merely lifted a brow. She had yet to meet the infamous Dutchman, but Jenny, clever as any parrot, would often quote him word for word. And all too often, those words were vividly blue.

"We're here." Alex burst onto the bridge, breathless with excitement. "Kevin, too."

"Welcome aboard." Nathaniel glanced up from the chart he was studying. His eyes fastened unerringly on Megan's.

"I was expecting Holt."

"He's helming the *Queen.*" He picked up his cigar, clamped it between his teeth, grinned. "Don't worry, Meg, I won't run you aground."

She wasn't concerned about that. Exactly. In his black sweater and jeans, a black Greek fisherman's cap on his head and that gleam in his eye, he looked supremely competent. As a pirate might, she mused, upon boarding a merchant ship. "I started on your books." There, she thought, the ground was steady under her feet.

"I figured you would."

"They're a disorganized mess."

"Yeah. Kevin, come on over and take a look. I'll show you where we're heading."

Kevin hesitated, clinging to his mother's hand another moment. But the lure of those colorful charts was too much for him. He dashed over, dozens of questions tripping off his tongue.

"How many whales will we see? What happens if they bump the boat? Will they shoot water up from that hole on their back? Do you steer the boat from way up here?"

Megan started to interrupt and gently tell her son not to badger Mr. Fury, but Nathaniel was already answering questions, hauling Jenny up on one hip and taking Alex's finger to slide over the lines of the chart.

Pirate or not, she thought with a frown, he had a way with children.

"Ready to cast off, Captain."

Nathaniel nodded to the mate. "Quarter speed astern." Still holding Jenny, he walked to the wheel. "Pilot us out of here, sailor," he said to her, and guided her eager hands.

Curiosity got the better of Megan. She inched closer to study the instruments. Depth sounders, sonar, ship-to-shore radio. Those, and all the other equipment, were as foreign to her as the cockpit of a spaceship. She was a woman of the plains.

As the boat chugged gently away from the docks, her stomach lurched, reminding her why.

She clamped down on the nausea, annoyed with herself. It was in her mind, she insisted. A silly, imaginary weakness that could be overcome through willpower.

Besides, she'd taken seasickness pills, so, logically, she couldn't be seasick.

The children cheered as the boat made its long, slow turn in the bay. Megan's stomach turned with it.

Alex was generous enough to allow Kevin to blow the horn. Megan stared straight out the bridge window, her eyes focused above the calm blue water of Frenchman Bay.

It was beautiful, wasn't it? she told herself. And it was hardly tilting at all.

"You'll see The Towers on the starboard side," Nathaniel was saying.

"That's the right," Jenny announced. "Starboard's right and port's left."

"Stern's the back and the bow's in front," said Alex, not to be outdone. "We know all about boats."

Megan shifted her eyes to the cliffs, struggling to ignore another twist in her stomach. "There it is, Kevin." She gripped the brass rail beneath the starboard window for balance. "It looks like it's growing right out of the rock."

And it did look like a castle, she mused as she watched it with her son beside her. The turrets spearing up into the blue summer sky, the somber gray rock glistening with tiny flecks of mica. Even the scaffolding and the antlike figures of men working didn't detract from the fairy-tale aura. A fairy tale, she thought, with a dark side.

And that, she realized, was what made it all the more alluring. It was hardly any wonder that Sloan, with his love of buildings, adored it.

"Like something you'd expect to see on some lonely Irish coast." Nathaniel spoke from behind her. "Or on some foggy Scottish cliff."

"Yes. It's even more impressive from the sea." Her eyes drifted up, to Bianca's tower. She shivered.

"You may want to put your jacket on," Nathaniel told her. "It's going to get chillier when we get out to sea."

"No, I'm not cold. I was just thinking. When you've heard all the stories about Bianca, it's hard not to imagine what it was like."

"She'd sit up there and watch the cliffs for him. For Christian. And she'd dream—guiltily, I imagine, being a proper lady. But propriety doesn't have a snowball's chance in hell against love."

She shivered again. The statement hit much too close to home. She'd been in love once, and had tossed propriety aside, along with her innocence.

"She paid for it," Megan said flatly, and turned away. To distract herself, she wandered over to the charts. Not that she could make heads or tails of them.

"We're heading north by northeast." As he had with Alex, Nathaniel took Megan's hand and guided it along the chart. "We've got a clear day, good visibility, but there's a strong wind. It'll be a little choppy."

Terrific, she thought, and swallowed hard. "If you don't come up with whales, you're going to have some very disappointed kids."

"Oh, I think I can provide a few." She bumped against him as bay gave way to sea. His hands came up to steady her shoulders, and remained. The boat might have swayed, but he stood solid as a rock. "You want to brace your feet apart. Distribute the weight. You'll get your sea legs, Meg."

She didn't think so. Already she could feel the light coating of chilly sweat springing to her skin. Nausea rolled in an answering wave in her stomach. She would not, she promised herself, spoil Kevin's day, or humiliate herself, by being sick.

"It takes about an hour to get out, doesn't it?" Her voice wasn't as strong, or as steady, as she'd hoped.

"That's right."

She started to move away, but ended by leaning dizzily against him.

"Come about," he murmured, and turned her to face him. One look at her face had his brows drawing together. She was pale as a sheet, with an interesting tinge of green just under the surface. Dead sick, he thought with a shake of his head. And they were barely under way.

"Did you take anything?"

There was no use pretending. And she didn't have the strength to be brave. "Yes, but I don't think it did any good. I get sick in a canoe."

"So you came on a three-hour trek into the Atlantic."

"Kevin had his heart set—" She broke off when Nathaniel put a steadying arm around her waist and led her to a bench.

"Sit," he ordered.

Megan obeyed and, when she saw that the children were occupied staring out the windows, gave in and dropped her head between her legs.

Three hours, she thought. They'd have to pour her into a body bag in three hours. Maybe bury her at sea. God,

what had made her think a couple of pills would steady
her? She felt a tug on her hand.

"What? Is the ambulance here already?"

"Steady as she goes, sugar." Crouched in front of her,
Nathaniel slipped narrow terry-cloth bands over her
wrists.

"What's this?"

"Acupressure." He twisted the bands until small metal
studs pressed lightly on a point on her wrist.

She would have laughed if she hadn't been moaning.
"Great. I need a stretcher and you offer voodoo."

"A perfectly valid science. And I wouldn't knock voodoo, either. I've seen some pretty impressive results. Now
breathe slow and easy. Just sit here." He slid open a
window behind her and let in a blast of air. "I've got to
get back to the helm."

She leaned back against the wall and let the fresh air
slap her cheeks. On the other side of the bridge, the children huddled, hoping that Moby Dick lurked under each
snowy whitecap. She watched the cliffs, but as they
swayed to and fro, she closed her eyes in self-defense.

She sighed once, then began to formulate a complicated trigonometry problem in her mind. Oddly enough,
by the time she'd worked it through to the solution, her
stomach felt steady.

Probably because I've got my eyes closed, she thought.
But she could hardly keep them closed for three hours,
not when she was in charge of a trio of active children.

Experimentally, she opened one. The boat continued
to rock, but her system remained steady. She opened the
other. There was a moment of panic when the children
weren't at the window. She jolted upright, illness forgotten, then saw them circled around Nathaniel at
the helm.

A fine job she was doing, she thought in disgust, sitting there in a dizzy heap while Nathaniel piloted the ship and entertained three kids. She braced herself for the next slap of nausea as she took a step.

It didn't come.

Frowning, she took another step, and another. She felt a little weak, true, but no longer limp and clammy. Daring the ultimate test, she looked out the window at the rolling sea.

There was a tug, but a mild one. In fact, she realized, it was almost a pleasant sensation, like riding on a smooth-gaited horse. In amazement, she studied the terry-cloth bands on her wrists.

Nathaniel glanced over his shoulder. Her color was back, he noted. That pale peach was much more flattering than green. ''Better?''

''Yes.'' She smiled, trying to dispel the embarrassment as easily as his magic bands had the seasickness. ''Thank you.''

He waited while she bundled the children, then herself, into jackets. On the Atlantic, summer vanished. ''First time I shipped out, we hit a little squall. I spent the worst two hours of my life hanging over the rail. Come on. Take the wheel.''

''The wheel? I couldn't.''

''Sure you could.''

''Do it, Mom. It's fun. It's really fun.''

Propelled forward by three children, Megan found herself at the helm, her back pressed lightly into Nathaniel's chest, her hands covered by his.

Every nerve in her body began to throb. Nathaniel's body was hard as iron, and his hands were sure and firm. She could smell the sea, through the open windows and on him. No matter how much she tried to concentrate on the water flowing endlessly around them, he was there, just there. His chin brushing the top of her head, his heartbeat throbbing light and steady against her back.

''Nothing like being in control to settle the system,'' he commented, and she made some sound of agreement.

But this was nothing like being in control.

She began to imagine what it might be like to have those hard, clever hands somewhere other than on the backs of hers. If she turned so that they were face-to-face, and she tilted her head up at just the right angle…

Baffled by the way her mind was working, she set it to calculating algebra.

''Quarter speed,'' Nathaniel ordered, steering a few degrees to port.

The change of rhythm had Megan off balance. She was trying to regain it when Nathaniel turned her around. And now she was facing him, her head tilted up. The easy grin on his face made her wonder if he knew just where her mind had wandered.

''See the blips on the screen there, Kevin?'' But he was watching her, all but hypnotizing her with those unblinking slate-colored eyes. Sorcerer's eyes, she thought dimly. ''Do you know what they mean?'' And his lips curved—closer to hers than they should be. ''There be whales there.''

''Where? Where are they, Nate?'' Kevin rushed to the window, goggle-eyed.

''Keep watching. We'll stop. Look off the port bow,'' he told Megan. ''I think you'll get your money's worth.''

Still dazed, she staggered away. The boat rocked more enthusiastically when stopped—or was it her system that was so thoroughly rocked? As Nathaniel spoke into the P.A. system, taking over the mate's lecture on whales, she slipped the camera and binoculars out of her shoulder bag.

"Look!" Kevin squealed, jumping like a spring as he pointed. "Mom, look!"

Everything cleared from her mind but wonder. She saw the massive body emerge from the choppy water. Rising, up and up, sleek and grand and otherworldly. She could hear the shouts and cheers from the people on the deck below, and her own strangled gasp.

It was surely some sort of magic, she thought, that something so huge, so magnificent, could lurk under the whitecapped sea. Her fingers rose to her lips, pressed there in awe as the sound of the whale displacing water crashed like thunder.

Water flew, sparkling like drops of diamond. Her camera stayed lowered, useless. She could only stare, an ache in her throat, tears in her eyes.

"His mate's coming up."

Nathaniel's voice broke through her frozen wonder. Hurriedly she lifted the camera, snapping quickly as sea parted for whale.

They geysered from their spouts, causing the children to applaud madly. Megan was laughing as she hauled Jenny up for a better view and the three of them took impatient turns with the binoculars.

She pressed herself to the window as eagerly as the children while the boat cruised, following the glossy humps as they speared through the sea. Then the whales sounded, diving deep with a flap of their enormous tails. Below, people laughed and shouted as they were drenched with water.

Twice more the *Mariner* sought out and found pods, giving her passengers the show of a lifetime. Long after they turned and headed for home, Megan stayed at the window, hoping for one more glimpse.

"Beautiful, aren't they?"

She looked back at Nathaniel, eyes glowing. "Incredible. I had no idea. Photographs and movies don't quite do it."

"Nothing quite like seeing and doing for yourself." He cocked a brow. "Still steady?"

With a laugh, she glanced down at her wrists. "Another minor miracle. I would never have put stock in anything like this."

"'There are more things in heaven and earth, Horatio.'"

A black-suited pirate quoting Hamlet. "So it seems," she murmured. "There's The Towers." She smiled. "Off the port side."

"You're learning, sugar." He gave orders briskly and eased the *Mariner* into the calm waters of the bay.

"How long have you been sailing?"

"All my life. But I ran off and joined the merchant marine when I was eighteen."

"Ran off?" She smiled again. "Looking for adventure."

"For freedom." He turned away then, to ease the boat into its slip as smoothly as a foot slides into an old, comfortable shoe.

She wondered why a boy of eighteen would have to search for freedom. And she thought of herself at that age, a child with a child. She'd cast her freedom away. Now, more than nine years later, she could hardly regret it. Not when the price of her freedom had been a son.

"Can we go down and get a drink?" Kevin tugged on his mother's hand. "We're all thirsty."

"Sure. I'll take you."

"We can go by ourselves," Alex said earnestly. He knew they were much too big to need an overseer. "I got money and everything. We just want to sit downstairs and watch everybody get off."

"All right, then, but stay inside." She watched them rush off. "They start spreading their wings so soon."

"Your boy's going to be flying back to you for a long time yet."

"I hope so." She cut herself off before she voiced the rest: *He's all I have.* "This has been a terrific day for him. For me, too. Thanks."

"My pleasure." They were alone on the bridge now, the lines secured, the plank down and the passengers disembarking. "You'll come again."

"I don't think I could keep Kevin away. I'd better go down with them."

"They're fine." He stepped closer, before she could evade. "You know, Meg, you forget to be nervous when the kids are around."

"I'm not nervous."

"Jumpy as a fish on a line. It was a pure pleasure watching your face when we sighted whale. It's a pure pleasure anytime, but when you're laughing and the wind's in your hair, it could stop a man's heart."

He took another step and backed her up against the wheel. Maybe it wasn't fair, but he'd think about that later. It was going to take him a good long time to forget the way she'd felt, her back pressed against him, her hands soft and hesitant under his.

"Of course, there's something to be said about the way you're looking right now. All eyes. You've got the prettiest blue eyes I've ever seen. Then there's all that peaches-and-cream." He lifted a finger to her cheek, skimmed it down. She felt as though she'd stepped on a live wire. "Makes a man crave a nice long taste."

"I'm not susceptible to flattery." She'd wanted to sound firm and dismissive, not breathless.

"Just stating a fact." He leaned down until his mouth was a whisper from hers. "If you don't want me to kiss you, you'd better tell me not to."

She would have. Absolutely. If she'd been able to speak. But then his mouth was on hers, warm and firm and every bit as clever as his hands. She would tell herself later that her lips had parted with shock, to protest. But it was a lie.

They opened greedily, with a surge of hunger that went deep, that echoed on a groan that a woman might make who had her first sampling of rich cream after years of thin water.

Her body refused to go rigid in denial, instead humming like a harp string freshly plucked. Her hands dived into his hair and urged him to take the kiss deeper.

He'd expected a cool response, or at least a hesitant one. Perhaps he'd seen a flash of passion in her eyes, deep down, like the heat and rumble in the core of a volcano that seems dormant from the surface.

But nothing had prepared him for this blast of fire.

His mind went blank, then filled with woman. The scent and feel and taste of her, the sound of the moan that caught in her throat when he nipped on her full lower lip. He dragged her closer, craving more, and had the dizzying delight of feeling every slim curve and line of Megan pressed against his body.

The scent of the ocean through the window had him imagining taking her on some deserted beach, while the surf pounded and the gulls screamed.

She felt herself sinking, and gripped him for balance.

There was too much, much too much, rioting through her system. It would take a great deal more than the little bands around her wrist to level her now.

It would take control, willpower, and, most of all…remembering.

She drew back, would have stumbled if his arms hadn't stayed clamped around her. "No."

He couldn't get his breath. He told himself he would analyze later why one kiss had knocked him flat, like a two-fisted punch. "You'll have to be more specific. No to what?"

"To this. To any of this." Panic kicked in and had her struggling away. "I wasn't thinking."

"Me, neither. It's a good sign you're doing it right, if you stop thinking when you're kissing."

"I don't want you to kiss me."

He slipped his hands into his pockets. Safer there, he decided, since the lady was thinking again. "Sugar, you were doing more than your share."

There was little use in hotly denying the obvious truth. She fell back on cool logic. "You're an attractive man, and I responded in a natural manner."

He had to grin. "Darling, if kissing like that's in your nature, I'm going to die happy."

"I don't intend for it to happen again."

"You know what they say about the road to hell and intentions, don't you?" She was tensed up again. He could see it in the set of her shoulders. He imagined her experience with Dumont had left plenty of scars. "Relax, Meg," he said, more kindly. "I'm not going to jump you. You want to take it slow, we'll take it slow."

The fact that his tone was so reasonable raised her hackles. "We're not going to take it any way at all."

Better, he decided. He didn't mind riling her. In fact, he was looking forward to doing it. Often.

"I'm going to have to say you're wrong. A man and woman set off a fire like that, they're going to keep coming back to the heat."

She was very much afraid he was right. Even now, part of her yearned to fan that blaze again. "I'm not interested in fires or in heat. I'm certainly not interested in an affair with a man I barely know."

"So, we'll get to know each other better before we have one," Nate responded, in an irritatingly reasonable tone.

Megan clamped her teeth together. "I'm not interested in an affair, period. I know that must be a blow to your ego, but you'll just have to deal with it. Now, if you'll excuse me, I'm going to get the children."

He stepped politely out of her way, waited until she'd reached the glass door leading onto the upper deck. "Meg?" It was only partly ego that pushed him to speak. The rest was pure determination. "The first time I make love with you, you won't think about him. You won't even remember his name."

Her eyes sliced at him, twin ice-edged swords. She abandoned dignity and slammed the door.

Chapter 4

"The woman'll be the death of me." Dutch took a bottle of Jamaican rum from his hidey-hole in the back of the pantry. "Mark my words, boy."

Nathaniel kicked back in the kitchen chair, sated and relaxed after the meal he'd enjoyed in the Calhoun dining room. The hotel kitchen was spotless, now that the dinner rush was over. And Coco, Nathaniel knew, was occupied with family. Otherwise, Dutch wouldn't have risked the rum.

"You're not thinking of jumping ship, are you, mate?"

Dutch snorted at the idea. As if he had to take French leave because he couldn't handle a fussy, snooty-nosed female. "I'm sticking." After one wary glance toward the door, he poured them both a healthy portion of rum. "But I'm warning you, boy, sooner or later that woman's going to get her comeuppance. And she's going to get it from yours truly." He stabbed a thick thumb at his wide chest.

Nathaniel downed a swig of rum, hissing through his teeth as it hit. Smooth as silk it wasn't. "Where's that bottle of Cruzan I got you?"

"Used it in a cake. This is plenty good enough for drinking."

"If you don't want a stomach lining," Nathaniel said under his breath. "So, what's the problem with Coco now?"

"Well, if it's not one thing, it's two." Dutch scowled at the kitchen phone when it rang. Room service, he thought with a sneer. Never had any damn room service aboard one of his ships. "Yeah, what?"

Nathaniel grinned into his rum. Tact and diplomacy weren't Dutch's strong points. He imagined that if Coco heard the man growl at guests that way, she'd faint. Or pop Dutch over the head with a skillet.

"I guess you think we've got nothing better to do down here?" he snarled into the phone. "You'll get it when it's ready." He hung up and snagged a plate. "Ordering champagne and fancy cake this time of night. Newlyweds. Ha! Haven't seen hide nor hair of the two in number three all week."

"Where's your romance, Dutch?"

"I leave that to you, lover boy." His ham-size fists delicately cut into the chocolate *gâteau*. "Seen the way you was eyeing that redhead."

"Strawberry blonde," Nathaniel corrected. "More gold than red." Bravely he took another sip of rum. "She's a looker, isn't she?"

"Never seen you go for one that wasn't." With an artist's flair, Dutch ladled vanilla sauce on the side of the twin slices of cake and garnished them with raspberries. "Got a kid, doesn't she?"

"Yeah." Nathaniel studied the cake and decided he

could probably force down a small piece. "Kevin. Dark hair, tall for his age." A smile curved his lips. Damned if the boy hadn't gotten to him. "Big, curious eyes."

"Seen him." Dutch had a weakness for kids that he tried to hide. "Okay-looking boy. Comes around with those other two noisy brats, looking for handouts."

Which, Nathaniel knew, Dutch dispensed with great pleasure behind the mask of a scowl.

"Got herself in trouble pretty young."

Nathaniel frowned at that. It was a phrase, too often used to his way of thinking, that indicated the woman was solely responsible for the pregnancy. "It takes two, Dutch. And the bastard was stringing her along."

"I know. I know. I heard about it. Not much gets past me." It wasn't hard to finesse information out of Coco— if he pushed the right buttons. Though he'd never admit it, that was something he looked forward to doing daily. He buzzed for a waiter, taking delight in holding his thumb down until the kitchen door swung open. "Make up a tray for number three," Dutch ordered. "Two gato's, bottle of house champagne, two flutes, and don't forget the damn napkins."

That done, he tossed back his own rum. "Guess you'll be wanting a piece of this now."

"Wouldn't turn it down."

"Never known you to turn down food—or a female." Dutch cut a slice—a great deal larger than those he'd cut for the newlyweds—and shoved the plate in front of Nathaniel.

"I don't get any raspberries?"

"Eat what's in front of you. How come you ain't out there flirting with that skinny girl?"

"I'm working on it," Nathaniel said with a mouthful of cake. "They're in the dining room, all of them. Family meeting." He rose, poured himself coffee, dumped the rest of his rum in it. "They found some old book. And she's not skinny." He had firsthand knowledge, now that he'd had Megan in his arms. "She's delicate."

"Yeah, right." He thought of Coco, those long, sturdy lines as fine as any well-crafted sloops. And snorted again. "All females are delicate—until they get a ring through your nose."

No one would have called the women in the dining room delicate—not with a typical Calhoun argument in full swing.

"I say we burn it." C.C. folded her arms across her chest and glared. "After everything we learned about Fergus from Bianca's journal, I don't know why we'd consider keeping his lousy account book around."

"We can't burn it," Amanda fired back. "It's part of our history."

"Bad vibes." Lilah narrowed her eyes at the book, now sitting in the center of the table. "Really bad vibes."

"That may be." Max shook his head. "But I can't go along with burning a book. Any kind of book."

"It's not exactly literature," C.C. mumbled.

Trent patted his wife's stiff shoulder. "We can always put it back where it came from—or give Sloan's suggestion some consideration."

"I think a room designed for artifacts, mementos—" Sloan glanced at Amanda "—the pieces of history that go with The Towers, would add something. Not only to the hotel, but for the family."

"I don't know." Suzanna pressed her lips together and tried to be objective. "I feel odd about displaying Fergus's things with Bianca's, or Aunt Colleen's, Uncle Sean's and Ethan's."

"He might have been a creep, but he's still a piece of the whole." Holt toyed with the last of his coffee. "I'm going with Sloan on this one."

That, of course, enticed a small riot of agreements, disagreements, alternate suggestions. Megan could only sit back and watch in amazement.

She hadn't wanted to be there at all. Not at a family meeting. But she'd been summarily outvoted. The Calhouns could unite when they chose.

As the argument swirled around her, she glanced at the object in question. When Amanda left it in her office, she'd eventually given in to temptation. After cleaning off the leather, she'd flipped through pages, idly totaling up columns, clucking her tongue at the occasional mistake in arithmetic. Of course, she'd scanned a few of the marginal notations, as well, and had found Fergus Calhoun a cold, ambitious and self-absorbed man.

But then, a simple account ledger hardly seemed worth this much trouble. Particularly when the last few pages of the books were merely numbers without any rhyme or reason.

She was reminding herself it wasn't her place to comment when she was put directly on the spot.

"What do you think, Megan, dear?" Coco's unexpected question had Megan blinking.

"Excuse me?"

"What do you think? You haven't told us. And you'd be the most qualified, after all."

"Qualified?"

"It's an account book," Coco pointed out. "You're an accountant."

Somehow, the logic in that defeated Megan. "It's really none of my business," she began, and was drowned out by a chorus of reasons why it certainly was. "Well,

I…'' She looked around the table, where all eyes were focused on her. "I imagine it would be an interesting memento—and it's kind of fascinating to review book-keeping from so long ago. You know, expenses, and wages for the staff. It might be interesting to see how it adds up, what the income and outgo was for your family in 1913.''

"Of course!" Coco clapped her hands. "Why, of course it would. I was thinking about you last night, Meg, while I was casting my runes. It kept coming back to me that you were to take on a project—one with numbers.''

"Aunt Coco," C.C. said patiently, "Megan is our accountant.''

"Well, I know that, darling." With a bright smile, Coco patted her hair. "So at first I didn't think much of it. But then I kept having this feeling that it was more than that. And I'm sure, somehow, that the project is going to lead to something wonderful. Something that will make all of us very happy. I'm so pleased you're going to do it.''

"Do it?" Megan looked helplessly at her brother. She got a flash of a grin in return.

"Study Fergus's book. You could even put it all on computer, couldn't you? Sloan's told us how clever you are.''

"I could, of course, but—''

She was interrupted by the cry of a baby through the monitor on the sideboard.

"Bianca?" Max said.

"Ethan," C.C. and Lilah said in unison.

And the meeting was adjourned.

What exactly, Megan wondered later, had she agreed to do? Somehow, though she'd barely said a word, she'd been placed in charge of Fergus's book. Surely that was a family matter.

She sighed as she pushed open the doors to her terrace and stepped outside. If she stated that obvious fact, in the most practical, logical of terms, she would be patted on the head, pinched on the cheek and told that she was family and that was all there was to it.

How could she argue?

She took a deep breath of the scented night air, and all but tasted Suzanna's freesias and roses. She could hear the sea in the distance, and the air she moved through was moist and lightly salty from it. Stars wheeled overhead, highlighted by a three-quarter moon, bright as a beacon.

Her son was dreaming in his bed, content and safe and surrounded by people who loved him.

Dissecting Fergus's book was a small favor that couldn't begin to repay what she'd been given.

Peace of mind. Yes, she thought, the Calhouns had opened the gates to that particular garden.

Too charmed by the night to close it out and sleep, she wandered down the curving stone steps to drift through the moon-kissed roses and star-sprinkled peonies, under an arbor where wisteria twisted triumphantly, raining tiny petals onto the path.

"'She was a phantom of delight when first she gleamed upon my sight.'"

Megan jolted, pressing a hand on her heart when a shadow separated itself from the other shadows.

"Did I startle you?" Nathaniel stepped closer, the red tip of his cigar glowing. "Wordsworth usually has a different effect."

"I didn't know you were there." And wouldn't have come out had she known. "I thought you'd gone home."

"I was passing a little time with Dutch and a bottle of rum." He stepped fully into the moonlight. "He likes to complain about Coco, and prefers an audience." He drew slowly on his cigar. For a moment, his face was misted by smoke, making it mysterious and beautiful. An angel cast from grace. "Nice night."

"Yes, it is. Well…"

"No need to run off. You wanted to walk in the garden." He smiled, reaching down to snap a pale pink peony from its bush. "Since it's nearly midnight, there's no better time for it."

She accepted the blossom, told herself she wouldn't be charmed. "I was admiring the flowers. I've never had much luck growing them."

"You have to put your heart in it—along with the water and fertilizer."

Her hair was down, waving softly over her shoulders. She still wore the neatly tailored blue jacket and slacks she'd had on at dinner. A pity, he thought. It would have suited the night, and his mood, if she'd drifted outside in a flowing robe. But then, Megan O'Riley wasn't the type of woman to wander midnight gardens in swirling silks.

Wouldn't let herself be.

The only way to combat those intrusive gray eyes, other than to run like a fool, was conversation. "So, do you garden, as well as sail and quote the classics?" she asked him.

"I've an affection for flowers, among other things." Nathaniel put a hand over the peony she held, and lifted it toward him so that he could enjoy its fragrance, and hers. He smiled at her over the feathered petals.

She found herself caught, as if in some slow-motion dream, between the man and the moonlight. The perfume of the garden seemed to rise up and swirl like the breeze, gently invading her senses. Shadows shifted over his face, highlighting all those fascinating clefts and ridges, luring her gaze to his mouth, curved now and inviting.

They seemed so completely alone, so totally cut off from the reality and responsibilities of day-to-day.

Just a man and a woman among star-dappled flowers and moonlit shadows, and the music of the distant sea.

Deliberately she lowered her lashes, as if to break the spell.

"I'm surprised you'd have time for poetry and flowers, with all the traveling."

"You can always make time for what counts."

The fact that the night held magic hadn't escaped him. But then, he was open to such things. There'd been times he'd seen water rise out of itself like a clenched fist, times he'd heard the siren song of mermaids through shifting fog—he believed in magic. Why else had he waited in the garden, knowing, somehow knowing, she would come?

He released the flower, but took her free hand, linking their fingers before she could think of a reason he shouldn't. "Walk with me, Meg. A night like this shouldn't be wasted."

"I'm going back in." She looked back up just as a breeze stirred in the air. Wisteria petals rained down.

"Soon."

So she was walking with him in the fairy-lit garden, with a flower in her hand and fragrant petals in her hair.

"I...really should check on Kevin."

"The boy have trouble sleeping?"

"No, but—"

"Bad dreams?"

"No."

"Well, then." Taking that as an answer, he continued

his stroll down the narrow path. "Does having a man flirt with you always make you turn tail and run?"

"I certainly wasn't running. And I'm not interested in flirtations."

"Funny. When you were standing out on the terrace a bit ago, you looked like a woman ready for a little flirting."

She stopped dead. "You were watching me."

"Mmm." Nathaniel crushed his cigar out into the sand of a nearby urn. "I was thinking it was a shame I didn't have a lute."

Annoyance warred with curiosity. "A lute?"

"A pretty woman standing on a balcony in the moonlight—she should be serenaded."

She had to laugh at that. "I suppose you play the lute."

"Nope. Wished I did, though, when I saw you." He began to walk again. The cliff curved downward, toward the seawall. "I used to sail by here when I was a kid and look up at The Towers. I liked to think there was a dragon guarding it, and that I'd scale the cliffs and slay him."

"Kevin still calls it a castle," she murmured, looking back.

"When I got older and took note of the Calhoun sisters, I figured when I killed the dragon, they'd reward me. In the way a sixteen-year-old walking hormone fantasizes."

She laughed again. "Which one of them?"

"Oh, all of them." Grinning, he sat on the low wall, drew her down beside him. "They've always been... remarkable. Holt had this thing for Suzanna, though he wouldn't admit it. Being as he was my friend, I

selflessly crossed her off my list. That left three for me
after I conquered that dragon.''

''But you never did face the dragon?''

A shadow passed over his face. ''I had another to deal
with. I guess you could say we left it at a draw, and I
went to sea.'' He shook off the mood, and the uncomfortable past. ''But I did have a brief and memorable
interlude with the lovely Lilah.''

Megan's eyes widened. ''You and Lilah?''

''Right before I left the island. She set out to drive me
crazy. I think she was practicing.'' He sighed at the memory. ''She was damn good at it.''

But they were so easy with each other, Megan thought.
So relaxed and friendly.

''You're so easy to read, Meg.'' He chuckled and
slipped his arm around her shoulders. ''We weren't exactly Romeo and Juliet. I kissed her a few times, did my
damnedest to convince her to do more. She didn't. And
she didn't break my heart. Well, dented it a little,
maybe,'' he mused.

''And Max isn't bothered?''

''Why would he be? He's got her. If we'd had a flaming affair—which we didn't—it would be a smoldering
matchstick compared to what they've got.''

He was right there. Each of the Calhoun women had
found her match. ''Still, it's interesting,'' she said quietly. ''All these connections within connections.''

''Are you thinking of me, or yourself?''

She stiffened, abruptly aware that she was sitting hip-
to-hip with him, his arm around her. ''That's not something I care to discuss.''

''Still raw?'' He tightened his arm, comforting. ''From
what I've heard of Dumont, I wouldn't think he'd be
worth it. Settle down,'' he said when she jerked away.

"We'll let it go. Too nice a night to uncover old wounds. Why don't you tell me how they talked you into taking on that old account book?"

"How do you know about that?"

"Holt and Suzanna filled me in." She was still rigid, he noted. But she wasn't running. "I saw them before they left."

She relaxed a little. It was comforting to discuss it with someone else who was just that small step outside the family. "I don't know how they talked me into it. I barely opened my mouth."

"Your first mistake."

She huffed out a breath. "I'd have had to shout to be heard. I don't know why they call it a meeting, when all they do is argue." Her brows knit. "Then they stop arguing and you realize you've been sucked in. If you try to pull yourself out, you find they've united in this solid wall that's impossible to beat."

"I know just what you mean. I still don't know if it was my idea to go into business with Holt. The notion came up, was debated, voted on and approved. The next thing I knew, I was signing papers."

Interesting, she mused, and studied his strong profile. "You don't strike me as someone who could be talked into anything."

"I could say the same."

She considered a moment, then gave up. "You're right. The book's fascinating. I can hardly wait to get at it."

"I hope you're not planning on letting it take up all your free time." He toyed with the ends of her blowing hair. No, not red, he mused. It was gold, enriched by quiet fire. "I want some of it."

Cautiously she inched away. "I explained to you, I'm not interested."

"What you are is worried because you are interested." He cupped a hand under her chin and turned her to face him. "I figure you had a rough time, and maybe it's helped you cope to lump all men in with the bastard who hurt you. That's why I said I'd be patient."

Fury flared in her eyes. "Don't tell me what I am or how I've coped. I'm not asking for your understanding or your patience."

"Okay."

He crushed his mouth to hers, without any patience at all. His lips were demanding, urgent, irresistible, conquering hers before she could draw the breath to deny it.

The embers that had smoldered inside her since the first time he'd kissed her burst into reckless flame. She wanted—craved—this flash point of feeling, this fireball of sensation. Hating herself for the weakness, she let herself burn.

He'd proved his point, Nathaniel thought as he tore his mouth from hers to press it against the thundering pulse in her throat. Proved his point, and wrapped himself up in nasty knots of need.

Needs that would have to wait, because she was far from ready. And because it mattered—she mattered— more than he'd expected.

"Now tell me you're not interested," he muttered against her lips, furious that he was unable to take what was so obviously his. "Tell me you didn't want me to touch you."

"I can't." Her voice broke in despair. She wanted him to touch her, to take her, to throw her on the ground and make wild love to her. And to take the decision, and the responsibility, out of her hands. That made her ashamed.

That made her a coward. "But wanting's not enough." Shaken, she pushed away, lurched to her feet. "It's never going to be enough for me. I've wanted before." She stood trembling in the moonlight, her hair blowing free, her eyes fierce and afraid.

Nathaniel cursed himself, then her for good measure. "I'm not Dumont. And you're not a seventeen-year-old girl."

"I know who I am. I don't know who you are."

"You're hedging, Megan. We recognized each other from the first instant."

She stepped back, because she knew he was right. Because it terrified her. "You're talking about chemistry."

"Maybe I'm talking about fate." He said it softly, as he rose. He'd frightened her, and he despised himself for it. Unnerving a woman was one thing, bullying another. "You need time to think about that. So do I. I'll walk you back."

She put out a hand to stop him. "I can find my own way." She whirled and raced up the moonlit path.

Nathaniel swore under his breath. He sat again and took out a fresh cigar, lit it. There wasn't any use heading home yet. He already knew he wouldn't sleep.

Late the following afternoon, Megan roused herself from her ledgers when a knock sounded on her office door.

"Come in."

"Sorry to interrupt." Coco poked her head in the door—a head, Megan noted with surprise, that was now topped with sleek ebony hair—she apparently was a woman who changed her hair color as often as she changed moods. "You didn't break for lunch," Coco said as she stepped through the door with a large and laden silver tray.

"You didn't have to bother." Megan glanced at her watch and was stunned to see it was after three. "You've got enough to do without waiting on me."

"Just part of the service." After setting the tray on a table, Coco began to arrange a place setting. "We can't have you skipping meals." She glanced over at the computer screen, the open ledgers, the calculator and the neatly stacked files. "My goodness, such a lot of numbers. Numbers have always unsettled me. They're so…unyielding."

"You don't have to let them push you around," Megan said with a laugh. "Once you know that one and one always equals two, you can do anything."

Coco studied the screen doubtfully. "If you say so, dear."

"I've just finished up the first quarter on Shipshape. It was…a challenge."

"It's wonderful that you think so." Coco turned her back on the numbers before they could give her a headache. "But none of us wants you overdoing things. Now, here's some iced tea and a nice club sandwich."

It did look tempting, particularly since she'd had no appetite for breakfast. A residual effect, she knew, of her encounter with Nathaniel.

"Thank you, Coco. I'm sorry I took you away from your work."

"Oh." Coco waved a dismissive hand as Megan rose to pick up her plate. "Don't give it a thought. To be frank, dear, I simply had to get out—away from that man."

"The Dutchman?" Megan smiled over her first bite of sandwich. "I met him this morning, when I was coming down. I made a wrong turn and ended up in the hotel wing.''

Restless, Coco began to fiddle with the thick gold links around her throat. ''I hope he didn't say anything to offend you. He's a bit…rough.''

''No.'' Megan poured two glasses of tea, offered one to Coco. ''He sort of glowered and told me I needed some meat on my bones. I thought he was going to start stuffing me with the Greek omelet he was fixing, but one of the busboys dropped a plate. I escaped while he was swearing at the poor kid.''

''His language.'' Coco seated herself, smoothed down her silk trouser leg. ''Deplorable. And he's always contradicting me on recipes.'' She shut her eyes, shuddered. ''I've always considered myself a patient woman—and, if I can be immodest for a moment, a clever one. I had to be both to raise four lively girls.'' Sighing, she tossed up her hands in a gesture of surrender. ''But as far as that man's concerned, I'm at my wits' end.''

''I suppose you could let him go,'' Megan said tentatively.

''Impossible. The man's like a father to Nathaniel, and the children, for reasons that escape me, are terribly fond of him.'' She opened her eyes again and smiled bravely. ''I can cope, dear, and I must admit the man has a way with certain rudimentary dishes.'' She patted her new hairdo. ''And I find little ways to distract myself.''

But Megan's attention was stuck back at Coco's first statement. ''I suppose Mr. Van Horne has known Nathaniel for some time.''

''Oh, more than fifteen years, I believe. They served together, sailed together, whatever you call it. I believe Mr. Van Horn took Nate under his wing. Which is something in his favor, I suppose. God knows the boy needed someone, after the miserable childhood he had.''

''Oh?'' It wasn't in Megan's nature to probe, but Coco needed little prompting.

''His mother died when he was very young, poor boy. And his father.'' Her lovely mouth went grim. ''Well, the man was little more than a beast really. I barely knew John Fury, but there was always talk in the village. And now and then Nathaniel would come along with Holt when Holt brought us fish. I'd see the bruises for myself.''

''Bruises,'' Megan repeated, horrified. ''His father beat him?''

Coco's soft heart had tears swimming in her eyes. ''I'm very much afraid so.''

''But—didn't anyone do anything about it?''

''Whenever there were questions, the man would claim the boy had fallen, or gotten into a fight with another child. Nathaniel never contradicted him. Sad to say, abuse was something people often overlooked back then. Still is, I'm afraid.'' Tears threatened her mascara. She dabbed at them with Megan's napkin. ''Nathaniel ran off to sea the moment he was of age. His father died a few years back. Nate sent money for the funeral, but didn't come. It was hard to blame him.''

Coco sighed, shook herself. ''I didn't mean to come in with such a sad story. But it has a good ending. Nate turned out to be a fine man.'' Coco's damp eyes were deceptively guileless. ''All he needs is the right woman. He's terribly handsome, don't you think?''

''Yes,'' Megan said cautiously. She was still trying to equate the abused child with the confident man.

''And dependable. Romantic, too, with all those tales

of the sea, and that air of mystery around him. A woman would be very lucky to catch his eye.''

Megan blinked her own eyes as the not-so-subtle hint got through. ''I couldn't say. I don't know him very well, and I don't really think about men that way.''

''Nonsense.'' Confident in her own matchmaking skills, Coco patted Megan's knee. ''You're young, beautiful, intelligent. Having a man in your life doesn't diminish those things, dear—or a woman's independence. The right man enhances them. And I have a feeling that you'll be finding that out, very soon. Now—'' she leaned over and kissed Megan's cheek ''—I have to get back to the kitchen, before that man does something horrid to my salmon patties.''

She started out the door, then paused—timing it, Coco thought, rather beautifully. ''Oh, dear, I'm such a scatterbrain. I was supposed to tell you about Kevin.''

''Kevin?'' Automatically Megan's gaze shifted to the window. ''Isn't he outside with Alex and Jenny?''

''Well, yes, but not here.'' Coco smiled distractedly—it was a pose she'd practiced for years. ''It's Nathaniel's day off, and he was by for lunch. Such a wonderful appetite he has, and never seems to gain an ounce. Of course, he does keep active. That's why he has all those marvelous muscles. They are marvelous, aren't they?''

''Coco, where is Kevin?''

''Oh, there I go, running off again. Kevin's with Nate. All of them are. He took the children with him.''

Megan was already on her feet. ''With him? Where? On a boat?'' Visions of squalls and towering waves of water swam through her head, despite the calm, cloudless blue of the sky.

''No, no, to his house. He's building a deck or something, and the children were dying to go along and help.

It would be such a favor to me if you could go by and
pick them up.'' And, of course, Coco thought cannily,
Megan would then see Nate's lovely little home, and his
charming way with children. ''Suzanna expects the children to be here, you see, but I didn't have the heart to
deny them. She won't be back until five, so there's no
hurry.''

''But, I—''

''You know where Suzanna and Holt's cottage is,
don't you, darling? Nathaniel's is only a half a mile past
it. Charming place. You can't miss it.''

Before Megan could form another word, the door
closed gently in her face.

A job, Coco thought as she strode down the corridor,
very well done.

Chapter 5

Kevin didn't know which was the coolest. It was a very close call between the small fire-breathing dragon on the back of Nathaniel's shoulder and the puckered white scar on the front. The scar was the result of the knife wound, which ought to have put it far ahead in the running. But a tattoo, a tattoo of a *dragon,* was pretty hard to beat.

There was another scar, just above Nathaniel's waist-line, near the hip. At Alex's eager questioning, Nathaniel had said it was from a moray eel he'd tangled with in the South Pacific.

Kevin could easily imagine Nathaniel, armed with only a knife clenched between his teeth, fighting to the death with a sea creature on the scale of the Loch Ness monster.

And Nathaniel had a parrot, a big, colorful bird who sat right inside the house on a wooden perch and talked. Kevin's current favorite was ''Off with her head.''

Kevin figured Nathaniel Fury was about the coolest man he'd ever met—a man who had traveled the seven seas like Sinbad, and had the scars and stories to prove it. A man who liked puppies and talking birds.

He didn't seem to mind when Kevin hung back while Alex and Jenny raced around the yard with the puppy and killed each other with imaginary laser pistols. It was more fun to crouch close while Nathaniel hammered nails into boards.

It took Kevin about six boards to start asking questions.

"How come you want a deck out here?"

"So I can sit on it." Nathaniel set another board in place.

"But you've already got one in the back."

"I'll still have it." Three strikes of the hammer and the nail was through board and joist. Nathaniel sat back on his haunches. He wore nothing but a bandanna twisted around his head and a pair of ragged cutoff jeans. His skin was bronzed by the sun and coated lightly with sweat. "See how the frame goes?"

Kevin followed the direction of the deck frame as it skirted around the side of the house. "Uh-huh."

"Well, we'll keep going till we meet the other deck."

Kevin's eyes brightened. "So it'll go all around, like a circle."

"You got it." Nathaniel hammered the next nail, and the next, then shifted positions. "How do you like the island?"

He asked the question in such a natural, adult fashion that Kevin first glanced around to see if Nathaniel was speaking to him. "I like it. I like it a lot. We get to live in the castle, and I can play with Alex and Jenny anytime."

"You had friends back in Oklahoma, too, right?"

"Sure. My best friend is John Curtis Silverhorn. He's

part Comanche. My mom said he could come visit anytime, and that we can write letters all we want. I already
wrote him about the whale.'' Kevin smiled shyly. ''I
liked that the best.''

''We'll have to go out again.''

''Really? When?''

Nathaniel stopped hammering and looked at the boy.
He realized he should have remembered from his expo-
sure to Alex and Jenny that when children were raised
with love and trust, they believed just about everything
you told them.

''You can come out with me whenever you want.
'Long as your mother gives the go-ahead.''

His reward for the careless offer was a brilliant smile.
''Maybe I can steer the boat again?''

''Yeah.'' Nathaniel grinned and turned Kevin's baseball cap backward. ''You could do that. Want to nail
some boards?''

Kevin's eyes widened and glowed. ''Okay!''

''Here.'' Nathaniel scooted back so that Kevin could
kneel in front of him. ''Hold the nail like this.'' He
wrapped his hands over Kevin's, showing him how to
hold both the hammer and the nail to guide the stroke.

''Hey!'' Alex rose from the dead on Planet Zero and
raced over. ''Can I do it?''

''Me too.'' Jenny leaped on Nathaniel's back, knowing
she was always welcome.

''I guess I got me a crew.'' Nathaniel figured that with
all the extra help it would only take about twice as long
to finish.

An hour later, Megan pulled up beside the long, classic
lines of the T-Bird and stared. The house itself surprised
her. The charming two-story cottage, with its neatly

painted blue shutters and its window boxes bright with pansies, wasn't exactly the image she had of Nathaniel Fury. Nor was the tidy green lawn, the trimmed hedge, the fat barking puppy.

But it was Nathaniel who surprised her most. She was a bit taken aback by all that exposed golden skin, the lithe, muscled body. She was human, after all. But it was what he was doing that really captured her attention.

He was crouched over her son on the partially finished deck, their heads close, his big hand over Kevin's small one. Jenny was sitting adoringly beside him, and Alex was playing highwire on a joist.

"Hi, Megan! Look, I'm the death-defying Alex." In his excitement, Alex nearly lost his balance and almost plunged a harrowing eight inches to the ground. He pinwheeled his arms and avoided disaster.

"Close call," she said, and grinned at him.

"I'm in the center ring, without a net."

"Mom, we're building a deck." Kevin caught his bottom lip between his teeth and pounded a nail. "See?"

"Yes, I do." Briefcase in tow, Megan stopped to pet the eager puppy who fell over backward in enthusiasm.

"And it's my turn next." Jenny batted her eyes at Nathaniel. "Isn't it?"

"That's right, sugar. Okay, Captain. Let's drive that baby home."

With a grunt of effort, Kevin sent the nail into the board. "I did it. I did the whole board." Proudly Kevin looked back at his mother. "We each get to do a board. This is my third one."

"It looks like you're doing a good job." To give the devil his due, she smiled at Nathaniel. "Not everyone could handle it."

"Just takes a steady eye and a sure hand. Hey, mates, where's my timber?"

"We'll get it." Alex and Kevin scrambled together to heave the next plank.

Standing back, Megan watched the routine they'd worked out. Nathaniel took the board, sighted down it, set it in place. He tapped, shifted, using a small block of wood to measure the distance between the last board and the new one. Once he was satisfied, Jenny wriggled in front of him.

She wrapped both little hands around the hammer, and Nathaniel, a braver soul than Megan had imagined, held the nail.

"Keep your eye on the target," Nathaniel warned, then sat patiently while her little strokes gradually anchored the nail. Then, wrapping his hand over hers, he rammed it home. "Thirsty work," he said casually. "Isn't it, mates?"

"Aye, aye." Alex put his hands to his throat and gagged.

Nathaniel held the next nail. "There's some lemonade in the kitchen. If someone was to go fetch the pitcher and a few glasses…"

Four pairs of eyes turned on her, putting Megan firmly in her place. If she wasn't going to be a carpenter, she'd have to be a gofer.

"All right." She set the briefcase down and crossed the finished portion of the deck to the front door.

Nathaniel said nothing, waited.

Seconds later, a shrill wolf whistle sounded from inside, followed by a muffled scream. He was grinning by the time Bird squawked out his invitation: "Hey, sugar, buy you a drink? Here's looking at you, kid." When Bird began to sing a chorus of "There Is Nothing Like a Dame," the children collapsed into fits of laughter.

A few minutes later, Megan carried out a tray of drinks. Bird's voice followed her. "'Give me a kiss, and to that kiss a score!'"

She arched a brow as she set the tray on the deck. "Bogart, show tunes and poetry. That's quite a bird."

"He has an eye for pretty women." Nathaniel picked up a glass and downed half the contents. He scanned Megan, taking in the tidy French twist, the crisp blouse and slacks. "Can't say I blame him."

"Aunt Coco says Nate needs a woman." Alex smacked his lips over the tart lemonade. "I don't know why."

"To sleep with him," Jenny said, and caused both Nathaniel and Megan to gape. "Grown-ups get lonely at night, and they like to have someone to sleep with. Like Mom and Daddy do. I have my bear," she continued, referring to her favorite stuffed animal. "So I don't get lonely."

"Break time." Nathaniel gamely swallowed his choke of laughter. "Why don't you guys take Dog for a walk down by the water?"

The idea met with unanimous approval. With war whoops and slapping feet, they raced off.

"Kid's got a point." Nathaniel rubbed the cold glass over his sweaty brow. "Nights can get lonely."

"I'm sure Jenny will lend you her bear." Megan stepped away from him, as if studying the house. "It's a very nice place, Nathaniel." She flicked a finger over the sassy petals of a pansy. "Homey."

"You were expecting a crow's nest, some oilcloth?"

She had to smile. "Something like that. I want to thank you for letting Kevin spend the day."

"I'd say the three of them are working as a team these days."

Her smile softened. She could hear their laughter from behind the house. "Yes, you're right."

"I like having them around. They're good company." He shifted on the deck, folding his legs Indian-style. "The boy's got your eyes."

Her smile faded. "No, Kevin's are brown." Like his father's.

"No, not the color. The look in them. Goes a lot deeper than brown or blue. How much have you told him?"

"I—" She brought herself back, angled her chin. "I didn't come here to discuss my personal life with you."

"What did you come here to discuss?"

"I came to get the children, and to go over your books."

Nathaniel nodded at her briefcase. "Got them in there?"

"Yes." She retrieved it, then, because she saw little choice, sat on the deck facing him. "I've finished the first quarter—that's January, February, March. Your outlay exceeded your income during that period, though you did have some cash flow through boat repairs. There is an outstanding account payable from February." She took out files, flipped through the neat computer-generated sheets. "A Mr. Jacques LaRue, in the amount of twelve hundred and thirty-two dollars and thirty-six cents."

"LaRue's had a tough year." Nathaniel poured more lemonade. "Holt and I agreed to give him some more time."

"That's your business, of course. Traditionally there

would be late charges on any outstanding account after thirty days.''

"Traditionally, on the island, we're a little friendlier."

"Your choice." She adjusted her glasses. "Now, as you can see, I've arranged the books into logical columns. Expenses—rent, utilities, office supplies, advertising and so forth. Then we have wages and withholding."

"New perfume."

She glanced over. "What?"

"You're wearing a new perfume. There's a hint of jasmine in it."

Distracted, she stared at him. "Coco gave it to me."

"I like it." He leaned closer. "A lot."

"Well." She cleared her throat, flipped a page. "And here we have income. I've added the weekly ticket sales from the tours to give you a month-by-month total, and a year-to-date. I see that you run a package deal with The Retreat, discounting your tour for hotel guests."

"Seemed friendly—and like good business."

"Yes, it's very smart business. On the average, eighty percent of the hotel guests take advantage of the package. I... Do you have to sit so close?"

"Yeah. Have dinner with me tonight, Meg."

"No."

"Afraid to be alone with me?"

"Yes. Now, as you can see, in March your income began an upswing—"

"Bring the boy."

"What?"

"Am I mumbling?" He smiled at her and slipped her glasses off her nose. "I said bring Kevin along. We'll take a drive out to this place I know. Great lobster rolls." He gave the word *lobster* a broad New England twist that made her smile. "I can't claim they're up to Coco's standards, but there's plenty of local color."

"We'll see."

"Uh-uh. Parental cop-out."

She sighed, shrugged. "All right. Kevin would enjoy it."

"Good." He handed her glasses back before he rose to heft another board. "Tonight, then."

"Tonight?"

"Why wait? You can call Suzanna, tell her we'll drop the kids off at her house on the way."

"I suppose I could." Now that his back was to her, she had no choice but to watch the ripple of muscles play as he set the board. She ignored the quick tug at her midsection, and reminded herself that her son would be along as chaperon. "I've never had a lobster roll."

"Then you're in for a treat."

He was absolutely right. The long, winding drive in the spectacular T-Bird was joy enough. The little villages they passed through were as scenic as any postcard. The sun dipped down toward the horizon in the west, and the breeze in the open car smelled of fish, then flowers, then sea.

The restaurant was hardly more than a diner, a square of faded gray wood set on stilts in the water, across a rickety gangplank. The interior decoration ran to torn fishnets and battered lobster buoys.

Scarred tables dotted the equally scarred floor. The booths were designed to rip the hell out of panty hose. A dubious effort at romantic atmosphere was added by the painted tuna can and hurricane globe set in the center of each table. The candles globbed in the base of the cans were unlit. Today's menu was scrawled on a chalkboard hanging beside the open kitchen.

"We got lobster rolls, lobster salad and lobster lobster," a waitress explained to an obviously frazzled family of four. "We got beer, we got milk, iced tea and soft drinks. There's French fries and coleslaw, and no ice cream 'cause the machine's not working. What'll you have?"

When she spotted Nathaniel, she abandoned her customers and gave him a hard punch in the chest. "Where you been, Captain?"

"Oh, out and about, Jule. Got me a taste for lobster roll."

"You came to the right place." The waitress, scarecrow-thin with a puff of steel gray hair, eyed Megan craftily. "So, who's this?"

"Megan O'Riley, her son Kevin. This is Julie Peterson. The best lobster cook on Mount Desert Island."

"The new accountant from The Towers." Julie gave a brisk nod. "Well, sit down, sit down. I'll fix you up when I get a minute." She swiveled back to her other customers. "You make up your mind yet, or are you just going to sit and take the air?"

"The food's better than the service." Nathaniel winked at Kevin as he led them to a booth. "You've just met one of the monuments of the island, Kevin. Mrs. Peterson's family has been trapping lobster and cooking them up for over a hundred years."

"Wow." He eyed the waitress, who, to almost-nine-year-old eyes, seemed old enough to have been handling that job personally for at least a century.

"I worked here some when I was a kid. Swabbing the decks." And she'd been kind to him, Nathaniel remembered. Giving him ice or salve for his bruises, saying nothing.

"I thought you worked with Holt's family—" Megan began, then cursed herself when he lifted a brow at her. "Coco mentioned it."

"I put in some time with the Bradfords."

"Did you know Holt's grandfather?" Kevin wanted to know. "He's one of the ghosts."

"Sure. He used to sit on the porch of the house where Alex and Jenny live now. Sometimes he'd walk up to the cliffs over by The Towers. Looking for Bianca."

"Lilah says they walk there together now. I haven't seen them." And it was a crushing disappointment. "Have you ever seen a ghost?"

"More than once." Nathaniel ignored the stiff kick Megan gave him under the table. "In Cornwall, where the cliffs are deadly and the fogs roll in like something alive, I saw a woman standing, looking out to sea. She wore a cape with a hood, and there were tears in her eyes."

Kevin was leaning forward now, rapt and eager.

"I started toward her, through the mist, and she turned. She was beautiful, and sad. 'Lost,' was what she said to me. 'He's lost. And so am I.' Then she vanished. Like smoke."

"Honest?" Kevin said in an awed whisper.

Honest wasn't the point, Nathaniel knew. The pull of the story was. "They called her the Captain's Lady, and legend is that her husband and his ship went down in a storm in the Irish Sea. Night after night while she lived, and long after, she walked the cliffs weeping for him."

"Maybe you should be writing books, like Max," Megan murmured, surprised and annoyed at the shiver that raced down her spine.

"Oh, he can spin a tale, Nate can." Julie plopped two beers and a soft drink on the table. "Used to badger me about all the places he was going to see. Well, guess you saw them, didn't you, Captain?"

"Guess I did." Nathaniel lifted the bottle to his lips. "But I never forgot you, darling."

Julie gave another cackling laugh, punched his shoulder. "Sweet-talker," she said, and shuffled off.

Megan studied her beer. "She didn't take our order."

"She won't. She'll bring us what she wants us to have." He took another pull of the beer. "Because she likes me. If you're not up for beer, I can charm her into switching it."

"No, it's fine. I suppose you know a lot of people on the island, since you grew up here."

"A few. I was gone a long time."

"Nate sailed around the whole world. Twice." Kevin slurped soda through his straw. "Through hurricanes and typhoons and everything."

"It must have been exciting."

"It had its moments."

"Do you miss it?"

"I sailed on another man's ship for more than fifteen years. Now I sail my own. Things change." Nathaniel draped his arm over the back of the booth. "Like you coming here."

"We like it." Kevin began to stab his straw in the ice. "Mom's boss in Oklahoma was a skinflint."

"Kevin."

"Granddad said so. And he didn't appreciate you. You were hiding your light under a bushel." Kevin didn't know what that meant, but his grandmother had said so.

"Granddad's biased." She smiled and ruffled her son's hair. "But we do like it here."

"Eat hearty," Julie ordered, and dropped three enormous platters on the table.

The long rolls of crusty bread were filled with chunks of lobster and flanked by a mound of coleslaw and a small mountain of French fries.

"Girl needs weight," Julie proclaimed. "Boy, too. Didn't know you liked 'em skinny, Captain."

"I like them any way I can get them," Nathaniel corrected, which sent Julie off into another gale of laughter.

"We'll never eat all of this." Megan stared, daunted, at her plate.

Nathaniel had already dug in. "Sure we will. So, have you looked over Fergus's book yet?"

"Not really." Megan sampled the first bite. Whatever the atmosphere, the food was four-star. "I want to get the backlog caught up first. Since Shipshape's books were the worst, I dealt with them first. I still have to work on your second quarter, and The Retreat's."

"Your mother's a practical woman, Kev."

"Yeah." Kevin managed to swallow a giant bite of lobster roll. "Granddad says she needs to get out more."

"Kevin."

But the warning came too late. Nathaniel was already grinning.

"Does he? What else does Granddad say?"

"She should live a little." Kevin attacked his French fries with the single-minded determination of a child. "'Cause she's too young to hole up like a hermit."

"Your granddad's a smart man."

"Oh, yeah. He knows everything. He's got oil for blood and horses on the brain."

"A quote from my mother," Megan said dryly. "She knows everything, too. But you were asking about Fergus's book."

"Just wondered if it had scratched your curiosity."

"Some. I thought I might take an hour or so at night to work on it."

"I don't think that's what your daddy meant by living a little, Meg."

"Regardless." She turned back to the safer topic of the account book. "Some of the pages are faded badly, but other than a few minor mistakes, the accounts are very accurate. Except for the last couple of pages, where there are just numbers without any logic."

"Really. They don't add up?"

"They don't seem to, but I need to take a closer look."

"Sometimes you miss more by looking too close." Nathaniel winked at Julie as she set another round of drinks on the table. It was coffee for him this time. She knew that when he was driving he kept it to one beer. "I wouldn't mind taking a look at it."

Megan frowned at her. "Why?"

"I like puzzles."

"I don't think it's much of a puzzle, but if it's all right with the family, I don't have any objection." She leaned back, sighed. "Sorry, I just can't eat any more."

"It's okay," Nathaniel switched his empty plate with hers. "I can."

To Megan's amazement, he could. It wasn't much of a surprise that Kevin had managed to clean his plate. The way he was growing he often seemed in danger of eating china and all when he sat down for a meal. But Nathaniel ate his meal, then half of hers, without a blink.

"Have you always eaten like that?" Megan asked when they were driving away from the restaurant.

"Nope. Always wanted to, though. Never could seem to fill up as a kid." Of course, that might have been because there was little to fill up on. "At sea, you learn to eat anything, and plenty of it, while it's there."

"You should weigh three hundred pounds."

"Some people burn it off." He shifted his eyes to hers. "Like you. All that nervous energy you've got just eats up those calories."

"I'm not skinny," she muttered.

"Nope. Thought you were myself, till I got ahold of you. It's more like willowy—and you've got a real soft feel to you when you're pressed up against a man."

She hissed, started to look over her shoulder.

"He conked out the minute I turned on the engine," Nathaniel told her. And, indeed, she could see Kevin stretched out in the back, his head pillowed on his arms, sleeping soundly. "Though I don't see what harm there is for the boy to know a man's interested in his mother."

"He's a child." She turned back, the gentle look in her eyes gone. "I won't have him think that I'm—"

"Human?"

"It's not your affair. He's my son."

"That he is," Nathaniel agreed easily. "And you've done a hell of a job with him."

She slanted him a cautious look. "Thank you."

"No need to. Just a fact. It's tough raising a kid on your own. You found the way to do it right."

It was impossible to stay irritated with him, especially when she remembered what Coco had told her. "You lost your mother when you were young. Ah...Coco mentioned it."

"Coco's been mentioning a lot of things."

"She didn't mean any harm. You know how she is, better than I. She cares so much about people, and wants to see them..."

"Lined up two by two? Yeah, I know her. She picked you out for me."

"She—" Words failed her. "That's ridiculous."

"Not to Coco." He steered easily around a curve. "Of course, she doesn't know that I know she's already got me scheduled to go down on one knee."

"It's fortunate, isn't it, that you're forewarned?"

Her indignant tone had a smile twitching at his lips. "Sure is. She's been singing your praises for months. And you almost live up to the advance publicity."

She hissed like a snake and turned to him. His grin, and the absurdity of the situation, changed indignation to amusement. "Thank you." She stretched out her legs, leaned back and decided to enjoy the ride. "I'd hate to have disappointed you."

"Oh, you didn't, sugar."

"I've been told you're mysterious, romantic and charming."

"And?"

"You almost live up to the advance publicity."

"Sugar—" he took her hand and kissed it lavishly "— I can be a lot better."

"I'm sure you can." She drew her hand away, refusing to acknowledge the rippling thrill up her arm. "If I wasn't so fond of her, I'd be annoyed. But she's so kind."

"She has the truest heart of anyone I've ever met. I used to wish she was my mother."

"I'm sorry." Before she could resist the urge, Megan laid a hand on his. "It must have been so hard, losing your mother when you were only a child."

"It's all right. It was a long time ago." Much too long for him to grieve. "I still remember seeing Coco in the village, or when I'd tag along with Holt to take fish up to The Towers. There she'd be, this gorgeous woman—looked like a queen. Never knew what color her hair would be from one week to the next."

"She's a brunette today," Megan said, and made him laugh.

"First woman I ever fell for. She came to the house a couple times, read my old man the riot act about his drinking. Guess she thought if he was sober he wouldn't knock me around so much." He took his eyes off the road again, met hers. "I imagine she mentioned that, too?"

"Yes." Uncomfortable, Megan looked away. "I'm sorry, Nathaniel. I hate when people discuss me, no matter how good their intentions. It's so intrusive."

"I'm not that sensitive, Meg. Everybody knew what my old man was like." He could remember, too well, the pitying looks, the glances that slid uneasily away. "It bothered me back then, but not anymore."

She struggled to find the right words. "Did Coco—did it do any good?"

He was silent a moment, staring out at the lowering sun and the bloodred light it poured into the water. "He was afraid of her, so he beat the hell out of me when she left."

"Oh, God."

"I'd just as soon she didn't know that."

"No." Megan had to swallow the hot tears lodged in her throat. "I won't tell her. That's why you ran away to sea, isn't it? To get away from him."

"That's one of the reasons." He reached over, ran a fingertip down her cheek. "You know, if I'd figured out the way to get to you was to tell you I'd taken a strap a few times, I'd have brought it up sooner."

"It's nothing to joke about." Megan's voice was low

and furious. "There's no excuse for treating a child that way."

"Hey, I lived through it."

"Did you?" She shifted back to him, eyes steady. "Did you ever stop hating him?"

"No." He said it quietly. "No, I didn't. But I stopped letting it be important, and maybe that's healthier." He stopped the car in front of The Towers, turned to her. "Someone hurts you, in a permanent way, you don't forget it. But the best revenge is seeing that it doesn't matter."

"You're talking about Kevin's father, and it's not at all the same. I wasn't a helpless child."

"Depends on where you draw the line between helpless and innocent." Nathaniel opened the car door. "I'll carry Kevin in for you."

"You don't have to." She hurried out herself, but Nathaniel already had the boy in his arms.

They stood there for a moment, in the last glow of the day, the boy between them, his head resting securely on Nathaniel's shoulder, dark hair to dark hair, honed muscle to young limbs.

Something locked deep inside her swelled, tried to burst free. She sighed it away, stroked a hand over her son's back and felt the steady rhythm of his breathing.

"He's had a long day."

"So have you, Meg. There are shadows under your eyes. Since that means you didn't sleep any better than I did last night, I can't say I mind seeing them there."

It was hard, she thought, so very hard, to keep pulling away from the current that drew her to him. "I'm not ready for this, Nathaniel."

"Sometimes a wind comes up, blows you off course.

You're not ready for it, but if you're lucky, you end up in a more interesting place than you'd planned.''

"I don't like to depend on luck."

"That's okay. I do." He shifted the boy more comfortably, and carried him to the house.

Chapter 6

"Don't see what all the damn to-do's about," Dutch grumbled as he whipped a delicate egg froth for his angel food cake surprise.

"Trenton St. James II is a member of the family." Running on nerves, Coco checked the temperature on her prime rib. She had a dozen things to deal with since the cucumber facial she'd indulged in had thrown off her timetable. "And the president of the St. James hotels." Satisfied that the beef was coming along nicely, she basted her roast duck. "As this is his first visit to The Retreat, it's important that everything run smoothly."

"Some rich bastard coming around to freeload."

"Mr. Van Horne!" Coco's heart lurched. After six months, she knew she shouldn't be shocked by the man. But, *really*. "I've known Mr. St. James for…well, a great number of years. I can assure you he is a successful businessman, an entrepreneur. *Not* a freeloader."

Dutch sniffed, gave Coco the once-over. She'd done

herself up good and proper, he noted. The fancy-shmancy dress glittered and flowed down, stopping plenty short to show off her legs. Her cheeks were all pink, too. And he didn't think it was from kitchen heat. His lips curled back in a sneer.

"So what's he, your boyfriend?"

The pink deepened to rose. "Certainly not. A woman of my...experience doesn't have boyfriends." Surreptitiously she checked her face in the stainless-steel exhaust hood on the stove. "Beaux, perhaps."

Beaux. Ha! "I hear he's been married four times and pays enough alimony to balance the national debt. You looking to be number five?"

Speechless, Coco pressed a hand to her heart. "You are—" She stumbled, stuttered, over the words. "Impossibly rude. Impossibly crude."

"Hey, ain't none of my never-mind if you want to land yourself a rich fish."

She squeaked. Though the rolling temper that caused red dots to swim in front of her eyes appalled her—she was, after all, a civilized woman—she surged forward to ram a coral-tipped nail into his massive chest. "I will not tolerate any more of your insults."

"Yeah?" He poked her right back. "Whatcha gonna do about it?"

She leaned forward until they were nose-to-nose. "I will fire you."

"Now that'll break my heart. Go ahead, fancy face, give me the boot. See how you get by with tonight's dinner rush."

"I assure you, I will 'get by' delightfully." Her heart was beating too fast. Coco wondered it didn't soar right out of her breast.

"Like hell." He hated her perfume. Hated that it made

his nostrils twitch and his mouth water. "When I came on board, you were barely treading water."

She couldn't get her breath, simply couldn't. "This kitchen doesn't need you, Mr. Van Horne. And neither do I."

"You need me plenty." How had his hands gotten onto her shoulders? Why were hers pressed to his chest? The hell with how or why, he thought. He'd show her what was what.

Her eyes popped hard when his hard, sneering mouth crushed down on hers in a very thorough kiss. But she didn't see a thing. Her world, so beautifully secure, tilted under her feet. That was why—naturally that was why—she clung to him.

She would slap his face. She certainly would.

In just a few minutes.

Damn women, Dutch thought. Damn them all. Especially tall, curvy, sweet-smelling females with lips like…cooking cherries. He'd always had a weakness for tartness.

He jerked her away, but kept his big hands firm on her shoulders. "Let's get something straight…." he began.

"Now look here…." she said at the same time.

They both leaped apart like guilty children when the kitchen door swung open.

Megan stood frozen in the doorway, her jaw dropping. Surely she hadn't seen what she thought she'd seen. Coco was checking the oven, and Dutch was measuring flour into a bowl. They couldn't have been…embracing. Yet both of them were a rather startling shade of pink.

"Excuse me," she managed. "I'm sorry to, ah…"

"Oh, Megan, dear." Flustered, Coco patted her hair. She was tingling, she realized. From embarrassment—

and annoyance, she assured herself. ''What can I do for you?''

''I just wanted to check a couple of the kitchen expenses.'' She was still goggling, her eyes shifting from Coco to Dutch and back. The tension in the room was thicker than Coco's split-pea soup. ''But if you're busy, we can do it later.''

''Nonsense.'' Coco wiped her sweaty palms on her apron. ''We're just a little frantic preparing for Trenton's arrival.''

''Trenton? Oh, I'd forgotten. Trent's father's expected.'' She was cautiously backing out of the room. ''We don't need to do this now.''

''No, no.'' Oh, Lord, Coco thought, don't leave me. ''Now's a perfect time. We're under control here. Let's do it in your office, shall we?' She took Megan firmly by the arm. ''Mr. Van Horne can handle things for a few minutes.'' Without waiting for his assent, she hurried from the room. ''Details, details,'' Coco said gaily, and clung to Megan as though she were a life raft in a churning sea. ''It seems the more you handle, the more there are.''

''Coco, are you all right?''

''Oh, of course.'' But she pressed a hand to her heart. ''Just a little contretemps with Mr. Van Horne. But that's nothing I can't deal with.'' She hoped. ''How are your accounts coming along, dear? I must say I'd hoped you'd find time to glance at Fergus's book.''

''Actually, I have—''

''Not that we want you working too hard.'' With the buzz going on in Coco's head, she didn't hear a word Megan said. ''We want you to feel right at home here, to enjoy yourself. To relax. After all the trouble and excitement last year, we all want to relax. I don't think any of us could stand any more crises.''

"I do not have, nor do I require, a reservation."

The crackling, irate voice stopped Coco in her tracks. The becoming flush in her cheeks faded to a dead white.

"Dear God, no. It can't be."

"Coco?" Megan took a firmer grip on Coco's arm. She felt the tremor and wondered if she could hold the woman up if she fainted.

"Young man." The voice rose, echoing off the walls. "Do you know who I am?"

"Aunt Colleen," Coco said in a shaky whisper. She let go one last shuddering moan, drew in a bracing breath, then walked bravely into the lobby. "Aunt Colleen," she said in an entirely different tone. "What a lovely surprise."

"Shock, you mean." Colleen accepted her niece's kiss, then rapped her cane on the floor. She was tall, thin as a rail and formidable as iron in a raw-silk suit and pearls as white as her hair. "I see you've filled the place with strangers. Better to have it burned to the ground. Tell this insolent boy to have my bags taken up."

"Of course." Coco gestured for a bellman herself. "In the family wing, second floor, first room on the right," she instructed.

"And don't toss those bags around, boy." Colleen leaned on her gold-tipped cane and studied Megan. "Who's this?"

"You remember Megan, Aunt Colleen. Sloan's sister? You met at Amanda's wedding."

"Yes, yes." Colleen's eyes narrowed, measured. "Got a son, don't you?" Colleen knew all there was to know about Kevin. Had made it her business to know.

"Yes, I do. It's nice to see you again, Miss Calhoun."

"Ha. You'd be the only one of this lot who thinks so." Ignoring them both, she walked to Bianca's portrait, studied it and the emeralds glistening in their case. She sighed, but so quietly no one could hear.

"I want brandy, Cordelia, before I take a look at what you've done to this place."

"Of course. We'll just go into the family wing. Megan, please, join us."

It was impossible to deny the plea in Coco's eyes.

A few moments later, they had settled into the family parlor. Here, the wallpaper was still faded, peeling in spots. There were scars on the floor in front of the fireplace where errant embers had seared and burned.

"Nothing's changed here, I see." Colleen sat like a queen in a wing chair.

"We've concentrated on the hotel wing." Nervous and babbling, Coco poured brandy. "Now that it's done, we're beginning renovations. Two of the bedrooms are finished. And the nursery's lovely."

"Humph." She'd come specifically to see the children—and only secondarily to drive Coco mad. "Where is everyone? I come to see my family and find nothing but strangers."

"They'll be along. We're having a dinner party tonight, Aunt Colleen." Coco kept the brilliant smile plastered on her face. "Trent's father's joining us for a few days."

"Aging playboy," Colleen mumbled into her brandy. "You." She pointed at Megan. "Accountant, aren't you?"

"Yes, ma'am."

"Megan's a whiz with figures," Coco said desperately.

"We're so grateful she's here. And Kevin, too, of course. He's a darling boy."

"I'm talking to the girl, Cordelia. Go fuss in the kitchen."

"But—"

"Go on, go on."

With an apologetic look for Megan, Coco fled.

"The boy'll be nine soon?"

"Yes, in a couple of months." She was prepared, braced, for a scathing comment on his lineage.

Tapping her fingers on the arm of the chair, Colleen nodded. "Get along with Suzanna's brood, does he?"

"Very well. They've rarely been apart since we arrived." Megan did her best not to squirm. "It's been wonderful for him. And for me."

"Dumont bothering you?"

Megan blinked. "I beg your pardon?"

"Don't be a fool, girl, I asked if that excuse for a human being has been bothering you."

Megan's spine straightened like a steel rod. "No. I haven't seen or heard from Baxter since before Kevin was born."

"You will." Colleen scowled and leaned forward. She wanted to get a handle on this Megan O'Riley. "He's been making inquiries."

Megan's fingers clenched on the snifter of brandy. "I don't understand."

"Poking his nose in, asking questions." Colleen gave her cane an imperious thump.

"How do you know?"

"I keep my ear to the ground when it comes to family." Eyes bright, Colleen waited for a reaction, got none. "You moved here, didn't you? Your son's been accepted as Alex and Jenny—and Christian's—brother."

Ice was forming in Megan's stomach, thin, brittle strips of it. "That has nothing to do with him."

"Don't be a fool. A man like Dumont thinks the world revolves around him. His eye's on politics, girl, and the way that particular circus is running, a few well-chosen words from you to the right reporter…" The idea was pleasant enough to make Colleen smile. "Well, his road to Washington would be a steeper climb."

"I've no intention of going to the press, of exposing Kevin to public attention."

"Wise." Colleen sipped again. "A pity, but wise. You tell me if he tries anything. I'd like to tangle with him again."

"I can handle it myself."

Colleen lifted one snowy brow. "Perhaps you can."

"How come I have to wear a dumb tie?" Kevin squirmed while Megan fumbled with the knot. Her fingers had been stiff and cold ever since her talk with Colleen.

"Because it's a special dinner and you need to look your best."

"Ties are stupid. I bet Alex doesn't have to wear a stupid tie."

"I don't know what Alex is wearing," Megan said, with the last of her patience. "But you're doing as you're told."

The sharp tone, rarely heard, had his bottom lip poking out. "I'd rather have pizza."

"Well, you're not having pizza. Damn it, Kevin, hold still!"

"It's choking me."

"*I'm* going to choke you in a minute." She blew her

hair out of her eyes and secured the knot. "There. You look very handsome."

"I look like a dork."

"Fine, you look like a dork. Now put your shoes on."

Kevin scowled at the shiny black loafers. "I hate those shoes. I want to wear my sneakers."

Exasperated, she leaned down until their faces were level. "Young man, you will put your shoes on, and you will watch your tone of voice. Or you'll find yourself in very hot water."

Megan marched out of his room and across the hall to her own. Snatching her brush from the dresser, she began to drag it through her hair. She didn't want to go to the damn dinner party, either. The aspirin she'd downed an hour before hadn't even touched the splitting headache slicing through her skull. But she had to put on her party face and go down, pretend she wasn't terrified and angry and sick with worry over Baxter Dumont.

Colleen might be wrong, she thought. After all, it had been nearly a decade. Why would Baxter bother with her and Kevin now?

Because he wanted to be a United States senator. Megan closed her eyes. She read the paper, didn't she? Baxter had already begun his campaign for the seat. And an illegitimate son, never acknowledged, hardly fit the straight-arrow platform he'd chosen.

"Mom."

She saw Kevin's reflection in the mirror. His shoes were on—and his chin was on his chest. Guilt squeezed its sticky fingers around her heart. "Yes, Kevin."

"How come you're so mad at everything?"

"I'm not." Wearily she sat on the edge of the bed. "I've just got a little headache. I'm sorry I snapped at you." She held out her arms, sighing when he filled them. "You're such a handsome dork, Kev." When he laughed, she kissed the top of his head. "Let's go down. Maybe Alex and Jenny are here."

They were, and Alex was just as disgusted with his tie as Kevin was with his. But there was too much going on for the boys to sulk for long. There were canapés to gobble, babies to play with and adventures to plan.

Everyone, naturally, was talking at once.

The volume in the room cut through Megan's aching head like a rusty saw. She accepted the flute of champagne Trenton II offered her, and did her best to pretend an interest in his flirtation. He was trim and tall and tanned, glossily handsome and charming. And Megan was desperately relieved when he turned his attentions on Coco.

"Make a nice couple, don't they?" Nathaniel murmured in her ear.

"Striking." She took a cube of cheese and forced it down.

"You don't look in the party mood, Meg."

"I'm fine." To distract him, she changed the subject. "You might be interested in what I think I might have walked in on this afternoon."

"Oh?" Taking her arm, he steered her toward the open terrace doors.

"Coco and Dutch."

"Fighting again? Saucepans at twenty paces?"

"Not exactly." She took a deep breath of air, hoping it would clear her head. "They were…at least I think they were…"

Nathaniel's brows shot up. He could fill in the blanks himself. "You're joking."

"No. They were nose-to-nose, with their arms around

each other.'' She managed to smile even as she rubbed at the throbbing in her temple. ''At my unexpected and ill-timed entrance, they jumped apart as if they'd been planning murder. And they were blushing. Both of them.''

''The Dutchman, blushing?'' Nathaniel started to laugh, but it began to sink in. ''Good God.''

''I think it's sweet.''

''Sweet.'' He looked back inside, where Coco, regally elegant, was laughing over something Trenton had whispered in her ear. ''She's out of his league. She'll break his heart.''

''What a ridiculous thing to say.'' Lord, why didn't her head just fall off her shoulders and give her some relief? ''Sporting events have leagues, not romances.''

''The Dutchman and Coco.'' It worried him, because they were two of the very few people in the world he could say he loved. ''You're the accountant, sugar, and you're going to tell me that adds up?''

''I'm not telling you anything,'' she shot back. ''Except I think they're attracted to each other. And stop calling me 'sugar.'''

''Okay, simmer down.'' He looked back down at her, focused on her. ''What's the matter?''

Guiltily she dropped her hand. She'd been massaging her temple again. ''Nothing.''

With an impatient oath, he turned her fully to face him, looked into her eyes. ''Headache, huh? Bad one?''

''No, it's— Yes,'' she admitted. ''Vicious.''

''You're all tensed up.'' He began to knead her shoulders. ''Tight as a spring.''

''Don't.''

''This is purely therapeutic.'' He rubbed his thumbs in gentle circles over her collarbone. ''Any pleasure either of us gets out of it is incidental. Have you always been prone to headaches?''

His fingers were strong and male and magical. It was impossible not to stretch under them. ''I'm not prone to headaches.''

''Too much stress.'' His hands skimmed lightly up to her temples. She closed her eyes with a sigh. ''You bottle too much up, Meg. Your body makes you pay for it. Turn around, let me work on those shoulders.''

''It's not—'' But the protest died away when his hands began to knead at the knots.

''Relax. Pretty night, isn't it? Moon's full, stars are out. Ever walk up on the cliffs in the moonlight, Megan?''

''No.''

''Wildflowers growing right out of the rock, the water thundering. You can imagine those ghosts Kevin's so fond of strolling hand in hand. Some people think it's a lonely place, but it's not.''

His voice and his hands were so soothing. She could almost believe there was nothing to worry about. ''There's a painting at Suzanna's of the cliffs in moonlight,'' Megan offered, trying to focus on the conversation.

''Christian Bradford's work—I've seen it. He had a feel for that spot. But there's nothing like the real thing. You could walk with me there after dinner. I'll show you.''

''This isn't the time to fool around with the girl.'' Colleen's voice cut through the evening air, and she stamped her cane in the doorway.

Though Megan tensed again, Nathaniel kept his hands where they were and grinned. ''Seems like a fine time to me, Miss Colleen.''

"Ha! Scoundrel." Colleen's lips twitched. Nothing she liked better than a handsome scoundrel. "Always were. I remember you, running wild through the village. Looks like the sea made a man of you, all right. Stop fidgeting, girl. He's not going to let loose of you. If you're lucky."

Nathaniel kissed the top of Megan's head. "She's shy."

"Well, she'll have to get over it, won't she? Cordelia's finally going to feed us. I want you to sit with me, talk about boats."

"It would be a pleasure."

"Well, come on, bring her. Lived on cruise ships half my life or more," Colleen began. "I'll wager I've seen more of the sea than you, boy."

"I wouldn't doubt it, ma'am." Nathaniel kept one hand on Megan and offered Colleen his arm. "With a trail of broken hearts in your wake."

She gave a hoot of laughter. "Damn right."

The dining room was full of the scents of food and flowers and candle wax. The moment everyone was settled, Trenton II rose, glass in hand.

"I'd like to make a toast." His voice was as cultured as his dinner suit. "To Cordelia, a woman of extraordinary talents and beauty."

Glasses were clinked. From his spy hole at the crack in the doorway, Dutch snorted, scowled, then stomped back to his own kitchen.

"Trent." C.C. leaned toward her husband, her voice low. "You know I love you."

He thought he knew what was coming. "Yes, I do."

"And I adore your father."

"Mmm-hmm…"

"And if he puts the moves on Aunt Coco, I'm going to have to kill him."

"Right." Trent smiled weakly and began on the first course.

At the other end of the table, sublimely ignorant of the threat, Trenton beamed at Colleen. "What do you think of The Retreat, Miss Calhoun?"

"I dislike hotels. Never use them."

"Aunt Colleen." Coco fluttered her hands. "The St. James hotels are world-famous for their luxury and taste."

"Can't stand them," Colleen said complacently as she spooned up soup. "What's this stuff?"

"It's lobster bisque, Aunt Colleen."

"Needs salt," she said, for the devil of it. "You, boy." She jabbed a finger down the table at Kevin. "Don't slouch. You want your bones to grow crooked?"

"No, ma'am."

"Got any ambitions?"

Kevin stared helplessly, and was relieved when his mother's hand closed over his. "I could be a sailor," he blurted out. "I steered the *Mariner*."

"Ha!" Pleased, she picked up her wine. "Good for you. I won't tolerate any idlers in my family. Too thin. Eat your soup, such as it is."

With a quiet moan, Coco rang for the second course.

"She never changes." Lazily content, Lilah rocked while Bianca suckled hungrily at her breast. The nursery was quiet, the lights were low. Megan had headed for it, figuring it would be the perfect escape hatch.

"She's..." Megan searched for a diplomatic phrase. "Quite a lady."

"She's a nosy old nuisance." Lilah laughed lightly. "But we love her."

In the next rocker, Amanda sighed. "As soon as she

hears about Fergus's book, she's going to start nagging you."

"And badgering," C.C. put in, cradling Ethan.

"And hounding," Suzanna finished up as she changed Christian's diaper.

"That sounds promising."

"Don't worry." With a laugh, Suzanna slipped Christian into his sleeper. "We're right behind you."

"Notice," Lilah added with a smile, "the direction is *behind.*"

"About the book." Megan flicked a finger over a dancing giraffe on a mobile. "I've made copies of several pages I thought you'd be interested in. He made a lot of notations, about business deals, personal business, purchases. At one point he inventories jewelry—Bianca's, I assume—for insurance purposes."

"The emeralds?" Amanda's brow rose at Megan's nod. "And to think of all the hours we spent going through papers, trying to find proof that they existed."

"There's a number of other pieces—hundreds of thousands of dollars' worth in 1913 dollars."

"He sold nearly everything," C.C. murmured. "We found the documents of sale. He got rid of anything that reminded him of Bianca."

"It still hurts," Lilah admitted. "Not the money, though God knows we could have used it. It's the loss of what was hers, what we won't be able to pass on."

"I'm sorry."

"Don't be." Amanda rose to lay a sleeping Delia in her crib. "We're too sentimental. I suppose we all feel such a close connection with Bianca."

"I know what you mean." It felt odd to admit it, but Megan was compelled. "I feel it, too. I suppose from seeing the references to her in the old book, and having her portrait right there in the lobby.'' A bit embarrassed, she laughed. ''Sometimes, when you walk down the halls at night, it's almost as if you could sense her.''

''Of course,'' Lilah said easily. ''She's here.''

''Excuse me, ladies.'' Nathaniel stepped inside, obviously comfortable in a nursery inhabited by babies and nursing mothers.

Lilah smiled slowly. ''Well, hello, handsome. What brings you to the maternity wing?''

''Just coming to fetch my date.''

When he took Megan's arm, she drew back. ''We don't have a date.''

''A walk, remember?''

''I never said—''

''It's a lovely night for it.'' Suzanna lifted Christian into her arms, cooed to him.

''I have to put Kevin to bed.''

She was digging in her heels, but it didn't seem to be doing any good.

''I've already tucked him in.'' Nathaniel propelled her toward the doors.

''You put Kevin to bed?''

''Since he'd fallen asleep in my lap, it seemed the thing to do. Oh, Suzanna, Holt said the kids are ready whenever you are.''

''I'm on my way.'' Suzanna waited until Megan and Nate were out of earshot before she turned to her sisters. ''What do you think?''

Amanda smiled smugly. ''I think it's working perfectly.''

''I have to agree.'' C.C. settled Ethan comfortably in his crib. ''I thought Lilah had lost her mind when she came up with the idea of getting those two together.''

Lilah yawned, sighed. "I'm never wrong." Then her eyes lit. "I bet we can see them from the window."

"*Spy* on them?" Amanda arched her brows. "Good idea," she said, and darted to the window.

They were outlined in the moonlight that sprinkled the lawn.

"You're complicating things, Nathaniel."

"Simplifying," he corrected. "Nothing simpler than a walk in the moonlight."

"That's not where you expect all this to end."

"Nope. But we're still moving at your pace, Meg." He brought her hand to his lips, kissed it absently, when they began the climb. "I seem to have this need to be around you. It's the damnedest thing. Can't shake it. So I figure, why try? Why not just roll with it?"

"I'm not a simple woman." She wished she could be, just for tonight, just for an hour in the starlight. "I have baggage and resentments and insecurities I didn't even realize were there until I met you. I'm not going to let myself be hurt again."

"No one's going to hurt you." In a subtle gesture of protection, he slipped an arm around her and looked up at the sky. "Look how big the moon is tonight. Just hanging there. You can see Venus, and the little star that dogs her. There's Orion." He lifted her hand, tracing the sky with it as he had once traced his charts. "And the Twins. See?"

"Yes." She watched their joined hands connect stars while the breeze lifted lovingly off the water and stirred the flowers that grew wild in the rock.

Romantic, mysterious, Coco had said. Yes, he was, and Megan realized she was much more susceptible to both than she would have believed.

For she was here, wasn't she, standing on a cliff with a seafaring man whose callused hand held hers, whose voice helped her see the pictures painted by the stars. His body was warm and solid against hers. And her blood was pumping fast and free in her veins.

Alive. The wind and the sea and the man made her feel so alive.

And perhaps there was something more—those ghosts of the Calhouns'. The cliffs seemed to invite spirits to walk, the air filled with contentment. And the glow of love that had outlasted time.

"I shouldn't be here like this." But she didn't move away, not even when his lips brushed over her hair.

"Listen," he murmured. "Close your eyes and listen, and you can hear the stars breathing."

She obeyed, and listened to the whisper and throb of the air. And of her own heart. "Why do you make me feel this way?"

"I don't have an answer. Not everything adds up neat, Meg." Because he had a great need to see her face, he turned her gently. "Not everything has to." And kissed her. His lips skimmed hers, journeyed up to her temple, over her brow and down. "How's the headache?"

"It's gone. Nearly."

"No. Keep your eyes closed." His lips traced over them, soft as air, before trailing slowly over her face. "Kiss me back, will you?"

How could she not, when his mouth was so tempting on hers? With a small sound of surrender, she let her heart lead. Just for tonight, she promised herself. Just for a moment.

That slow, melting change almost undid him. She went pliant in his arms, those hesitant lips heating, parting, offering. It took all his willpower not to drag her against him and plunder.

She wouldn't resist. Perhaps he'd known that there would be enough magic on those cliffs to bewitch them both, to seduce her into surrender—and to remind him to take care.

"I want you, Megan." He took his lips down her throat, up over her jaw. "I want you so much it's got me tied in knots."

"I know. I wish…" She pressed her face to his shoulder. "I'm not playing games, Nathaniel."

"I know." He stroked a hand down her hair. "It would be easier if you were, because I know all the rules." Cupping her face, he lifted it. "And how to break them." He sighed, kissed her again, lightly. "They make it damn hard for me, those eyes of yours." He stepped back. "I'd better take you in."

"Nathaniel." She laid a hand on his chest. "You're the first man who's made me…who I've wanted to be with since Kevin was born."

Something flashed in his eyes, wild, dangerous, before he banked it. "Do you think it makes it easier on me, knowing that?" He would have laughed, if he hadn't felt so much like exploding. "Megan, you're killing me." But he swung an arm around her shoulders and led her down the cliff path.

"I don't know how to handle this," she said under her breath. "I haven't had to handle anything like this before."

"Keep it up," he warned, "and you're over my shoulder, shanghaied straight to bed. Mine."

The image gave her a quick thrill, and a guilty one. "I'm just trying to be honest."

"Try lying," he said with a grimace. "Make it easier on me."

"I'm a lousy liar." She slanted a look at him. Wasn't it interesting, she mused, that for once he was the one at a disadvantage? "It doesn't seem logical that it would bother you to know what I'm feeling."

"I'm having a lot of trouble dealing with what I'm feeling." He took a long, steadying breath. "And I'm not feeling logical." Nor, he thought ruefully, would he sleep tonight. "'Desire hath no rest.'"

"What?"

"Robert Burton. Nothing."

They walked toward the lights of The Towers. The shouting reached them before they crossed the lawn.

"Coco," Megan said.

"Dutch." Taking firm hold of Megan's hand, Nathaniel quickened his pace.

"You're insulting and obnoxious," Coco snapped at Dutch, her chin up, her hands planted on her hips.

His massive arms were folded across his barrel of a chest. "I saw what I saw, said what I said."

"I was not draped all over Trenton like a…a…"

"Barnacle," Dutch said with relish. "Like a barnacle on the hull of a fancy yacht."

"We happen to have been dancing."

"Ha! That's what you call it. We got another name for it. Where I come from, we call it—"

"Dutch!" Nathaniel cut off the undoubtedly crude description.

"There." Mortified, Coco smoothed down her dress. "You've made a scene."

"You were the one making a scene, with that smooth-skinned rich boy. Flaunting yourself."

"F-f-flaunting." Enraged, she drew herself up to her

full, and considerable, height. "I have never flaunted in my life. You, sir, are despicable."

"I'll show you despicable, lady."

"Cut it out." Prepared for fists to fly, Nathaniel stepped between them. "Dutch, what the hell's wrong with you? Are you drunk?"

"A nip or two of rum never rattled my brain." He glared over Nathaniel's shoulder at Coco. "It's her that's acting snockered. Out of my way, boy, I've got a thing or two left to say."

"You've finished," Nathaniel corrected.

"Out of his way." All eyes turned to Coco. She was flushed, bright-eyed, and regal as a duchess. "I prefer to handle this matter myself."

Megan tugged gently on her arm. "Coco, don't you think you should go inside?"

"I do not." She caught herself and added a friendly pat. "Now, dear, you and Nate run along. Mr. Van Horne and I prefer to handle this privately."

"But—"

"Nathaniel," Coco said, interrupting her, "take Megan inside now."

"Yes, ma'am."

"Are you sure we should leave them alone?"

Nathaniel continued to steer Megan to the terrace doors. "You want to get in the middle of that?"

Megan glanced back over her shoulder. "No." She chuckled, shook her head. "No, I don't think so."

"Well, Mr. Van Horne," Coco began, when she was certain they were alone again. "Do you have something more to say?"

"I got plenty." Prepared for battle, he stepped forward. "You tell that slick-talking rich boy to keep his hands to himself."

She tossed back her head and enjoyed the mad flutter of her heart when her eyes met his. "And if I don't?"

Dutch growled like a wolf—like a wolf, Coco thought, challenging his mate. "I'll break his puny arms like matchsticks."

Oh, my, she thought. Oh, my goodness. "Will you, really?"

"Just you try me." He gave her a jerk, and she let herself tumble into his arms.

This time she was ready for the kiss, and met it head-on. By the time they broke apart, they were both breathless and stunned.

Sometimes, Coco realized, it was up to the woman. She moistened her lips, swallowed hard.

"My room's on the second floor."

"I know where it is." A ghost of a smile flitted around his mouth. "Mine's closer." He swept her into his arms—very much, Coco thought dreamily, like a pirate taking his hostage.

"You're a fine, sturdy woman, Coco."

She pressed a hand on her thundering heart. "Oh, Niels."

Chapter 7

It wasn't like Megan to daydream. Years of discipline had taught her that dreams were for sleeping, not for rainy mornings when the fog was drifting around the house and the windows ran wet, as if with tears. But her computer hummed, unattended, and her chin was on her fist as her mind wandered back, as it had several times over the past few days, toward moonlight and wildflowers and the distant thunder of surf.

Now and again she caught herself and fell back on logic. It wouldn't pay to forget that the only romance in her life had been an illusion, a lie that betrayed her innocence, her emotions and her future. She'd thought herself immune, been content to be immune. Until Nathaniel.

What should she do, now that her life had taken this fast, unexpected swing? After all, she was no longer a child who believed in or needed promises and coaxing words. Now that her needs had been stirred, could she satisfy them without being hurt?

Oh, how she wished her heart wasn't involved. How she wished she could be smart and savvy and sophisticated and indulge in a purely physical affair, without emotion weighing in so heavily.

Why couldn't attraction, leavened with affection and respect, be enough? It should be such a simple equation. Two consenting adults, plus desire, times understanding and passion, equals mutual pleasure.

She just wished she could be sure there wasn't some hidden fraction that would throw off the simple solution.

"Megan?"

"Hmm?" Dreamily she turned toward the sound of the voice. Her imaginings shattered when she saw Suzanna inside the office, smiling at her. "Oh, I didn't hear you come in."

"You were miles away."

Caught drifting, Megan fought back embarrassment and shuffled papers. "I suppose I was. Something about the rain."

"It's lovely—always sets my mind wandering." Suzanna thought she knew just where Megan's mind had wandered. "Though I doubt the tourists or the children think so."

"Kevin thought the fog was great—until I told him he couldn't climb on the cliffs in it."

"And Alex and Jenny's plans for an assault on Fort O'Riley have been postponed. The kids are in Kevin's room, defending the planet against aliens. It's wonderful watching them together."

"I know. They've blended together so well."

"Like a mud ball," Suzanna said with a laugh, and

eased a jean-clad hip on the edge of Megan's desk. "How's the work coming?"

"It's moving along. Amanda kept everything in order, so it's just a matter of shifting it into my own system and computerizing."

"It's a tremendous relief for her, having you take it over. Some days she'd be doing the books with a phone at her ear and Delia at her breast."

The image made Megan grin. "I can see it. She's amazingly organized."

"An expert juggler. Nothing she hates more than to bobble a ball. You'd understand that."

"Yeah, I do." Megan picked up a pencil and ran it between her fingers. "I worried about coming here, Suzanna, bringing Kevin. I was afraid I'd not only bobble a ball, but drop all of them, because I'd be so anxious not to say anything, even think anything, that would make you uncomfortable."

"Aren't we past that, Megan?"

"You were." Sighing, Megan set the pencil down again. "Maybe it's a little harder, being the other woman."

"Were you?" Suzanna said gently. "Or was I?"

Megan could only shake her head. "I can't say I wish I could go back and change things, because if I did I wouldn't have Kevin." She took a long breath, met Suzanna's eyes levelly. "I know you consider Kevin a brother to your children, and that you love him."

"Yes, I do."

"I want you to know that I think of your children as my family and I love them."

Suzanna reached over to lay a hand over Megan's. "I know you do. One of the reasons I dropped in was to ask if you'd mind if Kevin came along with us. I'm going to do some greenhouse work today. Alex and Jenny always enjoy it—especially since it includes pizza for lunch.''

"I can't think of anything he'd rather do. And it would make up for having to wear a tie the other night.''

Suzanna's eyes lit with humor. "I nearly had to strangle Alex to get him into his. I hope Aunt Coco doesn't plan any more formal dinner parties for some time to come.'' She tilted her head. "Speaking of Aunt Coco, have you seen her today?''

"Only for a minute, right after breakfast. Why?''

"Was she singing?''

"As a matter of fact, she was.'' Megan touched her tongue to her top lip. "She's been singing in the morning for several days now.''

"She was singing just now, too. And wearing her best perfume.'' Uneasy, Suzanna nibbled her lip. "I was wondering if Trent's father... Of course, he's gone back to Boston now, so I thought there was nothing to worry about. He's a lovely man, and we're all very fond of him, but, well, he's been married four times, and he doesn't seem able to keep his eye from roving.''

"I noticed.'' After a quick debate on privacy versus disclosure, Megan cleared her throat. "Actually, I don't think Coco's looking in that direction.''

"No?''

"Dutch,'' Megan said, and watched Suzanna's eyes go blank.

"Excuse me?''

"I think she and Dutch are...infatuated.''

"Dutch? Our Dutch? But she's always complaining about him, and he's snarling at her every chance he gets. They're always fighting, and...'' She trailed off, pressed her hands to her lips. "Oh…" she said, while her eyes danced over them. "Oh, oh, oh…"

They stared at each other, struggled dutifully for perhaps three seconds before bursting into laughter. Megan fell easily into the sisterly pleasure of discussing a family member. After she told Suzanna about walking in on Coco and Dutch in the kitchen, she followed it up with the scene on the terrace.

"There were sparks flying, Suzanna. At first I thought they were going to come to blows, then I realized it was more of a—well, a mating ritual."

"A mating ritual," Suzanna repeated in a shaky voice. "Do you really think they—?"

"Well." Megan wriggled her eyebrows. "She's been doing a lot of singing lately."

"She certainly has." Suzanna let the idea stew for a moment, found it simmered nicely. "I think I'll drop by the kitchen before I go. Check out the atmosphere."

"I hope I can count on a full report."

"Absolutely." Still chuckling, Suzanna rose to go to the door. "I guess that was some moon the other night."

"It was," Megan murmured. "Some moon."

Suzanna paused with her hand on the knob. "And Nathaniel's some man."

"I thought we were talking about Dutch."

"We were talking about romance," Suzanna corrected. "I'll see you later."

Megan frowned at the closed door. Good Lord, she thought, was she that obvious?

After spending the rest of the morning and the first part of the afternoon on The Retreat's accounts, Megan gave herself the small reward of an hour with Fergus's book. She enjoyed tallying up the costs of stabling horses, maintaining carriages. It was an eye-opener to see how much expense was involved in giving a ball at The Towers in 1913. And, by reading Fergus's margin notes, to come to understand his motives.

Invitations all accepted. No one dare decline. B. ordered flowers—argued about ostentation. Told her big display equals success and wife must never question husband. She will wear emeralds, not pearl choker as she suggested, show society my taste and means, remind her of her place.

Her place, Megan thought with pity for Bianca, had been with Christian. How sad that it had taken death to unite them.

Wanting to dispel the gloom, she flipped to the back pages. The numbers simply didn't make sense. Not expenses, she mused. Not dates. Account numbers, perhaps. Stock-market prices, lot numbers?

Perhaps it would be worth a trip to the library to see if she could unearth any information from 1913 that correlated. And on the way she could stop by Shipshape to drop off the completed spreadsheet for April and pick up any more receipts.

If she happened to run into Nathaniel, it would be purely coincidental.

It was a pleasure to drive in the rain. The slow, steady stream of drops had most of the summer people seeking indoor entertainment. A few pedestrians wandered the sidewalks, window-shopping under umbrellas. The water in Frenchman Bay was gray and misted, with the masts and sails of ships spearing through the heavy air.

She could hear the ring of bell buoys, the drone of

foghorns. It was as if the entire island were tucked under
a blanket, snug and safe and solitary. She was tempted
to keep driving, to take the twisting road to Acadia National Park, or the meandering one along the shore.

Maybe she would, she thought. After she completed
the day's business, she would take that drive, explore her
new home. And maybe she would ask Nathaniel to join
her.

But she didn't see his car outside Shipshape. Ridiculous to say it didn't matter whether she saw him or not,
she realized. Because it did matter. She wanted to see
him, to watch the way his eyes deepened and locked on
hers. The way his lips curved.

Maybe he'd parked around the corner, out of sight.
Snagging her briefcase, she dashed from her car into the
office. It was empty.

The first slap of disappointment was stunning. She
hadn't realized just how much she'd counted on him being there until he wasn't. Then she heard, faintly, through
the rear wall, the throb of bass from a radio. Someone
was in the shop attached to the back of the building, she
concluded. Probably working on repairs as the seas were
too rough for tours.

She wasn't going to check out who was back there,
she told herself firmly. She'd come on legitimate business
and she took out the latest spreadsheet and set it on the
overburdened desk. But on a purely practical level, she
would need to go over, with at least one of them, the
second quarter and the projections for the rest of the year.
But she supposed it could wait.

A long look around showed her a disorder she couldn't
comprehend. How could anyone work, or hope to concentrate, in such a mess?

She was tempted to organize, but turned her back on

the chaos and walked to the filing cabinets. She'd take what she needed and leave the rest. Then she would, casually, wander around back, to the shop.

When she heard the door open, she turned, ready with a smile. It faded a little when she saw a stranger in the doorway. "May I help you?"

The man stepped fully inside and shut the door behind him. When he smiled, something jittered inside Megan's brain. "Hello, Megan."

For an instant, time froze, and then it rewound. Slow motion for five years, six, then back a decade, to a time when she'd been young and careless and ready to believe in love at first sight.

"Baxter," she whispered. How odd, she thought dully, that she hadn't recognized him. He'd hardly changed in ten years. He was as handsome, as smooth and polished, as he'd been when she first saw him. A trim, Savile Row–suited Prince Charming with lies on his lips.

Baxter smiled down at Megan. For days he'd been trying to catch her alone. Frustration had pushed him to approach her here and now. Because he was a man concerned with his image, he'd checked the office thoroughly before he stepped through the door. It was easy to see she was alone in the small space. There were things he intended to settle with her once and for all. Calmly, of course, he thought as she stared at him. Reasonably. Privately.

"Pretty as ever, aren't you?" It pleased him to see her eyes go blank with shock. The advantage was with him, as he preferred it. After all, he'd been planning this reunion for several weeks now. "The years have improved your looks, Megan. You've lost that charming baby fat, and you've become almost elegant. My compliments."

When he stepped closer, she didn't move, couldn't

make her legs or her brain respond. Not even when he lifted a finger and trailed it down her cheek, under her chin, to tip it up in an old habit she'd made herself forget.

"You were always a beauty, Megan, with that wide-eyed innocence that makes a man want to corrupt."

She shuddered. He smiled.

"What are you doing here?" *Kevin* was all she could think. Thank God Kevin wasn't with her.

"Funny, I was going to ask you the same. Just what are you doing here, Megan?"

"I live here." She hated hearing the hesitancy in her voice, like the throb of an old scar. "I work here."

"Tired of Oklahoma, were you? Wanted a change of scene?" He leaned closer, until she backed into the filing cabinet. Bribery, he knew, wouldn't work with her. Not with the O'Riley money behind her. Intimidation was the next logical choice. "Don't take me for a fool, Megan. It would be a terrible, costly mistake."

When her back hit the filing cabinet, she realized she was cringing, and her shock melted away, her spine stiffening. She wasn't a child now, she reminded herself, but a woman. Aware, responsible. "It's none of your business why I moved here."

"Oh, but it is." His voice was silky, quiet, reasonable. "I prefer you in Oklahoma, Megan. Working at your nice, steady job, in the midst of your loving family. I really much prefer it."

His eyes were so cold, she thought with dull wonder. Odd, she'd never seen that, didn't remember that. "Your preferences mean nothing to me, Baxter."

"Did you think I wouldn't find out that you'd thrown your lot in with my ex-wife and her family?" he continued, in that same reasonable tone. "That I haven't kept tabs on you over the years?"

With an effort, she steadied her breathing, but when she tried to shift away, he blocked her. She wasn't afraid, yet, but the temper she'd worked so hard to erase from her character was beginning to bubble up toward the surface.

"I never gave a thought to what you'd find out. And no, I wasn't aware you were keeping tabs. Why should you? Neither Kevin nor I ever meant anything to you."

"You've waited a long time to make your move." Baxter paused, struggling to control the fury that had clawed its way into his throat. He'd worked too hard, done too much, to see some old, forgotten mistake rear up and slap him down. "Clever of you, Megan, more clever than I gave you credit for."

"I don't know what you're talking about."

"Do you seriously want me to believe you know nothing about my campaign? I'm not going to tolerate this pathetic stab at revenge."

Her voice was cooler now, despite the fact that she could feel her skin start to tremble with an intense mixture of emotions. "At the risk of repeating myself, I don't know what you're talking about. My life is of no concern to you, Baxter, and yours none of mine. You made that clear a long time ago, when you refused to acknowledge me or Kevin."

"Is that the tack you're going to take?" He'd wanted to be calm, but rage was working through him. Intimidation, he realized, simply wouldn't be enough. "The young, innocent girl, seduced, betrayed, abandoned? Left behind, pregnant and brokenhearted? Please, spare me."

"That's not a tack, it's truth."

"You were young, Megan, but innocent?" His teeth flashed. "Now, that's a different matter. You were willing enough, even eager."

"I believed you!" She shouted it—a mistake, as her own voice tore her composure to pieces. "I believed you loved me, that you wanted to marry me. And you played on that. You never had any intention of making a future with me. You were already engaged. I was just an easy mark."

"You certainly were easy." He pushed her back against the cabinet, kept his hands hard on her shoulders. "And very, very tempting. Sweet, Megan. Very sweet."

"Take your hands off me."

"Not quite yet. You're going to listen to me, carefully. I know why you've come here, linked yourself with the Calhouns. First there'll be whispers, rumors, then a sad story to a sympathetic reporter. The old lady put pressure on me about Suzanna." He thought of Colleen with loathing. "But I've made that work for me. In the interest of the children," he murmured. "Letting Bradford adopt them, selflessly giving up my rights, so the children could be secure in a traditional family."

"You never cared about them, either, did you?" Megan said in a husky voice. "Alex and Jenny never mattered to you, any more than Kevin."

"The point is," he continued, "the old woman has no reason to bother about you. So, Megan, you'd better mind your step and listen to me. Things aren't working out for you here, so you're going to move back to Oklahoma."

"I'm not going anywhere," she began, then gasped when his fingers dug in.

"You're going back to your quiet life, away from here. There will be no rumors, no tearful interviews with reporters. If you try to undermine me, to implicate me in any way, I'll ruin you. When I've finished—and believe me, with the Dumont money I can hire plenty of willing men who'll swear they've enjoyed you—when I've finished,'' he repeated, ''you'll be nothing more than an opportunistic slut with a bastard son.''

Her vision hazed. It wasn't the threat that frightened her, or even infuriated her so very much. It was the term *bastard* in connection with her little boy.

Before she fully realized her intent, her hand was swinging up and slapping hard across his face. ''Don't you ever speak about my son that way.''

When his hand cracked across her cheek, it wasn't pain she felt, or even shock, but rage.

''Don't push me, Megan,'' he said, breathing hard. ''Don't push me, because you'll be the one to take the fall. You, and the boy.''

As crazed as any mother protecting her cub, she lunged at him. The power of the attack rammed them both against the wall. She landed two solid blows before he threw her off.

''You still have that passionate nature, I see.'' He dragged her against him, infuriated, aroused. ''I remember how to channel it.''

She struck out again, a glancing blow, before he caught her arms and pinned them against her body. So she used her teeth. Even as Baxter cursed in pain, the door burst in.

Nathaniel plucked him off the floor as he might a flea off a dog. Through the haze of her own vision, Megan saw there was murder in his eye. Hot-blooded. Deadly.

''Nathaniel.''

But he didn't look at her. Instead, he rapped Baxter hard against the wall. ''Dumont, isn't it?'' His voice was viciously quiet, terrifyingly pleasant. ''I've heard how you like pushing women around.''

Baxter struggled for dignity, though his feet were inches off the ground. ''Who the hell are you?''

"Well, now, it seems only fair you should know the name of the man who's going to rip out your damn heart with his bare hands." He had the pleasure of seeing Baxter blanch. "It's Fury, Nathaniel Fury. You won't forget it—" he rammed a fist low, into the kidneys "—will you?"

When Baxter could breathe again, his words struggling out weakly, he wheezed, "You'll be in jail before the night's out."

"I don't think so." His head snapped around when Megan started forward. "Stay back," he said between his teeth. The hot leap of fire in his eyes had her coming to a stop.

"Nathaniel." She swallowed hard. "Don't kill him."

"Any particular reason you want him alive?"

She opened her mouth, shut it again. The answer seemed desperately important, so she offered the truth. "No."

Baxter drew in his breath to scream. Nathaniel cut it off neatly with a hand over the windpipe. "You're a lucky man, Dumont. The lady doesn't want me to kill you, and I don't like to disappoint her. We'll leave it to fate." He dragged Baxter outside, hauling him along as if the man were nothing more than a heavily packed seabag.

Megan raced to the door. "Holt." A shiver of relief worked down her spine when she spotted Suzanna's husband near the pier. "Do something."

Holt merely shrugged. "Fury beat me to it. You should go back in, you're getting wet."

"But—he's not really going to kill him, is he?"

Holt considered a moment, narrowing his eyes against the rain as Nathaniel carted Baxter down the pier. "Probably not."

"I hope to God you can't swim," Nathaniel muttered, then threw Baxter off the pier. He turned away and was striding to Megan before the sound of the splash. "Come on."

"But—"

He simply scooped her up in his arms. "I'm knocking off for the day."

"Fine." Holt stood, his thumbs in his pockets, a look of unholy glee in his eyes. "See you tomorrow."

"Nathaniel, you can't—"

"Shut up, Meg." He dumped her in the car. She craned her neck, and wasn't sure whether she was relieved or disappointed to see Baxter heaving himself back onto the pier.

He needed quiet to pull himself back from violence. He detested the temper that lurked inside him, that made him want to raise his fists and pummel. He could rationalize it, under the circumstances, but it always left him sick inside to know what he was capable of if pushed.

There was no doubt in his mind that he would have come very close to murder if Megan hadn't stopped him.

He'd trained himself to use words and wit to resolve a fight. It usually worked. When it didn't, well, it didn't. But he continued, years after the last blow he'd taken from his father, to remember, and regret.

She was shivering by the time he parked the car in his driveway. It didn't occur to him until that moment that he'd forgotten Dog. Holt would see to him, Nathaniel figured, and plucked Megan from her seat.

"I don't—"

"Just be quiet." He carried her in, past the bird, who squawked greetings, and up the stairs. Megan was ready to babble in shock by the time he dumped her in a chair in the bedroom. Without a word, he turned away to rummage through his dresser drawers. "Get out of those wet clothes," he ordered, tossing her a sweatshirt and sweatpants. "I'm going to go down and make you some tea."

"Nathaniel—"

"Just do it!" he shouted, gritting his teeth. "Just do it," he repeated quietly, and shut the door.

He didn't slam it; nor, when he was down in the kitchen, did he put his fist through a wall. He thought about it. But instead, he put on the kettle, got out the brandy. After a moment's consideration, he took a pull of the fiery liquid, straight from the bottle. It didn't calm him very much, but it took the edge off his sense of self-disgust.

When he heard Bird whistle and invite Megan to come to the Casbah, he set her spiked tea on the table.

She was pale, he noted, and her eyes were too big. So were the sweats. He nearly smiled at the picture she made, hesitating in the doorway, with the shirt drooping off her shoulders and the pants bagging at her ankles.

"Sit down and have something to drink. You'll feel better."

"I'm all right, really." But she sat, and lifted the mug in both hands, because they tended to shake. The first sip had her sucking in her breath. "I thought this was tea."

"It is. I just gave it a little help." He sat across from her, waited until she sipped again. "Did he hurt you?"

She stared down at the table. The wood was polished so brightly she could see her own face in it. "Yes."

She said it calmly. She thought she was calm, until Nathaniel put his hand over hers. Her breath hitched once, twice, and then she put her head on the table and wept.

So much washed out with the tears—the hopes she'd

once had, the dreams, the betrayal and the disillusionment, the fears and the bitterness. He didn't try to stop her, only waited it out.

"I'm sorry." She let her cheek rest against the table a moment, comforted by the cool, smooth feel of the wood on her skin and Nathaniel's hand on her hair. "It all seemed to happen so fast, and I wasn't prepared." She straightened, started to wipe the tears away, when a new fear glazed her eyes. "Kevin. Oh, God, if Bax—"

"Holt will take care of Kevin. Dumont won't get near him."

"You're right." She gave a shuddering sigh. "Of course, you're right. Holt would see to Suzanna and all the children right away. And all Baxter wanted to do in any case was frighten me."

"Did he?"

Her eyes were still wet, but they were steady. "No. He hurt me, and he infuriated me, and he made me sick that I'd ever let him touch me. But he didn't frighten me. He can't."

"Attagirl."

She sniffled, smiled weakly. "But I frightened him. That's why he came here today, after all this time. Because he's frightened."

"Of what?"

"Of the past, the consequences." She drew another, deeper breath and smelled Nathaniel—tobacco and salt spray. How oddly comforting it was. "He thinks our coming here is some sort of plot against him. He's been keeping track of me all this time. I didn't know."

"He's never contacted you until today?"

"No, never. I suppose he felt safe when I was in Oklahoma and hadn't any connection with Suzanna. Now, not only is there a connection, but I'm living here.

And Kevin and Alex and Jenny... Well, he doesn't seem to understand it has nothing to do with him.''

She picked up her tea again. Nathaniel hadn't asked anything, he'd simply sat and held her hand. Perhaps that was why she felt compelled to tell him.

''I met him in New York. I was seventeen, and it was my first real trip away from home. It was during the winter break, and several of us went. One of my friends had relatives there. I guess you've been to New York.''

''A time or two.''

''I'd never experienced anything like it. The people, the buildings. The city was so exciting, and so unlike the West. Everything crowded in and colorful. I loved it—rushing along Fifth Avenue, having coffee in some hole-in-the-wall in Greenwich Village. Gawking. It sounds silly.''

''No, it sounds normal.''

''I guess it was,'' she said with a sigh. ''Everything was normal, and simple, before... It was at this party, and he looked so handsome and romantic, I suppose. A young girl's dream, with those movie-star looks and that sheen of sophistication. And he was older—just enough older to be fascinating. He'd been to Europe.'' She stopped herself, squeezed her eyes shut. ''Oh, God, how pathetic.''

''You know you don't have to do this now, Meg.''

''No, I think I do.'' Steadying herself, she opened her eyes again. ''If you can stand listening to it.''

''I'm not going anywhere.'' He gave her hand a comforting squeeze. ''Go ahead, then, get rid of it.''

''He said all the right things, made all the right moves. He sent a dozen roses the next day, and an invitation to dinner.''

She paused to choose her words and pushed absently

at a pin that had loosened in her hair. It wasn't so horrible, she realized, to look back. It seemed almost like a play, with her as both actor and audience. Vitally involved and breezily detached.

"So I went. There was candlelight, and we danced. I felt so grown-up. I think you only really feel that way when you're seventeen. We went to museums and window-shopping and to shows. He told me he loved me, and he bought me a ring. It had two little diamond hearts, interconnected. It was very romantic. He slipped it on my finger, and I slipped into his bed."

She stopped, waited for Nathaniel to comment. When he didn't, she worked up the courage to continue.

"He said he would come to Oklahoma, and we'd make our plans for the future. But, of course, he didn't come. At first, when I called, he said he'd been delayed. Then he stopped answering my calls altogether. I found out I was pregnant, and I called, I wrote. Then I heard that he was engaged, that he'd been engaged all along. At first I didn't believe it, then I just went numb. It took me a while before I made myself believe it, made myself understand and deal with it. My family was wonderful. I never would have gotten through it without them. When Kevin was born, I realized I couldn't just feel grown-up. I had to *be* grown-up. Later on, I tried to contact Bax one last time. I thought he should know about Kevin, and that Kevin should have some sort of relationship with his father. But…" She trailed off. "When there was absolutely no interest, only anger and hostility, I began to understand that it was best that that didn't happen. Today, maybe for the first time, I was absolutely sure of it."

"He doesn't deserve either of you."

"No, he doesn't." She managed a small smile. Now that she'd said it all, for the first time in so very long, she felt hollowed out. Not limp, she realized. Just free. "I want to thank you for charging to the rescue."

"My pleasure. He won't touch you again, Meg." He took her hand, brought it to his lips. "You or Kevin. Trust me."

"I do." She turned her hand in his, gripped. "I do trust you." Her pulse was starting to skip, but she kept her eyes on his. "I thought, when you carried me in and upstairs... Well, I didn't think you were going to make me tea."

"Neither did I. But you were trembling, and I knew if I touched you before I cooled off, I'd be rough. That it wouldn't be right, for either of us."

Her heart stuttered, then picked up its pace. "Are you cooled off now?"

His eyes darkened. "Mostly." Slowly, he rose, drew her to her feet. "Is that an invitation, Megan?"

"I—" He was waiting, she realized, for her to agree or refuse. No seduction, no pretty promising words. No illusions. "Yes," she said, and met his lips with hers.

When he swept her up this time, she gave a quick, nervous laugh. It slid back down her throat when she met the look in his eyes.

"You won't think of him," Nathaniel said quietly. "You won't think of anything but us."

Chapter 8

She could hear her own heartbeat pounding, pounding, in counterpoint to the rain that pounded against the windows. She wondered whether Nathaniel could hear it, too, and if he did, whether he knew that she was afraid. His arms were so strong, his mouth was so sure each time it swooped down to claim hers again.

He carried her up the stairs as if she weighed no more than the mist that swirled outside the cottage.

She would make a mistake, she would do something foolish, she wouldn't be what either of them wanted. The doubts pinched at her like fingers as he swept her into his bedroom, where the light was dim and the air was sweet with wisteria.

She saw the spear of purple blooms in an old bottle on a scarred wooden chest, the undraped windows that were opened to welcome the moist breeze. And the bed, with its sturdy iron headboard and taut cotton spread.

He set her down beside it, so that she was all too aware

of the weakness in her knees. But she kept her eyes on his and waited, terrified and aching, for him to make the first move.

"You're trembling again." His voice was quiet, the fingers he lifted to stroke her cheek were soothing. Did she think he couldn't see all those fears in her eyes? She couldn't know that they stirred his own.

"I don't know what to do." The moment the words were out, she closed her eyes. She'd done it already, she realized. The first mistake. Determined, she dragged his head down to hers for an aggressive kiss.

A fire kindled in his gut, flames leaping and licking at the ready fuel of his need. Muscles tensed in reaction, he fought back the urge to shove her back on the bed and take, take quickly, fiercely. He kept his hands easy, stroking her face, her shoulders, her back, until she quieted.

"Nathaniel."

"Do you know what I want, Meg?"

"Yes— No." She reached for him again, but he caught her hands, kissed them, fingertip by fingertip.

"I want to watch you relax. I want to watch you enjoy." His eyes on hers, he lowered her hands to her sides. "I want to watch you fill up with me." Slowly he began to take the pins from her hair, setting them on the table beside the bed. "I want to hear you say my name when I'm inside you."

He combed his fingers through her hair, contenting himself with the silky texture. "I want you to let me do all the things I've been dreaming of since I first laid eyes on you. Let me show you."

He kissed her first, his mouth soft, smooth, seductive. Endlessly patient, he parted hers with teasing nips and nibbles, with the persuasive caress of his tongue. Degree by torturous degree, he deepened the kiss, until her hands clutched weakly at his waist and her shudders gave way to pliancy.

The lingering taste of brandy, the faint and very male scrape of a day's beard against her cheek, the patter of rain and the drifting scent of flowers. All this whirled in her head like a drug, both potent and possessing.

His lips left hers to journey over her face, to trace the line of her jaw, to nuzzle at her ear, waiting, patiently waiting, until he felt her slip over to the next stage of surrender.

He stepped back, only an inch, and slipped the shirt up her torso, over her head, let it drop to the floor. His muscles coiled like a snake. She thought she saw the lightning flash of desire that darkened his eyes to soot. But he only skimmed a fingertip down her throat, to the aching tip of her breast.

Her breath caught; her head lolled back.

''You're so beautiful, Meg. So soft.'' He pressed a kiss to her shoulder while his hands gently molded, caressed, aroused. ''So sweet.''

He was afraid his hands were too big, too rough. As a result, his touch was stunningly tender, humming over her heating skin. They slicked down her sides, leaving tremors in their wake as he eased the loose pants from her hips.

Then those fingertips moved over her, gliding over curves until her shaking breathing turned to unsteady moans.

He undressed, watching her heavy eyes flutter open, seeing the misty blue focus on him, the pupils dilate.

Now, she thought, and her heart stuttered madly in her throat. He would take her now, and ease this glorious ache he'd stirred to life inside her. Sweet and eager, her mouth lifted to his. He gathered her close, laid her on the bed as gently as he might have laid her in a pool of rose petals. She arched to him, accepting, braced for the torrent. He used only his lips, soft as the rain, savoring her flesh as though it were a banquet of the most delicate flavors. Then his hands, big and hard-palmed, skimmed, lingered, discovered.

Nothing could have prepared her. If she'd had a hundred lovers, none could have given more, or taken more. She was lost in a gently rocking sea of sensation, undone by patience, weakened by tenderness.

Her breathing slowed, deepened, even as her heart rate soared. She felt the brush of his hair on her breast before his mouth claimed it, heard his quiet, satisfied groan of pleasure as he suckled. Heard his sigh as he circled and teased with his tongue.

She sank, fathoms deep, in warm, clear waters.

She didn't know when those waters began to churn. The storm gathered so slowly, so subtly. It seemed one moment she was drifting, and the next floundering. She couldn't get her breath, no matter how deeply she gasped for air. Her mind, suddenly reeling, struggled for the surface, even as her body coiled and tensed.

"Nathaniel." She grabbed at him, her fingers digging into his flesh. "I can't—"

But he covered her mouth with his, swallowing her gasps, savoring her moan, as the first dizzy climax racked her.

She reared against his hand, instinctively urging him on as hot red waves of pleasure swept her up. Her neat, rounded nails scored his shoulders before her hands, her body, even her mind, went limp.

"Megan. God." She was so hot, so wet. He pressed his lips to her throat as he fought to level his own breathing. Pleasuring a woman had always pleasured him. But not like this. Never like this. He felt like a king and a beggar all at once.

Her stunned response aroused him unbearably. All he could do was wallow in her, absorbing her shock waves, and his own, feeling each and every nerve in his body sizzle and spark.

He wanted to give her more. Had to give her more. Strapping down his own grinding needs, he slipped inside her, letting himself rock with the pleasure of her quick shudder, her broken sigh.

She was so small. He had to remind himself again and again that she was small, all delicate bones and fragile skin. That she was innocent, and nearly as untouched as a virgin. So while the blood pounded in his head, his heart, his loins, he took her gently, his hands fisted on the bedspread for fear he would touch her and bruise.

He felt her body contract, explode. And then she said his name.

He pressed his lips to hers again, and followed her over.

The rain was still drumming. As she slowly swam back to reality, she heard its steady beat on the roof. She lay still, her hand tangled in Nathaniel's hair, her body glowing. She realized she had a smile on her face.

She began to hum.

Nathaniel stirred himself, pushed back lazily to lean on his elbow. "What are you doing?"

"Singing. Sort of."

He grinned, studying her. "I like your looks, sugar."

"I'm getting used to yours." She traced the cleft in his chin with a fingertip. Her lashes lowered. "It was all right, wasn't it?"

"What?" He waited, wisely holding back a chuckle until she looked at him again. "Oh, that. Sure, it was okay for a start."

She opened her mouth, closed it again with a little humming sound that wasn't at all musical. "You could be a little more...flattering."

"You could be a little less stupid." He kissed her frowning mouth. "Making love isn't a quiz, Meg. You don't get graded."

"What I meant was... Never mind."

"What you meant was..." He hauled her over until she was splayed on top of him. "On a scale of one to ten..."

"Cut it out, Nathaniel." She laid her cheek on his chest. "I hate it when you make me feel ridiculous."

"I don't." Possessively he ran a hand down her back. "I love to make you feel ridiculous. I love to make you feel."

He nearly followed that up with a very simple "I love you." But she wouldn't have accepted it. He'd barely done so himself.

"You did." She kept her head over his heart. "You made me feel things I never have before. I was afraid."

Trouble clouded his eyes. "I don't want you to be afraid of me."

"I was afraid of me," she corrected. "Of us. Of letting this happen. I'm glad it did." It was easier than she'd imagined to shift, to smile, to press her mouth to his. For a moment, she thought he tensed, but she dismissed that as foolish and kissed him again.

His system snapped to full alert. How could he want her again, so desperately, so quickly? he wondered. How could he resist those sweet, tantalizing lips?

"Keep that up," he managed, "and it's going to happen again."

The shiver of excitement was glorious. "Okay." She shared her anticipation in the kiss, torturing his mouth, teasing his tongue. Amazed that there could be more, she gave a low sound of delight when he rolled, shoving her beneath him and crushing her mouth.

For a heady moment, he let those violent needs hold sway, trapping her beneath him, devouring her lips, her skin, dragging a hand through her tousled hair until her throat was exposed to his hungry teeth and tongue.

She moaned, writhed under him. Whimpered.

Rolling away, he lay on his back, cursing himself, while his heart pounded the blood through his veins.

Confused, shivering with needs freshly aroused but unmet, Megan laid a tentative hand on his arm. He jerked away.

"Don't." The order came out harsh. "I need a minute."

Her eyes went dead. "I'm sorry. I did something wrong."

"No, you didn't." He scrubbed his hands over his face and sat up. "I'm just not ready. Look, why don't I go down and rustle us up something to eat?"

He was only inches away. It might as well have been miles, and she felt the sharp sting of rejection. "No, that's all right." Her voice was cool and calm again. "I really should get going. I need to pick up Kevin."

"Kevin's fine."

"Regardless." She brushed at her hair, tried to smooth it. She wished desperately for something to wrap around her nakedness.

"Don't pull that door shut on me now." He battled back fury, and a much more dangerous passion.

"I haven't shut any door. I thought—that is, I assumed you wanted me to stay. Since you don't, I'll—"

"Of course I want you to stay. Damn it, Megan." He whirled on her, and wasn't surprised when she jerked back. "I need a bloody minute. I could eat you alive, I want you so much."

In defense, she crossed an arm over her breasts. "I don't understand you."

"Damn right you don't understand me. You'd run like hell if you did." He fought for control, gained a slippery hold. "We'll be fine, Meg, if you wait until I pull myself together."

"What are you talking about?"

Gripped by frustration, he grabbed her hand, pressed it against his, palm to palm. "I've got big hands, Megan. Got them from my father. I know the right way to use them—and the wrong way."

There was a glint in his eyes, like the honed edge of a sword. It should have frightened her, but it only excited. "You're afraid of me," she said quietly. "Afraid you'll hurt me."

"I won't hurt you." He dropped his hand, left it fisted on the bed.

"No, you won't." She lifted a hand to touch his cheek. His jaw was tight, urging her fingers to stroke and soothe. There was a power here, she realized, a power she'd been unaware of possessing. She wondered what they could make between them if she set it free.

"You want me." Feeling reckless, she edged closer, until her mouth slid over his. "You want to touch me." She lifted his fisted hand to her breast, her heart pounding like a drum as his fingers opened, cupped. "And for me to touch you." Her hands stroked down his chest, felt the quiver of his stomach muscles. So much strength, she thought, so ruthlessly chained. What would it be like if those links snapped free?

She wanted to know.

"Make love with me now, Nathaniel." Eyes half-closed, she linked her arms around his neck, pressed her eager body to his. "Show me how much you want me."

He held himself in check, concentrating on the flavor of her mouth. It would be enough, he told himself, to make her float again.

But she had learned quickly. When he sought to soothe, she enticed. Where he tried to gentle, she enraged.

With an oath, he dragged her up until they were kneeling, body-to-body. And his mouth was wild.

She answered avidly each urgent demand, each desperate moan. His hands were everywhere, hard and possessive, taking more only when she cried out for it. There was no calm water to sink in now, but a violent tempest that spun them both over the bed in a tangle of hot flesh and raging needs.

He couldn't stop, no longer gave a damn about control. She was his, and by God, he would have all of her. With something like a snarl, he clamped her hands above her head and ravished her flesh.

She arched like a bow, twisted, and still he plundered, invading that hot, wet core with probing tongue until she was sobbing his name.

And more, still more, wrestling over the bed with her hands as rough and ready as his, her mouth as bold and ravenous.

He drove himself into her, hard and deep, hissing with triumph, eyes glazed and dark. His hands locked on hers as she rose to meet him.

She would remember the speed, and the wild freedom,

of their mindless mating. And she would remember the
heady flavor of power as they plunged recklessly off the
edge together.

She must have slept. When she woke, she was
sprawled on her stomach across the bed. The rain had
stopped and night had fallen. When her mind cleared, she
became aware of dozens of small aches, and a drugged
sense of satisfaction.

She thought of rolling over, but it seemed like too
much trouble. Instead, she stretched out her arms, searching the tumbled bed, knowing already that she was alone.

She heard the bird squawk slyly. "You know how to
whistle, don't you, Steve?"

She was still chuckling when Nathaniel stepped back
into the room.

"What do you do, run old movies for him all day?"

"He's a Bogart fan. What can I tell you?" It amazed
him that he felt awkward, holding a dinner tray while a
naked woman lolled in his bed. "That's a pretty good
scar you've got there, sugar."

She was much too content to be embarrassed when she
saw where his eyes had focused. "I earned it. That's a
pretty good dragon you've got."

"I was eighteen, stupid, and more than a little buzzed
on beer. But I guess I earned it, too."

"Suits you. What have you got there?"

"Thought you might be hungry."

"I'm starving." She braced herself on both elbows and
smiled at him. "That smells terrific. I didn't know you
cooked."

"I don't. Dutch does. I cadge handouts from the
kitchen, then nuke them."

"Nuke them?"

"Zap them in the microwave." He set the tray down on the sea chest at the foot of the bed. "We've got some Cajun chicken, some wine."

"Mmm..." She roused herself enough to lean over and peer at it. "Looks wonderful. But I really need to get Kevin."

"I talked to Suzanna." He wondered if he could talk her into eating dinner just as she was, gloriously naked. "Unless she hears from you, Kevin's set to spend the night with them."

"Oh. Well."

"She says he's already knee-deep in video games with Alex and Jenny."

"And if I called, I'd spoil his party."

"Pretty much." He sat on the edge of the bed, ran a fingertip down her spine. "So, how about it? Sleep with me tonight?"

"I don't even have a toothbrush."

"I can dig up an extra." He broke off a piece of chicken, fed it to her.

"Oh." She swallowed, blew out a breath. "Spicy."

"Yeah." He leaned down to sample her lips, then lifted a glass of wine to them. "Better?"

"It's wonderful."

He tipped the glass so that a few drops of wine spilled on her shoulder. "Oops. Better clean that up." He did so with a lingering lick of his tongue. "What do I have to do to convince you to stay?"

She forgot the food and rolled into his arms. "You just did."

In the morning, the mists had cleared. Nathaniel watched Megan pin up her hair in a beam of sunlight. It seemed only right that he move behind her and press his lips to the base of her neck.

He thought it was a sweetly ordinary, sweetly intimate gesture that could become a habit.

"I love the way you polish yourself up, sugar."

"Polish myself up?" Her curious eyes met his in the glass. She had on the same tailored suit she'd worn the day before—now slightly wrinkled. Her makeup was sketchy at best, courtesy of the small emergency cosmetic kit she carried in her purse, and her hair was giving her trouble, as she'd lost half of her pins.

"Like you are now. Like some pretty little cupcake behind the bakery window."

"Cupcake." She nearly choked. "I'm certainly not a cupcake."

"I've got a real sweet tooth." To prove it, he nibbled his way to her ear.

"I've noticed." She turned, but put her hands against his chest to hold him off. "I have to go."

"Yeah, me too. I don't suppose I could talk you into coming with me."

"To sight whales?" She cocked her head. "No more than I could talk you into sitting with me in my office all day, running figures."

He winced. "Guess not. How about tonight?"

She yearned, wished, longed. "I have to think of Kevin. I can't spend my nights here with you while he spends them somewhere else."

"I had that figured. I was thinking if you were to leave your terrace doors open…"

"You could come sneaking in?" she asked archly.

"More or less."

"Good thinking." She laughed and drew away. "Now, are you going to drive me back to my car?"

"Looks that way." He took her hand, holding it as they walked downstairs. "Megan..." He hated to bring it up when the sun was shining and his mood was light. "If you hear from Dumont, if he tries to see you or Kevin, if he calls, sends a damn smoke signal, does anything, I want you to tell me."

She gave his hand a reassuring squeeze. "I doubt I will, after the dunking you gave him. But don't worry, Nathaniel, I can handle Baxter."

"Off with his head," Bird suggested, but Nathaniel didn't smile.

"It's not a matter of what you can handle." He pushed the door open, stepped outside. "Maybe you don't figure that last night gives me the right to look out for you and your boy, but I do. I will. So we'll put it this way." He opened the car door for her. "Either you promise me that you'll tell me, or I go after him now."

She started to protest, but the image, absolutely vivid, of the look on Nathaniel's face when he'd rammed Baxter against the wall stopped her. "You would."

"Bank on it."

She tried to separate annoyance from the simple pleasure of being protected. And couldn't. "I want to say I appreciate the concern, but I'm not sure I do. I've been taking care of myself, and of Kevin, for a long time."

"Things change."

"Yes," she said carefully, wondering what was behind those calm, unblinking gray eyes. "I'm more comfortable when they change slowly."

"I'm doing my best to keep at your pace, Meg." Whatever frustrations he had, he told himself, he could handle. "Just a simple yes or no on this'll do."

It wasn't just herself, Megan thought. There was Kevin. And Nathaniel was offering them both a strong, protecting arm. Pride meant nothing when compared to the welfare of her son.

Not at all sure why she was amused, she turned to him once he'd settled into the driver's seat. ''You have an uncanny knack for getting your own way. And when you do, you just accept it as inevitable.''

''It usually is.'' He backed out of the drive and headed for Shipshape.

There was a small greeting party waiting for them. Holt and, to Megan's surprise, her brother, Sloan.

''I dropped the kids off at The Towers,'' Holt told her, before she could ask. ''They've got your dog, Nate.''

''Thanks.'' She'd barely stepped from the car when Sloan grabbed her by the shoulders, stared hard into her eyes.

''Are you all right? Why the hell didn't you call me? Did he put his hands on you?''

''I'm fine. Sloan, I'm fine.'' Instinctively she cupped his face, kissed him. ''I didn't call because I already had two white knights charging into battle. And he may have put his hands on me, but I put my fists on him. I think I split his lip.''

Sloan said something particularly foul about Dumont and hugged Megan close. ''I should have killed him when you first told me about him.''

''Stop it.'' She pressed her cheek to his. ''It's over. I want it put aside. Kevin's not to hear about it. Now come on, I'll drive you back to the house.''

''I've got some things to do.'' He gave Nathaniel a steely stare over Megan's shoulder. ''You go on up, Meg. I'll be along later.''

''All right, then.'' She kissed him again. ''Holt, thanks again for looking after Kevin.''

''No problem.'' Holt tucked his tongue in his cheek

when Nathaniel scooped Megan up for a long, lingering kiss. A glance at Sloan's narrowed eyes had him biting that tongue to keep from grinning.

"See you, sugar."

Megan flushed, cleared her throat. "Yes…well. Bye."

Nathaniel tucked his thumbs in his pocket, waited until she'd driven off before he turned to Sloan. "Guess you want to talk to me."

"Damn right I want to talk to you."

"You'll have to come up to the bridge. We've got a tour going out."

"Want a referee?" Holt offered, and earned two deadly glances. "Too bad. I hate to miss it."

Smoldering, Sloan followed Nathaniel up the gangplank, waited restlessly while he gave orders. Once they were on the bridge, Nathaniel glanced over the charts and dismissed the mate.

"If this is going to take longer than fifteen minutes, you're in for a ride."

"I've got plenty of time." Sloan stepped closer, braced his legs like a gunslinger at high noon. "What the hell were you doing with my sister?"

"I think you have that figured out," Nathaniel said coolly.

Sloan bared his teeth. "If you think I'm going to stand back while you move in on her, you're dead wrong. I wasn't around when she got tangled up with Dumont, but I'm here now."

"I'm not Dumont." Nathaniel's own temper threatened to snap, a dry twig of control. "You want to take out what he did to her on me, that's fine. I've been looking to kick someone's ass ever since I caught that bastard tossing her around. So you want to take me on?" he said invitingly. "Do it."

Though the invitation tempted some elemental male urge, Sloan pulled back. "What do you mean, he was tossing her around?"

"Just what I said. He had her up against the wall." The rage swept back, almost drowning him. "I thought about killing him, but I didn't think she could handle it."

Sloan breathed deep to steady himself. "So you threw him off the pier."

"Well, I punched him a few times first, then I figured there was a chance he couldn't swim."

Calmer, and grateful, Sloan nodded. "Holt had a few words with him when he dragged his sorry butt out. They've tangled before." He'd missed his chance that time, as well, he thought, thoroughly disgusted. "I don't think Dumont'll come back, chance running into any of us again." Sloan knew he should be glad of it, but he regretted, bitterly, not getting his own licks in.

"I appreciate you looking out for her," he said stiffly. "But that doesn't get us past the rest. She'd have been upset, vulnerable. I don't like a man who takes advantage of that."

"I gave her tea and dry clothes," Nathaniel said between his teeth. "It would have stopped right there, if that was what she wanted. Staying with me was her choice."

"I'm not going to see her hurt again. You might look at her and see an available woman, but she's my sister."

"I'm in love with your sister." Nathaniel snapped his head around when the bridge door opened.

"Ready to cast off, Captain."

"Cast off." He cursed under his breath as he stalked to the wheel.

Sloan stood back while he gave orders and piloted the boat into the bay.

"You want to run that by me again?"

"Have you got a problem with plain English?" Nathaniel tossed back. "I'm in love with her. Damn it."

"Well, now." More than a little taken aback, Sloan sat on the bench closest to the helm.

He wanted to think that one through. After all, Megan had barely met the man. Then again, he remembered, he'd fallen for Amanda in little more time than it took her to snap his head off. If he'd been able to choose a man for his sister, it might have been someone very much like Nathaniel Fury.

"Have you told her that?" Sloan asked, his tone considerably less belligerent.

"Go to hell."

"Haven't," he decided, and braced his booted foot on his knee. "Does she feel the same way about you?"

"She will." Nathaniel set his teeth. "She needs time to work it out, that's all."

"Is that what she said?"

"That's what I say." Nathaniel ran a frustrated hand through his hair. "Look, O'Riley, either mind your own damn business or take a punch at me. I've had enough."

Sloan's smile spread slow and easy. "Crazy about her, aren't you?"

Nathaniel merely grunted and started out to sea.

"What about Kevin?" Sloan studied Nathaniel's profile as he probed. "Some might have a problem taking on another man's son."

"Kevin's Megan's son." His eyes flashed to Sloan's, burned. "He'll be mine."

Sloan waited a moment until he was sure. "So, you're going to take on the whole package."

"That's right." Nathaniel pulled out a cigar, lit it. "You got a problem with that?"

"Can't say as I do." Sloan grinned and accepted the

cigar Nathaniel belatedly offered him. "You might, though. My sister's a damn stubborn woman. But seeing as you're almost a member of the family, I'll be glad to offer any help."

A smile finally twitched at Nathaniel's mouth. "Thanks, but I'd like to handle it on my own."

"Suit yourself." Sloan settled back to enjoy the ride.

"Are you sure you're all right?"

Megan had no more than stepped in the door of The Towers when she found herself surrounded by concern.

"I'm fine, really." Her protests hadn't prevented the Calhouns from herding her into the family kitchen and plying her with tea and sympathy. "This has gotten blown out of proportion."

"When somebody messes with one of us," C.C. corrected, "he messes with all of us."

She glanced outside, where the children were playing happily in the yard. "I appreciate it. Really. But I don't think there's anything more to worry about."

"There won't be." Colleen stepped into the room, her gaze scanning each face in turn. "What are you all doing in here, smothering the girl? Get out."

"Aunt Colleen…" Coco began.

"Out, I said, all of you. You, go back to your kitchen and flirt with that big Dutchman you've got sneaking into your room at night."

"Why, I—"

"Go. And you." Now her cane gestured threateningly at Amanda. "You've got a hotel to run, don't you? Go weed some flowers," she ordered Suzanna. "And you go tinker with an engine." She flicked her gaze from C.C. to Lilah.

"Tougher with me, isn't it, Auntie?" Lilah said lazily.

"Take a nap," Colleen snapped.

"Got me," Lilah said with a sigh. "Come on, ladies, we've been dismissed."

Satisfied when the door swung shut behind them, Colleen sat heavily at the table. "Get me some of that tea," she ordered Megan. "See that it's hot."

Though she moved to obey, Megan wasn't cowed. "Do you always find rudeness works to your advantage, Miss Calhoun?"

"That, old age, and a hefty portfolio." She took the tea Megan set in front of her, sipped, nodded grudgingly when she found it hot and strong. "Now then, sit down and listen to what I have to say. And don't prim your mouth at me, young lady."

"I'm very fond of Coco," Megan told her. "You embarrassed her."

"Embarrassed her? Ha! She and that tattooed hulk have been mooning around after each other for days. Gave her a prod is what I did." But she eyed Megan craftily. "Loyal when it's deserved, are you?"

"I am."

"And so am I. I made a few calls this morning, to some friends in Boston. Influential friends. Hush," she ordered when Megan started to speak. "Detest politics myself, but it's often necessary to dance with the devil. Dumont should be being made aware, at this moment, that any contact with you, or your son, will fatally jeopardize his ambitions. He will not trouble you again."

Megan pressed her lips together. She wanted her voice to be steady. No matter what she had said, how she had pretended, there had been an icy fear, like a cold ax balanced over her head, of what Baxter might do. In one stroke, Colleen had removed it.

"Why did you do it?"

"I loathe bullies. I particularly loathe bullies who interfere with the contentment of my family."

"I'm not your family," Megan said softly.

"Ha! Think again. You stuck your toe in Calhoun waters, girl. We're like quicksand. You're a Calhoun now, and you're stuck."

Tears rushed into her eyes, blinding her. "Miss Calhoun—" Megan's words were cut off by the impatient rap of Colleen's cane. After a sniffle, Megan began again. "Aunt Colleen," she corrected, understanding. "I'm very grateful."

"So you should be." Colleen coughed to clear her own husky voice. Then she raised it to a shout. "Come back in here, the lot of you! Stop listening at the door!"

It swung open, Coco leading the way. She walked to Colleen, bent, kissed the papery cheek.

"Stop all this nonsense." She waved her grandnieces away. "I want the girl to tell me how that strapping young man tossed that bully in the drink."

Megan laughed, wiped her eyes. "He choked him first."

"Ha!" Colleen rapped her cane in appreciation. "Don't spare the details."

Chapter 9

B. behaving oddly. Since return to island for summer she is absentminded, daydreaming. Arrived late for tea, forgot luncheon appointment. Intolerable. Unrest in Mexico annoying. Dismissed valet. Excess starch in shirts.

Unbelievable, Megan thought, staring at the notes Fergus had written in his crabbed hand beside stock quotations. He could speak of his wife, a potential war and his valet in the same faintly irritated tone. What a miserable life Bianca must have had. How terrible to be trapped in a marriage, ruled by a despot and without any power to captain your own destiny.

How much worse, she thought, if Bianca had loved him.

As she often did in the quiet hours before sleep, Megan flipped through the pages to the series of numbers. She had time now to regret that she'd never made it to the library.

Or perhaps Amanda was a better bet. Amanda might know whether Fergus had had foreign bank accounts, safe-deposit boxes.

Peering down, she wondered whether that was the answer. The man had had homes in Maine and in New York. These could be the numbers of various safe-deposit boxes. Even combinations to safes he'd kept in his homes.

That idea appealed to her, a straightforward answer to a small but nagging puzzle. A man as obsessed with his wealth and the making of money as Fergus Calhoun had been would very likely have kept a few secret stores.

Wouldn't it be fantastic, she thought, if there was some dusty deposit box in an old bank vault? Unopened all these years, she imagined. The key lost or discarded. The contents? Oh…priceless rubies or fat, negotiable bonds. A single faded photograph. A lock of hair wound with a gold ribbon.

She rolled her eyes and laughed at herself. "Imagination's in gear, Megan," she murmured. "Too bad it's so farfetched."

"What is?"

She jumped like a rabbit, her glasses sliding down to her chin. "Damn. Nathaniel."

He was grinning as he closed and locked the terrace doors at his back. "I thought you'd be happy to see me."

"I am. But you didn't have to sneak up on me that way."

"When a man comes through a woman's window at night, he's supposed to sneak."

She shoved her glasses back in place. "They're doors."

"And you're too literal." He leaned over the back of the chair where she sat and kissed her like a starving man. "I'm glad you talk to yourself."

"I do not."

"You were, just now. That's why I decided to stop watching you and come in." He strolled to the hallway door, locked it. "You looked incredibly sexy sitting there at your neat little desk, your hair scooped up, your glasses sliding down your nose. In that cute, no-nonsense robe."

She wished heartily that the practical terry cloth could transform into silk and lace. But she had nothing seductive to adorn herself in, and had settled for the robe and Coco's perfume.

"I didn't think you were coming after all. It's getting late."

"I figured there'd be some hoopla over yesterday, and that you'd need to settle Kevin for the night. He didn't get wind of it, did he?"

"No." It touched her that he would ask, that it would matter to him. "None of the children know. Everyone else has been wonderful. It's like thinking you're alone in a battle and then finding yourself surrounded by a circle of shields." She smiled, tilted her head. "Are you holding something behind your back?"

His brows rose, as if in surprise. "Apparently I am." He drew out a peony, a twin to the one he'd given her before. "'A rose,'" he said, "'without a thorn.'"

He crossed to her as he spoke, and all she could think for one awed moment was that this man, this fascinating man, wanted her. He started to take its faded twin from the bud vase on her desk.

"Don't." She felt foolish, but stayed his hand. "Don't throw it out."

"Sentimental, Meg?" Moved that she had kept his token, he slipped the new bud in with the old. "Did you sit here, working late, looking at the flower and thinking of me?"

"I might have." She couldn't fight the smile in his eyes. "Yes, I thought of you. Not always kindly."

"Thinking's enough." He lifted her hand, kissed her palm. "Nearly." To her surprise, he plucked her from the chair, sat himself down and nestled her in his lap. "But this is a whole lot better."

It seemed foolish to disagree, so she rested her head on his shoulder.

"Everyone's getting prepped for the big Fourth of July celebration," she told him idly. "Coco and Dutch are arguing about recipes for barbecue sauce and the kids are bitterly disappointed we won't let them have small, colorful bombs to set off."

"They'll end up making two kinds of sauce and asking everyone to take sides." It was nice sitting like this, he thought, alone and quiet at the end of the day. "And the kids won't be disappointed after they see the fireworks display Trent organized."

Kevin had talked of nothing else all evening, she remembered. "I've heard it's going to be quite a show."

"Count on it. This bunch won't do anything halfway. Like fireworks, do you, sugar?"

"Almost as much as the kids." She laughed and snuggled against him. "I can't believe it's July already. All I have to do is get about two dozen things out of the way so I can compete in the great barbecue showdown, keep the kids from setting themselves on fire and enjoy the show."

"Business first," he murmured. "Working on Fergus's book?"

"Mmm-hmm... I had no idea how much of a fortune

he'd amassed, or how little he considered people. Look here.'' She tapped her finger to the page. ''Whenever he made a note about Bianca, it's as if she were a servant or, worse, a possession. He checked over the household accounts every day, to the penny. There's a notation about how he docked the cook thirty-three cents for a kitchen discrepancy.''

''A lot of people think more of money than souls.'' He flipped idly through the book. ''I can be sure you're not sitting on my lap because of my bank balance—since you know it down to the last nickel.''

''You're in the black.''

''Barely.''

''Cash flow is usually thin the first few years in any business—and when you add in the outlay in equipment you've purchased, the down payment for the cottage, insurance premiums and licensing fees—''

''God, I love it when you talk profit and loss.'' Letting the book close, he nipped playfully at her ear. ''Talk to me about checks and balances, or quarterly returns. Quarterly returns make me crazy.''

''Then you'll be happy to know you and Holt underestimated your federal payments.''

''Mmm…'' He stopped, narrowed his eyes. ''What do you mean?''

''You owe the government another two hundred and thirty dollars, which can be added to your next quarter due, or, more wisely, I can file an amended return.''

He swore halfheartedly. ''How come we have to pay them in advance, anyway?''

She gave him a light kiss in sympathy. ''Because, Nathaniel, if you don't, the IRS will make your life a living hell. I'm here to save you from them. I'm also, if your system can take the excitement, going to suggest you open a Keogh—a retirement account for the self-employed."

"Retirement? Hell, Meg, I'm thirty-three."

"And not getting a day younger. Do you know what the cost-of-living projections are for your golden years, Mr. Fury?"

"I changed my mind. I don't like it when you talk accountant to me."

"It's also good tax sense," she persisted. "The money you put in won't be taxable until you're of retirement age. When, usually, your bracket is lower. Besides, planning for the future might not be romantic, but it is rewarding."

He slid a hand under the terry cloth. "I'd rather have instant gratification."

Her pulse scrambled. "I have the necessary form."

"Damn right you do."

"For the Keogh. All you need to— Oh." The terry cloth parted like water under his clever hands. She gasped, shuddered, melted. "How did you do that?"

"Come to bed." He lifted her. "I'll show you."

Just past dawn, Nathaniel strolled down the curve of the terrace steps, his hands in his pockets and a whistle on his lips. Dutch, in a similar pose, descended the opposite curve. both men stopped dead when they met in the center.

They stared, swore.

"What are you doing here at this hour?" Dutch demanded.

"I could ask you the same question."

"I live here, remember?"

Nathaniel inclined his head. "You live down there." He pointed toward the kitchen level.

"I'm taking the air," Dutch said, after a fumble for inspiration.

"Me too."

Dutch flicked a glance toward Megan's terrace. Nathaniel gave Coco's a studying look. Each decided to leave well enough alone.

"Well, then. Suppose you want some breakfast."

Nathaniel ran his tongue around his teeth. "I could do with some."

"Come on, can't dawdle out here all morning."

Relieved with the solution, they walked down together in perfect agreement.

She overslept. It was a breach in character that had her racing out of her room, still buttoning her blouse. She stopped to peek into Kevin's bedroom, spotted the haphazardly made bed and sighed.

Everyone was up and about, it seemed, but her.

She made a dash toward her office, crossing breakfast with her son off her list of small pleasures for the day.

"Oh, dear." Coco fluttered her hands when Megan nearly mowed her down in the lobby. "Is something wrong?"

"No, I'm sorry. I'm just late."

"Did you have an appointment?"

"No." Megan caught her breath. "I meant I was late for work."

"Oh, my, I thought there was a problem. I just this minute left a memo on your desk. Go ahead in, dear, I don't want to hold you up."

"But—" Megan found herself addressing Coco's retreating back, so she turned into her office to read the message.

Coco's idea of an interoffice memo was something less than professional.

Megan, dear, I hope you slept well. There's fresh coffee in your machine, and I've left you a nice basket of muffins. You really shouldn't skip breakfast. Kevin ate like a young wolf. It's so rewarding to see a boy enjoy his food. He and Nate will be back in a few hours. Don't work too hard.

Love, Coco

P.S. The cards say you have two important questions to answer. One with your heart, one with your head. Isn't that interesting?

Megan blew out a breath, and was reading the memo again when Amanda popped in. "Got a minute?"

"Sure." She handed over the paper she held. "Do you think you could interpret this for me?"

"Ah, one of Aunt Coco's convoluted messages." Lips pursed, Amanda studied it. "Well, the coffee and muffins are easy."

"I got that part." In fact, Megan helped herself to both. "Want some?"

"No, thanks, she already delivered mine. Kevin ate a good breakfast. I can vouch for that. When I saw him, he was scarfing down French toast, with Nathaniel battling him for the last piece."

Megan bobbled her coffee. "Nathaniel was here for breakfast?"

"Eating and charming Aunt Coco, while telling Kevin some story about a giant squid. They'll be back in a few hours," she continued, tapping the note, "because Kevin talked Nate into taking him out on the tour again. It didn't

take much talking,'' she added with a smile. "And we
didn't think you'd mind.''

"No, of course not.''

"And the bit about the cards defies interpretation.
That's pure Aunt Coco.'' Amanda set the memo down
again. "It's spooky, though, just how often she hits the
mark. Been asked any questions lately?''

"No, nothing in particular.''

Amanda thought of what Sloan had related to her about
Nathaniel's feelings. "Are you sure?''

"Hmmm? Yes. I was thinking about Fergus's book. I
suppose it could loosely be considered a question. At
least there's one I want to ask you.''

Amanda made herself comfortable. "Shoot.''

"The numbers in the back. I mentioned them before.''
She opened a file, handing a copy of the list to Amanda.
"I was wondering if they might be passbook numbers,
or safe-deposit boxes, safe combinations. Lot numbers,
maybe, on some real estate deal?'' She moved her shoulders. "I know it's silly to get so hung up on them.''

"No.'' Amanda waved the notion away. "I know just
what you mean. I hate it when things don't fit into place.
We went through most of the papers from this year when
we were looking for clues to find the necklace. I don't
recall anything that these figures might connect to, but I
can look through the material again.''

"Let me do it,'' Megan said quickly. "I feel like it's
my baby.''

"Glad to. I've got more than enough on my plate, and
with the big holiday tomorrow, barely time to clean up.
Everything you'd want is in the storeroom under Bianca's
tower room. We've got it all boxed according to year and
content, but it's still a nasty, time-consuming job.''

"I live for nasty, time-consuming jobs.''

"Then you'll be in heaven. Megan, I hate to ask, but it's the nanny's day off, and Sloan's up to his ears in plywood or something. We've been playing pass-the-babies this morning, but I've got an appointment in the village this afternoon. I could reschedule."

"You want me to baby-sit."

"I know you're busy, but—"

"Mandy, I thought you'd never ask me." Megan's eyes lit up. "When can I get my hands on her?"

Kevin figured this was the best summer of his life. He missed his grandparents, and the horses, and his best friend, John Silverhorn, but there was too much to do for him to be really homesick.

He got to play with Alex and Jenny every day, had his own fort, and lived in a castle. There were boats to sail, and rocks to climb—and Coco or Mr. Dutch always had a snack waiting in the kitchen. Max told him really neat stories. Sloan and Trent sometimes let him help with the renovations, and Holt had let him drive the little powerboat.

All his new aunts played games with him, and sometimes, if he was really, really careful, they let him hold one of the babies.

It was, to Kevin's thinking, a really good deal.

Then there was Nathaniel. He snuck a look at the man who sat beside him, driving the big convertible up the winding road to The Towers. Kevin had decided that Nathaniel knew something about everything. He had muscles and a tattoo and most always smelled like the sea.

When he stood at the helm of the big tour boat, his eyes narrowed against the sun and his broad hands on the wheel, he was every little boy's idea of a hero.

"Maybe…" Kevin trailed off until Nathaniel glanced down at him.

"Maybe what, mate?"

"Maybe I could go back out with you sometime," Kevin blurted out. "I won't ask so many questions next time, or get in the way."

Was there ever a man, Nathaniel wondered, who could defend himself against the sweetness of a child? He stopped the car at the family entrance. "I'll pipe you aboard my ship anytime." He flicked a finger down the brim of the captain's hat he'd carelessly dropped on Kevin's head. "And you can ask all the questions you want."

"Really?" Kevin pushed the brim back up, so that he could see.

"Really."

"Thanks!" Kevin threw his arms around Nathaniel in a spontaneous hug that had Nathaniel's heart sliding down the slippery chute toward love. "I gotta tell Mom. Are you going to come in?"

"Yeah." He let his hands linger on the boy a moment before they dropped away.

"Come on." Bursting with tidings, Kevin scrambled out of the car and up the steps. He hit the door running. "Mom! I'm back!"

"What a quiet, dignified child," Megan commented as she stepped into the hallway from the parlor. "It must be my Kevin."

With a giggle, Kevin darted to her, rising on his toes to see which baby she was holding. "Is that Bianca?"

"Delia."

Kevin squinted and studied. "How can you tell them apart? They look the same."

"A mother's eyes," she murmured, and bent to kiss him. "Where've you been, sailor?"

"We went way, way out in the ocean and back, twice. We saw nine whales. One was like a baby. When they're all together, they're called a pod. Like what peas grow in."

"Is that so?"

"And Nate let me steer and blow the horn, and I helped chart the course. And this man on the second deck was sick the whole time, but I wasn't 'cause I've got good sea legs. And Nate says I can go with him again, so can I?"

Nearly nine years as a mother had Megan following the stream of information perfectly. "Well, I imagine you can."

"Did you know whales mate for life, and they're not really fish at all, even though they live in the water? They're mammals, just like us and elephants and dogs, and they've got to breathe. That's how come they come up and blow water out of their spouts."

Nathaniel walked in on the lecture. And stopped, and looked. Megan stood, smiling down at her son, his hand in hers and a baby on her hip.

I want. The desire streamed through Nathaniel like sunlight, warm, bright. The woman—there had never been a question of that. But he wanted, as Sloan had said, the whole package. The woman, the boy, the family.

Megan looked over and smiled at him. His heart all but stopped.

She started to speak, but the look in Nathaniel's eyes had her throat closing. Though she took an unconscious step back, he was already there, his hand on her cheek, his lips on hers with a tenderness that turned her to putty.

The baby laughed in delight and reached for a fistful of Nathaniel's hair.

"Here we go." Nathaniel took Delia, hefted her high so that she could squeal and kick her feet. When he settled her on his hip, both Megan and Kevin were still staring at him. He jiggled the baby and cocked his head at the boy. "Do you have a problem with me kissing your mom?"

Megan made a little strangled sound. Kevin's gaze dropped heavily to the floor. "I don't know," he mumbled.

"She sure is pretty, isn't she?"

Kevin shrugged, flushed. "I guess." He wasn't sure how he was supposed to feel. Lots of men kissed his mother. His granddad and Sloan—and Holt and Trent and Max. But this was different. He knew that. After all, he wasn't a baby. He shot a look up, lowered his eyes again. "Are you going to be her boyfriend now?"

"Ah…" Nathaniel glanced at Megan, was met with a look that clearly stated that he was on his own. "That's close enough. Does that bother you?"

Because his stomach was suddenly jittery, Kevin moved his thin shoulders again. "I don't know."

If the boy wasn't going to look up, Nathaniel figured it was time to move down. He crouched, still holding the baby. "You can take plenty of time to think about it, and let me know. I'm not going anywhere."

"Okay." Kevin's eyes slid up toward his mother's, then back to Nathaniel's. He sidled closer and leaned toward Nathaniel's ear. "Does she like it?"

Nathaniel clamped down on a chuckle and answered solemnity with solemnity. "Yeah, she does."

After a long breath, Kevin nodded. "Okay, I guess you can kiss her if you want."

"I appreciate it." He offered Kevin a hand, and the man-to-man shake had the boy's chest swelling like a balloon.

"Thanks for taking me today." Kevin took off the captain's hat. "And for letting me wear this."

Nathaniel dropped the hat back on Kevin's head, pushed up the brim. "Keep it."

The boy's eyes went blank with shocked pleasure. "For real?"

"Yeah."

"Wow. Thanks. Thanks a lot. Look, Mom, I can keep it. I'm going to show Aunt Coco."

He raced upstairs with a clatter of sneakers. When Nathaniel straightened again, Megan was eyeing him narrowly.

"What did he ask you?"

"Man talk. Women don't understand these things."

"Oh, really?" Before she could disabuse him of that notion, Nathaniel hooked his fingers in her waistband and jerked her forward.

"I've got permission to do this now." He kissed her thoroughly, while Delia did her best to snuggle between them.

"Permission," Megan said when she could breathe again. "From whom?"

"From your men." He strolled casually into the parlor, laid Delia on her play rug, where she squealed happily at her favorite stuffed bear. "Except your father, but he's not around."

"My men? You mean Kevin and Sloan." Realization dawned, and had her sinking onto the arm of a chair. "You spoke to Sloan about…this?"

"We were going to beat each other up about it, but it didn't come to that." Very much at home, Nathaniel walked to the side table and poured himself a short whiskey from a decanter. "We straightened it out."

"You did. You and my brother. I suppose it didn't occur to either of you that I might have some say in the matter."

"It didn't come up. He was feeling surly about the fact that you'd spent the night with me."

"It's none of his business," Megan said tightly.

"Maybe it is, maybe it isn't. It's water under the bridge now. Nothing to get riled about."

"I'm not riled. I'm irritated that you took it upon yourself to explain our relationship to my family without discussing it with me." And she was unnerved, more than a little, by the worshipful look she'd seen in Kevin's eyes.

Women, Nathaniel thought, and tossed back his whiskey. "I was either going to explain it to Sloan or take a fist in the face."

"That's ridiculous."

"You weren't there, sugar."

"Exactly." She tossed back her head. "I don't like to be discussed. I've had my fill of that over the years."

Very carefully, Nathaniel set his glass down. "Megan, if you're going to circle back around to Dumont, you're just going to get me mad."

"I'm not doing that. I'm simply stating a fact."

"And I stated a fact of my own. I told your brother I was in love with you, and that settled it."

"You should have…" She trailed off, gasped for air that had suddenly gone too thin. "You told Sloan you were in *love* with me?"

"That's right. Now you're going to say I should have told you first."

"I...I don't know what I'm going to say." But she was glad, very glad, that she was already sitting down.

"The preferred response is 'I love you, too.'" He waited, ignored the slow stroke of pain. "Can't get your tongue around that."

"Nathaniel." Be calm, she warned herself. Reasonable. Logical. "This is all moving so fast. A few weeks ago, I didn't even know you. I never expected what's happened between us. And I'm still baffled by it. I have very strong, very real feelings for you, otherwise I couldn't have stayed with you that first night."

She was killing him, bloodlessly. "But?"

"Love isn't something I'll ever be frivolous about again. I don't want to hurt you, or be hurt, or risk a misstep that could hurt Kevin."

"You really think time's the answer, don't you? That no matter what's going on inside you, if you just wait a reasonable period, study all the data, balance all the figures, the right answer comes up."

Her shoulders stiffened. "If you're saying do I need time, then yes, I do."

"Fine, take your time, but add this into your equation." In two strides he was in front of her, dragging her up, crushing her mouth with his. "You feel just what I feel."

She did—she was very much afraid she did. "That's not the answer."

"It's the only answer." His eyes burned into hers. "I wasn't looking for you, either, Megan. My own course was plotted out just fine. You changed everything for me. So you're going to have to adjust your nice neat columns and make room for me. Because I love you, and I'm going to have you. You and Kevin are going to belong to me." He released her. "Think about it," he said, and walked out.

* * *

Idiot. Nathaniel continued to curse himself as he spun his wheels pulling up in front of Shipshape. Obviously he'd found a new way to court a woman: Yell and offer ultimatums. Clearly the perfect way to win a heart.

He snatched Dog out of the back seat and received a sympathetic face bath. "Want to get drunk?" he asked the wriggling ball of fur. "Nope, you're right, bad choice." He stepped inside the building, set the dog down and wondered where he might find an alternative.

Work, he decided, was a wiser option than a bottle.

He busied himself with an engine until he heard the familiar blat of a horn. That would be Holt, bringing in the last tour of the day.

His mood still sour, Nathaniel went out and down to the pier to help secure lines.

"The holiday's bringing in a lot of tourists," Holt commented when the lines were secured. "Good runs today."

"Yeah." Nathaniel scowled at the throng of people still lingering on the docks. "I hate crowds."

Holt's brow lifted. "You were the one who came up with the Fourth of July special to lure them in."

"We need the money." Nathaniel stomped back into the shop. "Doesn't mean I have to like it."

"Who's ticked you off?"

"Nobody." Nathaniel took out a cigar, lit it defiantly. "I'm not used to being landlocked, that's all."

Holt very much doubted that was all, but, in the way of men, shrugged his acceptance and picked up a wrench. "This engine's coming along."

"I can pick up and go anytime." Nathaniel clamped the cigar between his teeth. "Nothing holding me. All I got to do is pack a bag, hop a freighter."

Holt sighed, accepted his lot as a sounding board. "Megan, is it?"

"I didn't ask for her to drop in my lap, did I?"

"Well..."

"I was here first." Even when he heard how ridiculous that sounded, Nathaniel couldn't stop. "Woman's got a computer chip in her head. She's not even my type, with those neat little suits and that glossy briefcase. Who ever said I was going to settle down here, lock myself in for life? I've never stayed put anywhere longer than a month since I was eighteen."

Holt pretended to work on the engine. "You started a business, took out a mortgage. And it seems to me you've been here better than six months now."

"Doesn't mean anything."

"Is Megan dropping hints about wedding bells?"

"No." Nathaniel scowled around his cigar and snarled. "I am."

Holt dropped his wrench. "Hold on a minute. Let me get this straight. You're thinking of getting married, and you're kicking around here muttering about hopping a freighter and not being tied down?"

"I didn't ask to be tied down, it just happened." Nathaniel took a deliberate puff, then swore. "Damn it, Holt, I made a fool of myself."

"Funny how we do that around women, isn't it? Did you have a fight with her?"

"I told her I loved her. She started the fight." He paced the shop, nearly gave in to the urge to kick the tool bench. "What happened to the days when women wanted to get married, when that was their Holy Grail, when they set hooks for men to lure them in?"

"What century are we in?"

The fact that Nathaniel could laugh was a hopeful sign. "She thinks I'm moving too fast."

"I'd tell you to slow down, but I've known you too long."

Calmer, he took up a ratchet, considered it, then set it down again. "Suzanna took her lumps from Dumont. How'd you get past it?"

"I yelled at her a lot," Holt said, reminiscing.

"I've tried that."

"Brought her flowers. She's got a real weakness for flowers." Which made him think that perhaps he'd stop on the way home and pick some up.

"I've done that, too."

"Have you tried begging?"

Nathaniel winced. "I'd rather not." His eyes narrowed curiously. "Did you?"

Holt took a sudden, intense interest in the engine. "We're talking about you. Hell, Nate, quote her some of that damn poetry you're so fond of. I don't know. I'm not good at this romance stuff."

"You got Suzanna."

"Yeah." Holt's smile spread. "So get your own woman."

Nathaniel nodded, crushed out his cigar. "I intend to."

Chapter 10

The sun had set by the time Nathaniel returned home. He'd overhauled an engine and repaired a hull, and he still hadn't worked off his foul mood.

He remembered a quote—Horace, he thought—about anger being momentary insanity. If you didn't figure out a way to deal with momentary insanity, you ended up in a padded room. Not a cheerful image.

The only way to deal with it, as far as he could see, was to face it. And Megan. He was going to do both as soon as he'd cleaned up.

"And she'll have to deal with me, won't she?" he said to Dog as the pup scrambled out of the car behind him. "Do yourself a favor, Dog, and stay away from smart women who have more brains than sense."

Dog wagged his tail in agreement or sympathy, then toddled away to water the hedges.

Nathaniel slammed the car door and started across the yard.

"Fury?"

He stopped, squinted into the shadows of dusk, toward the side of the cottage. "Yeah?"

"Nathaniel Fury?"

He watched the man approach, a squat, muscled tank in faded denim. Creased face, strutting walk, a grease-smeared cap pulled low over the brow.

Nathaniel recognized the type. He'd seen the man, and the trouble he carried with him like a badge, in dives and on docks the world over. Instinctively he shifted his weight.

"That's right. Something I can do for you?"

"Nope." The man smiled. "Something *I* can do for *you.*"

Even as the first flash of warning lit in Nathaniel's brain, he was grabbed from behind, his arms viciously twisted and pinned. He saw the first blow coming, braced, and took a heavy fist low in the gut. The pain was incredible, making his vision double and waver before the second blow smashed into his jaw.

He grunted, went limp.

"Folded like a girl. Thought he was supposed to be tough." The voice behind him sneered, giving him the height and the distance. In a fast, fluid movement, Nathaniel snapped his head back, rapping his skull hard against the soft tissue of a nose. Using the rear assailant for balance, he kicked up both feet and slammed them into a barrel chest.

The man behind him cursed, loosened his grip enough for Nathaniel to wrest himself away. There were only seconds to judge his opponents and the odds.

He saw that both men were husky, one bleeding profusely now from his broken nose, the other snarling as he wheezed, trying to get back his breath after the double

kick to his chest. Nate snapped his elbow back, had the
momentary pleasure of hearing the sound of bone against
bone.

They came at him like dogs.

He'd been fighting all his life, knew how to mentally
go around the pain and plow in. He tasted his own blood,
felt the power sing up his arm as his fist connected. His
head rang like church bells when he caught a blow to the
temple. His breath burned from another in the ribs.

But he kept moving in as they circled him, lashing out,
dripping sweat and blood. Avoiding a leap at his throat
with a quick pivot, he followed through with a snapping,
backhanded blow. The flesh on his knuckles ripped, but
the pain was sweet.

He caught the quick move out of the corner of his eye
and turned into it. The blow skimmed off his shoulder,
and he answered it with two stinging jabs to the throat
that had one of the men sinking bonelessly to his knees.

"Just you and me now." Nathaniel wiped the blood
from his mouth and measured his foe. "Come on."

The loss of his advantage had his opponent taking a
step in retreat. Facing Nathaniel now was like facing a
wolf with fangs sharp and exposed. His partner was useless, and the man shifted his eyes for the best route of
escape.

Then his eyes lit up.

Lunging, he grabbed one of the boards waiting to be
nailed to the deck. He was grinning now, advancing and
swinging the board like a bat. Nathaniel felt the wind
whistle by his ear as he feinted left, then the wood slapping on his shoulder on the return swing.

He went in low. The rushing power took them both
over the deck and smashing through the front door.

"Fire in the hole!" Bird shouted out. "All hands on

déck!'' His wings flapped frantically as the two men hurtled across the room.

A small table splintered like toothpicks under their combined weight. The wrestling wasn't pretty, nor was there any grace in the short body punches or the gouging fingers. The cottage rang with smashing furniture and harsh breathing.

Something new crept into the jungle scent of sweat and blood. When he recognized fear, Nathaniel's adrenaline pumped faster, and he used the new weapon as ruthlessly as his fists.

He closed his hand around the thick throat, thumb crushing down on the windpipe. The fight had gone out of his opponent. The man was flailing now, gagging.

"Who sent you?" Nathaniel's teeth were bared in a snarl as he grabbed the man by the hair and rapped his head hard on the floor.

"Nobody."

Breathing through his teeth, Nathaniel hauled him over, twisted his arm and jerked it viciously up his back. "I'll snap it like a twig. Then I'll break the other one, before I start on your legs. Who sent you?"

"Nobody," the man repeated, then screamed thinly when Nathaniel increased the pressure. "I don't know his name. I don't!" He screamed again, almost weeping now. "Some dude outa Boston. Paid us five hundred apiece to teach you a lesson."

Nathaniel kept the arm twisted awkwardly, his knee on the man's spine. "Draw me a picture."

"Tall guy, dark hair, fancy suit." The squat man babbled out curses, unable to move without increasing his own agony. "Name of God, you're breaking my arm."

"Keep talking and it's all I'll break."

"Pretty face—like a movie star. Said we was to come

here and look you up. We'd get double if we put you in the hospital.''

"Looks like you're not going to collect that bonus." After releasing his arm, Nathaniel dragged the man up by the scruff of his neck. "Here's what you're going to do. You're going to go back to Boston and tell your pretty-faced pal that I know who he is and I know where to find him." For the hell of it, Nathaniel rammed the man against the wall on the way out the door. "Tell him not to bother looking over his shoulder, because if I decide he's worth going after, he won't see me coming. You got that?"

"Yeah, yeah, I got it."

"Now pick up your partner." The other man was struggling onto his hands and knees. "And start running."

They didn't need any more urging. Pressing a hand to his ribs, Nathaniel watched until they'd completed their limping race out of sight.

He gave in to a groan then, hobbling painfully through the broken door and into the house.

"I have not yet begun to fight," Bird claimed.

"A lot of help you were," Nathaniel muttered. He needed ice, he thought, a bottle of aspirin and a shot of whiskey.

He took another step, stopping, then swearing, when his vision blurred and his legs wobbled like jelly. Dog came out of the corner where he'd huddled, whimpering, and whined at Nate's feet.

"Just need a minute," he said to no one in particular, and then the room tilted nastily on its side. "Oh, hell," he murmured, and passed out cold.

Dog licked at him, tried to nuzzle his nose, then sat,

thumped his tail and waited. But the smell of blood made him skittish. After a few moments, he waddled out the door.

Nathaniel was just coming to when he heard the footsteps approaching. He struggled to sit up, wincing at every blow that had gone unfelt during the heat of battle. He knew that if they'd come back for him, they could tap-dance on his face without any resistance from him.

"Man overboard," Bird announced, and earned a hissing snarl from Nathaniel.

Holt stopped in the doorway and swore ripely. "What the hell happened?" Then he was at Nathaniel's side, helping him to stand.

"Couple of guys." Too weak to be ashamed of it, Nathaniel leaned heavily on Holt. It began to occur to him that he might need more than aspirin.

"Did you walk into a robbery?"

"No. They just stopped by to beat me to a pulp."

"Looks like they did a good job of it." Holt waited for Nathaniel to catch his breath and his balance. "Did they mention why?"

"Yeah." He wiggled his aching jaw and saw stars. "They were paid to. Courtesy of Dumont."

Holt swore again. His friend was a mess, bruised, bloodied and torn. And it looked as though he were too late to do anything other than mop up the spills.

"Did you get a good look at them?"

"Yeah, good enough. I kicked their butts back to Boston to deliver a little message to Dumont."

Half carrying Nathaniel to the door, Holt stopped, took another survey. "You look like this, and you won?"

Nathaniel merely grunted.

"Should have known." The news made Holt marginally more cheerful. "Well, we'll get you to the hospital."

"No." Damned if he'd give Dumont the satisfaction. "Son of a bitch told them they'd get a bonus if they put me in the hospital."

"Then that's out," Holt said with perfect understanding. "Just a doctor then."

"It's not that bad. Nothing's broke." He checked his tender ribs. "I don't think. Just need some ice."

"Yeah, right." But, being a man, Holt was in perfect sympathy with the reluctance to be bundled off to a doctor. "Okay, we're going to the next-best place." He eased Nathaniel into the car. "Take it slow, ace."

"I can't take it otherwise."

With a snap of his fingers, Holt ordered Dog into the car. "Hold on a minute while I phone Suzanna, let her know what's going on."

"Feed the bird, will you?"

Nathaniel drifted between pain and numbness until Holt returned.

"How'd you know to come by?"

"Your dog." Holt started the car and eased it as gently as possible out of the drive. "He played Lassie."

"No fooling?" Impressed, Nathaniel made the effort to reach back and pat Dog on the head. "Some dog, huh?"

"It's all in the bloodlines."

Nathaniel roused himself enough to probe his face with cautious fingers. "Where are we going?"

"Where else?" Holt headed for The Towers.

Coco squealed at the sight of him, pressing both hands to her cheeks, as Nathaniel hobbled into the family kitchen with one arm slung over Holt's supporting shoulders.

"Oh, you poor *darling!* What happened? Was there an accident?"

"Ran into something." Nathaniel dropped heavily into a chair. "Coco, I'll trade you everything I own, plus my immortal soul, for a bag of ice."

"Goodness."

Brushing Holt away, she took Nathaniel's battered face in her hands. In addition to bruises and scrapes, there was a jagged cut under one eye. The other was bloodshot and swelling badly. It didn't take her longer than a moment to see that the something he'd run into was fists.

"Don't you worry, sweetheart, we'll take care of you. Holt, run up to my room. There's a bottle of painkillers in the medicine chest, from when I had that nasty root canal."

"Bless you," Nathaniel managed. He closed his eyes, listening to her bustling around the kitchen. Moments later he hissed and jerked when a cool cloth dabbed the cut under his eye.

"There, there, dear," she cooed. "I know it hurts, but we have to get it clean so there's no infection. I'm going to put a little peroxide on it now, so you just be brave."

He smiled, but found that did nothing to help his torn lip. "I love you, Coco."

"I love you, too, sweetie."

"Let's elope. Tonight."

Her answer was to lay her lips gently on his brow. "You shouldn't fight, Nathaniel. It doesn't solve anything."

"I know."

Breathless from the run, Megan burst into the kitchen. "Holt said— Oh, God." She streaked to Nathaniel's side, grabbed his sore hand so tightly he had to bite down to suppress a yelp. There was blood drying on his face, and there were bruises blooming. "How bad are you hurt? You should be in the hospital."

"I've had worse."

"Holt said two men came after you."

"Two?" Coco's hand paused. "*Two* men attacked you?" All the softness fled from her eyes, hardening them to tough blue steel. "Why, that's reprehensible. Someone should teach them how to fight fair."

Despite his lip, Nathaniel grinned. "Thanks, beautiful, but I already did."

"I hope you knocked their heads together." After a huffing breath, Coco went back to work on his face. "Megan, dear, fix Nate an ice bag for his eye. It's going to swell."

Megan obeyed, torn into dozens of pieces, by the damage to his face, by the fact that he hadn't even looked at her.

"Here." She laid the cool bag against his eye while Coco cleaned his torn knuckles.

"I can hold it. Thanks." He took it from her, let the ice numb the pain.

"There's antiseptic in the left-hand cupboard, second shelf," Coco said.

Megan, feeling weepy, turned to get it.

The door opened again, this time letting in a crowd. Nathaniel's initial discomfort with the audience turned to reluctant amusement as the Calhouns fired questions and indignation. Plans for revenge were plotted and discarded while Nathaniel suffered the sting of iodine.

"Give the boy air!" Colleen commanded, parting her angry grandnieces and nephews like a queen moving through her court. She eyed Nathaniel. "Banged you up pretty good, did they?"

"Yes, ma'am."

Her eyes were shrewd. "Dumont," she murmured, so that only he could hear.

Nathaniel winced. "Right the first time."

She glanced at Coco. "You seem to be in able hands, here. I have a call to make." She smiled thinly. It helped to have connections, she thought as she tapped out of the room with her cane. And through them she would see that Baxter Dumont knew he had put a noose around his own neck, and that one false move would mean his career would come to an abrupt and unpleasant stop.

Nobody trifled with Colleen Calhoun's family.

Nathaniel watched Colleen go, then took the pill Coco held out to him and gulped it down. The movement sent fresh pain radiating up his side.

"Let's get that shirt off." Trying to sound cheerful, Coco attacked the torn T-shirt with kitchen shears. The angry mutters died away as Nathaniel's bruised torso was exposed.

"Oh." Tears stung Coco's eyes. "Oh, baby."

"Don't pamper the boy." Dutch came in holding two bottles. Witch hazel and whiskey. One look at Nathaniel had him gritting his teeth together so hard they ached, but he kept his voice careless. "He ain't no baby. Take a shot of this, Captain."

"He's just taken a pill," Coco began.

"Take a shot," Dutch repeated.

Nathaniel winced once as the whiskey stung his lip. But it took the edge off a great many other aches. "Thanks."

"Look at ya." Dutch snorted and dumped the witch hazel onto a cloth. "Let 'em pound all over you, like some city boy with sponges where his fists should be."

"There were two of them," Nathaniel muttered.

"So?" Dutch gently swabbed the bruises. "You getting so outa shape you can't take two?"

"I kicked their butts." Experimentally Nathaniel probed a tooth with his tongue. It hurt, but at least it wasn't loose.

"Better had," Dutch returned, with a flash of pride. "Tried to rob you, did they?"

Nathaniel's gaze flashed to Megan. "No."

"Ribs're bruised." Ignoring Nathaniel's curse, Dutch prodded and poked until he was satisfied. "Not cracked though." He crouched, peered into Nathaniel's eyes. "D'ya pass out?"

"Maybe." It was almost as bad as another thumping to admit it. "For a minute."

"Vision blurred?"

"No, Doc. Not now."

"Don't get smart. How many?" He held up two thick fingers.

"Eighty-seven." Nathaniel would have reached for the whiskey again, but Coco shoved it aside.

"He's not drinking any more on top of the pill I gave him."

"Women think they know every damn thing." But Dutch sent her a look, reassuring her that their charge would be all right. "Bed's what you need now. A hot soak and cool sheets. Want I should carry you?"

"Hell, no." That was one humiliation he could do without. He took Coco's hand, kissed it. "Thanks, darling. I'd do it all again if I knew you'd be my nurse." He looked back at Holt. "I could use a ride home."

"Nonsense." Coco disposed of that idea instantly. "You'll stay here, where we can look after you. You may very well have a concussion, so we'll take shifts waking you up through the night to be sure you don't slip into a coma."

"Wives' tales," Dutch grunted, but nodded at her behind Nathaniel's back.

"I'll turn down the bed in the rose guest room," Amanda stated. "C.C., why don't you run our hero a nice hot bath? Lilah, bring that ice along."

He didn't have the energy to fight the lot of them, so he sat back as Lilah walked over and touched her lips gently to his. "Come on, tough guy."

Sloan moved over to help him to his feet. "Two of them, huh? Puny guys?"

"Bigger than you, pal." He was floating just a little as he hobbled up the stairs between Sloan and Max.

"Let's get those pants off," Lilah said, when they'd eased him down to sit on the side of the bed.

He still had the wit to arch a brow at her. "You never said that when it counted. No offense," he added to Max.

"None taken." With a chuckle, Max bent down to pull off Nathaniel's shoes. He knew what it was to be nursed back to health by the Calhoun women, and he figured that once Nathaniel got past the worst of the pain, he'd realize he'd landed in heaven. "Need some help getting in the tub?"

"I can handle it, thanks."

"Give a call if you run into trouble." Sloan held the door open, waiting until the room cleared. "And, when you're more up to it, I'd like the whole story."

Alone, Nathaniel managed to ease himself into the hot water. The first flash of agony passed, transforming gradually into something closer to comfort. By the time he'd climbed out again, the worst seemed to be over.

Until he looked in the mirror.

There was a bandage under his left eye, another on his

temple. His right eye looked like a rotting tomato. That
left the bruises, the swollen lip, the nasty scrape on his
jaw. All in all, he thought, he looked like hell.

With a towel slung around his waist, he stepped back
into the bedroom, just as Megan came in the hallway
door.

"I'm sorry." She pressed her lips together to keep
herself from saying all manner of foolish things.
"Amanda thought you might want another pillow, some
more towels."

"Thanks." He made it to the bed and lay back with a
sigh of relief.

Grateful for something practical to do, she hurried to
the bed, plumped and arranged pillows for him, smoothed
the sheets. "Is there anything I can get you? More ice?
Some soup?"

"No, this is fine."

"Please, I want to help. I need to help." She couldn't
bear it any longer, and she laid a hand to his cheek.
"They hurt you. I'm so sorry they hurt you."

"Just bruises."

"Damn it, don't be so stupid—not when I'm looking
right at you, not when I can see what they did." She
pulled back on the need to rage and looked helplessly
into his eyes. "I know you're angry with me, but can't
you let me do something?"

"Maybe you'd better sit down." When she did, he
took her hand in his. He needed the contact every bit as
much as she did. "You've been crying."

"A little." She looked down at his damaged knuckles.
"I felt so helpless downstairs, seeing you like this. You
let Coco tend you, and you wouldn't even look at me."
Drenched with emotion, her eyes came back to his. "I

don't want to lose you, Nathaniel. It's only that I've just found you, and I don't want to make another mistake.''

''It always comes back to him, doesn't it?''

''No, no. It comes back to me.''

''What he did to you,'' Nathaniel corrected grimly.

''All right, yes.'' She brought his hand to her cheek. ''Please, don't walk away from me. I don't have all the answers yet, but I know when Holt said you'd been hurt—my heart just stopped. I've never been so frightened. You mean so much to me, Nathaniel. Let me just take care of you until you're better.''

''Well.'' He was softening, and he reached out to stroke her hair. ''Maybe Dumont did me a favor this time.''

''What do you mean?''

He shook his head. Maybe his brain was a little addled by the drug and the pain. He hadn't meant to tell her, at least not yet. But he thought she had the right to know.

''The two guys that jumped me tonight. Dumont hired them.''

Every ounce of color faded from her cheeks. ''What are you saying? You're saying that Baxter paid them to attack you? To—''

''Rough me up, that's all. I'd say he was sore about me tossing him in the water and was looking for some payback.'' He shifted, winced. ''He'd have been smarter to put his money on a couple of pros. These two were real amateurs.''

''*Baxter* did this.'' Megan's vision hazed. She shut her eyes until she was sure it had cleared again. ''My fault.''

''Like hell. None of it's been yours, not from the start. He did what he did to you, Suzanna, the kids. Chicken-hearted bastard couldn't even fight for himself. Hey.'' He tugged on her hair. "I won, remember. He didn't get what he'd paid for."

"Do you think that matters?"

"It does to me. If you want to do something for me, Megan, really want to do something for me, you'll push him right out of your head."

"He's Kevin's father," she whispered. "It makes me sick to think it."

"He's nothing. Lie down here with me, will you?"

Because she could see that he was fighting off the drug, she did as he asked. Gently she shifted his head so that it rested on her breast.

"Sleep for a while," she murmured. "We won't think of it now. We won't think of anything."

He sighed, let himself drift. "I love you, Megan."

"I know." She stroked his hair and lay wakeful while he slept.

Neither of them saw the little boy with shattered eyes and pale cheeks in the open doorway.

Nathaniel woke to the rhythm of his own pain. There was a bass drum in his head, pounding low in the skull, with a few more enthusiastic riffs at the left temple. It was more of a snare along his ribs, a solid rat-a-tat that promised to remain steady and persistent. His shoulder sang along in a droning hum.

Experimentally, he sat up. Stiff as a week-old corpse, he thought in disgust. With slow, awkward movements, he eased out of the bed. Except for the pounding in his head, it was clear. Maybe too clear, he thought with a wince as he limped into the shower. His one pleasure was that he knew his two unexpected visitors would be suffering more than he was at the moment.

Even the soft needles of spray brought a bright bloom

of pain to the worst of his bruises. Teeth clenched, he waited out the pain until it mellowed to discomfort.

He'd live.

Naked and dripping, he stepped out of the shower, then filled the basin with icy water. Taking one bracing breath, he lowered his face into it until the shocking cold brought on a blessed numbness.

Steadier, he went back into the bedroom, where fresh clothes had been left folded on a chair. With a great deal of swearing, he managed to dress. He was thinking of coffee, aspirin and a full plate when the door creaked open.

"You shouldn't be up." Coco, a tray balanced in both hands, clucked her tongue. "Now get that shirt off and get back into bed."

"Darling, I've been waiting all my life to hear you say that."

"You must be feeling a little better," Coco said, and laughed, then set the tray on the bedside table and fluffed at her hair. It occurred to Nathaniel as he followed the familiar gesture that her hair hadn't changed color in a couple weeks, maybe more. Must be some mood she was in, he decided.

"I'll do."

"Poor dear." She lifted a hand to gently touch the bruises on his face. He looked even worse this morning, but she didn't have the heart to say so. "At least sit down and eat."

"You read my mind." More than willing, he eased himself into a chair. "I appreciate the service."

"It's the least we can do." Coco fit the legs of the bedside table over the chair and unfolded his napkin. Nathaniel thought she would have tucked it into his collar if he hadn't taken it himself. "Megan told me what happened. That Baxter hired those—those thugs. I've a mind to go to Boston myself and deal with that man.''

The fierce look in her eyes warmed Nathaniel's heart. She was like some fiery Celtic goddess. ''Sugar, he wouldn't have a chance against you.'' He sampled his eggs, closed his eyes on the simple pleasure of hot, delicious food. ''We'll let it go, darling.''

''Let it go! You can't. You have to contact the police. Of course, I'd prefer if all you boys got together and took a trip down to blacken that man's eyes...'' She pressed a hand to her heart as the image caused it to beat fast. ''But,'' she continued with some regret, ''the proper thing to do is contact the authorities and have them handle it.''

''No cops.'' He scooped up delicately fried hash brown potatoes. ''Dumont's going to suffer a lot more, not knowing what I'll do or when I'll do it.''

''Well...'' Considering that, Coco began to smile. ''I suppose he would. Like waiting for the other shoe to drop.''

''Yeah. And bringing the police in would make it tough for Megan and the boy.''

''You're right, of course.'' Gently she brushed a hand over his hair. ''I'm so glad they have you.''

''I wish she felt the same way.''

''She does. She's just afraid. Megan's had so much to handle in her life. And you—well, Nathaniel, you're a man who'd leave any woman a bit addled.''

''You think so, huh?''

''I know so. Are you having much pain this morning, dear? You can take another pill.''

''I'll settle for aspirin.''

''I thought you might.'' Coco took a bottle out of her apron pocket. ''Take these with your juice.''

"Yes, ma'am." He obeyed, then went back to his eggs. "So, you've seen Megan this morning?"

"It was nearly dawn before I could convince her to leave you and get some sleep."

That information went down even better than the food. "Yeah?"

"And the way she looked at you..." Coco patted his hand. "Well, a woman knows these things. Especially when she's in love herself." A becoming blush bloomed on her cheeks. "I suppose you know that Niels and I— that we're...involved."

He made some sound. He didn't want the image in his brain of them together in the dark. Coco and Dutch were as close to parents as he'd ever had, and no child, even at thirty-three, wanted to think about that side of a parental relationship.

"These past few weeks have been wonderful. I had a lovely marriage, and there are memories I've cherished and will cherish all of my life. And over the years, I've had some nice, compatible relationships. But with Niels..." The dreamy look came into her eyes. "He makes me feel young and vital, and almost delicate. It's not just the sex," she added, and had Nathaniel wincing.

"Aw, jeez, Coco." He took a sip of coffee, as he was rapidly losing his appetite. "I don't want to know about that."

She chuckled, adoring him. "I know how close you are to Niels."

"Well, sure." He was beginning to feel trapped in the chair, barred by the tray. "We sailed together a long time, and he's..."

"Like a father to you," she said gently. "I know. I just wanted you to know I love him, too. We're going to be married."

"What?" His fork clattered against china. "*Married?*
You and the Dutchman?"

"Yes." Nervous now, because she couldn't tell
whether his expression was horrified or simply shocked,
Coco fiddled with the jet beads at her throat. "I hope you
don't mind."

"Mind?" His brain had gone blank. Now it began to
fill again—the restless movements of her hands, the tone
of her voice, the anxious look in her eyes. Nathaniel
shifted the table away from his chair and rose. "Imagine
a classy woman like you falling for that old tar. Are you
sure he hadn't been slipping something into your soup?"

Relieved, she smiled. "If he has, I like it. Do we have
your blessing?"

He took her hands, looked down at them. "You know,
for nearly as far back as I can remember, I wanted you
to be my mother."

"Oh." Her eyes filled, overflowed. "Nathaniel."

"Now I guess you will be." His gaze lifted to hers
again before he kissed her, one cheek, the other, then her
lips. "He'd better be good to you, or he'll answer to
me."

"I'm so happy." Coco sank, weeping, into his arms.
"I'm so very happy, Nate. I didn't even see it coming in
the cards." Her breath hitched as she pressed her wet
face to his throat. "Or the tea leaves, even the crystal. It
just happened."

"The best things usually do."

"I want you to be happy." Drawing back, she fumbled
in her pocket for one of her lace-trimmed hankies. "I
want you to believe in what you have with Megan, and
not let it slip away. She needs you, Nate. So does
Kevin."

"That's what I told her." He smiled a little as he took

the hankie and dried Coco's tears himself. "I don't guess she was ready to hear it."

"You just keep saying it." Her voice became firm. "Keep right on saying it until she is." And if Megan needed an extra push, Coco thought, she'd be happy to supply it herself. "Now, then." She smoothed down her hair, her slacks. "I have a million things to do. I want you to rest, so you'll be up to the picnic and the fireworks."

"I feel okay."

"You feel as if you've been run over by a truck." She marched to the bed, busying herself with smoothing sheets and fluffing pillows. "You can lie down for another hour or two, or you can sit out on the terrace in the sun. It's a lovely day, and we can fix you up a nice chaise. When Megan wakes up, I'll have her come give you a rubdown."

"Now that sounds promising. I'll take the sun." He started toward the terrace doors, but then he heard footsteps hurrying down the hall.

Megan rushed in. "I can't find Kevin," she blurted out. "No one's seen him all morning."

Chapter 11

She was pale as ice, and struggling to be calm. The idea
of her little boy running away was so absurd that she
continued to tell herself it was a mistake, a prank. Maybe
a dream.

"No one's seen him," she repeated, bracing a hand on
the doorknob to stay upright. "Some—some of his
clothes are gone, and his knapsack."

"Call Suzanna," Nathaniel said quickly. "He's probably with Alex and Jenny."

"No." She shook her head slowly, side to side. Her
body felt like glass, as though it would shatter if she
moved too quickly. "They're here. They're all here.
They haven't seen him. I was sleeping." She said each
word deliberately, as if she were having trouble understanding her own voice. "I slept late, then I checked his
room, like I always do. He wasn't there, but I thought
he'd be downstairs, or outside. But when I went down,
Alex was looking for him." The fear began to claw at

her, little cat feet up and down her spine. "We hunted around, then I came back up. That's when I saw that some of his things…some of his things…"

"All right, dear, now don't you worry." Coco hurried over to slip a supporting arm around Megan's waist. "I'm sure he's just playing a game. There are so many places to hide in the house, on the grounds."

"He was so excited about today. It's all he could talk about. He's supposed to be playing Revolutionary War with Alex and Jenny. He—he was going to be Daniel Boone."

"We'll find him," Nathaniel told her.

"Of course we will." Gently Coco began to ease Megan along. "We'll organize a search party. Won't he be excited when he finds out?"

An hour later, they were spread throughout the house, searching corners and hidey-holes, retracing and backtracking. Megan kept a steel grip on her composure and covered every inch, starting in the tower and working her way down.

He had to be here, she reassured herself. Of course, she would find him any minute. It didn't make sense otherwise.

Bubbles of hysteria rose in her throat and had to be choked down.

He was just playing a game. He'd gone exploring. He loved the house so much. He'd drawn dozens of pictures of it to send back to Oklahoma so that everyone could see that he lived in a castle.

She would find him behind the next door she opened.

Megan told herself that, repeating it like a litany, as she worked her way from room to room.

She ran into Suzanna in one of the snaking hallways.

She felt cold, so cold, though the sun beat hot against the windows. "He doesn't answer me," she said faintly. "I keep calling him, but he doesn't answer."

"It's such a big house." Suzanna took Megan's hands, gripped hard. "Once when we were kids we played hide-and-seek and didn't find Lilah for three hours. She'd crawled into a cabinet on the third floor and had a nap."

"Suzanna." Megan pressed her lips together. She had to face it, and quickly. "His two favorite shirts are missing, and both pairs of his sneakers. His baseball caps. The money he'd been saving in his jar is gone. He's not in the house. He's run away."

"You need to sit down."

"No, I—I need to do something. Call the police. Oh, God—" Breaking, Megan pressed her hands to her face. "Anything could have happened to him. He's just a little boy. I don't even know how long he's been gone. I don't even know." Her eyes, swimming with fear, locked on Suzanna's. "Did you ask Alex, Jenny? Maybe he said something to them. Maybe—"

"Of course I asked them, Megan," Suzanna said gently. "Kevin didn't say anything to them about leaving."

"Where would he go? Why? Back to Oklahoma," she said on a wild, hopeful thought. "Maybe he's trying to get back to Oklahoma. Maybe he's been unhappy, just pretending to like it here."

"He's been happy. But we'll check it out. Come on, let's go down."

"Been over every bit of this section," Dutch told Nathaniel. "The pantries, the storerooms, even the meat locker. Trent and Sloan are going over the renovation areas, and Max and Holt are beating the bushes all over the grounds.''

There was worry in his eyes, but he was brewing a pot of fresh coffee with steady hands.

''Seems to me if the kid was just playing and heard all this shouting and calling, he'd come out to see what the excitement was all about.''

''We've been over the house twice.'' Nathaniel stared grimly out the window. ''Amanda and Lilah have combed every inch of The Retreat. He's not in here.''

''Don't make a lick of sense to me. Kevin's been happy as a clam. He's in here every blessed day, getting under my feet and begging for sea stories.''

''Something's got him running.'' There was a prickle at the back of his neck. Rubbing it absently, Nathaniel looked out toward the cliffs. ''Why does a kid run? Because he's scared, or he's hurt, or he's unhappy.''

''That boy ain't none of those things,'' Dutch said staunchly.

''I wouldn't have thought so.'' Nathaniel had been all three at that age, and he believed he would have recognized the signs. There had been times he ran, too. But he'd had nowhere to go.

The tickle at the back of his neck persisted. Again, he found his gaze wandering toward the cliffs. ''I've got a feeling,'' he said almost to himself.

''What?''

''No, just a feeling.'' The prickle was in his gut now. ''I'm going to check it out.''

It was as though he were being pulled to the cliffs. Nathaniel didn't fight it, though the rocky ground jarred the pain back into his bones and the steep climb stole his breath. With one hand pressed to his aching ribs, he continued, his gaze sweeping the rocks and the high wild grass.

It was, he knew, a place that would draw a child. It had drawn him as a boy. And as a man.

The sun was high and white, the sea sapphire blue, then frothy where it lashed and foamed on the rocks. Beautiful and deadly. He thought of a young boy stumbling along the path, missing a step, slipping. The nausea churned so violently he had to stop and choke it back.

Nothing had happened to Kevin, he assured himself. He wouldn't let anything happen to Kevin.

He turned, started to climb higher, calling the boy's name as he searched.

It was the bird that caught his eye. A pure white gull, graceful as a dancer, swooped over the grass and rock, circled back with a musical call that was almost human, eerily feminine. He stood, staring at it. For one sunstruck second, Nathaniel would have sworn the gull's eyes were green, green as emeralds.

It glided down, perched on the ledge below and looked up, as if waiting for him.

Nathaniel found himself clambering down, ignoring the jolts to his abused body. The thunder of the surf seemed to fill his head. He thought he smelled a woman, sweet, soft, soothing, but then it was only the sea.

The bird wheeled away, skyward, joined its mate— another gull, blindingly white. For a moment they circled, calling together in something like joy. Then they winged out to sea.

Wheezing a bit, Nathaniel gained the ledge, and saw the shallow crevice in the rock where the boy was huddled.

His first instinct was to scoop the child up, hold him.

But he checked it. He wasn't altogether certain he wasn't the reason Kevin had run.

Instead, he sat down on the ledge and spoke quietly. "Nice view from here."

Kevin kept his face pressed to his knees. "I'm going back to Oklahoma." It was an attempt at defiance that merely sounded weary. "I can take a bus."

"I guess so. You'd see a lot of the country that way. But I thought you liked it here."

His answer was a shrug. "It's okay."

"Somebody give you a hard time, mate?"

"No."

"Did you have a fight with Alex?"

"No, it's nothing like that. I'm just going back to Oklahoma. It was too late to take the bus last night, so I came up here to wait. I guess maybe I fell asleep." He hunched his shoulder, kept his face averted. "You can't make me go back."

"Well, I'm bigger than you, so I could." He said it gently, touched a hand to Kevin's hair. But the boy jerked away. "I'd rather not make you do anything until I understand what's on your mind."

He let some time pass, watching the sea, listening to the wind, until he sensed Kevin relaxing a little beside him.

"Your mother's kind of worried about you. Everybody else is, too. Maybe you ought to go back and tell them goodbye before you leave."

"She won't let me go."

"She loves you a lot."

"She should never have had me." There was bitterness in the words, words that were much too sharp for a little boy.

"That's a stupid thing to say. I figure you've got a

right to get mad if you want but there's not much point in just being stupid."

Kevin's head shot up. His face was streaked with tears and dirt, and it sliced through Nathaniel's heart.

"If she hadn't had me, things would be different. She always pretends it doesn't matter. But I know."

"What do you know?"

"I'm not a baby anymore. I know what he did. He made her pregnant, then he went away. He went away, and he never cared. He went away and married Suzanna, and then he left her, too. And Alex and Jenny. That's how come I'm their brother."

Those were stormy seas, Nathaniel thought, that needed to be navigated with care. The boy's eyes, hurt and angry, latched on to his.

"Your mother's the one who has to explain that to you, Kevin."

"She told me that sometimes people can't get married and be together, even when they have kids. But he didn't want me. He never wanted me, and I hate him."

"I'm not going to argue with you about that," Nathaniel said carefully. "But your mother loves you, and that counts for a lot more. If you take off, it's going to hurt her, bad."

Kevin's lips trembled. "She could have you if I was gone. You'd stay with her if it wasn't for me."

"I'm afraid I'm not following you, Kevin."

"He—he had you beaten up." Kevin's voice hitched as he fought to get the words out. "I heard last night. I heard you and Mom, and she said it was her fault, but it's mine. 'Cause he's my father and he did it and now you hate me, too, and you'll go away."

"Little jerk." On a flood of emotion, Nathaniel yanked the boy to his knees and shook him. "You pulled this stunt because I got a few bruises? Do I look like I can't take care of myself? Those other two wimps had to crawl away."

"Really?" Kevin sniffed and rubbed at his eyes. "But still—"

"Still, hell. You didn't have anything to do with it, and I ought to shake you until your teeth fall out for worrying us all this way."

"He's my father," Kevin said, tilting his chin up. "So that means—"

"That means nothing. My father was a drunk who used to kick my butt for the pleasure of it, six days out of seven. Does that make me like him?"

"No." Tears began to roll more freely now. "But I thought you wouldn't like me anymore, and you'd never stay and be my father now, like Holt is with Alex and Jenny."

Nathaniel's hands gentled as he drew the sobbing boy into his arms. "You thought wrong." He rubbed his lips over Kevin's hair, absorbed the jolt of love. "I ought to hang you from the yardarm, sailor."

"What's that?"

"I'll show you later." He tightened his grip. "Did you stop and think that I might be hoping you'd be my son? That I want you and your mom to be mine?"

"Honest?" Kevin's voice was muffled against Nathaniel's chest.

"Do you figure I've been training you to take the helm just to have you walk off?"

"I don't know. I guess not."

"I've been looking for you, Kevin, longer than just today."

With a sigh, Kevin let his head rest in the curve of

Nathaniel's shoulder. "I was awful scared. But then the bird came."

"Bird?" Remembering, Nathaniel glanced around. But the rocks were empty.

"Then I wasn't so scared. She stayed all night. She was there whenever I woke up. She flew away with the other one, but then you came. Is Mom mad at me?"

"Probably."

Kevin sighed again—a long-suffering sound that made Nathaniel smile. "I guess I'm in trouble."

"Well, let's get your things and go back and face the music."

Kevin picked up his knapsack and put his hand trustingly in Nathaniel's. "Does it hurt?" he asked, studying Nathaniel's face.

"You bet."

"Later, can I see all your bruises?"

"Sure. I've got some beauts."

Nathaniel felt every one of them as they climbed back up to the cliff path and started down the rocky slope toward home. It was worth it, worth every jar and wince, to see the look on Megan's face.

"Kevin!" She flew across the lawn, hair blowing, cheeks tracked with tears.

"Go on," Nathaniel murmured to the boy. "She'll want to hug you first."

With a nod, Kevin dropped his knapsack and raced into his mother's arms.

"Oh, Kevin…" She couldn't hold him tight enough, even kneeling on the grass, pressing him close, rocking and weeping in terrible relief.

"Where'd you find him?" Trent asked Nathaniel quietly.

"Up on the cliffs, holed up in a crevice in the rocks."

"Good God." C.C. shuddered. "Did he spend the night up there?"

"Looked that way. I had this feeling, I can't explain it. And there he was."

"A feeling?" Trent exchanged a look with his wife. "Remind me to tell you sometime how I found Fred when he was a puppy."

Max gave Nathaniel a pat on the back. "I'll go call the police, let them know we've found him."

"He'll be hungry." Coco swallowed fresh tears and burrowed closer to Dutch. "We'll go fix him something to eat."

"You bring 'em in when she's finished slobbering over him—" Dutch camouflaged the break in his voice with a cough. "Women. Always making a fuss."

"Come on, let's go in." Suzanna tugged on Alex and Jenny's hands.

"But I want to ask if he saw the ghosts," Alex complained.

"Later." Holt solved the problem by hoisting Alex onto his shoulders.

With a shuddering sigh, Megan drew back, ran her hands over Kevin's face. "You're all right? You're not hurt?"

"Nuh-uh." It embarrassed him that he'd cried in front of his brother and sister. After all, he was nearly nine. "I'm okay."

"Don't you *ever* do that again." The swift change from weeping mother to fierce parent had Nathaniel's brows rising. "You had us all worried sick, young man. We've been looking for you for hours, even Aunt Colleen. We've called the police."

"I'm sorry." But the thrill of knowing the police had been alerted overpowered the guilt.

"Sorry isn't enough, Kevin Michael O'Riley."

Kevin's gaze hit the ground. It was big-time trouble when she used all his names. "I won't ever do it again. I promise."

"You had no business doing it this time. I'm supposed to be able to trust you, and now— Oh." On another hitching sob, she pressed his head to her breast. "I was so scared, baby. I love you so much. Where were you going?"

"I don't know. Maybe Grandma's."

"Grandma's." She sat back on her heels and sighed. "Don't you like it here?"

"I like it best of anything."

"Then why did you run away, Kevin? Are you mad at me?"

He shook his head, then dropped his chin on his chest. "I thought you and Nate were mad at me because he got beaten up. But Nate says it's not my fault and you're not mad. He says it doesn't matter about *him*. You're not mad at me, are you?"

Her horrified eyes flew to Nate's, held there as she drew Kevin close again. "Oh, no, baby, I'm not. No one is." She looked at her son again, cupping his face in her hands. "Remember when I told you that sometimes people can't be together? I should explain that sometimes they shouldn't be together. That's the way it was with me and—" She couldn't refer to him as Kevin's father. "With me and Baxter."

"But I was an accident."

"Oh, no." She smiled then, kissed his cheeks. "An accident's something you wish hadn't happened. You were a gift. The best one I ever had in my life. If you ever think I don't want you again, I guess I'll have to stuff you into a box and tie it up with a bow so you'll get the point.''

He giggled. "I'm sorry."

"Me too. Now let's go get you cleaned up." She rose, gripped her son's hand in hers and looked at Nathaniel. "Thank you."

In the way of children, Kevin bounced back from his night on the cliffs and threw himself into the holiday. He was, for the moment, a hero, desperately impressing his siblings with his tales of the dark and the sea and a white bird with green eyes.

In keeping with the family gathering, all the dogs attended, so Sadie and Fred raced with their puppies and the children over the rolling lawn. Babies napped in playpens or rocked in swings or charmed their way into willing arms. A few hotel guests wandered over from their own feast provided by The Retreat, drawn by the laughter and raised voices.

Nathaniel passed, reluctantly, on the impromptu softball game, figuring one slide into third would have him down for the count. Instead, he designated himself umpire and had the pleasure of arguing with every batter he called out.

"Are you blind or just stupid?" C.C. tossed down her bat in disgust. "A sock in the eye's no excuse for missing that call. That ball was outside a half a mile."

Nathaniel clamped his cigar in his teeth. "Not from where I'm standing, sugar."

She slapped her hands on her hips. "Then you're standing in the wrong spot." Jenny took the opportunity to attempt a cartwheel over home plate, and earned some applause from the infield.

"C.C., you've got one of the best-looking strike zones I've ever had the pleasure of seeing. And that was strike three. You're out."

"If you weren't already black-and-blue..." She swallowed a laugh, and sneered instead. "You're up, Lilah."

"Already?" In a lazy gesture, Lilah brushed her hair away from her face and stepped into the box.

From her position at short, Megan glanced at her second baseman. "She won't run even if she connects."

Suzanna sighed, shook her head. "She won't have to. Just watch."

Lilah skimmed a hand down her hip, cast a sultry look back at Nathaniel, then faced the pitcher. Sloan went through an elaborate windup that had the children cheering. Lilah took the first strike with the bat still on her shoulder. Yawned.

"We keeping you up?" Nathaniel asked her.

"I like to wait for my pitch."

Apparently the second one wasn't the one she was waiting for. She let it breeze by, and earned catcalls from the opposing team.

She stepped out of the box, stretched, smiled at Sloan. "Okay, big guy," she said as she took her stance again. She cracked the low curveball and sent it soaring for a home run. Amid the cheers, she turned and handed her bat to Nathaniel. "I always recognize the right pitch," she told him, and sauntered around the bases.

When the game broke for the feast, Nathaniel eased down beside Megan. "You've got a pretty good arm there, sugar."

"I coached Kevin's Little League team back in Oklahoma." Her gaze wandered to her son, as it had dozens of times during the afternoon. "He doesn't seem any the worse for wear, does he?"

"Nope. How about you?"

"The bats in my stomach have mellowed out to butterflies." She pressed a hand to them now, lowered her voice. "I never knew he thought about Baxter. About…any of it. I should have."

"A boy's got to have some secrets, even from his mother."

"I suppose." It was too beautiful a day, she decided, too precious a day, to waste on worry. "Whatever you said to him up there, however you said it, was exactly right. It means a lot to me." She looked over at him. "You mean a lot to me."

Nathaniel sipped his beer, studied her. "You're working up to something, Meg. Why don't you just say it?"

"All right. After you left yesterday, I spent a lot of time thinking. About how I'd feel if you didn't come back. I knew there'd be a hole in my life. Maybe I'd be able to fill it again, part of the way, but something would always be missing. When I asked myself what that would be, I kept coming up with the same answer. No matter how many ways I looked at it or juggled it around, the answer never changed."

"So what's the answer, Meg?"

"You, Nathaniel." She leaned over and kissed him. "Just you."

Later, when the sky was dark and the moon floated over the water, she watched the fireworks explode. Color bloomed into color. Waterfalls of glowing sparks rained from sky to water in a celebration of freedom, new beginnings and, Megan thought, hope.

It was a dazzling display that had the children staring upward, wide-eyed and openmouthed. The echoing booms shivered the air until, with a machine-gun crescendo, color and light spewed high in the finale. For a heart-pounding interlude, the sky was bright with golds and reds, blues and blinding whites, circles and spirals, cascades and towers, that shattered into individual stars over the sea.

Long after it was over, the dregs of the party cleared away, the children tucked into bed, she felt the power of the celebration running through her blood. In her own room, she brushed her hair until it flowed over her shoulders. Anticipation vibrating inside her, she belted her borrowed robe loosely at her waist. Quietly she slipped out the terrace doors and walked to Nathaniel's room.

It hadn't taken much pressure to persuade him to stay another night. He'd been tired and aching, and he hadn't relished even the short drive home. But the long soak in the tub hadn't relaxed him, as he hoped. He was still filled with restless urges, and with flashing images of Megan's face, lit with the glow of rockets.

Then he stepped into the bedroom and saw her.

She wore a silky robe of deep blue that flowed down her body and clung to her curves. Her hair glinted, golden fire, and her eyes were as dark and mysterious as sapphires.

"I thought you could use a rubdown." She smiled hesitantly. "I've had a lot of experience loosening stiff muscles. With horses, anyway."

He was almost afraid to breathe. "Where did you get that?"

"Oh." Self-consciously she ran a hand down the robe. "I borrowed it from Lilah. I thought you'd like it better than terry cloth." When he said nothing, her nerve began to slip. "If you'd rather I go, I understand. I don't expect that you'd feel well enough to— We don't have to make love, Nathaniel. I just want to help."

"I don't want you to go."

Her smile bloomed again. "Why don't you lie down, then? I'll start on your back. Really, I'm good at this." She laughed a little. "The horses loved me."

He crossed to the bed, touched her hair, her cheek. "Did you wear silk robes to work the stock?"

"Always." She eased him down. "Roll onto your stomach," she said briskly. Pleased with the task, she poured liniment into her hands, then rubbed her palms together to warm it. Carefully, so that the movement of the mattress didn't jar him, she knelt over him. "Tell me if I hurt you."

She started on his shoulders, gently over the bruises, more firmly over knotted muscles. He had a warrior's body, she thought, tough and tight, and carrying all the marks of battle.

"You overdid it today."

He only grunted, closing his eyes and letting his body reap the pleasure of her stroking hands. He felt the brush of silk against his skin when she shifted. Drifting through the sharp scent of liniment was her subtle perfume, another balm to the senses.

The aches began to fade, then shifted into a deeper, more primal pain that coursed smoothly through his blood when she lowered her lips to his shoulder.

"Better?" she murmured.

"No. You're killing me. Don't stop."

Her laugh was low and soft as she eased the towel from his hips, and pressed competent fingers low on his spine. "I'm here to make you feel better, Nathaniel. You have to relax for me to do this right."

"You're doing just fine." He moaned as her hands moved lower, circling, kneading. Then her lips, skimming, whisper-soft.

"You have such a beautiful body." Her own breathing grew heavy as she stroked and explored. "I love looking at it, touching it." Slowly she took her lips up his spine, over his shoulder again, to nuzzle at his ear. "Turn over," she whispered. "I'll do the rest."

Her lips were there to meet his when he shifted, to linger, to heat. But when he reached up, groaning, to cup her breasts, she drew back.

"Wait." Though her hands trembled, she freshened the liniment. With her eyes on his, she spread her fingers over his chest. "They put marks on you," she murmured.

"I put more on them."

"Nathaniel the dragon-slayer. Lie still," she whispered, and bent close to kiss the scrapes and bruises on his face. "I'll make it all go away."

His heart was pounding. She could feel it rocket against her palm. In the lamplight, his eyes were dark as smoke. The robe pooled around her knees when she straddled him. She massaged his shoulders, his arms, his hands, kissing the scraped knuckles, laving them with her tongue.

The air was like syrup, thick and sweet. It caught in his lungs with each labored breath. No other woman had ever made him feel helpless, drained and sated, all at once.

"Megan, I need to touch you."

Watching him, she reached for the belt of the robe, loosened it. In one fluid movement, the silk slid from her shoulders. Beneath she wore a short slip of the same color and texture. As he reached up, one thin strap spilled off her shoulder.

She closed her eyes, let her head fall back, as his hands stroked over the silk, then beneath. The colors were back, all those flashing, dazzling lights that had erupted in the sky. Stars wheeled inside her head, beautifully hot. Craving more, she rose over him, took him into her with a delicious slowness that had them both gasping.

She shuddered when he arched up, gripping her hips in his hands. Now the colors seemed to shoot into her blood, white-hot, and her skin grew damp and slick. Suddenly greedy, she swooped down, devouring his lips, fingers clutching the bruised flesh she'd sought to soothe.

"Let me." She moaned and pressed his hands against her breasts. "Let me."

With a wildness that staggered him, she drove him hard, riding him like lightning. He called out her name as his vision dimmed, as the frantic need convulsed like pain inside him. Release was like a whiplash that stung with velvet.

She tightened around him like a fist and shattered him.

Weak as water, she flowed down, rested her head on his chest. "Did I hurt you?"

He couldn't find the strength to wrap his arms around her and let them lie limp on the bed. "I can't feel anything but you."

"Nathaniel." She lifted her head to press a kiss to his thundering heart. "There's something I forgot to tell you yesterday."

"Hmm... What's that?"

"I love you, too." She watched his eyes open, saw the swirl of emotion darken them.

"That's good." His arms, no longer weak, circled her, cradled her.

"I don't know if it's enough, but—"

He turned his lips to hers to quiet her. "Don't mess it up. 'For love's sake only,' Megan. That's enough for tonight." He kissed her again. "Stay with me."

"Yes."

Chapter 12

Fireworks were one thing, but when the Calhouns put their heads together planning Coco's engagement party, there promised to be plenty of skyrockets.

Everything from a masked ball to a moonlight cruise had been considered, with the final vote going to dinner and dancing under the stars. With only a week to complete arrangements, assignments were handed out.

Megan squeezed time out of each day to polish silver, wash crystal and inventory linens.

"All this fuss." Colleen thumped her way to the closet where Megan was counting napkins. "When a woman her age straps herself down to a man, she should have the sense to do it quietly."

Megan lost count and patiently began again. "Don't you like parties, Aunt Colleen?"

"When there's a reason for them. Never considered putting yourself under a man's thumb reason to celebrate."

"Coco's not doing that. Dutch adores her."

"Humph. Time will tell. Once a man's got a ring on your finger, he doesn't have to be so sweet and obliging." Her crafty eyes studied Megan's face. "Isn't that why you're putting off that big-shouldered sailor? Afraid of what happens after the 'I-dos'?"

"Of course not." Megan laid a stack of linens aside before she lost count again. "And we're talking about Coco and Dutch, not me. She deserves to be happy."

"Not everybody gets what they deserve," Colleen shot back. "You'd know that well, wouldn't you?"

Exasperated, Megan whirled around. "I don't know why you're trying to spoil this. Coco's happy, I'm happy. I'm doing my best to make Nathaniel happy."

"I don't see you out buying any orange blossoms for yourself, girl."

"Marriage isn't the answer for everyone. It wasn't for you."

"No, I'm too smart to fall into that trap. Maybe you're like me. Men come and go. Maybe the right one goes with the rest, but we get by, don't we? Because we know what they're like, deep down." Colleen eased closer, her dark eyes fixed on Megan's face. "We've known the worst of them. The selfishness, the cruelty, the lack of honor and ethics. Maybe one steps into our lives for a moment, one who seems different. But we're too wise, too careful, to take that shaky step. If we live our lives alone, at least we know no man will ever have the power to hurt us."

"I'm not alone," Megan said in an unsteady voice.

"No, you have a son. One day he'll be grown, and if you've done a good job, he'll leave your nest and fly off to make his own."

Colleen shook her head, and for one moment she

looked so unbearably sad that Megan reached out. But the old woman held herself stiff, her head high.

"You'll have the satisfaction of knowing you escaped the trap of marriage, just as I did. Do you think no one ever asked me? There was one," Colleen went on, before Megan could speak. "One who nearly lulled me in before I remembered, before I turned him away, before I risked the hell my mother had known."

Colleen's mouth thinned at the memory. "He tried to break her in every way, with his rules, his money, his need to own. In the end, he killed her, then he slowly, slowly, went mad. But not with guilt. What ate at him, I think, was the loss of something he'd never been able to fully own. That was why he rid the house of every piece of her, and locked himself in his own private purgatory."

"I'm sorry," Megan murmured. "I'm so sorry."

"For me? I'm old, and long past the time to grieve. I learned from my experience, as you learned from yours. Not to trust, never to risk. Let Coco have her orange blossoms, we have our freedom."

She walked away stiffly, leaving Megan to flounder in a sea of emotion.

Colleen was wrong, she told herself, and began to fuss with napkins again. She wasn't cold and aloof and blocked off from love. Just days ago she'd declared her love. She wasn't letting Baxter's shadow darken what she had with Nathaniel.

Oh, but she was. Wearily she leaned against the doorjamb. She was, and she wasn't sure she could change it. Love and lovemaking didn't equal commitment. No one knew that better than she. She had loved Baxter fully, vitally. And that was the shadow. Even knowing that what she felt for Nathaniel was fuller, richer, and much, much truer, she couldn't dispel that doubt.

She would have to think it through, calmly, as soon as she had time. The answer was always there, she assured herself, if you looked for it long enough, carefully enough. All she had to do was process the data.

She tossed down her neatly counted napkins in disgust. What kind of woman was she? she wondered. She was trying to turn emotions into equations, as if they were some sort of code she had to decipher before she could know her own heart.

That was going to stop. She was going to stop. If she couldn't look into her own heart, it was time to…

Her thoughts trailed off, circled back, swooping down on one errant idea like a hawk on a rabbit.

Oh, God, a code. Leaving the linens in disarray, she flew down the hall to her own bedroom.

Fergus's book was where she'd left it, lying neatly on the corner of her desk. She snatched it up and began flipping frantically through pages.

It didn't have to be stock quotations or account numbers, she realized. It didn't have to be anything as logical as that. The numbers were listed in the back of the book, after dozens of blank sheets—after the final entry Fergus had written. On the day before Bianca died.

Why hadn't she seen it before? There were no journal entries, no careful checks and balances after that date. Only sheet after blank sheet. Then the numbers, formed in a careful hand.

A message, Megan wondered, something he'd been compelled to write down but hadn't wanted prying eyes to read. A confession of guilt, perhaps? Or a plea for understanding?

She sat and took several clearing breaths. They were numbers, after all, she reminded herself. There was nothing she couldn't do with numbers.

An hour passed, then two. As she worked, the desk became littered with discarded slips of paper. Each time she stopped to rest her eyes or her tired brain, she wondered whether she had tumbled into lunacy even thinking she'd found some mysterious code in the back of an old book.

But the idea hooked her, kept her chained to the desk. She heard the blast of a horn as a tour boat passed. The shadows lengthened from afternoon toward evening.

She grew only more determined as each of her efforts failed. She would find the key. However long it took, she would find it.

Something clicked, causing her to stop, sit back and study anew. As if tumblers had fallen into place, she had it. Slowly, painstakingly, she transcribed numbers into letters and let the cryptogram take shape.

The first word to form was *Bianca.*

"Oh, God." Megan pressed her hand to her lips. "It's real."

Step by step she continued, crossing out, changing, advancing letter by letter, word by word. When the excitement began to build in her, she pushed it back. This was an answer she would find only with her mind. Emotions would hurry her, cause mistakes. So she thought of nothing but the logic of the code.

The figures started to blur in front of her eyes. She forced herself to close them, to sit back and relax until her mind was clear again. Then she opened them again, and read.

Bianca haunts me. I have no peace. All that was hers must be put away, sold, destroyed. Do spirits walk? It is nonsense, a lie. But I see her eyes, staring at me as she fell. Green as her emeralds. I will leave

her a token to satisfy her. And that will be the end
of it. Tonight I will sleep.

Breathless, Megan read on. The directions were very
simple, very precise. For a man going mad with the enor-
mity of his own actions, Fergus Calhoun had retained his
conciseness.

Tucking the paper in her pocket, Megan hurried out.
She didn't consider alerting the Calhouns. Something was
driving her to finish this herself. She found what she
needed in the renovation area in the family wing. Hefting
a crowbar, a chisel, a tape measure, she climbed the
winding iron steps to Bianca's tower.

She had been here before, knew that Bianca had stood
by the windows and watched the cliffs for Christian. That
she had wept here, dreamed here, died here.

The Calhouns had made it charming again, with
plump, colorful pillows on the window seat, delicate tables and china vases. A velvet chaise, a crystal lamp.

Bianca would have been pleased.

Megan closed the heavy door at her back. Using the
tape measure, she followed Fergus's directions. Six feet
in from the door, eight from the north wall.

Without a thought to the destruction she was about to
cause, Megan rolled up the softly faded floral carpet, then
shoved the chisel between the slats of wood.

It was hard, backbreaking work. The wood was old,
but thick and strong. Someone had polished it to a fine
gleam. She pried and pulled, stopping only to flex her
straining muscles and, when the light began to fail, to
switch on the lamps.

The first board gave with a protesting screech. If she'd
been fanciful, she might have thought it sounded like a
woman. Sweat dripped down her sides, and she cursed

herself for forgetting a flashlight. Refusing to think of spiders, or worse, she thrust her hand into the gap.

She thought she felt the edge of something, but no matter how she stretched and strained, she couldn't get a grip. Grimly resigned, she set to work on the next board.

Swearing at splinters and her own untried muscles, she fought it loose. With a grunt, she tossed the board aside, and panting, stretched out on her stomach to grope into the hole.

Her fingertip rang against metal. She nearly wept. The handle almost slipped out of her sweaty hand, but she pulled the box up and free and set it on her lap.

It was no more than a foot long, a foot wide and a few pounds in weight, and it was grimy from the years it had spent in the darkness. Almost tenderly, she brushed away the worst of the dust. Her fingers hovered at the latch, itching to release it, then dropped away.

It wasn't hers to open.

"I don't know where she could be." Amanda strode back into the parlor, tossing up her hands. "She's not in her office, or her room."

"She was fussing in a closet when I saw her last." Colleen tipped back her glass. "She's a grown woman. Might be taking a walk."

"Yes, but…" Suzanna trailed off with a glance at Kevin. There was no point in worrying the child, she reminded herself. Just because Megan was never late, that was no reason to assume something was wrong. "Maybe she's in the garden." She smiled and handed the baby to Holt. "I can go look."

"I'll do it." Nathaniel stood up. He didn't really believe Megan had forgotten their date for dinner and gone walking in the garden, but looking was better than worrying. "If she comes in while I'm gone—" But then he heard her footsteps and glanced toward the doorway.

Her hair was wild, her eyes were wide. Her face and clothes were smeared with dirt. And she was smiling, brilliantly. "I'm sorry I'm late."

"Megan, what on earth?" Dumbfounded, Sloan stared at her. "You look as if you've been crawling in a ditch."

"Not quite." She laughed and pushed a hand through her disordered hair. "I got a little involved, lost track of the time. Sloan, I borrowed some of your tools. They're in the tower."

"In the—"

But she was crossing the room, her eyes on Colleen. She knelt at the old woman's feet, set the box in her lap. "I found something that belongs to you."

Colleen scowled down at the box, but her heart was thrumming in her ears. "Why would you think it belongs to me?"

Gently Megan took Colleen's hand, laid it on the dusty metal. "He hid it under the floor of the tower, her tower, after she died." Her quiet voice silenced the room like a bomb. "He said she haunted him." Megan pulled the transcribed code out of her pocket, set it on top of the box.

"I can't read it," Colleen said impatiently.

"I'll read it for you." But when Megan took the sheet again, Colleen grabbed her wrist.

"Wait. Have Coco come in. I want her here."

While they waited, Megan got up and went to Nathaniel. "It was a code," she told him, before turning to face the room. "The numbers in the back of the book. I don't know why I didn't see it...." Then she smiled. "I was looking too hard, too closely. And today I knew. I just knew." She stopped, lifted her hands, let them fall. "I'm sorry. I should have told you as soon as I'd solved it. I wasn't thinking."

"You did what you were meant to do," Lilah corrected. "If one of us was supposed to find it, we would have."

"Is it like a treasure hunt?" Kevin wanted to know.

"Yes." Megan drew him close to ruffle his hair.

"I really don't have time right now, dear." Coco was arguing as Amanda dragged her into the room. "It's the middle of the dinner rush."

"Sit and be quiet," Colleen ordered. "The girl has something to read. Get your aunt a drink," she said to C.C. "She may need it. And freshen mine, while you're at it." She lifted her eyes, bird-bright, to Megan's. "Well, go on. Read it."

As she did, Megan slipped her hand into Nathaniel's. She heard Coco's quick gasp and sigh. Her own throat was raw with unshed tears when she lowered the page again.

"So...I went up and I pried up some floorboards. And I found it."

Even the children were silent when Colleen placed her thin hands on the box. They trembled once, then steadied as she worked the latch free, and opened the lid. Now it was her lips that trembled, and her eyes filled. She drew out a small oval frame, tarnished black with age.

"A photograph," she said in a thick voice. "Of my mother with me and Sean and Ethan. It was taken the year before she died. We sat for it in the garden in New York." She stroked it once, then offered it to Coco.

"Oh, Aunt Colleen. It's the only picture we have of all of you."

"She kept it on her dressing table, so that she could look at it every day. A book of poetry." Colleen drew out the slim volume, caressed it. "She loved to read poetry. It's Yeats. She would read it to me sometimes, and tell me it reminded her of Ireland. This brooch." She took out a small, simple enamel pin decorated with violets. "Sean and I gave it to her for Christmas. Nanny helped us buy it, of course. We were too young. She often wore it."

She caressed a marcasite watch, its pin shaped like a bow, and a carved jade dog hardly bigger than her thumb.

There were other small treasures—a smooth white stone, a pair of tin soldiers, the dust of an ancient flower. Then the pearls, an elegant choker of four delicate strands that had slept the decades away in a black velvet pouch.

"My grandparents gave her these as a bridal gift." Colleen ran a fingertip over the smooth orbs. "She told me it would be mine on my wedding day. He didn't like her to wear it. Too plain, he said. Too ordinary. She kept them in the pouch, in her jewel case. She would often take them out and show them to me. She said that pearls given with love were more precious than diamonds given for show. She told me to treasure them as she did, and to wear them often, because—" Her voice broke, and she reached for her glass, sipped to clear her throat. "Because pearls needed warmth."

She closed her eyes and sat back. "I thought he'd sold them, disposed of them with the rest."

"You're tired, Aunt Colleen." Suzanna went quietly to her side. "Why don't I take you upstairs? I can bring you a dinner tray."

"I'm not an invalid." Colleen snapped the words out, but her hand covered Suzanna's and squeezed. "I'm old, but I'm not feeble. I've wit enough to make some bequests. You." She pressed the brooch into Suzanna's hand. "This is yours. I want to see you wear it."

"Aunt Colleen—"

"Put it on now. Put it on." She brushed Suzanna away and picked up the book of poetry. "You spend half your time dreaming," she said to Lilah. "Dream with this."

"Thank you." Lilah bent down, kissed her.

"You'll have the watch," she said to Amanda. "You're the one who's always worrying about what time it is. And you," she continued, looking at C.C. and waving Amanda's thanks away, "take the jade. You like to set things around that gather dust."

Her eyebrow cocked at Jenny.

"Waiting for your turn, are you?"

Jenny smiled guilelessly. "No, ma'am."

"You'll have this." She offered Jenny the stone. "I was younger than you when I gave this to my mother. I thought it was magic. Maybe it is."

"It's pretty." Delighted with her new treasure, Jenny rubbed it against her cheek. "I can put it on my windowsill."

"She'd have been pleased," Colleen said softly. "She kept it on hers." With a harsh cough, she cleared her voice to briskness again. "You boys, take these, and don't lose them. They were my brother's."

"Neat," Alex whispered, reverently holding a perfectly detailed soldier. "Thanks."

"Thanks," Kevin echoed. "It's just like a treasure box," he said, grinning at her. "Aren't you going to give anything to Aunt Coco?"

"She'll have the photograph."

"Aunt Colleen." Overcome, Coco reached for her hankie. "Really, you mustn't."

"You'll take it as a wedding gift, and be grateful."

"I am grateful. I don't know what to say."

"See that you clean that tarnish off the frame." Bracing her weight on the cane, Colleen rose and turned to Megan. "You look pleased with yourself."

Megan's heart was too full for pretense. "I am."

For a moment, Colleen's damp eyes twinkled back. "You should be. You're a bright girl, Megan. And a resourceful one. You remind me of myself, a very long time ago." Gently she picked up the pearls, letting the glowing strands run through her bent fingers.

"Here." Megan stepped toward her. "Let me help you put them on."

Colleen shook her head. "Pearls need youth. They're for you."

Stunned, Megan dropped her hands again. "No, you can't give them away like that. Bianca meant them for you."

"She meant them to be passed on."

"Within the family. They...they should go to Coco, or—"

"They go where I say they go," Colleen said imperiously.

"It isn't right." Megan searched the room for help, but found only satisfied smiles.

"It seems perfectly right to me," Suzanna murmured. "Amanda?"

Amanda touched a hand to the watch she'd pinned to her lapel. "Completely."

"Lovely." Coco wept into her hankie. "Just lovely."

"Fits like a glove," C.C. agreed, and glanced at Lilah.

"Destined." She tilted her face up to Max. "Only a fool fights destiny."

"Then we're agreed?" Suzanna took a quick survey and received nods from the men. "The vote's in."

"Ha!" Though she was enormously proud, Colleen scowled. "As if I needed approval to dispose of what's mine. Take them.'' She thrust them into Megan's hands. ''Go upstairs and clean yourself up. You look like a chimney sweep. I want to see you wearing them when you come down.''

''Aunt Colleen…''

''No blubbering. Do as you're told.''

''Come on.'' Suzanna took Megan's arm to lead her from the room. ''I'll give you a hand.''

Satisfied, Colleen sat again, thumped her cane. ''Well, where's my drink?''

Later, when the waning moon had tipped over the edge of the sea, Megan walked with Nathaniel to the cliffs. The breeze whispered secrets in the grass and teased the wildflowers.

She wore blue, a simple summer dress with a full skirt that swirled in the wind. The pearls, glowing like small, perfect moons, circled her throat.

''You've had quite a day, Megan.''

''My head's still spinning. She gave it all away, Nathaniel. I can't understand how she could give away all the things that mattered so much.''

''She's a hell of a woman. It takes a special one to recognize magic.''

''Magic?''

''My practical, down-to-earth Megan.'' He tugged on her hand until they sat on a rock together, looking out over the churning water. ''Didn't you wonder, even for a moment, why each gift was so perfectly suitable? Why eighty years ago Fergus Calhoun would have been compelled to select just those things to hide away? The flower brooch for Suzanna, the watch for Amanda, Yeats for Lilah and the jade for C.C.? The portrait for Coco?''

"Coincidence," Megan murmured, but there was doubt in her voice.

He only laughed and kissed her. "Fate thrives on coincidence."

"And the pearls?"

"These." He lifted a finger to trace them. "A symbol of family, endurance, innocence. They suit you very well."

"They— I know I should have found a way not to accept them, but when Suzanna put them on me upstairs, they felt as though they were mine."

"They are. Ask yourself why you found them, why, with all the months the Calhouns searched for the emeralds, they never came across a hint of the strongbox. Fergus's book turns up after you move into The Towers. There's a numbered code. Who better to solve it than our logical CPA?"

Megan shook her head and blew out a laughing breath. "I can't explain it."

"Then just accept it."

"A magic rock for Jenny, soldiers for the boys." She rested her head against Nathaniel's shoulder. "I suppose I can't argue with that kind of coincidence. Or fate." Content, she closed her eyes and let the air caress her cheeks. "It's hard to believe that just a few days ago I was frantic with worry. You found him near here, didn't you?"

"Yes." He thought it best for her peace of mind not to mention the dicey climb down to the ledge. "I followed the bird."

"The bird?" Puzzled, she drew back. "That's odd. Kevin told me about a bird. A white one with green eyes that stayed with him that night. He's got a good imagination."

"There was a bird," Nathaniel told her. "A white gull with emerald eyes. Bianca's eyes."

"But—"

"Take magic where you find it." He slipped an arm around her shoulders so that they both could enjoy the sounds of the surf. "I have something for you, Megan."

"Mmm?" She was comfortable, almost sleepy, and she moaned in protest when he shifted away.

Nathaniel reached inside his jacket and drew out a sheaf of papers. "You might have a hard time reading them in this light."

"What's this?" Amused, she took them. "More receipts?"

"Nope. It's a life insurance policy."

"A— For heaven's sake. You shouldn't be carrying this around. You need to put it in a safe-deposit box, or a safe. Fireproof."

"Shut up." His nerves were beginning to stretch, so he stood, then paced to the edge of the cliff and back. "There's a hospitalization policy, too, my mortgage, a couple of bonds. And a damn Keogh."

"A Keogh." Megan held the papers as if they were diamonds. "You filled out the form."

"I can be practical, if that's what it takes. You want security, I'll give you security. There are plenty of figures there for you to tally."

She pressed her lips together. "You did this for me."

"I'd do anything for you. You'd rather I invest in municipal bonds than slay dragons? Fine."

She stared at him as he stood with the sea and sky at his back, his feet braced as if he were riding the deck of a ship, his eyes lit with a power that defeated the dark. And with bruises fading on his face.

"You faced your dragon years ago, Nathaniel." To

keep her hands occupied, she smoothed the papers. "I've had trouble facing my own." Rising, she walked to him, slipped the papers back into his pocket. "Aunt Colleen cornered me today. She said a lot of things, how I was too smart to take risks. How I'd never make the mistake of letting a man be too important. That I'd be better off alone than giving someone my trust, my heart. It upset me, and it frightened me. It took me a while to realize that's just what she'd meant to do. She was daring me to face myself."

"Have you?"

"It's not easy for me. I didn't like everything I saw, Nathaniel. All these years I've convinced myself that I was strong and self-reliant. But I'd let someone so unimportant shadow my life, and Kevin's. I thought I was protecting my son, and myself."

"You did a hell of a good job, from where I'm standing."

"Too good, in some ways. I closed myself off because it was safer. Then there was you." She reached up to lay a hand on his cheek. "I've been so afraid of what I feel for you. But that's over. I love you, Nathaniel. It doesn't matter if it was magic or fate, coincidence or sheer luck. I'm just glad I found you."

She lifted her face to his, reveled in the freedom of the kiss, the scent of the sea, the promise of his arms.

"I don't need retirement plans and insurance policies, Nathaniel," she murmured. "Not that you don't. It's very important that you... Stop laughing."

"I'm crazy about you." Still laughing, Nathaniel scooped her off her feet and swung her in dizzying circles.

"Crazy period." She struggled to catch her breath and clung to him. "We're going to fall off the cliff."

"Not tonight we're not. Nothing can happen to us tonight. Can't you feel it? We're the magic now." He set her on her feet again and held her close, so that even the air couldn't come between them. "I love you, Meg, but damned if I'm going to get down on one knee."

She went very still. "Nathaniel, I don't think—"

"Good. Don't think. Just listen. I've sailed around the world more than once, and seen in a decade more than most people see in their lifetimes. But I had to come home to find you. Don't say anything," he murmured. "Sit."

He led her back to the rock and sat with her. "I have something more for you than paperwork. That was just to smooth the path. Take a look at it," he said as he drew a box from his pocket. "Then tell me it wasn't meant."

With trembling fingers, she opened the box. With a sound of wonder, she lifted her eyes to his. "It's a pearl," she whispered.

"I was going to go for the traditional diamond. Seemed like the right thing. But when I saw this, I knew." He took it out of the box. "Coincidence?"

"I don't know. When did you buy this?"

"Last week. I thought about walking here with you, that first time. The moon and the stars." He studied the ring, the single glowing pearl surrounded by small, bright diamonds. "The moon and the stars," he said again, taking her hands. "That's what I want to give you, Megan."

"Nathaniel." She tried to tell herself it was too fast, too foolish, but the thought wouldn't lodge. "It's lovely."

"It's meant." He touched his lips to hers. "Just as we're meant. Marry me, Megan. Start a life with me. Let me be Kevin's father and make more children with you. Let me grow old loving you."

She couldn't find the logic, or think of all the reasons they should wait. So she answered with her heart. "Yes. Yes to everything." Laughing, she threw her arms around him. "Oh, Nathaniel. Yes, yes, yes…"

He squeezed his eyes tight on relief and joy. "You sure you don't want to qualify that?"

"I'm sure. I'm so sure." Drawing back, she held out her left hand. "Please. I want the moon and the stars. I want you."

He slipped the ring on her finger. "You've got me, sugar."

When he drew her close again, he thought he heard the air sigh, like a woman.

Epilogue

"Mom! We're here!"

Megan glanced up from her desk just as Kevin flew in the office door. She lifted her brow at the suit jacket and tie he wore.

"My, my, don't you look handsome!"

"You said I had to dress up 'cause it's Aunt Colleen's birthday dinner. I guess it's okay." He stretched his neck. "Dad showed me how to tie the tie by myself."

"And you did a fine job." She restrained herself from smoothing and straightening the knot. "How was the tour business today?"

"It was great. Calm seas and a freshening breeze. We sighted the first whale off the port bow."

"Oh, I love that nautical talk." She kissed his nose.

"If I didn't have to go to school, I could work with Dad and Holt every day, and not just on Saturday."

"And if you didn't go to school, you'd never know

much more than you do today. Saturdays will have to do.'' She gave his hair a tug. ''Mate.''

He'd expected as much. And, really, he didn't mind school. After all, he was a whole year in front of Alex. He grinned at his mother. ''Everybody's here. When are the new babies coming?''

''Mmm…'' With the Calhoun sisters in varying stages of pregnancy, it was an interesting question. ''I'd say on and off starting next month and through the New Year.''

He ran a fingertip over the corner of her desk. ''Who do you think's going to be first? C.C. or Suzanna?''

''Why?'' She glanced up from the ledger, and her eyes narrowed. ''Kevin, you are not betting on who has the next baby.''

''But, Mom—''

''No betting,'' she repeated, and smothered a laugh. ''Give me just a minute to finish up here, and I'll be along.''

''Hurry up.'' Kevin was bouncing. ''The party's already started.''

''All right, I'll just—'' Just nothing, she thought, and closed the ledger with a snap. ''Office hours are over. Let's go party.''

''All right!'' Grabbing her hand, Kevin hauled her out of the room. ''Alex said Dutch made this really big cake and it's going to have about a hundred candles on it.''

''Not quite a hundred,'' Megan said with a laugh. When they neared the family wing, she glanced toward the ceiling. ''Honey, I'd better check upstairs first.''

''Looking for someone?'' Nathaniel came down the steps. There was a twinkle in his eye and a tiny pink bundle in his arms.

''I should have known you'd wake her up.''

''She was awake. Weren't you, sugar?'' He bent his head to kiss his daughter's cheek. ''She was asking for me.''

''Really.''

''She can't talk yet,'' Kevin informed his father. ''She's only six weeks old.''

''She's very advanced for her age. Smart, like her mama.''

''Smart enough to know a sucker when she sees one.'' They made such a picture, she thought, the big man with a boy at his side and a baby in his arms. Her picture, she thought, and smiled. ''Come here, Luna.''

''She wants to go to the party, too,'' Kevin declared, reaching up to stroke a finger over his sister's cheek.

''Sure she does. That's what she told me.''

''Oh, Dad.''

Grinning, Nathaniel ruffled Kevin's hair. ''I could eat a pod of whales, mate. How about you?''

''Aye, aye.'' Kevin made a dash for the parlor. ''Come on, come on, everybody's waiting.''

''I've got to do this first.'' Nathaniel leaned over his daughter to kiss Megan.

''Jeez.'' With a roll of his eyes, Kevin headed for the noise, and the real fun.

''You're looking awfully pleased with yourself,'' Megan murmured.

''Why shouldn't I? I've got a beautiful wife, a terrific son, an incredible daughter.'' He ran his knuckles over Megan's pearl choker. ''What else could I ask for? How about you?''

Megan lifted her hand to pull his mouth back to hers. ''I've got the moon and the stars.''

From No. 1 *New York Times* bestselling author Nora Roberts

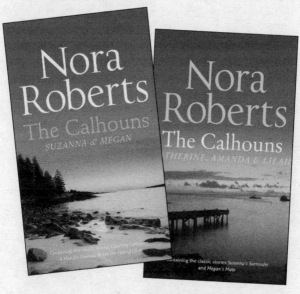

Atop the rocky coast of Maine sits the Towers, a magnificent family mansion that is home to a legend of long-lost love, hidden emeralds – and four determined sisters.

Catherine, Amanda & Lilah
Featuring *Courting Catherine*, *A Man for Amanda* and *For the Love of Lilah*

Suzanna & Megan
Featuring *Suzanna's Surrender* and *Megan's Mate*

From No. 1 *New York Times* bestselling author Nora Roberts

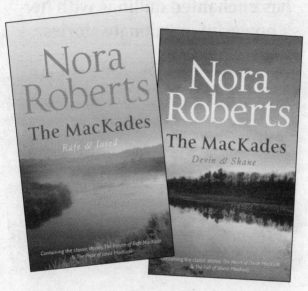

The irresistible MacKade brothers are back and once again stirring the heart of every female that crosses their path.

Rafe and Jared
Featuring *The Return of Rafe MacKade* and *The Pride of Jared MacKade*

Devin and Shane
Featuring *The Heart of Devin MacKade* and *The Fall of Shane MacKade*

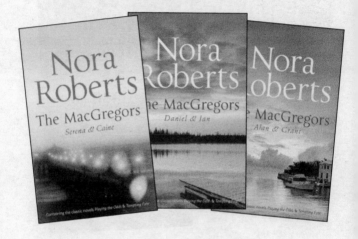

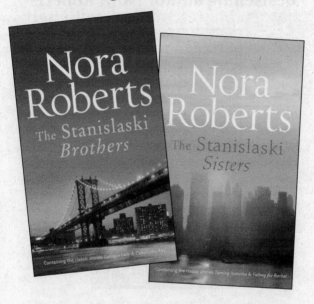

From No. 1 *New York Times* bestselling author Nora Roberts

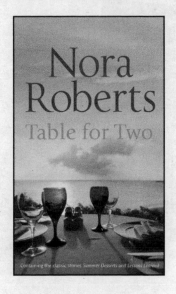

*Two world class chefs discover an
irresistible recipe for romance*

Features

Summer Desserts

and

Lessons Learned